AN...
"ONE OF TH...

Publishers Weekly

"NORTON CAN STILL EVOKE THAT
MYSTERIOUS AND DIFFICULT-TO-DEFINE
SENSE OF WONDER."
Fantasy Review

SCENT OF MAGIC
"SKILLED STORYTELLING AND A
NEW TWIST ON MAGIC . . .
Norton brings together a varied cast of
appealing characters caught in an intricate web
of intrigue and treachery."
Library Journal

"WELL-IMAGINED FANTASY . . .
Norton at her near-best."
Booklist

"STURDILY CONSTRUCTED,
FETCHINGLY RENDERED;
a top-notch outing for the
grandmasterly author."
Kirkus Reviews

"VERY COMPELLING . . . FABULOUS MAGICS."
Starlog

"MEMORABLE . . .
INTRIGUING AND CAPTIVATING . . .
An adventure, a distant civilization, and a chance
to experience a time and place in a new way—
no more than one expects from one of the
Grand Masters of science fiction and fantasy."
SF Site

Avon Books are available at special quantity discounts for bulk
purchases for sales promotions, premiums, fund raising or educa-
tional use. Special books, or book excerpts, can also be created to
fit specific needs.

For details write or telephone the office of the Director of Special
Markets, Avon Books, Inc., Dept. FP, 1350 Avenue of the Americas,
New York, New York 10019, 1-800-238-0658.

ANDRE NORTON

SCENT of MAGIC

AVON · EOS

AVON BOOKS, INC.
1350 Avenue of the Americas
New York, New York 10019

Copyright © 1998 by Andre Norton
Cover art by Kinuko Craft
Excerpt from *Signal to Noise* copyright © 1998 by Eric S. Nylund
Excerpt from *The Death of the Necromancer* copyright © 1998 by Martha Wells
Excerpt from *Scent of Magic* copyright © 1998 by Andre Norton
Excerpt from *The Gilded Chain* copyright © 1998 by Dave Duncan
Excerpt from *Krondor the Betrayal* copyright © 1998 by Raymond E. Feist
Excerpt from *Mission Child* copyright © 1998 by Maureen F. McHugh
Excerpt from *Avalanche Soldier* coypright © 1999 by Susan R. Matthews
Inside back cover author photograph by Jay Kay Klein
Published by arrangement with the author
Library of Congress Catalog Card Number: 98-18173
ISBN: 0-380-78416-5
www.avonbooks.com/eos

First Avon Eos Paperback Printing: August 1999
First Avon Eos Hardcover Printing: October 1998

AVON EOS TRADEMARK REG. U.S. PAT. OFF. AND IN OTHER COUNTRIES, MARCA REGISTRADA, HECHO EN U.S.A.

Printed in the U.S.A.

WCD 10 9 8 7 6 5 4 3 2 1

For the support system which has meant so much
to me this past year—

Rose Wolf
Ann Crispin
Mary Schaub
eluki bes shahar
Lyn McConchie
Marj Krueger
and
Caroline Fike

1   The great bell in the central watchtower of Kronengred boomed the
same warning as it had for more years than the most dili-
gent scholars could remember. A heavy vibration of sound
penetrated every one of the aged buildings huddled comfortably together, rising even to the castle on a mount
which rivaled the height of the bell tower. Though the
dark of the passing winter season still held in thick blots
around alleys and doorway, yet the bell's call now sounded
to all responsible citizens—those who had kept Kronengred's prosperity and safety alive—to be up and about
the day's labors.

His Highness, the Duke, might wriggle deeper into the
covers of his great bed, but in the tiny cupboard (one
could certainly not dignify it with the title of "room")
off the vast kitchen of the Wanderers Inn, Willadene
sighed herself into sitting up, the musty straws pricking
through the ragged cover of the pallet beneath her, meeting
her every movement with familiar scratching.

Her first real act was always the same. Before she
reached for undersmock her hands went to that small bag,
warm between her small breasts, and lifted it to her tormented nose. A deep sniff of the crushed spices and herbs

1

within cleared her head, but the dull ache from last night's long service in the taproom did not go away.

Now she dressed hurriedly, pulling on clothing which had been cobbled down from a much larger size, so worn that its color was now a uniform muddy gray. Smells—it was always the smells against which she had to brace herself each morning. She was sure sometimes that those invaded her very dreams, bringing shadows of nightmares. The kitchen was no flower garden for the pleasuring of some lord's daughter, that was certain.

She was still twisting her lank hair up under a kerchief when she heard, as she had feared, the clang of pans harshly slammed down together on the long table. Aunt Jacoba was the only one who dared to use those utensils without order, and, by the sound of it, she had a monumental temper to work off this morning.

"Willa—get you here, you lazy slut!" That voice, which even sounded like a badly scrubbed kettle, arose on the end of one crash. Certainly Aunt Jacoba had deliberately swung the big porridge kettle on its hanger so that it had rebounded from the smoke-darkened stone of the wide hearth.

Willadene (sometimes she forgot she had once been called that—it had been years now since the great plague had decimated the inhabitants of the city and she had been grudgingly accepted under the orders of the district Reeve by her father's cousin as a scullery maid, or scullery drudge) hurried into the kitchen.

Wisely she had been on guard and so dodged the heavy tankard which might have struck her senseless if it had landed true. There was no easy greeting from Jacoba when she was in this foul mood. Swiftly the girl reached well over her head and pulled down a flitch of bacon. She had to fight with all her strength against the smell of the meat—it was never of the first quality and always kept too long. Jacoba pinched each pence when it came to supplies for the majority of those eating early in the morning. Perhaps they were still so drowsy they were able to choke it down in a dull fog of half sleep.

Jacoba had turned to the stirring of the vast pot of porridge which had been set to cook slowly the night before. Figis, the waiting boy, his face still masked with most of yesterday's grime, was slamming bowls onto a tray. He did not look up, but Willadene sighted the bruise near his eye. There was an ever-going feud between Figis and Jorg, the horseboy.

She sawed away at the bacon with a knife which Figis should have sharpened yesterday. What she turned off now were not smooth slices but ragged hunks to be put in the footed skillet, when she knelt in the ashes which had drifted out from the fire to thrust her burden close enough to the flames for its contents to begin to sputter.

Longing to pull out her spice bag and use it as a defense against the heavy odor of the now-crisping meat, Willadene hunched her shoulders and held on, grimly determined not to attract any attention from Jacoba.

The big woman was sawing at rounds of yesterday's black bread—now near stone hard. These were the plates waiting to hold the bacon and wedges of cheese. The fare might be of third or even fourth grade, but Jacoba did not stint on portions.

Then she turned to ladling out porridge—there were five bowls waiting. Willadene haunched in upon herself.

So fortune had not favored her. Wyche *had* stayed the night. When she had crept away as the last two candles were near to guttering out in the taproom he had still been there, the huge bulk of his body half sprawling out of the one large chair which the inn owned. The odor of mulled cider of the strongest had not been enough to hide that other stench exuding from him. It was not only that of unclean flesh and/or filthy clothing but something else of which she was aware but could not put name to—though now and then the inn sheltered other patrons who carried the same odor and mostly they had been an ugly lot.

She must ask Halwice—

"Burn you that and you'll feel the fire yourself."

Willadene jerked the skillet back, its three legs grating on the stone. She had wrapped her hand as tightly as she could against the bite of the flames, but she still could feel the heat as she approached the table, striving to hold the heavy pan straight. Jacoba took her time inspecting the bacon.

At length she spiked hunks onto the waiting bread, for the most part impartially, though the last portion was doubled. For Wyche, of course. Tilting the skillet now with caution Willadene poured a measure of the sizzling grease over each slab of plate bread.

Figis had gone off with the tray of bowls and the pot of honey for the sweetening of their coarse contents. Now he returned for the rest of the meal.

"The merchant from Bresta," he said, keeping well away from Jacoba as he spoke, "said as how he found him a roach in his bowl. See—" He had put the bowl on the table and there was no mistaking the black creature. "Said as how he was going to speak to the Reeve—something about meat he had not ordered—" The boy sniggered, easily evading Jacoba's doubled fist. Catching up the second tray of bread, meat, and a large round of cheese he was gone before his mistress could round the table.

Figis had little sense, Willadene thought. Jacoba had a very retentive memory. Sooner or later the boy would pay for his pertness. Though what he warned might well be true—a few more complaints to the district Reeve and Jacoba could find herself in trouble.

In fact, Willadene had come to wonder, through the days of her servitude here, why the cook had so long escaped any real censure for her lack of cleanliness and her questionable products.

The Wanderers Inn was, of course, Jacoba's own. But no building in Kronengred was really owned by anyone but the Duke, even though the same family might shelter in it for generations. The Duke undoubtedly had more important things to think over than the lacks and temper of an innkeeper.

It had been five years since the great plague, which had seated Uttobric on the ducal highseat. He had been a relatively unknown and distant member of the family, but the only male fortunate enough to escape the all too devastating death. The only male—but there was one far closer to that honor—the last Duke's daughter, Lady Saylana. She had been widowed also by the march of the disease, but she had a son (luckily away from the city when disaster struck), and there were those who lifted an eyebrow significantly, or perhaps even dared to whisper behind a hand, when his name was spoken in passing. Thus Uttobric had a rival—or the threat of one—though Kronen law did not change and by all rights the rule was his.

"Get you in to the tap, slut," Jacoba said. "Wyche wants to clear his morning throat. Be sure you draw the best— Hmm—" There was something in that "Hmm" which kept Willadene from immediate obedience.

"You are but one and twenty days away from Reeve listing as a full woman, scrawny and stupid as you are. Upchucking good food and saying it makes you sick. Sick! It is only that stubborn will of yours tryin' to lie to your betters. No—you've no looks to you. But you're young and might wash up better. Wyche was taken a fancy to you, girl. Don't you give him any black looks. As one set over you by the Reeve himself I has the right to choose a man to take you off my hands. Wyche must be mazed to want *you*. Now get in there and, as I have said, do the pretty for him. Be glad you are gettin' a man as has a full purse—sure he has offered enough wed bounty for you to promise that."

Somehow the inn mistress had talked herself into a good humor. Now she laughed, roaring coarsely. Willadene was well aware that her utter horror of this promised fate must be read on her face.

Halwice—if she could only get to Halwice!—though she could not be sure the Herbmistress would even listen to any plea. She thought longingly of that quiet shop and of all it had seemed to promise since she had first found it. If—if she could serve as Halwice's cook maid—she could cook and well when she had the chance—that would be heaven. But twenty days lay between her and any free choice, and Wyche was waiting, Jacoba moving toward her, a big fist raised. Willadene went, her hands pressed tightly against her bosom as if the faint scent still rising from her bag could arm her against the future.

She scuttled around the edge of the wide door, intent on reaching the shelf by the already tapped barrel so she could fill a flagon as soon as possible. Giving a quick glance over her shoulder, she saw that the big chair was empty, and she looked a little wildly ahead to her goal— hoping that Wyche was not lying in wait there.

However, his broad back fronted those in the room as he stood by the major window, curtaining the light from those behind him. Four of them—all dressed in that sturdy travel-worn leather and heavy cloth favored by out-city merchants. They were all wearing badges, which meant they were legal and registered wayfarers, protected by tradition from any trouble within the borders of Kronen— except, of course, from those inhabitants now outside the same laws.

The eldest of the three was picking with his belt eating-knife at the half-charred bacon before him, disgust plain to be read on his face. He was trimly neat, his short gray hair curling up in the back about the border of his bowl cap. There was a flash of ring on his knife hand, and it was plain he was prosperous in his trade. Now he pushed aside the slab of greasy bread and uttered a sound deep in his throat which brought the full attention of his three companions. Two of them were plainly of lesser rank in their guild, but the youngest had the same wide nose above a smallish mouth and shared the older man's other features to a degree which made it very possible they were father and son.

"The road guard has been thinned again." There was an angry note in the older man's statement. "We passed a full half company coming down from the west hills, bag and baggage—and not on leave either. I tell you whoever gives such orders delivers us like geese to the poulterer!"

Both of those seated, one on either side of him, nodded. But the youngest one moved his head in the smallest suggestion of a shake as he stared straight at their leader.

"The affairs of the highborn," one of the others remarked, "seldom are settled to *our* satisfaction. Remember there are more disasters than the plague. There has never been Kronen blood turned against Kronen blood. However. . . ." His voice trailed away and he shrugged.

In Willadene's hands the flagon was now brimming full, but she shrank from crossing toward that bulky back, sniffing its foul odor. However, Wyche had not changed position. She was determined now that he was entirely intent on what lay beyond the bubbled glass of that window. Dare she ease her way to that small side table almost within his reach to empty the flagon into the waiting tankards, slip back before he was aware of her?

Only, fortune failed her now. He shrugged his huge width of shoulder and turned his head. In his fat, puffed face his small dark eyes looked like a pair of dry, shriveled raisins. But his mouth gaped in what he might consider a welcoming smile.

"Good fare for the belly, wench." He swung farther away from the window and stuck out his bristly paw of a hand. Swiftly Willadene passed him the tankard. However, when he raised it to his mouth and was gulping its contents he deliberately raised his other hand to slap palm to the wall, cutting off her flight. His blubber lips had pursed, and, bringing down the tankard after that hefty pull, he eyed her from head to foot and back again.

It seemed to Willadene then that that odor she had never been able to identify strengthened until she wanted to gag.

"Skinny," Wyche remarked, "but you're young and Jacoba swears you are still a maid. Though that state will not be with you for long now." Before she could do more than flatten herself against the wall, her hands again seeking her amulet, his huge face loomed above her, and her skin shrank from the rough touch of his lips.

"Yes, a bargain, I'm thinking. There won't be any youngsters hanging around gawking at such as you. Jacoba says you can cook—and a full table before him and a warmer for his bed at night is all any man wants. You're as skittish as a spring lamb." The tip of a fat tongue passed over those thick lips which she felt had left a kind of scum on her own skin. "I likes 'em so—it don't take long to tame 'em—"

What more threats he might have added Willadene did not know. Those she had just heard had sickened her. But Wyche's survey of her was interrupted, and she felt the door to the left—the one giving on the outer world— opening. Did she have a chance? But to run without any protector of rank was folly. She could be named vagabond and driven out of Kronengred—though she was sure that Jacoba would not willingly lose the bride price. She heard the tinkle of a small silvery bell as two cloaked and veiled women came in, a girl in a drab cloak at their heels, in her hand a basket already laden heavy enough to draw her childish body to one side.

"Food for those in hunger as is the second commandment." The first of the women to cross the threshold swung her bell again, its tinkle echoed by the one in the hand of her companion.

Stools scraped across the flagstones as the four merchants got to their feet and bowed. Their leader advanced, digging one hand in his belt purse, and Willadene caught the glint of what could only be a silver coin.

"Well has your Great One favored me." The first of

the cloaked Sisters of Bright Star was already bringing forth a plump bag of her own into which he dropped his offering, his fellows swift to follow his example.

"What prayer would you have us set for you?" the woman asked. It was difficult to see her features so deeply she was veiled.

"That of safe travel—for me, Jaskar of Bresta, and for these, my companions. Such petitions are needed in our present days, Sister."

"Evil always awaits beyond the bonds of light," she returned as Jacoba came into the room.

"What's to do—?" the inn mistress began and then, catching full sight of the women, she stopped short. "You"—her attention swung to Willadene—"if the guests be through, then clear the table."

Thankfully Willadene put room between her and Wyche. The girl with the basket lugged her burden up to the board, and Willadene hastily crammed in those rounds of well-greased bread. By the looks of what already lay within the basket the Sisters had had good fortune in their begging round of the taverns and noble houses of the section this morning.

"Fortune favor you, goodwife," the Sister commented, but when her small serving maid tried to raise the basket she near sent it and its contents toppling to the floor.

"It would please the Great One," the Star follower added a moment later, "if you would lend us this girl of yours to our aid. We have only one more place to cry for alms and she would be quickly back."

Willadene knew very well that Jacoba wanted to answer that with one of her angry outbursts. Yet no one refused a Sister, for that Great Mistress was well-known to rule the whims of fortune itself.

"Come back, wench"—there was a threat of trouble to come—"as fast as you can. We have dawdled away to near the Second Bell and nothing is done."

Willadene eagerly took half share of the handle, and the

basket swung between her and the girl as they left. Oddly enough, Wyche was back to the window as if to watch them out of sight.

She was breathing fast. Just as there were odors which clung to evil, so there were fragrances which matched good. She had sniffed those many times in Halwice's domain. And there was a strain of what might even be flowers—a mere whiff—as she and the girl maneuvered their way with their burden out of the inn door.

Wyche was watching, but she thought that she knew the house the Sisters would seek out now—the section Reeve lived three doors away in the direction the Sisters were taking. His wife was well-known to be both pious and bountiful. She could cut through the alley beside the Reeve's house and, though it was near time for the Second Bell to summon all shopkeepers to the business of the day, she thought she could reach Halwice's without being seen.

What would happen then she could not foresee. She had received both kindness and training from the Herbmistress in the past—ever since Jacoba sent her monthly for the scant supply of spices to hide the age of the meat.

Now she walked obediently behind the Begging Sisters, fitting her pace to that of the maid whose burden she shared. The girl had not done more than glance at her once, following the rule of the Star's outventuring—eyes to the pavement and no worldly gazing at anything on either side.

They had turned the corner to approach the Reeve's kitchen door, as was the custom. As Willadene heard the silver notes of the bells she tensed. The moment she saw the door thrown open and heard a brisk welcome for the Sisters, she herself looked to the girl.

There was no time for any explanation—she would just have to go! Shifting her grasp off the basket handle so swiftly that the other girl had to grasp at the house wall to steady herself, Willadene ran.

She thought to hear voices behind her and was amazed

that such did not come. But the Great One of the Star—
perhaps *She* would spread *her* shining cloak between those
in the house and this fugitive.

Turn left here—yes, she could catch sight of the great
Maninger House—two streets over and around another
corner—Halwice's. She had never taken this way to the
Herbmistress's shop before, but she was sure.

The morning chill whipped about her and caught at her
toes left bare by her house sandals. Willadene was gasping
a little, aware of every lighted window, every movement
on the street. She tried to force herself to fall to a walk,
but within a step or so her pace quickened again.

She could not reckon now when she had discovered this
haven. It went back to the shadowy days before the plague,
for she had known the Herbmistress a very long time.

Halwice had a place on the Guild Council. She was far
more learned in the properties of her wares than were
many of the doctors who strutted in answer to a distress
call, their badged robes of fine cut worn with a flick and
flourish of hem, their brimmed hats with a dangle of face
mask ready to use when one might be called to enter a
disease-tainted room, their pride in their calling sometimes—most times—spilling over into arrogance. Yet it
was to Halwice that these same "masters of healing" must
send for the mixtures they drew upon speedily enough.

But healing—though Willadene knew well the importance Halwice placed on such knowledge—was not the
only product sold in that shop where spice vied with fragrances and with sharp odors of oils. Those scents themselves had their place of importance.

Willadene rubbed her knuckles across her nose. Already
she could almost anticipate the feast awaiting her. She
always stood just within the door of Halwice's shop for a
long moment or two, drawing into her lungs the medley
of odors. It was as if she could bathe herself in the freshest
air of spring, the headiest perfume of summer, the spice
of autumn. She could feel it scrub across her salt-sweated

skin, her sticky hair—freeing her from Jacoba's hold, somehow stirring within her new thoughts and firming good memories.

For Willadene had "the nose." Although each and every one of her kind wore such a feature, only to a very few was the privilege given—the ability to recognize and name the most subtle of mixed scents. Just as the foul odors which haunted Jacoba's kitchen assaulted her to the point of choking and nausea, so could inhaling the perfume of a skillfully blended cream, a packet of dried leaves and petals, liquids so precious they must be dripped one drop at a time from small glass tubes, bring her a kind of freedom and pleasure.

She could remember Halwice's first testing of her "nose," the holding of a small jar of ointment from which there had risen a moisture—golden, luxuriant as any treasure from a jewel casket. And Willadene had confidently named each ingredient of that cream—measures of this and that.

Those of the ducal court paid well for their choices from Halwice's array of bottles and jars. Though Willadene was sent only for the coarsest and cheapest of spices, she would linger as long as she dared to drink in a nearly distilled scent, to listen to Halwice's explanations, to regard longingly the lines of tubes and bottles, the stands of narrow drawers—each compartmented and meant to hold powered leaves, petals, snippets of dried fruit rind. She had even drawn back to her a near lost skill in reading by studying the symbols lettered on each container.

If Jacoba would only— That frustration which was like a pain never left the girl. For two years now the Herbmistress had made regular offers to buy Willadene's apprenticeship. The cook's spiteful answer was always the same—that her scullery maid had been officially assigned to her from among the children orphaned by the great plague and as a relative she had accepted the Reeve's fee for taking such an unhandy servant.

Why the innkeeper wished to hold on to a serving maid who was always deserving of punishment, who was as sickly as a winter-born lamb, Willadene could never understand. There would be a fine-fee for such a change, yes, but she had even heard Halwice offer to pay that. Was the answer what she had learned today—that Jacoba could get a bride price for her?

She had sometimes thought that the cook had held on to her from pure spite. Jacoba had this twisted desire to torment. Willadene often thought that she was sent to the herb shop on trifling errands just to tantalize her.

But all things come to an end in time. In twenty days she would be of age and Jacoba could not hold her against her will. Then—not yet had she dared suggest to Halwice that perhaps the Herbmistress would take her into her employ. She would not even expect a full apprenticeship—willing to work any number of hours without more pay than a chance to be in the shop, to learn—if Halwice came to think her worthy.

The Herbmistress was of calm and unruffled temperament—but she was not cup friend to any of her neighbors. Pleasant to all but not welcoming chances for idle gossip. For the most part she was a silent woman, as if her thoughts occupied her more than her customers. Yet she was ready to serve all, listening to the complaints of those who ailed, mixing cordials and salves which served their purposes so well that all Kronen-bred knew their value.

She certainly was not noble born. However, though Halwice went plain of dress and quiet of demeanor, Willadene had seen her more than once reduce some fretful or upnosed housemistress to uneasy deference. She dealt with courtiers as well as stall keepers, and treated both with the same quiet courtesy.

The girl gave a start now as the Second Bell boomed out the orders for the day. She slipped out of an alley and hurried down the street. There was rising clatter and sound as the merchants unshuttered their shops, calling greetings from one to the other.

Halwice's shop was the ground floor of a three-story building. And while its neighbors were hung with banners urging this or that product upon the possible customer, her windows were trimmed with boxes—some green and lacy with ferns, others bright with flowers. Even her roof, Willadene knew, had been put to use with racks of shelves each bearing trays of plants, while Halwice's back door gave upon a stretch of well-nourished and tilled land, producing more healthy crops than one might usually find in the heart of a city.

Willadene slowed. Jacoba could well guess where she would head. And already she might well be reported to the Reeve for straying. Could she be bringing down trouble on Halwice?

The shop shutters were still up and there was no sign that the Herbmistress was starting her day. Willadene's head suddenly came up. That scent—it had the same evil promise that she knew meant trouble.

She was at the closed door. Only— The latch cord was out—then why were the shutters closed? With caution, the girl raised her hand to the door. There was something wrong—she stifled a gagging protest.

Though she had not been aware of it, she had given the door a nudge and it was swinging open. All the crowding scents she loved were loosed—but with them something dark and dangerous she could not name. . . . Halwice?

The shop was dim with the shutters closed. She could see only the bulk of counter and shelves. And she stepped within as warily as if she were certain some trap waited beyond.

2

The great bell's first sounding had not awakened the man who had left coverlets trailing behind him from the bed as he had crossed to draw the heavy curtain a little aside and look out on a dawn-grayed city. Uttobric of Kronen had never been an impressive figure even when decked out in the robes of formal ceremony. He was still less so now as he chewed his lower lip, his mind awhirl with the thoughts which had given him very little sleep this past night.

His scanty stock of gray-brown hair stood on end above a narrow face worn by deep crevices of wrinkles, two bracketing each side of his thin-lipped mouth, others furrowing his forehead. He stared shortsightedly out into the gloom where the twinkle of a few lights below marked the coming of a new day of—

Of course he had regretted the ravages of the plague, as any just man would; however, he certainly was not responsible for becoming the only male left in the straight line of descent. Now he could acknowledge to himself that he had both feared and envied his predecessor on the ducal throne. Wubric had been everything he was not—a ruler secure enough to be able to turn his attention to other matters.

Uttobric did not have to turn his head now and look back at the table, where two candles were fast guttering out, to remember what lay there: reports—too many of them. . . . Between them they would pull him to bits if they might.

Whom could he trust? Sometimes he even suspected Vazul—though that Chancellor, if Uttobric were swept away, would certainly fall with his lord, since he was not of the old nobility but rather the merchant class, a man of keen wit and wily action, all seemingly at the Duke's service.

It was Vazul who had made that suggestion the night before—one which had shocked Uttobric at first. The Duke still thought of his daughter as a child, content to amuse herself with a handful of carefully selected companions, of no proper service to him because of her gender. But what had Vazul pointed out? That very gender might be put to use now.

Uttobric loosened his hold on the curtain and padded back to the high-standing bulk of his craven bed. He picked up the holder of an unlighted candle and the miniature which lay beside it on the bedside shelf and then, lighting the candle from one of the dying ones, he dropped into the chair nearby and held the miniature of his daughter closer to his eyes.

It was his secret belief that commissioned artists always flattered their subjects; that was only good business for them. Yet Vazul had assured him—and it was true that Mahart took most of her looks from his wife's now-extinct line. He could see the soft rolls of dark brown hair, the slightly triangular face (that pointed chin was certainly his). But above that the mouth was generous, curving in the hint of a smile. Large eyes of an unexpected green were lashed thickly, and the brows delicately marked. Yes, this was no longer the face of a child, and he had to admit to himself that if the artist had not lied with his brush his daughter was possibly fair looking.

Beauty might snare the passing attention of a man, but anyone shrewd enough to provide what he, Uttobric, might have to demand could well wish more than just a pretty face and the fluttering attentions of a green girl. Dowry—

Uttobric tossed the miniature onto the table among the papers. Favorable port treatment? That would be too ambiguous. No, he would have to make it plain that on the wedding day he would proclaim the groom his accepted heir.

The small man in the tall-backed chair sighed. Could it be done? King Hawkner was over blessed with sons, it was true. He might be willing to provide for, say, a third or fourth one of them in this way, and Kronengred was a rich prize. Once the alliance was set, then changes could be safely made. For Hawkner's army was idle, and idle soldiers need to be occupied lest they view what lay about them and make a few decisions of their own.

Uttobric scowled at one shifting pile of reports. Of course he knew that he was stripping the western frontier and the mountain territory dangerously of trained manpower. The complaints of merchants grew louder and longer all the time. Let this Prince of the Blood Royal bring with him enough guards and that could be easily remedied.

If—again the Duke bit down upon his lip. If they had time! Saylana—now his mouth twisted as if he would spit—her backing—even Vazul could not pierce deeply into her ranks with his expertly trained spies to learn for certain who would rise for her if there came a day which actually tested them in open opposition. Wubric's daughter, unable by law to claim the throne—though she had a son, Barbric, around whom all her plotting was twisted.

However, with Mahart wed to a Prince Royal who could call upon Hawkner's own forces, one would think several times about any treachery. He glanced at the miniature. He had never really understood women. Her mother he had first seen at their own wedding—fair enough, yet he had always been pricked by the thought that she led some kind of secret life into which he had no entrance. Though he had not really cared. Then the plague and all his doubts were ended. The fact his daughter had survived had just been one of those jests of fate the raging disease had played throughout the city.

He expected no trouble from Mahart. The girl had been close kept all these years and had had no chance to form any interest in some boy of her own age. The thought of being a Princess Royal would be enough to dazzle her into welcome compliance. Yes, he would summon Vazul and—

He was startled by the discreet tapping at the door. Though he was no trained warrior he was out of his chair in an instant and reaching for the pillow sword resting each night as the ceremonial defense at the foot of his bed.

He flushed as he realized he had to clear his throat before he could harshly answer. "Enter!"

The door did not open very far, just enough for a very tall and thin figure, robes wrapped about him to aid in speed, to sidle in.

The robes shone in the dim light, which also picked out the heavy, gemmed gold chain which lay on the man's narrow shoulders, the signet at its end dangling near his belt.

"What's to do, Vazul?"

For the Chancellor to seek him out in this fashion was against all custom. Now the visitor was closing the door tightly behind him, almost as if he feared some follower.

"Your decision, Highness?"

In this gloom it was almost impossible to see the face of the speaker, only his height (for which Uttobric secretly could not forgive him) as he loomed over his master as he approached the table.

"Why must you come at *this* hour to know?" demanded the Duke testily.

"Time never waits for men—men are its servants." The rich voice was that of a practical speechmaker, one who was able to sway his fellows if the need arose. "And time is running out, Highness. The Bat has not returned."

Uttobric took a tighter grip on the sword he had not yet relinquished.

"Taken?"

Vazul shrugged. "Who knows? But he has never failed to report within the promised time before. He is mind blocked to the best of our ability, but we do not know what resources they may have. There are indications that Her Grace has had contact with several from overseas during the last year. Each land has its men of secrets, and some remain secret save to him who uses them. But this means, Highness, that you must move swiftly."

The Chancellor stood in the full light of the candle now. He was thin nearly to the point of emaciation, and his robe of crimson patterned on the breast with the ducal arms appeared nearly too heavy for him to support. His hair was cropped short as if he were a fighter, but his incurved cheeks were covered with a short-trimmed beard, while his pale gray eyes appeared to possess the same gleam as a sword blade showed. Only because he knew that Vazul would rise and fall with him, did the Duke trust him. The man had a wily mind, seemed sometimes almost able to read the future—at least light upon some of the perils lying in wait there.

"But if the Bat did not report—" the Duke now said slowly.

"How do I deduce that an alarm is sounding?" The Chancellor shrugged. "Because I know him as you should as well, Highness. He is the best of your eyes and ears, and there has never been any fault in the information which he has brought. We know that he crossed the border two days ago—he made touch with our man there. He should have reported at sunset last eve. Whatever chanced to delay him lies within your own realm, Highness, perhaps even here in Kronengred."

Uttobric slammed the sword back in its sheath and returned, his lips curved downward in sullen pout, to the chair he had earlier arisen from. With a wave of his hand he beckoned Vazul to another on the opposite side of the table.

But before the Chancellor joined him Vazul picked up a triple candle stand and lit all three candles so that there was enough light that each of them could well see the other.

"So we do not even know now whether the plan is feasible," the Duke said, blinking in the glow of light. "He was to tell us how matters lay with Hawkner. What do we do now, approach the King openly with our suggestion? He may take it in one of his whimsical moods and think it a jest, an improper one."

Uttobric squirmed in his chair. He had met King Hawkner on only two occasions—one his wedding—and both times he had felt overshadowed and almost a lackey awaiting the King's pleasure, though Kronen was *not* part of his kingdom—Oberstrand—and never had been.

Oddly enough, there was movement on one of the Chancellor's shoulders which continued down his right arm until, from under the heavy embroidery of his wide cuff, there appeared a sleek black head. So dark was the fur that covered it that one could only catch a gleam now and then of yellow reflecting the candlelight from two eyes above a narrow pointed snout. The Duke watched distastefully as the whole of Vazul's pet appeared—though the creature seemed more than just an animal and certainly its lithe, long-bodied shape, the very short legs sharply clawed, could not be seen anywhere else in Kronen that Uttobric knew of. He hated the creature, still something had always prevented him from ordering the Chancellor to at least keep the thing out of the ducal presence. It sat up now and licked down its chest.

The Duke made an effort to ignore it. Instead he returned to his querulous question of earlier.

"Do I go, hat in hand, and approach Hawkner through

Lord Perfer? Our ambassador is a fool, and we do not know how much he can be trusted.''

"Not quite yet." Vazul was drawing his hand down the back of the creature. "Has Your Highness spoken with the Lady Mahart? She is certainly of an age to be thinking of marriage—of a handsome prince—''

"She chatters like a hoobird if I welcomed it," snapped the Duke. "Possibly within a breath she would spill it all to that Lady Zuta and then it would be common knowledge."

"Just so. However"—the Chancellor continued to stroke his pet—"I did not mean make free with the heart of the matter, merely speak to her of marriage. Who knows such a rumor might bring the Lady Saylana's attention and push her supporters out of their holes to your advantage."

The Duke chewed a fingernail; his glance swept from the Chancellor to those piles of reports. Yes, if they could just stir the pot a little some useful steam might arise.

"Well enough," he said. "That much can certainly be done. Summon Burris—one might as well get to the thing.''

The Chancellor arose and went to pull the bell rope which would bring the Duke's personal servant. He neither smiled nor displayed any change in feature. It was becoming very easy to bring Uttobric to his way of thinking—but overconfidence was a sin.

The great bell's boom broke into the most pleasant of dreams. Mahart had never seen the world outside these ancient walls since she was a very small girl, but tonight she had skimmed away from her tower to a place she barely remembered when awake—a great open field in which brilliant gems of flowers bent under a breeze which carried the scent of summer itself.

The scent of summer—her brows drew together in a faint frown of one seeking a memory. Of course! Now she squirmed free of the tangle of silk and velvet and sat up. Her attention was on the small brazier which sat on the edge of her wide dressing table. No fragrant smoke threads arose upward from it now, but, as she stretched her arms wide, she felt she could purr like one of the guard cats who kept the castle free of vermin.

She was indeed a Herbmistress—that Halwice—to produce an incense which supplied such peaceful and comforting dreams. They said she was a mistress of scents so powerful that they could draw or repel another. Mahart's dissatisfied gaze went on to the array of fancifully fashioned bottles on that same dressing table. Many of those held rare fragrances from overseas—her father was very apt on Winter Turn day to present her with something new of that sort. It was as if in his mind a bottle of scent was an excellent substitute for the dolls of an earlier day—though he had actually continued to present those before someone, probably Vazul, had pointed out that she was at last grown up.

She did not ring for Julta, her maid. Rather, she freed herself from the cocoon of covers, thrust her feet into her waiting fur-lined slippers, and crossed to seat herself on the bench of the dressing table, bending at once to sniff at the last faint remains of the burnt incense.

The candles were hardly used and she snap-lighted them—all four—to lean forward a little to study her reflection in the wide mirror. Her hair was still night braided, but its dull brown shade was certainly not her best feature. She envied Zuta those sleek black strands that looked like lengths of satin. But—she was not too plain! For the first time Mahart allowed herself to believe that.

There were a number of powders and creams available. She knew that Zuta was zealous in using such, but she had hesitated to try, thinking always of the tittering of maids who *always* discussed the actions of their mistresses behind their backs, or even arousing amusement in Zuta, who would be entirely too kind to tell her the truth. What would she do without Zuta!

It seemed to Mahart that her companion lady was born knowing what Mahart had to learn. She could always say the right thing, do the gracious act, and had been quick when Mahart was younger to cover any awkwardness her mistress might cause. Though sometimes—sometimes Mahart wished that she still had Nurse.

Nurse had known and served her mother and had been her refuge in childhood whenever her father's impatient avoidance had hurt. But Nurse was of childhood, too, gone away with a generous pension to take care of her daughter's family back in Bresta. Then Zuta had come, dazzling with her sophistication, though she was only three years older. She was an orphan of the plague but of high rank, and seemed well satisfied with her present lot.

It had been Zuta who had told her of Halwice, the Herbmistress. Though she was so close kept in this shell, Mahart sighed and wished away all the fantastical carved furniture and comfort around her; perhaps it might be possible sometime to actually meet this purveyor of dreams and mistress of fragrance.

Only—she was tired—tired—tired— Her mouth drooped at the corners and the growing depression of the last few months gripped her again. She was tired of her life, feeling stifled at times. If it were not that she had in the past discovered the great library what would she have known at all of the world around her—outside that shell her father had forged?

Page by page she had traveled to far countries, confronted strange beasts and stranger peoples—and learned of Kronen of the past and the part her family had played in it. She believed that her father never entered the library; she was very certain that the Lady Saylana did not, though from time to time one of her serving people had come to search out a book, always on the shelves of the oldest ones where the leather backs left dust of decay upon the hands of would-be readers.

There was her daily walk, of course, but it was strictly

confined to the pocket-sized garden from which even the gardeners were warned away during that time. And her meals were in the stately, hollow magnificence of that dining room, where her father ate in hasty gulps, sometimes with Vazul, neither of them paying any attention to her.

She encouraged Zuta to mingle with the other ladies of the court. The gossip she brought back was always enlightening. But, of course, there was no mingling of her own with Saylana's chosen servants. Though that assembly had shrunk in size since the death of the late Duke, his daughter still had her adherents and visitors.

Mahart had seen Barbric, her son, from a distance and had not been greatly impressed. His shambling walk and foolish high laugh were certainly not that of a prospective Duke who would do justice to Kronen, but then—what of her father?

At each meal he sat beneath the state portrait of her distant cousin and the difference grew more apparent every time she had viewed the two in such contrast.

The mighty presence of the former Duke was certainly enough to overshadow most of the men she had seen. Captain Rangle of the Guard would come the closest to the firm jaw, that high-held head, that warrior's stance. Had Wubric really presented that overawing aspect to his subjects or was that his fancied idea of himself?

Mahart continued to stare into the mirror. One could see how she appeared—to herself at least. Did she appear with the same nonentity to others? Take away her position here and who would bow and curtsey, ply her with shallow compliments?

She rubbed her hand across her forehead wonderingly. Never before this morning had she asked so many such questions of herself. It was as if her dream—though it might not have freed her body—had lit a candle cluster in a dusky part of her mind.

She leaned over once again to the brazier to see if she

could catch any lingering trace of that fragrance just as a discreet knock on her door announced that she no longer had her privacy and would not for the rest of this long day.

It was Julta, of course, her noiseless glide in contrast to her stiff-held back—Julta, who was able to express her reaction to anything by a down curve of lip or a lift of eyebrow. But Zuta had said that the maid was as close-mouthed among the servants as she was with her mistress; and she was quiet, deft, and sometimes seemed to fade into the background as if she had stepped into one of the many time-faded tapestries.

She placed the silver tray she carried on the dressing table and poured from its matching pot the morning infusion of herbs supposed to enliven one for the day.

"Your Grace rested well?"

"As ever, Julta."

"There is a message from His Highness. He wishes your presence in his cabinet before Second Bell."

"Thank you," Mahart said as she sipped the tea. Well, this day was one which was beginning surprisingly. She could count on her fingers the number of times her father had ever summoned her to that chamber which was the heart of his own cramped life. "I will wear the vine dress, Julta."

The maid had already turned to the tall wardrobe. The vine dress—of a leaf green with its embroidered borders of silver vines—always gave Mahart confidence. And today there was something about its freshness which warred with the dark age of the room and reminded her of the open field and its gems of flowers.

She suffered the pinning and pulling of her hair into the new style suggested by Zuta—divided into two braids which were then coiled one over each ear to be anchored with fine silver nets, the pins holding such sometimes a threat to one's scalp. The rest of the ritual of washing and dressing continued as usual—Julta as closemouthed as always, leaving Mahart to her scrambling of thoughts.

What had she done lately which might have actually stirred her father into not only remembering he had a daughter but summoning her at this hour for speech? But her conscience was clear enough. So it was not some misconduct of the past but some new regulation of the future that she was facing.

As she selected from the jewel casket Julta held open the simple chain of silver leaves which she always wore with this gown there was a second knock at the door. Mahart was allowed to fasten the necklace for herself as Julta went to let in Zuta—though it was early for the lady-companion to appear.

As usual Mahart immediately felt drab. Zuta's gown outlined her form as closely as if she wore no chemise beneath. Its dark blue satin, the same shade as her heavy-lidded eyes, was not, however, cut as low at the bodice as those of the ladies who attended Saylana appeared to find in fashion, and her hair had been all but completely hidden by a gold-patterned baglike headdress.

She curtseyed and rose smiling.

"I see I chose well, Your Grace. You arose refreshed this morning." She glanced from Mahart to the brazier.

"True," Mahart agreed, "it was all you promised, Zuta. Surely this Herbmistress has great knowledge. I wish," before she thought (and why did she suddenly believe that this was a thought she did not wish to share?) "that I might visit this famous shop for myself."

With a slight frown, Zuta shook her head. "That is not the way, Your Grace. Should you wish to know more of what the Herbmistress has to offer, summon her and ask that she bring samples—if His Highness will approve. After all, he has always allowed you to select from Master Gorgias the best material for your gowns, and did he not give you last name day the moss lily scent you liked so well? Remind him of that when you ask to meet the Herbmistress, for it, too, came from her distilling. Now—what is your will?"

She stood waiting by the door. Mahart denied herself a last glance in the mirror as she answered.

"His Highness desires my presence in his cabinet before Second Bell. I shall have to wait to break my fast this morning, Zuta."

For a moment she thought she saw Zuta's lips begin to form a question. If the lady-companion wanted to know why this out-of-custom demand had been ordered, she was trained well enough in etiquette not to ask.

So Mahart went alone down the staircase into the busier section of the castle. Guardsmen she was hardly aware of snapped to attention as she passed until she reached the door she sought. There the guardsman thudded the butt of his spear of ceremony on the floor loud as any fist against that portal.

There was a muffled answer from within and the guardsman unbent enough from his statue pose to open the door and announce: "Her Grace, the High Lady Mahart, Your Highness."

Mahart took a deep breath and stepped forward. The heavy draperies at all the windows had been pulled open, and there was a measure of daylight added to by candles on the wide desk. He was not alone; standing to one side and curving forward in a formal bow was Vazul.

Mahart's eyes widened, but she swept the deep, formal court curtsey to her father. Why the Chancellor should be present was an added puzzle.

"Give you a fair day, Father, and may fortune favor you." She was glad that her voice sounded steady enough.

"Yes, yes—" The Duke waved an impatient hand, and his aspect was certainly not welcoming. But he stared at her strangely. His eyes actually seemed to open the wider, as if she were some curiosity being presented to his notice.

"Sit—" He jerked his hand again, this time toward a chair which the Chancellor had drawn forward.

Sit she did, but now uneasiness was fully awake in her.

What *did* they want of her? That Vazul was a part of her being here she did not doubt.

"You are of age." Uttobric was now shuffling papers back and forth on the desktop as if he were discovering that he was finding it difficult to select the proper words. "Of age," he repeated quickly, "to be betrothed."

Mahart's folded hands tightened on each other. She knew well that in this subject she had no choice at all.

He paused and was looking at her expectantly.

"Yes, Father." She pinched out the answer he seemed to have been waiting for as he now continued.

"As a woman matters of statecraft are beyond your judgment. But this is something which you *must* understand, for it means the safety of the duchy. As you well know, I was not in the direct line of descent but was elevated to serve Kronen by fate when my second cousin and the other male heirs died in the plague.

"By law the rule could not pass to the High Lady Saylana, as no woman ever rules, nor could it go to that son of hers"—his mouth twisted as if he could have added a few scathing words to describe Barbric—"as I lived. But though fortune favored me in one way, it scanted me in another. Your mother bore me only a daughter."

He made that sound, Mahart thought, as if in some way her only faintly remembered mother had deliberately arranged such a mishap.

"Now listen closely, girl, to what our good Chancellor has found in his lengthy search of the laws—for there are sometimes twists and turns in old decrees which can bring proper solutions."

Vazul moved into the full light of the window as if he needed to capture her attention and hold it. One of his shoulders seemed higher, and then she made out the inky black of that creature he was never seen without and which was held in dislike by all the court.

"In the reign of Duke Kathbric the Second"—his voice had a certain hypnotic quality and she was strangely eager for him to continue—"a similar situation arose. He had only a daughter, the High Lady Rothanna. The next heir, a distant cousin, was one who had betrayed his royal blood over and over by dastardly actions. Duke Kathbric appealed to the House of the Star. Those Chosen Ones prayed and petitioned in his behalf, and at last she who was abbess at that time was given a vision at the very altar. Others witnessed the silver beam, but only she saw who stood within.

"Thus the Star Dweller made answer: if the Lady Rothanna wed with one of equal blood who would enter into Kronen not as a visitor but as native to spend his life here, then the Duke, after that marriage or when his last days arrived, could proclaim this son-in-law now a son by blood.

"They sought for such a man and discovered him in Arsena across the sea. He was in exile, expelled from his land by the great conqueror Lantee, his former kingdom completely swallowed up by that Emperor's act.

"He had been first son to the king of his own land, but now was the only survivor of his line. His descent was proven by those from Kronen who searched. And he was brought here, married to Rothanna, and subsequently proclaimed son by descent."

Vazul's hand, raised to stroke the creature, seemed to move in rhythm with his words. Now he paused.

That strange feeling of another self opening within her moved Mahart daringly to speak.

"If this happened once—why not again? The High Lady Saylana—"

"The High Lady Saylana"—her father's grating voice almost made that a threat—"has, unfortunately for her, a strong will. She refused to follow the proper orders of *her* father and married Lord Aliken—entranced by his looks and the fact he was a public hero after putting down the outlaws at their stronghold at Volon. At the plague time she discovered to her cost what she had done. Her father and her lord were both swept away, and the latter had only been a noble for five generations and so was well outside any royal line.

"Such folly"—her father was continuing—"will not occur again. You have heard Vazul, praise the Star, he found this divine precedent—now you will do your duty."

Mahart suddenly shivered. Marriage was always, she understood, among those of the blood a gamble like the tossing of Fate Stones. Few girls ever even saw their intended before the wedding day. But to face this fate suddenly was frightening.

"Who—" she began when her father cut her short.

"All things will come in order at the proper time."

"Your Highness." Vazul's voice was soft but had in it the force of a reminder.

"Yes, yes." Uttobric slapped his hand down on the paper-strewn desk. "You are not fitted yet for court; there will be lessons. And then there will come a visitor whom you will meet with all goodwill. Now, go—I have much to do."

He waved his hand in dismissal. Vazul in two swift strides was at the door bowing as he opened it. As she passed she caught a faint whisper: "You will have more freedom, High Lady—take care how you use it."

3 That scent which made Willadene's flesh prickle was strong. But for a moment she had to blink to adjust her sight to the very dim light within the shop. The lamp which always burned all night at the other end of the room was the only glimmer here now, except for the sliver of daylight stretching out from the half-open door.

Willadene's sandaled foot nearly nudged a huddled shape on the floor—Halwice? Her hands flew to her lips, but she did not utter that scream which filled her throat. Why, she could not tell, but that it was necessary to be quiet now was like an order laid upon her.

Her eyes were drawn beyond that huddled body to a chair which did not belong in the shop at all but had been pulled from the inner room. In that sat the Herbmistress, unmoving and silent. Dead—?

Willadene's hands were shaking, but somehow she pulled herself around that other body on the floor toward where one of the strong lamps, used when one was mixing powders, sat. Luckily the strike light was also there, and after two attempts she managed to set spark to the wick.

With the lamp still in hands which quivered, the girl swung around to face that silent presence in the chair.

Eyes stared back at her, demanding eyes. No, Halwice lived but something held her in thrall and helpless. There were herbs which could do that in forbidden mixture, but Halwice never dealt with such.

Those eyes— Willadene somehow found a voice which was only a whisper.

"What—?" she began.

The eyes were urgent as if sight could write a message on the very air between them. They moved—from the girl to the half-open door and then back with an urgency Willadene knew she must answer. But how— Did Halwice want her to summon help?

"Can you"—she was reaching now for the only solution she could think of—"answer? Close your eyes once—"

Instantly the lids dropped and then rose again. Willadene drew a deep breath, almost of relief. By so much, then, she knew they could still communicate.

"Do I go for Doctor Reymonda?" He was the nearest of the medical practitioners who depended upon Halwice for their drugs.

The eyelids snapped down, arose, and fell again.

"No?" Willadene tried to hold the lamp steady. She had near forgotten the body on the floor.

She stared so intensely as if she could force the answer she needed out of the Herbmistress. Now she noted that the other's gaze had swept beyond her and was on the floor. Once more the silent woman blinked twice with almost the authority of an order. Willadene made a guess.

"Close the door?" That quick, single affirmative blink was her answer. She carefully edged about the body to do just that. Halwice did not want help from outside—but what evil had happened here? And was the silent form on the floor responsible for the Herbmistress's present plight?

With the door shut some instinct made the girl also, one-handedly as she held the lamp high, slide the bolt bar across it, turning again to find Halwice's gaze fierce and intent on her. The Herbmistress blinked. Yes, she had been right—Halwice wanted no one else here.

Then that gaze turned floorward, as far as nature would let the eyes move, to fasten on the body. Willadene carefully set the lamp down beside the inert stranger and then knelt.

It was a man lying facedown. His clothing was traveler's leather and wool as if he were just in from some traders' caravan. Halwice dealt often with traders, spices, and strange roots; even crushed clays of one sort or another arrived regularly here. But what had happened—?

Willadene's years of shifting iron pots and pans and dealing with Jacoba's oversize aids to cooking had made her stronger than her small, thin body looked. She was able to roll the stranger over.

Under her hand his flesh was cool, and she could see no wound or hurt. It was as if he had been struck down instantly by one of those weird powers which were a part of stories told to children.

He was young with dark hair which curled thickly over his head as she gingerly touched, seeking an injury which might be hid by the thick locks. His face was well featured but gaunt with the shadow of beard beginning to show. Altogether, there was nothing to differ him from any minor merchant she might serve in the inn. Willadene drew back her hand and wiped it on her ragged apron. That he was dead she was almost certain, but she was no healer. Questioningly she looked up at Halwice.

Again those wide eyes held hers. And, as if the Herbmistress so made sure that she had the girl's full attention, the eyes turned downward to the body on the floor. Once more the gaze was raised to Willadene and this time, very slowly, as if the Herbmistress was using every bit of the will she could summon, the eyes shifted away from Willadene and the body to that curtain which cloaked the entrance to the back room.

Three times Halwice went through that sequence. Again Willadene had to guess.

"Him—back there—that's what you want?" She pointed toward the inner room.

The blink which answered her was like a snap. Yes, that was what the woman wanted. He was to be hidden from anyone coming to the shop unwittingly as she had done.

She set the lamp back on the counter and then worked her way between the body and the angle of Halwice's chair. Stooping, she hooked hands in the armpits of that inert corpse—though every nerve in her shrank from what she was doing.

It was hard, but she managed to drag him into the second room, pausing now and then but always beginning doggedly again. The back room was large, for one end of it was a bedchamber and the other a cooking place, far cleaner and better smelling than that Jacoba ruled.

Willadene stood staring down at the body. The thought grew in her that it was foolish to leave him so, in plain sight. The bed was a cupboard one and so no hiding place there. She stared about until she noted the settle at one side of the fireplace.

It was a massive piece of furniture and the seat was deep. If the area below was as wide— Luckily the back windows had been thrown open; scents from the wide herb garden hidden behind the shop mingled and she felt refreshed, almost as if her mind had so been cleared and she could again think purposefully. The settle it would be.

However, getting her burden in place there was no easy task, and once it was done and she had made sure he could not be sighted by anyone casually glancing into the room, the girl was breathing as heavily as if she had been racing like a noble's trained mare.

She had to keep one hand against the side of the doorway as she looped up the curtain in order to steady herself as she returned to Halwice. Coming to stand directly before the Herbmistress she made her report.

"He is under the settle—there was no better hiding place."

Again she was answered by a single blink, but she continued: "Is there that I can do to aid *you*, mistress?"

The eyes blinked their yes. And Willadene studied the moving gaze with care. There was a drawer in the tall cupboard which, it seemed to her, Halwice had centered on. Her hand moved down those drawers, until an effective blink stopped her search.

This contained rarities, she knew, many from lands so far few had heard of them. The girl drew open that drawer. There were three small packets within, each wrapped in preservative oiled skin. She held up each until the blink signified the proper one.

Now the eyes were moving again—this time to the array of bottled oils and fragrance flasks on the shelf. Once more she went through the process of touching each until a signal came.

She waited for her next search but then became aware that Halwice was staring at a brazier on a lower shelf. Willadene lifted that up and placed it on the counter. No, the eyes went from where it stood to mark another spot directly before the motionless woman. Willadene moved it.

Once more she reached for the small bottle and that packet. Blink—yes! She undid the packet. The scent which arose from it— She was startled. This was something like that whiff of fragrance which that morning she had met as she walked with the Begging Sisters. The very opposite of the evil stench, fading now (or else she was more used to it) which she had met in this room earlier.

That all such must be used with discretion she well knew. She set a spark to the waiting fire tablets at the bottom of the brazier, and then she held up the opened paper in full sight of the Herbmistress. One pinch of the rough powder within she took up. The blink answered yes,

and to a second also, but the eyes refused a third. Willadene tossed what she held in the palm of her hand from
her and quickly caught up the flask.

It was one of those Halwice had made particularly for
her uses from which only one drop at a time would issue.
Now the eyes ordered three drops over what had already
begun to smoke in the brazier.

The smoke thickened. It seemed to take the form of a
cord which grew ever denser. When it had reached near
Willadene's own height it began to spiral, and that spiral
moved—to surround Halwice, hiding her totally from
sight.

Willadene stumbled back against the counter. The scent
was full fragrance of the richest kind, almost enough to
smother one. And she was not even within its hold.

For a moment, which seemed to last past an hour, it
curtained Halwice from sight. Then, as one might snap
fingers, it was gone. Halwice was moving, raising her
hands from her lap, turning her head from side to side, as
if she was testing the disappearance of her bondage.

Then she spoke, "Star sent you here this day. But this
coil is not yet untwined." She tried to stand but collapsed
once more onto the chair. "Time, I need time, and I think
there is very little of that left. Child, clear away all this—"
she nodded at the brazier, the flask, and the packet "—to
their proper places. We can at least hope that the one who
set the dark spell does not learn—or at least soon—that
there is the means of breaking it under this roof.

"You came for spices." Her voice grew ever brisker
as she spoke. "Will you be missed?"

Willadene's flight seemed very long ago, wiped out by
her labors here.

"I was not sent, mistress, I—I ran," she confessed.

"From what?"

"Jacoba. She would sell me for a good bride price to
Wyche— I think that is why she has kept me." Willadene

twisted her hands in the rags of her apron. "And, mistress, she has such a right, the Reeve will say so."

"So. Wyche—" Halwice repeated the name as if it stood for some offal. "Jacoba is no member of the council to say that the Reeve will allow her to dispose of you so. It is not quite as easy as she believes. I have not gone against her for these past few years—for reasons which are quite removed—but now, now I will take a hand!" She said that with the authority of one well used to giving orders and having them straightway obeyed.

"However—first there will be a game we must play." She made another effort to rise from the chair; however, it was very apparent that some weakness defeated her and her usually emotionless face showed an increasing frown.

"What about him—the dead man?" Willadene pointed to the curtain of the inner room.

Halwice, with great determination, had managed to get on her feet, and Willadene hurried to offer her support, her question unanswered. It was not until Halwice, leaning heavily on her, reached the counter to which she swiftly transferred her hold that the Herbmistress spoke.

"He is not dead—and can be dealt with later. But for now— Can you manage the shutters?" She nodded toward the still-closed front of the shop. "Try to attract as little attention as possible. It must seem to any watcher to be as always—ready for business." However, there was a look of strain on her face now, and the girl could see that her hold on the edge of the counter was tight.

That tenseness was shared by Willadene. She could make no possible guess at what had happened, or was going to happen, but she was very willing to follow any orders in order to please the gaunt-faced woman struggling in her own battle.

Outside in the street she tried not to fumble too much in the unfamiliar task set her. There were three other nearby shops, but luckily their proprietors were out of sight within and there seemed to be only a few passersby—none of them, she assured herself by a quick glance now and then, paying any attention to her.

When the last of those night barriers swung back, ready to be secured within, she slipped around the narrow crack she had left for her return and speedily snapped the shutter bolts into place. Before her, making her stretch some distance to finish her task, was the display shelf to show off the most enticing wares, and those were in place—small bottles, boxes with gem-set lids, pomanders ready to swing from neck or girdle—all treasures to be filled with Halwice's products, eye-catching enough to attract customers to the shop.

There was light enough here now, and Halwice had blown out the lamp, pushing it back to its stand. She was frowning at the chair which had been her prison.

"Push that into the far corner," she ordered. "It must be seen as part of what is rightfully here when they come."

Willadene, struggling with the heavy chair, wanted to ask who "they" might be, but she had a feeling that Halwice was in full command now and she was best off doing as the Herbmistress bade with no more questions.

When she had maneuvered the chair into the shadowed back corner Halwice had suggested, her attention was caught by a spark of color on the floor near where she had struggled with the inert body to be hidden within.

Stooping, she picked up what at first she thought was a coin, for it was round and about the size of a one noble piece. However, when she turned it over she could see the small hook on the edge; clearly it had been meant to hang from a chain as an ornament. Nor was it the coin she thought it; rather, on both surfaces front and back, it bore a symbol—widespread wings centered by a shield on which was engraved a sword and a staff crossed. That was a badge she had seen several times—it belonged to the Chancellor.

"Give that here!" Halwice's voice did not rise any

louder, but it was clear that she was even more disturbed. As Willadene quickly handed over her find she saw Halwice loose one of her handholds on the counter to tuck it quickly between the lacings of her bodice into hiding.

"This is not to be spoken of—"

Willadene nodded. Perhaps it was the property of that body (she still found it hard to believe Halwice's assurance he was not dead) loosened when she had dragged him behind the curtain.

"Now, listen with care, girl, and prove you have that within you which is needed. The watch will come—they should be here very soon now. What you found here was a trap—for me—for that one inside. So I can well believe that the district Reeve's own guard will visit us. You have come to get spices for Jacoba as always. Measure out the proper ones in the usual amounts—"

The woman gripped the counter with both hands again as the girl drew a small square of discarded paper from a shelf under that counter, smoothed it out on the surface above, and took down a box close at hand. Carefully she used the small scoop within and shook what looked like the usual amount of condiments onto the paper.

She had just time enough to slide that box back into place when she heard, from the street outside, the tramp of heavy boots drilled into unison of step. Halwice had been right! That was surely the Reeve's guard. Willadene rounded the counter to face the Herbmistress. She felt a growing need to hold on to the polished wood for support even as Halwice was doing.

If Jacoba had reported her already as a runaway she would speedily be taken. Her only hope was that the inn lay in another section of the town and that the Reeve who had jurisdiction in that quarter would not have been able to already pass the news to his peers.

There was a man in the doorway but Halwice did not look to him; instead she was scowling at Willadene.

"Tell Jacoba that there is no herb on earth which will

make her slop worth the eating. Her account is already high—when does she plan to pay?''

Willadene, so conscious of the man who was now nearly at her shoulder, fought to control her voice.

''Mistress, I be but the cook maid. The inn mistress does not tell me anything save go and get spice for the meat. Please, mistress''—she hunched herself together as if she already feared the smack of Jacoba's cane across her bony shoulders—''let me have what she has asked for—she is already angered.''

''Who are you!'' The voice in her ear was harsh, the hand which fell on her shoulder to pull her around was heavy enough to bruise.

Willadene did not have to call on any power of acting; she was already frightened enough. The man who jammed her back against the counter was of the guard right enough. His mail shirt, his helm shadowing the upper part of his broad face on which a mustache bristled fiercely, were more than warning—rather perhaps dire disaster.

''She is the cook maid for the Wanderers Inn''—Halwice's voice was as calm as if they were exchanging some pleasantries concerning a fine day—''she was sent here for spices—''

Willadene dared not stir. The man glanced only briefly at the Herbmistress; his eyes were sweeping swiftly about the shop, while two of his fellows crowded in behind him.

Again Halwice spoke. ''I am known well to the Reeve; also I have a seat on the Guild Council. Why do you come into my shop in this fashion? Do I not supply His Highness himself and all others of noted families—?'' Her voice was growing heated, as might that of any honest shopkeeper so used. ''My taxes are paid—given into the hands of the Reeve himself. I have offended no one and abide by the guild laws—''

The leader of the guard looked to her again. He indicated with a thumb the curtained doorway to the inner room.

"What lies there, mistress?" His voice was not quite as aggressive as it had been.

"My living quarters and beyond that the garden where I grow some of my stock. Look for yourself. But what do you hunt? I am indeed an honest woman and as such am not to be used in this manner. Be sure I shall report to the Reeve—"

The leader continued to stare at her.

"There has been information laid against this shop—against you," he repeated stolidly. "It was given to us on good authority that a rogue we seek would be found here dead—killed, mistress"—now his mustache seemed to rise straight out from the roots like the bristles of a boar—"by an evil potion."

Halwice drew herself up, her features set. "What kind of a talemonger's fashion is this? Do you see a dead man? Look you—look well!"

Willadene's heart was beating so she was sure it would soon shake her body, for Halwice was actually pointing to the curtain of the second room.

"But listen well, Sergeant. Do you, or any of these clumsy followers of yours, do any damage to my wares I shall not take it only in complaint to the Reeve but to His Highness himself. Look you there—" She pointed to where a glass bottle fashioned only large enough to fit perhaps into the palm of Willadene's hand and in the form of a rose, rested under a glass dome. "That is Breath of Roses for the High Lady Mahart. Know you the cost of that? It is worth more than half your year's pay with the lady's displeasure into the bargain?"

"Our information"—but the girl noted he was eyeing that bottle warily and had moved several steps away from its vicinity—"came from a source which does not rumor monger. Since you yourself bid us do so—we look."

He brushed by and swept the curtain roughly aside. Willadene stared down at the top of the counter, at that packet of spice she was supposed to be buying, and waited for the sergeant to make his find. Only, he did not but came tramping back to the shop room in just a moment or two. Perhaps Halwice's warning had had its effect.

"Well," the Herbmistress demanded, "where is your dead man? Look in the garden if you must—there is no recent delving to be seen there. Make very sure I shall enter on the Reeve's record my answer to this charge and the disturbance of my trade. Why should a dead man be found in *my* shop? I have taken oath before the altar of the Star and been examined by the High Priestess, who can detect any evil through her powers. She has proclaimed me free of all dealing which can cause ill to anyone. Do you dare to dispute that judgment?

"If there came one by night to seize my wares—where then could he sell them? And do I not have an alarm bell justified by the city laws to ring if any attempts to do this? Who heard my bell—where is there any intruder— have I made complaint?"

Her voice became harder and harder as she bombarded him with this string of questions. The man's full cheeks were blazing red and his two followers had retreated to the front door, keeping an eye to either side as if fearful of unwittingly causing some damage. That the sergeant was angry was plain. Willadene could almost feel the heat of his wrath. However, his own eyes told him there was nothing out of the ordinary to see in the shop. And certainly Halwice's free expression of influence both with the Reeve of this section and even the Duke himself sank home. She would not give such warnings unless she could back them up.

"I shall make my report, mistress." He was obviously trying to save face by putting a tone of warning into that.

"Do—and be about your rightful business and let me get about mine," she replied sharply.

He did go—several steps behind the members of his squad, who were now in the street. When they could no longer be seen through the small panes of the window

Halwice turned to the girl. She had already drawn another square of paper from a pile under the counter and was folding it together.

"Good, they have gone west. Now, listen well. Take this as if you were indeed on the errand you were supposed to go on. Once you are outside the door, go the opposite way—east. You know where Doctor Dobblier's house is?"

Willadene nodded.

"Follow the alley at its back and come down to the fence about my garden. Count to five the boards as you pass them and then press on the next two; they will open for you. Knock three times on the back door."

Willadene drew a deep breath. "Then I am to come back?" she half whispered.

Halwice looked at her measuringly. "Have you not wanted to?"

"Yes, oh, yes!"

"Then be quick about it. We have much which is to be done."

And Willadene sped through the street door as if she expected to meet some sharp punishment for being late about her errand.

4 Mahart's life, which she had once likened to that of a state prisoner, altered in a hurry. Though she noted that she was still kept from any close contact with the High Lady Saylana's courtiers, she began to be visited more and more by Vazul, who brought a number of ladies of an earlier generation to be presented and spend some hours of stilted conversation and very formal manners in her private sitting room.

She knew that she was an object of curiosity to most of them, and, though she squirmed inside, she made herself become outwardly unperturbed by the stares from behind the shadows of fans—measuring stares.

Zuta was always present and, at the end of such trials of public life, was only too ready to discuss each visitor—sometimes exceeding the boundaries of what was supposed to be suitable for a young girl to hear. Such revelations were to Mahart like the stories she had read in books but had never before really associated with living persons.

Her wardrobe doubled and the sewing maids were daily busied. She had to spend tedious hours standing as one or another of them encircled the hem of a shirt, marking it for stitching.

Though Zuta continued to urge brighter colors and

richer materials on her, Mahart kept to those shades in which she felt the most comfortable—paler colors in ranges of greens, rose, and creams. And she discouraged much embroidery or heavy trimmings of fur and metallic thread.

She was early made aware of the reason for all this glory, being rained unasked upon her, by Vazul, who, upon one early morning visit, was followed by one in the uniform of a bodyguard, who carried a good-sized chest. With the air of a showman about to astound his audience, the Chancellor unlocked it and threw back its lid, to disclose a treasury of jewelry. It seemed to blaze almost as brightly as a lamp, and Mahart stared at it, queerly repelled. There was too much of it—surely it could not be real. However, Vazul quickly assured her that these were the ducal jewels of state, not belonging to any one member of the family but kept as legacies to be worn on occasions of high state.

One such occasion was about to be proclaimed. For years—since the plague, in fact—there had never been a ducal court held, one in which the daughters and heirs of the noble houses first made their meeting with their overlord. Uttobric considered such affairs a waste of valuable time, since the preparation for such occupied most of the castle inhabitants for several weeks; in addition, he was never sure of such meetings with nobility he did not altogether trust.

However, it was not Uttobric this time who was to be the center of pomp. He had announced that, since the High Lady Mahart was of suitable age, her initiation into her duties would begin with such an event.

Between Vazul and Zuta, Mahart had to submit to being coached for such an affair. This would be worse than entertaining all the elder women at her teas. The audience watching her for any misstep would be avidly intent. Thus she set herself to learn a role she had no desire to play but which appeared to be part of her uncertain heritage.

"The High Lady Saylana will be present," Zuta announced. "She will occupy the lower seat. It is Your Grace who enters first, and she must curtsey—though not as low, of course, before she seats herself. She will have at least three of her favorite ladies with her, and they will stand on the lowest step of the dais to the far right.

"I shall be your chief lady—with your favor—" She paused and Mahart nodded quickly. "And it is best that you invite the Lady Famina of the House of Ranavice, which so far has not openly committed itself to sponsorship of either side of our old inheritance dispute. Then there is the Lady Geuverir of Krutz—her father is one who is very loyal to His Highness.

"With Your Grace's permission, these two have been summoned this very day to be presented to you. You remember that Lady Honora." Zuta smiled mischievously.

Mahart surely did and with a prick of irritation. The pompous dame had sailed into her presence several weeks ago, giving off very clearly that she was only doing her duty and the object of that duty was not to be highly considered.

"The Lady Honora is Lady Geuverir's mother. And Lady Geuverir is said to have inherited certain traits of the maternal character."

Mahart grinned. "Thank you kindly, Zuta, for your warning."

She duly met her new attendants.

To Mahart's taste they were overdressed, and she noted that the Lady Geuverir gave a sidewise look, which was not complimentary, at what she herself was wearing. On her the Lady Honora's imperious features were certainly repeated. The Lady Famina was round cheeked and pearls of sweat on her forehead wet down her fringe of hair. When she spoke—only in answer to some direct question—she had a slight stammer.

Mahart's own short experience of contact with the court had quickened her ability to sense some things, and she was very much aware that High Lady Saylana's attendants would far outshine these two. But she could count upon Zuta at least to catch eyes—unless they would all be centered on Mahart herself!

The court was indeed a trial. It was held, as had been usual, before the last bell in the late afternoon so that the great throne room was lighted not only by forests of candles in high, standing holders but also all by the westering sky through the windows at the meeting of wall and ceiling.

Mahart had refused nearly a third of the jeweled pieces urged upon her, but even so, a look into her mirror made her think of some little town girl tricked out far too much. Her cream satin gown was draped with a netting of pale gold in which was caught a heavy sprinkling of diamonds. A wide necklace of the same stones covered most of the skin displayed by the low-cut neckline, and a flashing tiara weighed on her head, making her uneasy about its safety. She continued to hold her head stiffly upward to assure that it would not slip.

The only part of what the maids and Zuta had done to her that she really enjoyed was the fragrance which had come from the most beautiful jeweled bottle she had in her collection—a recent gift from the Duke, fashioned like an open rose.

Somehow the fragrance stiffened her determination to make this indeed a court to be remembered as she led the way, with Zuta two steps behind, dressed in a shade of her favorite rose, and the other two ladies tricked out with flounces, ribbons, and gems enough to avert Mahart's attention from them quickly.

She made her entrance at the stately pace she had practiced for so many hours in her room, acknowledging the deep bow of the Chancellor with a raise of her hand, which she then laid on his arm as he led her up the five steps to the ducal throne. For this hour she was the chosen representative of their ruler, and the deference of those assembled in the room was rightly centered upon her.

The other chair, one step below her throne, was empty, but High Lady Saylana was already advancing with what seemed a lengthy train of followers. Most of them melted into the crowd of waiting courtiers, but she was escorted by a trio of mature and perfectly gowned beauties.

Saylana herself had chosen satin and netting also, but hers was moonlight gray and the stones caught in the overdress, rubies—like the bright-red eyes of forest animals. A choker of the same stones was clasped around her throat. Lapping a little over that were hints of flesh rolls. And there were wrinkles no cosmetic magic could hide about her mouth and at the corners of her eyes.

Those eyes were as bright and seemingly as fiery as the rubies. And she did not lower the head on which her hair was confined with jeweled bands. Her gaze holding steady and with the faintest of mocking smiles about her reddened lips, she sank into the deep court curtsey which Mahart readily recognized as being subtly insulting, her three ladies also sinking in a whirl of wide skirts behind her.

The whole affair was a wearying ordeal. At least twenty maidens of high blood were handed to the foot of the dais by one of the heralds, her name and house announced clearly. Mahart tried to manufacture smiles which were as close to welcoming and pleasant as possible and murmur correctly the name over the young lady who was bent in the awkward position of the lowest point of obedience.

She had to listen and remember those names, be sure that none was offended and slighted. Then that portion was finished, and the herald by the far door announced the heirs to be recognized.

Mahart had been able to ignore Saylana during this press of duties, but she was well aware now that the other stirred in her chair and was leaning forward a little.

No wonder—the first bedecked popinjay issued into place before Mahart was Barbric, Saylana's son. He was tall, but he carried himself awkwardly and had a slack mouth—certainly no prince to ride in a maid's dreams. Nor did she like the way he eyed her as he straightened from his bow—as if she were some sort of prize for the winning. There were many tales circulating in the castle about Barbric, and none of them carried to Mahart by Zuta had been edifying. She was glad now to see him move on.

As for the rest, they were just faces—one or two comely, the rest Mahart, used only to her father and Vazul, found childishly young.

The affair came to an end at last, and she must make her own exit, a little dubious about her long, wide skirt as she descended the steps. She had only to stumble to make Saylana's attendance a pleasure instead of a duty.

Once she was back in her chamber Mahart spoke more sharply than she ever had to Julta.

"Rid me of this!" She was already tugging at the tiara which she was sure was what was making her head ache so. Then she had to stand patiently as they unwrapped her from jewels and dress. Here in her room where there were not so many other odors to conceal it—for it seemed to her the entire court had been doused in warring perfumes—she could smell again that refreshing rose scent.

All right: she had performed as her father and Vazul had wished—dared she ask a favor in return? Zuta had said the Herbmistress could be summoned to the castle. But, by the Star, she herself was deadly tired of these walls and the bindings her birth had put upon her!

By the Star. On her bench while they rebraided her hair into its usual fashion a thought struck her.

"Zuta," she said eagerly, "have you ever been to the Abbey of the Star Sisters? I know that they welcome ones who seek answers—"

"Never, Your Grace. But—" she favored Mahart with a keen gaze "—several Duchesses and High Ladies in the past have sought them out."

"So it is a permitted thing!" Mahart exclaimed. Why

had this idea never come to her before? "I think that I shall petition my father to allow me to do this. It would be well, since he seems to wish to shift some of his formal burdens onto me, that I make the acquaintance of one who is supposed to know all which passes—the Abbess of the Star."

Vazul, his attendant creature wreathed around his neck like a second chain of office, bowed himself into the Duke's presence. Somehow at this hour, since tasting the splendor of the full court display, the Chancellor secretly found his master even more meager and without presence.

"Well?" the Duke snapped even as his Chancellor straightened again. "How did it go? Did she make a fool of herself and are half the court now laughing behind their hands?"

Vazul allowed himself a small smile, one suggesting satisfaction.

"Her Grace, Highness, was all you could wish her to be. It passed as if she had done this duty many times before."

The Duke stared at him under his eyebrows. "So—did those various eyes and ears you keep about pick up any comments later?"

"Only the most favorable ones, Highness. And in her court dress the High Lady looked truly at ease on the throne."

The Duke shuffled some of those papers which always seemed to gather about him. "And that she-wolf—did she show?"

"The High Lady Saylana made her proper appearance, Highness. She acknowledged your daughter in the most correct fashion. However, among the scions of high birth presented Barbric was the first."

"She would parade him like a new war horse, would she? I take it he has little resemblance to his sire?"

"None that could be ascertained during such presentation, Highness." Vazul stroked his pet. "He certainly does not present the appearance of a leader of. valiant men."

The Duke snorted. "If he can stick on a horse and wave a sword, she will have it he is his heroic father's true son. Now—" he scrabbled among the papers until he found one which he held close to his weak eyes "—I see the Bat was helpful as usual. But what happened to him that delayed this report? Oh, sit down, man, you must have a story to offer for that." He waved the Chancellor into another chair.

Vazul's slight smile was gone. "I think, Highness," he said slowly, "we have a Bat wearing other colors some-where among us."

The paper crunched between the Duke's hands. "He was taken, then?" he demanded, his voice rising.

"There was an attempt which near succeeded. He has those who will give him cover when necessary. One such is a woman you know well—Halwice the Herbmistress. She herself has a network of informers who have served us very well in the past, for her products are not all of Kronengred, but much comes from abroad.

"The Bat was given a packet to deliver to her, and he knew, or believed that he did, the seal set on it. It gave him a reason for going undercover in her house until he could contact me. But that packet was tampered with.

"When she opened it he was struck as if dead and she made prisoner within a helpless body. Had it not been for chance, that an inn brat she had befriended came to her aid, she and the Bat would have been taken up by the Reeve's guard."

"*He* set the trap?" The Duke's thin face flushed. "By the Star." His fist thudded on the table. "City law or no city law I'll have the fellow to rigorous question!"

Vazul was shaking his head. "The Reeve was but a tool himself. A message was sent him under a seal that he had reason to believe made a visit to the shop imperative— my seal—or a rough copy of it.

"However, from this we have learned something which is"—he paused—"unsettling. Somewhere there is one with herb knowledge, someone operating outside the sworn rules of the guild. Halwice has warned of such. Twice, if you remember, she detected foreign material among deliveries made to her. But this attack was stronger, she says, than anything she believed might be done. As one who works always among potions she has made herself immune to the known noxious materials which she might chance upon. Yet this struck her down as if she had no defense at all. And her wakening of the Bat was a lengthy and arduous task. One, she says frankly, she doubts she could have accomplished had it not been for the inn girl."

The Duke frowned. "Who might also have been planted."

"She has been vouched for, Highness. Her record is very clear from any contact with those we have reason to believe wish to deal ill with us. Before the plague struck, she lived with her parents. Her father was a member of the frontier guard and so away for lengths of time. Her mother was a midwife whom to this day is greatly missed by those survivors who knew her.

"Being alone she was gathered up with the other orphans in her ward and arbitrarily apprenticed to the cook-owner of the Wanderers Inn, an unsavory place but one with which the Reeve's guard can find no overt fault especially since they are blood kin. This cook is one of those bullies who welcome a victim, and the girl has been hers ever since. Now she threatens to wed the girl to a suspicious character we have been watching carefully, as she wants the bride price. The girl fled for aid to Halwice, who has tested her and discovered she has a natural talent for her own work. Halwice has appealed to the Reeve's court to reassign the girl to her care and a suggestion"—he smiled again—"from a high quarter has made this now a fact. No, set your fears to rest, my lord, she is not one of the spiders' netting.''

''If you say so.'' The Duke shrugged. ''Now as to this news from abroad—so Prince Lorien is at odds with his father, King Hawkner?''

''So much so,'' Vazul said, ''that he and his followers—all well trained, some of them former border guards—have withdrawn to the hold of Keesal.''

The Duke dropped the paper he was holding, swept it aside with a number of others to uncover a map. He picked up a round glass from the desk and held it over the northwest corner of the map.

''Near the border,'' he commented.

''Near something else also, Highness,'' Vazul remarked. ''Look to the left of Mount Nastor—''

''A red dot,'' the Duke replied, and then lifted his head swiftly to meet his Chancellor eye to eye. ''That is the Red Wolf's den!''

Vazul nodded approvingly. ''Just so. Of late, the Red Wolf's pickings have been lean. Since you withdrew the garrison at Krantz—''

''Which I had to do!'' snapped the Duke. ''If we do not keep the main highways free of despoilers the merchants will begin to ask awkward questions again.''

''The Wolf is beginning to hunger, yes. And the Prince's party is small. This outlaw is bold-thoughted enough to plan a quick raid across the border, maybe believing that he will not be pursued and that it would take time to send our troops thither.''

''Lorien's men are veterans, you say?'' The Duke leaned back in his chair and rubbed his chin with one hand.

''The Prince is not a berserker out for war on all fronts. However, he is well-known to admire feats of arms and has voluntarily served two terms with the Borderers. In fact, his present quarrel with the King began from the fact that he absents himself from court too much and there are questions raised contrasting his abilities with the heir who is of a rather indolent nature.''

"Can it be done?'' The Duke leaned forward in his chair.

"It is far from impossible,'' Vazul was replying when there came a diffident tap at the door.

"In with you!'' the Duke cried out, loud enough to be heard. The door swung open only far enough to admit a page, looking as wide-eyed as a cornered puppy surrounded by evil-tempered hunting hounds. The small silver tray he bore shook as the Chancellor plucked off the folded paper there before it fluttered to the floor.

"For Your Highness.'' He bowed as he held out the message.

"All right, all right. Away with you, boy, this is no morning for interruptions.''

Thankfully the page bowed himself hastily out, shutting the door behind him with a sound which was close to a slam.

Already the Duke had unfolded the paper. His flush grew a little deeper as he tossed it to the table. "It is always so with women—they can never be satisfied.''

Vazul picked the paper up, read the few lines with more ease than the Duke had done, and then, to his master's complete surprise, said: "Well done. She has learned her part well. It has been true that all High Ladies of the family, Highness, meet with the Abbess of the Star. They, in fact, provide some funds for the poor. Yes, the Abbey lies without these walls, but the High Lady will go in a measure of state, giving the commoners a chance to see her. There can be no more tales that she is crippled or a monster of ugliness—''

"What!'' The Duke's flush had now deepened alarmingly, and he half arose from his chair, both fists planted on the desktop as he leaned forward to face the Chancellor.

"Who has said such of *my daughter*? He will choke on those lies when he swings from the north wall!''

"Rumor has said it—and doubtless that rumor was helped along by some we can name. You have kept her so pent that few have ever seen her. Now you have displayed her to the court and those of noble birth, let her also be known and seen by the people."

Mahart sat, the all-important paper stretched between her two hands. She could hardly yet believe that her daring to address her father with a request had served her so well. Now she rubbed her thumb over his seal at the bottom of that short page and passed to the second part of her plan.

She had never been taught to ride and the second way to reach her goal was to be hidden from sight by the curtains of a horse litter. But her reading in the library had provided her with an argument against that. Pilgrimage—that was it!

Not one in which one made many days' travel into the mountains in the west where the Star first was manifest. No, but she *could* cite that her first visit to the all-important Abbey here could be counted a pilgrimage.

Other Duchesses and High Ladies had certainly gone on foot from castle to Abbey in the days past, and it was taken as only fit and proper that they should approach the greatest shrine in Kronen in a mock-humble manner. Mahart was well aware that she would never be allowed to make such a journey alone—actually walking through the streets of the city she had only seen during all these years from balconies as a spread of roofs below.

She would have guards. However, such, being armed men, could not enter the inner courts of the Abbey—that she knew. She would take Zuta—luckily those two who had been added to her retinue at the court had not been pressed upon her as daily companions—but, yes, she would accept even their company also if necessary. She somehow doubted that either of them was well-known behind the Abbey walls.

"I shall go as a pilgrim—" She spoke her decision aloud.

"But, Your Grace, His Highness—he will not allow you to walk so the streets!" Zuta was quick to answer.

"Even my father cannot stand against well-rooted custom. My mother herself went so to meet the Abbess Gofrera before the plague. No, let Julta lay out my gray overrobe and the plainest of my cloaks. I think I shall make this pilgrimage today." Before, she said to herself, my father may change his mind.

There was certainly a stir among those who had been added to make up a miniature court of her own since she had taken a part in public affairs. However, precedent had its way. She was able to recite quellingly the names of those near the ducal throne who had done likewise in times past. But she was forced to delay her venture for another day, since the guard captain himself came to tell her that such streets as she would traverse must be readied for her procession.

"It is only fit, Your Grace. Those who live under the ducal protection will want to view Your Grace, and we must be ready to counter any surge of crowds. His Highness would not allow it otherwise."

So she had to wait two tedious days, fearing each hour would bring a denial from her father. Zuta, with her subtle ability to collect information, reported that there were conferences being held in the Duke's study. Messengers had gone out, and there was even a hint that the senior officers had been brought into at least one conference. However, none of this appeared to have any connection with Mahart, and she blessed the business which perhaps had even once more made the Duke forget he had a daughter.

Thus on the fourth day, dressed in the plainest gown of her wardrobe, she, herself, bearing a casket in which lay her personal gift to the Abbey's charity, for the first time she could really remember, set foot on the cobbles—discreetly covered, of course, by procession carpets—of Kronengred.

There were crowds—even as the guard captain had promised—and they raised a hail which for a moment or two she could not believe was meant to honor her. Children squirmed and ran along the edges of the carpet just beyond the reaches of the guards, and Mahart found herself laughing freely at their antics, daring to smile at the townspeople.

This was a far different world from the somber castle, and she reveled in what she could see even as she heard such cries as "The Star bless Your Grace."

The procession wound through several streets, so she caught glimpses of shops behind the crowds and wished she could explore those on her own. But the Abbey loomed above them all too soon.

Here was another crowd gathered, not the well-clad, prosperous-looking people who had crowded to cheer. No, here was an old man bent nearly double, his wrapped body supported by two sticks; a woman whose dress was fashioned by patch cobbled upon patch; a blind man led by a small girl with yellow eyes and the look of one who had too great a burden laid upon her young—and others like them. They cowered back at the sight of the guardsmen as Mahart approached the wide door of the Abbey being thrown open for her to enter.

"Beggars." Zuta had moved up until she was hardly a step behind Mahart. "They have come for the daily bread."

Mahart had no time to answer, to even sort out her thoughts about the unfortunates before the gate. For there was a tall, thronelike chair set up only a few steps farther on, where a woman in a dull gray robe and cloak, with only a glittering star-shaped crystal, sat with the same— or more—authority than her father sat on the ducal throne.

Remembering what she had read of such meetings Mahart sank into a curtsey as deep as that she would make to the Duke himself on some formal occasion.

The woman on the seat extended a silver rod which

seemed to emit a gleam of its own, and Mahart kissed the second crystal star at its tip.

The face, within the muffled swathing which covered all the hair, was wrinkled and worn by years, but the lips curved in a smile which was open and welcoming.

"In the Star's sight, Your Grace is welcome." That voice was surprisingly hearty. "It is well, my daughter, that you have chosen to come."

Mahart turned a little, to hand the casket she had carried to another caped and robed figure whose hood was pulled so far forward that she could not see any face.

"For the poor—" Mahart began, and then added almost before she thought, "Lady Abbess, they wait now at the gate. Let them not be cheated by my coming, but let me also serve those who ill fortune has crushed."

The Abbess nodded. Mahart jerked her sleeve free from the grasp Zuta had caught and turned around, her other ladies retreating. There were Sisters by the gate now, each with a basket in her hand. Mahart, brushing by those who had followed her, waved to the guards.

"Back—let the Sisters do as is set upon us by the Star."

The men withdrew, visibly reluctant, but at last some of the beggars dared to approach. Mahart dipped her own hand into the basket of the nearest Sister, her fingers closing on a round of greasy bread which she held out to the small girl clinging to the patched dress of the woman. The child seized upon it as if she feared that it would be taken away from her again. The mother dipped in an awkward curtsey.

"Star's shine upon you, Your Grace." She was staring at Mahart now in open awe.

"And upon you also, goodwife," answered Mahart.

Thus, before the eyes of many in Kronengred was seen that day that the Duke's daughter, about whom foul rumors had spread, was fair of face, straight of body, and kind of heart. Vazul's advice had accomplished even more than he had thought.

At the toll of the First Bell Willadene awoke in the nest of covers in the trundle bed, covers which were clean and smelled of lavender and sweet clover. She loved the way they seemed to smooth her skin and somehow trap her in dreams in which no shadows crouched. So much had changed in the last twenty days—it was as if she had passed through a door to enter a new and glorious world.

She rubbed her hands together. The creams Halwice brewed were fast taking away the small scars and roughness the years of kitchen service had engraved into her skin.

And it had all started when she had obeyed Halwice's orders and had left the shop on the morning which seemed so far away now, made her trembling way down the alley, found those swinging boards in what looked like a forbidding fence, and so had come into this Star-blessed place.

She had crept into the house that day and had been instantly aware of voices in the outer room, though that dark-shadowed form under the settle had not moved. But more than mere curiosity had led her to peer around the edge of the door curtain.

Halwice had stood behind her counter, but Willadene

had noted that she still kept a hold on its edge. Her voice, however, had been as strong and vibrant as usual.

"Not so, steward," she had been saying. "Yes, we get such fragrances now and then from overseas. But as you well know the merchant caravans are not as plentiful as they were—and much of what I await is fragile and easily broken.

"What you ask for at the request of your mistress is no longer mine to sell." She had tapped a finger lightly on the top of that rose bottle. "His Highness had already ordered it for his daughter's name day."

The man had shrugged. His livery overjerkin had been dark blue, bearing on both breast and back entwined silver symbols Willadene could not distinguish.

"Her Grace pays well—also she had heard that you yourself, mistress, can distill scents fully equal to those from overseas."

"To each his or her trade, steward. The blending of a new oil or fragrance often takes years of labor. Unfortunately Kronen is not blessed with wide gardens. Most of my herbs grown here are for healing or cooking." She had smiled, not altogether a friendly smile, Willadene had shrewdly judged.

"Of course, should I ever be Star-blessed enough to find the Heart-Hold—then indeed I would have a treasure to offer."

"The Heart-Hold," he had repeated. "Pray tell what that may be."

Halwice had shrugged. "The tale is very old, perhaps mostly forgotten by now. But it was said that once a Star-blessed healer in Kronen chanced upon a flower so perfect in form, so soothing in scent, that she kept it immersed in oil, sealed well against the air. And she discovered that those who looked upon it must come again and again, so her business prospered. But, at last, at year's turn she was sent a dream that not for any gain in this world was Heart-

Hold intended. And with the morrow she took it as an offering to Hasker—''

''Hasker! But that—''

''The Abbey was assaulted by night, by wolf heads, men said. Its treasures were taken, the Star-servers put to the sword. And that was well over three hundred years ago. Never since has Heart-Hold been found. But there are tales—one lady who dipped but the tip of her finger within the oil which preserved it was so sought after that she wed far above her station and her lord was firmly faithful for all his life. But that is all legend now. And—to return to your desire, steward, if I get another such Breath of Roses I shall send a message to the High Lady Saylana. You may take my word for that.''

It was plain that he had to be satisfied, though he had been scowling as he had taken silver pieces from his belt pouch and rung them down on the counter. However, Willadene had noted that the wrapped package he'd taken up in return he had handled with care. It had been some long moments after he had left before Halwice had moved. Her head had been turned toward the open door, as if by some means of her own she could see beyond walls to watch him out of sight.

Then she had slowly gone to that door, shut it firmly, having hung a small signboard on its outer side. Only when she had dropped the bar latch had she turned toward the inner room.

She had pushed aside the curtain and nodded to Willadene without comment as if she had fully expected to find the girl right there.

''Light the lamps—'' she had ordered. ''We must have full sight.''

The girl had hastened to obey, and, with five lamps ablaze, every shadow had been banished and she could easily see the curve of body beneath the settle. Halwice had said he lived, but he had certainly not moved since her labor had stuffed him there.

"Bring him out." The Herbmistress had subsided onto a stool, leaving an open space on the floor.

That had been more easily ordered than done, but at length Willadene had the limp man stretched out faceup. In this very bright light she had been able to make out more of his features. He was, she had decided, much younger than she had first supposed, nor was he uncomely. His features were sharp and fine, and there was none of the lumpishness and blotched skin which had plagued Figis at the inn.

Halwice had surveyed him intently—he might have been some subtle problem in the combining of two of her treasured substances. She had sighed.

"Well, let us to it. Go to the bed cupboard, press twice with the palm of your hand just beyond where the sliding door now stands—toward the rear wall of the room."

Willadene had hesitated, and Halwice's glance at her had become a stare. "What keeps you, girl? Time is our enemy now."

"Mistress, you make me very free of your secrets," the girl had said slowly. "I am not even signed to your service."

Halwice had smiled. "But that is what you want in your heart—have wanted—is it not?"

At Willadene's vigorous nod she had continued. "That can well be arranged. Yes, I am making you free of secrets, but I do that because—by the Star—I know of what material you are wrought. Some of us are favored from birth with gifts. If we would truly serve as we were meant to do, then we use those—"

"The nose—" ventured Willadene.

"Yes, the nose—but yours is not only for scenting what lies about you in flask and jar, pot and pan, but also within. What did you smell when you pushed in the door at your morning's coming?"

"Evil!" The word had been out of her lips before she had truly thought it.

As one who was satisfied with her own opinion, Halwice had nodded. ''Do you smell such now?''

Willadene had tested the air about, which to her was soaked with such a wealth of scents it would have taken her a goodly time to list. But that which the Herbmistress had brought to her mind was gone.

''You see?'' Halwice had not waited for her answer. ''Even as you—I, also, possess, by Star's Grace, that gift. You can be trusted; and you will be, for you have been swept into matters which are both great and dire. Now, bring me what you find within the niche there.''

Willadene had placed her hands as she had been ordered, and the seemingly solid board had given, sliding away even as the outer doors to the bed. Inside had been a box, and from it had issued a scent Willadene had never encountered before—it had been sharp and clear, almost like fresh, prickling brine. She had brought it to the Herbmistress, who had balanced it on her knees before she had opened it.

Like the shelves in the shop cupboards without, the interior of the box had been divided into many compartments, each with its own lid, while fastened within the coffer of the chest itself had been a flat dishlike platter no larger than two hands pressed together.

''This''—Halwice had wrestled it loose from its hold—''must be placed on him heart-high.''

Willadene had taken it quickly and had done just that, seeing that it rested steadily. Halwice had already been opening the compartments. One or two she hesitated over and reclosed, but from the chatelaine clipped to her girdle she had already freed another small but deeper measure, and into this, with the spoon chained to its edge, she had shifted first this and that—

The tingling sharp scent had grown ever stronger. Yet it had not been unpleasant. Instead, it had appeared to clear the head, made Willadene, in an unprecedented way, much more aware of all about her.

The spoon had then been used to stir the powders together. Halwice, her hands so busied, had pointed with her chin.

"Beneath the bed pillow—a bag. Bring it!"

It had not been as large as a purse, and Willadene had found it was full of what felt like pebbles.

"Open"—Halwice had been still stirring—"but take care."

Willadene had untied the knot of the drawstring, and open it she did—to shake into hand that which caught and reflected the light as if they glowed with inner fire. Jewels—but none had been cut to use. They were like fragments of larger pieces which had been deliberately shattered.

"Now"—Halwice had edged her stool a fraction forward—"you must set a pattern, and it must be even as I tell you, for this can only be done once—and without fault. Search what you hold for two white crystals and place them above the crown of Nicolas's head."

Willadene had obeyed; at least the stranger had at last been given a name.

"Now choose blue, each one to be put halfway between those already set," continued the Herbmistress.

Last of all, Halwice had held out the bowl whose contents she had been energetically stirring all the while.

"Shake what lies within this on the heart plate, gently— it must not spread too far."

Diligently the girl had done just that. It had not puffed out as she had expected such ashy material to do, but formed a small mound.

"Look you now for the starred crystal," came the next order, and that she had done.

There had been such, not so unformed as the others, and smoother-edged but centered with an unmistakable star-shaped heart.

"Thrust that into the powder!"

Willadene had obeyed. It had been as if she had applied

a snap light, for smoke had begun to rise. About a hand's space above its source it had split into six equal trails, and each one of those had set out to touch a jewel.

The sharp clean scent had made Willadene feel that she herself, if she wished it, could have risen from the floor where she crouched, taken on wings, and soared beyond the world she had always known. Halwice had been speaking again, but not to give her an order.

Instead, the Herbmistress's voice had risen and fallen in a chant which had been like a song, needing no harp to keep in mastering tune. The words had been strange, and the crooning had seemed to slur them together at times.

Now the smoke had woven a cloud above nearly half of the quiet body. The girl could no longer see his face. Halwice's body had rocked back and forth slightly as she'd continued to chant.

Willadene had caught a glimpse of the Herbmistress's features across the inert body. The woman had plainly been under great strain, yet she herself dared not move to give her any aid.

The smoke forming that sight-repelling mask had moved again. Willadene had been sure she could detect tendrils drawing back into their source. And she had been right. But there had been nothing on the plate, not even scorch marks of any burning. And the brilliance of the gems had dimmed.

Halwice's head had fallen on her breast as if she could no longer hold it upright. Without orders Willadene had leaned over to gather up the gems and restore them to the bag. Then that dark-haired head had moved, and eyes of a gray of a steel blade and with the same grim threat in them had stared up at her.

"Who by the Horns of Gratch are you?" His voice had been low, hardly clearer than a whisper, and it had come like a cat's challenging hiss.

Willadene had hurriedly hunched back as he'd used his

elbows to lever himself to a near-sitting position. He had looked around, caught sight of Halwice, and frozen in that awkward pose. Then his head had swung again so he could see Willadene, and in that moment she had realized just what he was viewing—the grimy, tatter-clad drudge of the inn.

Then he had moved swiftly, with far more speed than she could have thought possible for that supine body of moments earlier. Before she'd been able to draw herself farther back his fingers had twisted in her hair, bringing pain as he jerked her upward until they were both standing.

Still keeping his tight grip on her he had begun a careful survey of the whole room, which ended by centering on the Herbmistress.

"What have you wrought here!" He had jerked the girl's head back and forth by that hold in her hair, and those steel eyes had been sword points to strike her.

"Let be!" Halwice had straightened on her stool. "You are always too ready to leap for answers—I thought you had learned the folly of that, Nicolas. Loose Willadene! Had it not been for her aid— How long does a man last in the Deep Sleep?"

"What does she *here*?" he had demanded, but he had loosened his grip and she was able to pull her head back and away from so close a vicinity so that he could not so seize upon her again.

"The Will of the Star." Halwice had the sharp tone of an adult dealing with a child. "Had it not been for her provident coming to the shop, we would both be deep in that she-serpent's net." Swiftly she had outlined what Willadene had discovered, and her efforts on their behalf thereafter. The girl had longed to interrupt that it was Halwice's welfare she had been concerned with and not that of this boor.

"I brought the packet from Arwa—as usual. He met me at the Fork's Border Inn and showed me the seal upon it, knowing I was coming to Kronengred. It was no different—'' Then he had paused and scowled. ''So they used me, did they— Arwan—'' His hand had gone to the belt where rode a sheathed knife longer than any ever intended for an eating tool.

''Arwan's part in this we shall learn in due time.'' Halwice still had a note of impatience in her voice. ''The important thing is here and now. You came over border with a message. You have already been delayed since well beyond First Bell in the delivery of it. I suggest that first things be met in the proper order. And this, I believe—'' her hands had groped among her bodice lacings to bring out the coin-shaped seal Willadene had found on the floor ''—is yours. Best be on your way.''

But it had seemed that he had not been ready to yield to the authority Halwice used.

''The girl—'' Now he had looked once more at Willadene.

''She is my affair, Nicolas. I warn you, one does not meddle with the moves of fate. Now go.''

And go he had, not through the shop but out back to traverse the herb garden, clearly in search of the same entrance which had brought Willadene there earlier.

''Nicolas serves his master well,'' the Herbmistress had begun when he was gone. ''Now—you will forget him!''

Willadene had blinked and then nodded. Curiosity might be alive in her, but she had had good reason to sense that this was no time for questions. Halwice had surveyed her up and down, and once more the girl had been aware of the grubby appearance she must have presented at that moment.

''Get the kettle, the largest one''— Halwice had gestured toward the hearth—''and set a fire for it. So Jacoba would take bride price for you from Wyche? That can be speedily taken care of. For your own sake, girl, you must be under my hand. There is this much true—good gold would be paid for noting what had passed here when repeated to the right person.''

Willadene had stiffened. Nicolas might well have been a spy—perhaps even so Halwice—but *she* was no tale-bearer and never had been. She *knew*—knew by the aid of her gift—that there was no evil in the woman facing her, and whatever she had done earlier she might truly confess to the Star and go unchided.

"Yes. We know—for, girl, we are of the same breed, only I have been forged like a fine smith's weapon, and you are but raw material. I know you have long wanted to come to me, but there was a reason that I should not arouse Jacoba's malice fully against the two of us. Today has changed all that.

"Bring me now one of the small measures and the third bottle from the left on the second shelf near the window of the shop."

When Willadene had returned Halwice had tried to take both objects from her, but the woman's hands had been shaking so hard she had not been able to manage to hold either safely.

"Age comes to all of us," she had said bleakly as if she spoke the thought aloud. "Take this, pour you from the bottle into the measure until it reaches this line graven in the glass—do it!"

The girl had nodded emphatically, and with the care she had always seen the Herbmistress use in putting together any mixture, she had allowed a green liquid to fall hardly more than a couple of drops at a time into the measure. Around her had wafted a fresh, clean scent she could not have put name to but which she wished would wash every smirch, every bruise, every scar from her body, for she had a strong feeling it might well be able to do just that.

Halwice had taken the measure in both shaking hands and held it to her lips. She had drunk steadily until the last green drop was gone. For another moment she had sat quietly and then she was on her feet moving as briskly as Willadene had always seen her do.

"Well enough." She reached out to take the bottle from the girl's hand. "Now the immediate affairs are our own."

Setting the bottle carefully on the table, she had moved to a chest so old that time had scrubbed away nearly all the painted patterns from its wood. When she had lifted the lid there had been another rush of scent which Willadene recognized came from herbs laid up to preserve clothing from moth and mildew.

Halwice had brought out a bundle tied together with a length of narrow cloth. She had set this on the table and then pointed toward a very large basin, nearly as tall as Willadene herself, where it leaned against the back wall.

"I have no scullery maid," Halwice had announced. "Those who serve me from time to time go in better guise. Take the kettle water to warm that from the bucket and let us see what lies under all that which plasters you now. Then dress yourself in these." She had thumped the bundle. "In that box is soap. See that you use it well on both body and hair. No one with the *nose* can wish to remain as you are now. I shall be in the shop. It has been closed too long. We are very near the time of the noon bell, and when I go out on errands I am seldom gone past that."

She had looped aside the curtain, and Willadene had set about obeying orders. Though the basin was no bath such as a noblewoman could soak herself in, the girl had found she could crouch in its water warmed by the supply from the kettle, and she had set about such a scrubbing with the soft soap scooped from the box as she had not been able to do for years. Though as she'd bathed, washed her hair, and washed it yet a second time, she had begun to remember times when she had been as free with water and soap as she was now.

There had been a rough towel; and she had moved closer to the small fire as she'd rubbed herself dry, ashamed of her hands where the skin seemed still cracked with gray lines in spite of all her efforts. The bundle had yielded a chemise which had not been too large that she could not pull it snugly about her. Then there had been a shirt with short sleeves, made for a worker who needed full use of her hands. It had had a line of green braid, which Willadene had caressed with a loving finger. Last had been a skirt, full and a little too wide for her waist, but she had been able to belt it in with the same piece of material which had held the bundle together. And they'd all been *clean,* fragrant from dried flowers which had fluttered in the air as she'd pulled free each garment.

So had begun her life in Halwice's shop and home. And Willadene found that to be equal to that life in brightness and beauty which the Star promised the faithful.

Of course, the Reeve's messenger appeared and with Halwice she had been summoned to face all the majesty of the law which had been indifferently placed on Jacoba's side. But to the girl's astonishment the innkeeper was subdued, her roaring anger hidden—if it still existed. She had tried to bring up the point that Willadene was a bespoken bride, but two or three skillful questions had dismissed that, since it had been apparent the girl had had no say in the matter.

That was the last of Jacoba, Willadene had thought, with a great feeling of being free of a smothering burden, as she had left with Halwice, her apprenticeship duly countersigned by two Reeves now—that of Jacoba's quarter and that who kept the Duke's peace in Halwice's.

It certainly had been plain at this meeting that the Herbmistress was of consequence in Kronengred and that her word was accepted without question.

However, during the days which followed, questions she hardly spelled out even for herself troubled Willadene from time to time. The trade in the shop was brisk, and, yes, strange merchants or their assistants came from time to time to deliver products from far beyond Kronen.

Among these were what Willadene came to consider special ones. Two had been delivered once after nightfall by the back alleyway and those who brought them had been given a number of coins which they promptly hid about their persons. Most of these visitors hardly ever seemed to even realize that the girl was there, and she kept mouse still, busying herself with some task of sorting, labeling, or generally setting the shop in order.

However, as much as she tried to efface herself, their quarters were cramped and there was little chance for any true privacy, so she listened. What passed between Halwice and many of these visitors was cryptic, making no sense to Willadene, but about none of them ever clung the cloying, rotten smell of evil.

Twice Nicolas had turned up—once openly in the shop, wearing a fine dark-red jerkin bearing the Chancellor's arms on both shoulder and breast, with an ordinary request for a product which calmed nerves and allowed sleep. He scowled when Halwice directed Willadene to make up the dosage. It was plain that he had no trust even yet in the girl.

"I hear," Halwice said, "that Her Grace did well for herself at the court. She is comely enough and appears to carry her position well."

Nicolas made a sound which was not far from a snort.

"Yes, it made a fine show. Even the High Lady Saylana could find little fault, I understand. But this is true, mistress: the Duke may have come to his rule cross-sidely but he will make every effort to hold it. And what is in a father may also lie in a child."

"The Lady Zuta still stands at her right hand?"

He was frowning now. "How else can it be? His Highness kept all others from Her Grace. But it is with that Lady Zuta as it is with my Lord Chancellor—only if His Highness remains in position to grant favors will she herself prosper."

"There are some strange tales from over the border—" Halwice continued placidly. "It would seem that the royal family there also has its problems."

"That is none of the business of Kronen." Nicolas shrugged. Then suddenly he changed the subject. "Is it indeed true, mistress, that there be scents which can en-snarl a man—not blast him, mind you, as was attempted here—but weave him to the purpose of another without his knowledge of what is happening?"

"There are said to be such—woman's weapons—" Hal-wice replied.

His teeth showed in a very unpleasant smile. She re-garded him steadily until that smile faded. "Well you should know what it means to fall even to the lightest of such traps. I would consider such a subject with care if I were you."

He grinned again, this time like the youth he seemed to be. "Well enough—there are rumors aplenty always flying about to mystify a man— Who needs to believe such? My lord's thanks for your services—"

Willadene had carefully stuffed the small pillow she had been busied with, now sealing it with a paste which would unite that opening past all forcing. She slid it across the counter to him.

His next visit was three days later and this time after nightfall, heralded by a soft knocking at the back door. Willadene looked to the Herbmistress, and at her nod slipped out the bar latch. This time Nicolas wore no well-cut and fitted clothing, certainly no identifying tabard of the Lord Chancellor. Instead, a long black cloak muffled him from chin, with rolls of a thrown-back cowl, to his booted ankles.

Halwice, without a word, went to a cupboard and brought out a pouch too rounded certainly to carry much wealth and giving forth no clink as she handled it. Nicolas caught it and it vanished beneath his cloak.

"The border?" That was no statement, rather a question.

"Mistress, no one can track well a night flyer." He

laughed, almost the joyous laugh of one about to engage in mischief. "If this one succeeds you will soon hear strange news—"

With no more farewell he was gone. Halwice sat down slowly on the chair they had dragged back from the shop, the former seat of her imprisonment. She was shaking her head, not at Willadene but at something perhaps only she could see.

"May the Star light him through! One can take such risks against fate but not forever." She sighed and then spoke directly to Willadene. "Bring me the book which stands at the far end of the knowledge shelf and take care; it is so old that someday it may turn to dust in one's hands."

Willadene obeyed quickly. There was an odd smell to what she held—the decay of ancient leather and parchment, and beyond that a medley of scents she did not have time to identify before Halwice had it from her, laid on the table between two lighted lamps so that the full glow was turned on the pages she so carefully turned.

"One can only try," she muttered as she searched. "Oh, get you to bed, Willadene. I may be half the night about this business."

And again, though questions nearly choked her, the girl obeyed.

"Were she younger I would have my cane across her back." Duke Uttobric snarled. "Making a show of herself before the whole of Kronengred, and I can well believe that most of the city was there to gape at her doing it!"

Vazul pursed his lips as he faced his master, and his black-furred companion made the faintest of chittering sounds from where she hung in one of her favorite positions around the man's neck. Sometimes—mentally Vazul hoped for patience and firmly banked down his impatience—Uttobric tried a man near to the far limits.

"Highness"—he picked his words now with care as he answered—"instead of Her Grace proving a barrier to your wishes, she has, on the contrary, played her part as well as if she had been trained to it from youth. With her own hands she has fed the hungry, standing with those pious Sisters of the Star. Not a task, I will grant you, that many of her blood have ever done in the past, but one which made all who watched it believe that she has the good of Kronen in her heart."

The Duke scowled, that dark twitch of skin and eyebrows fading slowly. "What say the court?" he then demanded. "Do they mutter behind their hands that one of the Old Blood so forgets her place as to mingle with beggars?"

Within himself Vazul sighed, but his tone was conciliating as he replied. "Highness, have we not been gathering rumors for more than a year now that those who oppose you are secretly building their own net to bring you down? And where is any army they can summon? Who can raise enough coin to import even one company of mercenaries? And, as all know, those are apt to turn upon their employers if their pay is not forthcoming as promised. Therefore any support your enemies could hope to gather would be from the dissatisfied, the unruly, the night flitters, of Kronengred itself. In every city there are those who will rise at the thought of loot.

"So far we have sifted very carefully all strangers coming into the city. The majority are honest merchants. Those, we wish to encourage, for our very life depends upon trade. But—" he leaned forward a little and drew from his belt a roll of paper he proceeded to pull taut enough to be read "—we also know that there are others who find their way through and out again our gates, that there are ties rooted within this city itself which lead to the outlaws. In the past year five small caravans have disappeared entirely as if the earth swallowed them, and attacks on two well-guarded larger ones were beaten off only with loss of life, and, what is more, of merchants' confidence that we are strong enough to protect them.

"We must hold the city. Just as you have graciously made concessions to the most powerful among the merchants, accepted—at least outwardly—suggestions from the Reeves, so must the people themselves believe that their welfare is a matter of heart interest for you. Thus— Her Grace's act at the Abbey—news of which, I assure you, has already spread through the city and even grown in the telling—is such which will serve you now as well as a full corps marching down from the castle. I repeat, Highness, Her Grace Mahart is one of your best weapons at present and must be well used. Twenty days hence is her birthday—to make such a holiday this year, Her Grace appearing perhaps to give thanks for the generous recognition of your pleasure in it—''

The Duke's gaze had gone from the narrow face of his Chancellor to the wall where a particularly drab stretch of tapestry celebrated a victory won long before his own birth.

''Very well—a feasting—alms—all the usual, I suppose,'' he said grudgingly. ''Her Grace and I will proceed to the Abbey to give thanks— Do you realize what a hole this will leave in my purse?'' he ended snappishly.

''But it shall be done with all propriety—'' promised Vazul. If he was going to add to that promise, he was stopped by his furred companion, whose chittering now reached the point it could be well heard by the Duke also.

The animal had slewed around on Vazul's shoulder and her whiskered snout was now pointing to the wall. With a speed which was out of place in him usually, the Chancellor was on his feet and at that wall, his hand outstretched so that the fingers pressed there in a certain pattern.

With no sound—the latch was too well oiled for that— a panel slid back and presented an opening through which a full-sized man could come only if he were bent double as the newcomer was.

He straightened to his full height, which was more than the Duke's and a little less than Vazul's. His cloak swept back a little as his hand came free to sketch what might be a salute of sorts, but he showed no other formal deference to the company in which he now found himself.

''Prince Lorien,'' he reported, ''has reached the lodge. Two nights ago a shepherd was slain just within the borders there. His flock was all killed, an act which will arouse the country people—on *both* sides of the border. It seemed that the Red Wolf held high feast for a comrade.''

"That comrade being?" the Duke demanded. "Noble or baseborn?"

"He did not appear openly but kept to the Wolf's own quarters, and none ventures there except under orders. The Wolf rules with the lash and the stake."

"Yet he rules," Vazul said quietly. "With such as he commands, it takes a man of unusual personality to hold so close rein. There was no way of finding out the identity of the visitor?" He spoke now to the newcomer.

"Chancellor, for that I ride—tonight. The network is well in place as usual."

For the first time the Duke's lips formed one of his sour smiles. "Good speed" was his farewell.

When the panel had closed behind their visitor, the Duke looked to Vazul. "You put great trust in this Bat of yours—has it not always been your plaint to me that to trust entirely weakens one?"

Vazul was smoothing the fur of his creature. "Your Highness, the Bat has good reason to hate as we hate— and is there not truth in the saying he who has the same enemy is in some manner a comrade? Yes, I trust this night journeyer of mine because he not only carries a burning hate within him, but one he has learned to control, that he may accomplish best what is asked of him."

The Duke was now eyeing him thoughtfully. "I have you, Vazul, because we both well know whatever fate the future holds will serve us equally. However—now that you have made clear the worth of my daughter to our plans—does she have any confidante who might be seduced into betrayal if such a moment of need arose?"

"Highness, the principal lady—in fact the only lady for the past four years—who serves Her Grace, is Zuta of Lakley."

"Lakley? But that— She is kin to Darmond?"

"She is a victim of Lord Darmond's greed," Vazul returned calmly. "By rights she should be lady there— with the coming of the plague he moved upon his grandfa-

ther's hold with force enough to hold it. It was given out
that all those of the true bloodline died from the sickness.
Sickness—*and* steel—as has been whispered. She could
not have inherited the title and ruled there—being female.
But she was entitled to daughter's share, and that was
worth a little bloodletting—her father having been very
lucky in several ventures overseas. It was her nurse who
saw her safely into the hands of Lady Janis of Ille. When
the plague brought down that guardian my sources ap-
praised me—'' He continued to stroke his pet, and the
Duke uttered one of his snickering laughs.

"Always you see the future worth of any deal, Vazul.
You administer her birth funds, of course."

But the Chancellor shook his head. "Unluckily no—
Darmond being what he is and having false witnesses to
say she is not the true heir. However, as all of us, she can
hope for a less burdensome future. She has funds to draw
upon, from her mother's line though they may not be her
own, and she is very clever. Her Grace has been safe these
past few years because they were so closely united."

"Another of your eyes and ears, Vazul? If so, she is
acceptable—you will nourish a traitor no more quickly
than I would."

"No. She knows nothing of our shadow servants, High-
ness. But she is my source of information concerning Her
Grace and all which pertains to her. Concerning Her
Grace, Highness, there is another matter—"

"That being?"

"When she made her pilgrimage to the Abbey she
walked it. To have ventured into the heart of the city in
a horse litter would not have served the purpose. Now—
Her Grace must learn to ride, Highness."

"Ride!" The Duke blinked rapidly several times. "But
there is no need for her to make any journey."

"Except through the city, Highness. Think now, when
the feast day you have planned comes and you ride forth—
will it not seem strange to all that your daughter is carried

in a litter? The people now know she is no invalid and will wonder why she journeys half hidden from them."

"Ride!" repeated the Duke with a snort. "How, pray you, can she learn such a feat within less than twenty days? The girl has never been near a horse!"

"Highness, your Master of Horse is counted the best in all Kronen. There is that large court where the guards drill—it can be made private for periods of Her Grace's instruction."

"All right. If it must be done to humor the baseborn in the streets, let it be so. You always have such good reasons for your suggestions, Vazul."

"That is why I am of service to you, Highness," returned the Chancellor.

So now Mahart, whether she wished or no, became introduced to what might give her in the future another form of freedom. Her lessons were well supervised by an elderly man, who plainly considered these hours of instruction in a way a reflection upon his status. But he knew his job well, and she was eager for any new knowledge. There always remained in the back of her mind that dream she had now dreamed three times over—of being free in flowered meadows under the open sky. Learning to govern this animal, which was presented to her each morning at the same hour, might well be another key to the outer world.

Luckily she proved to be a very apt pupil, graduating from boring rounds on a very placid old mare to at last a younger and less sluggish mount. Though the Master of Horse never expressed any satisfaction at her progress she could guess by the slight changes in his attitude that she was in some ways measuring up to what he considered a credible performance.

If she came to enjoy this new learning she could not say the same for Zuta. The practice place was seldom in full sun and since the year now advanced to harvest it was chill for anyone who merely stood enshawled, watching the action but not taking part in it. Mahart, catching sight of a cold-pinched nose and not missing the accompanying shivers, finally suggested that her companion withdraw into the tack room beyond. Then she became so absorbed in what she must remember to do properly that she completely forgot Zuta. Nor did anyone know that the lady-in-waiting was joined there by one dressed in simple garb but of noble materials—carrying no house shield adornment.

Mahart continued to make her solemn rounds. Apparently the fact that she could stay in the saddle, arranging her wide, divided skirt in proper falls; keep a straight back; and have her rein signals obeyed was all that was going to be required of her. The lessoning had become such a routine that she found herself able to occupy at least a fraction of her mind with other things.

Her eighteenth birthday was looming ahead. She could only remember very faintly when that had been a date of note. These past years, the full of a celebration had consisted of the good year wishes of Julta at her rising, similar ones with a small gift from Zuta, and the appearance of a footman sometime during the morning bearing a salver on which rested her father's remembrance, formal good wishes delivered in a monotone by memory from the bearer.

Now she was going to be, she gathered, the center of festivities of some extent. She would appear in the heaviest of formal court dress with her father on the west balcony, to be shown off properly to any of those in Kronengred who were interested. Then, later, she would practice this new art of hers in public, riding behind her father to the Abbey, to present a birthday gift to the Abbess.

She already knew that she was going to be walled by half the guard, protected carefully from any contact such as she had rebelliously indulged in before. But at least her father could not forbid her meeting with the Abbess, and so perhaps with some others of those who supported the shrine.

Mahart had already discovered that the scented candles of the inner shrine and the incense alight there were the product of the Herbmistress she had heard so much of. And, if protocol would not allow her to visit Halwice's own shop, there could be a good chance of such an encounter at the shrine—though she knew better now than to try personally to bring that about.

Her hour's exercise done, she allowed the Master to help her dismount, thanked him civilly as she always did for his efforts on her behalf, and headed for the tack room. There were other entrances to this exercise court, of course, but one could not clear out barracks and interrupt military matters so that no guardsman could get good sight of Her Grace—and the Duke's decree in this matter had been strictly followed.

She looked for Zuta, but the room was empty and it was a full moment before the lady-in-waiting appeared. She still had a shawl bundled closely around her chin, above which her face was a little flushed.

"It is done for the day," Mahart said. "Now what have we before us?"

"The Mistress of the Robes, Your Grace. As you remember, at last fitting your train would not lie flat."

Mahart sniffed. "Might as well clothe me in armor—these state robes are near as heavy. Very well—let us go."

She was always glad to get away from this guard section. There was a grimness about it which made her uneasy, and twice she raised the pomander which swung on its girdle chain to sniff at the fragrance it held.

"Your Grace?"

Mahart looked inquiringly at her companion. At least Zuta had dropped that fold of shawl so she could see her plainly.

"Yes?" she prompted when the girl did not continue.

"It is nothing—only just talk as usual. Concerning the

ball. The High Lady Saylana—she is sometimes in despair of her son—''

Mahart grinned. ''As well she might be, lumbering fool!''

To her surprise Zuta glanced swiftly around. ''Your Grace''—now her voice was hardly above a whisper. ''It is said—and has been proven—that castle walls have ears—and tongues.''

Mahart grasped the pomander more tightly. That was really a bald hint as far as Zuta was concerned. Mahart hesitated before she asked in as low a voice as the other had used: ''It is that perhaps the High Lady has some plan?''

Marriage—her father had spoken of marriage! Could it be that he would strive to brace up what he considered to be a shaky ducal throne by uniting her with Barbric? Her jaw set a little. She had been her father's tool, but there were some things—

''It is to favor the Lord Barbric.'' Zuta's now-whispered words came in a rush. ''When you open the ball, all know the Duke will not lead you out—as is usual. It has always been known that he disdains such niceties.''

''And I certainly cannot dance alone.'' Mahart tried to think of pacing through the stately steps allowed the ducal family and almost laughed at the picture her imagination painted of her father indulging in such a show. No, he would remain firmly on his throne, as uncomfortable there as ever, enduring that he *must* be present.

''His Highness must signify that you choose your partner,'' Zuta was continuing.

''And Barbric will be well ahead of the line,'' Mahart snapped.

''He will be the only one protocol will permit you to select,'' Zuta said. ''Your Grace knows well that His Highness has enemies in plenty. Should you choose without due thought, you might well alienate some family he wishes to bring into his party.''

That was true enough, Mahart had to conclude. So be it—Barbric must be her choice. Luckily in the stately paces of the opening dance one did not have to approach one's partner past the touching of hands at the end of outstretched arms. It was deadly dull, as she knew from the hours she had been drilled in its turns—deep curtsey to answer deeper bows, and the final delivery of her to her proper dais seat.

She shrugged now. "I shall remember, Zuta. But what will be my father's answer to this bit of diplomacy?"

"His Highness cannot deny your choice, Your Grace. It will be the only proper one."

It seemed in the days which passed all too swiftly that there were a great many proper choices to be remembered. She hated the heavy robes which weighed so on her slender body. They had a session in which her hair had to be tamed into a coiffure which would allow a wide tiara to be anchored to it. At least the Master of Horse had at last released her, doubtless having reported to her father that she would not disgrace their name by sliding out of the saddle.

Twice she ordered Zuta to see that she was supplied with that night-burning incense which produced in her soothing and restful dreams, and the last supply sent was one large enough that she could have it burnt for three nights running.

The feeling she had every time she was loosed into that place was comforting, but also it became more and more one of anticipation. She was never in the dream inclined to walk, if walk she could, away from where she entered. Yet she became surer and surer that she was the goal of another's journeying—though no shadow ever broke the stretches of field. She was never afraid, only ready to welcome, and now she awoke disappointed when that other promised traveler did not appear.

Sometimes it seemed that time flew, and others that it

dragged sluggishly. Vazul began to ask for audiences, and at first she wanted to refuse. There was that about the Chancellor which always made her feel tense and wary when she was in his presence. Then, as the subjects he advanced in those meetings delved deeper and deeper into matters of which she had been unaware but which now aroused her curiosity to a pitch, she looked forward to his coming.

To her father she had always seemed a non-person— something to be forgotten as soon as she was out of his sight. But Vazul was treating her from the first as someone with thoughts and not just a mirror image of a proper simple child who happened by fate to have been the daughter of the Duke.

This new and exciting interest had come on his first visit to her, and looking back she was sure that the key to it was the actions of his strange pet. For when she had waved him to a seat, uncertain as to what rebuke he must carry from her father, the sinuous black-furred thing had appeared from within his sleeve, ran across his knee, and leaped lightly to the floor over which it went like a flicker of shadow to come to her own feet. Beneath the billows of her skirt her toes had tried to curl within her slippers, and she did not know what she could do if the creature sprang at her.

She dared not raise her eyes from it lest it catch her so unawares, and she longed for the Chancellor to recall it. But the longer she studied it—the thing had raised the forepart of its body, its paws crossed over its upper belly, its head held at a sharp angle as the rippling of its long whiskers suggested that it was testing the air—Mahart found that its strangeness no longer seemed to hold any menace. Impulsively she detached the chain of her pomander from her girdle and dangled it down toward that questing nose.

There was a chittering sound, very faint. One of those forepaws came forward and claws hooked in the filigreed side of the ball, drawing it closer to the nose. She believed she could actually see the small form swell as if it drew in as deep a breath as its small lungs would allow.

"From the Herbmistress Halwice, Your Grace?" Mahart had been so engrossed by the actions of the creature that Vazul's question gave her a start.

"Yes, Chancellor. It is of her making. She is well-known for such things."

"As for healing also," he commented. But he made no attempt to recall his pet.

The creature at last made the leap Mahart had been fearing, landing on her lap, the pomander held between teeth which looked extremely sharp and menacing, small as they were.

Then its head pushed against one of her hands, and she felt the silken softness of fur she could not help but smooth. There was a vibration through the long body in return which she was certain signified pleasure. Still petting the creature, she looked to the Chancellor.

"What is its name?"

All within the castle knew of it, but never had any name been mentioned.

Vazul was leaning forward, his usually half-lidded eyes very wide, his gaze seeming to search within her as if he would count her very bones. For the first time, she saw him startled out of that usual armor he ever presented to any of the court.

"Ssssaaa." The sound coming from him was more a hiss than any true word. But she took it for what it must be—his answer to her question. "She would be a friend worth greeting."

"Ssssaaa." Mahart attempted as best she could to give the sound the same quality as he had done. And felt warmth as the creature seemed to slide in some way up her arm to her shoulder and there chitter into her very ear.

It appeared to her that Vazul was still startled out of his carefully preserved outer shell.

"You have no fear—" It was not a question but a statement. "Your Grace, you have won such a supporter as you will not be able to understand until a dire time comes—"

"A dire time?"

"Yes, time—for time itself works against us. Listen, Your Grace, and listen well, for there is much you must understand before you are totally engulfed by this court as necessity orders you must be."

He began to talk, keeping his voice very low, as Mahart listened and caressed the creature which had come to her. Her hours spent in the library had laid the foundation for much he now spoke of—but not all, for the accounts there were not of the immediate past but stretched much further back. That her father's ascension to the ducal throne was questioned she had always been aware, just as she had been early warned against the High Lady Saylana. But now she heard other names, Vazul pausing at some as if allowing her time to memorize each.

His steady voice, pitched even as it would be if he talked to someone his equal in years and knowledge, was in its way like those dreams of the meadow—opening out her world. It was a dark world and there was little in it over which one could rejoice—thus being far from the meadow of her dreams—but her intelligence, already awakened, was sharpened by all she heard now.

"But, my lord, if Kronen is so ridden by this rot what can be done? If merchants cannot trust our roadways they will cease to come. The trade will fail—" She hesitated, thinking of the beggars at the Abbey gate—she had done what she could since her confrontation there to give aid. "It will be again as the plague—"

Ssssaaa hissed in her ear, uncoiled, and was down her knee making a leap across to Vazul.

"Except death will come more slowly," the Chancellor said. "But—for this moment—we must play another's game—or seem to—"

"Her Grace Saylana," she guessed, but he gave her no yes or no.

Three more such meetings she held with Vazul. On the second and again on the fourth he brought with him packets of herbs, and it was on the last such meeting he agreed that on her birthday visit to the Abbey she might well meet the Herbmistress, since Halwice was one of the guild masters who would gather there in honor of the occasion.

Finally the day came—it would be a long one, Mahart knew. First the appearance in state with her father on the foresteps of the castle. Then the procession to the Abbey— the tedium afterward of a formal dinner and then the ball. Her dress for each occasion waited, hung along the wall on a heavy cord so no crease or wrinkle would mar its splendor.

There was her father's usual gift awaiting on the dressing table—more elaborate this year—a flagon like a half-opened rose which, in spite of its stopper, gave forth perfume. But in her mind Mahart desired more of that which had been in those packets Vazul had delivered—those which took her—*elsewhere*. She knew that Zuta wished to question how such reached her, and she had put her off with an explanation that such were delivered by her father's orders so she might be mind-clear and prepared for all that lay before her. Only—she had never yet seen the stranger who was meant to meet her in that place—in fact, now to her unease, he seemed far too long delayed.

There were flags and banners, loopings of flowers and branches all along the way, as she rode later, a pace or so behind her father, through the streets. And the cheers of the people brought a flush to her face. Vazul's information had sunk deep; she knew just on what a perilous foundation this gala in Kronengred rested.

But the serenity which lay within the Abbey gates held none of that feverish excitement. She made her curtsey to the Abbess even as she had before. But this time the elderly Sister, leaning a fraction on her staff, brought her on into the aisle of the Star House.

There was the rustle of a crowd there too, but subdued. She knew that the guild masters were in place. Mahart knelt at the Star altar, and the offering she set there might be bringing a frown to her father's face—she did not try to see. For she set the perfect rose bottle within the pure light which played along all points of the Star.

Once more there were presentations, and each of the guild masters had an offering—some fine example of the work his people did—to display. It was the fifth one who approached her who awoke Mahart from the haze of formality which had encompassed her.

This was a woman, her dress of rich green cloth but without any overlay of lace or metallic thread. She made dignified bow to the Duke and then to Mahart.

The girl could not have set any age to her. Though the woman's fine skin showed no wrinkling, those eyes which she boldly raised to meet the girl's gaze were strange indeed. Were they actually—yellow? Or only brown like autumn-touched forest leaves?

Mahart did not need the herald's introduction. She could not remember now what she had expected heretofore— perhaps some cronelike figure more suited to grubbing in a garden than appearing in courtly guise. But this woman had an ease of presence which even Saylana lacked for all her posturing. And she was one toward whom some inner, deep-buried part of Mahart reached in a half-awed need for friendship.

7 Willadene was weighing out tiny spoonsful of a powder which made her eyes water. This was surely more potent than any pepper she had ever dealt with in Jacoba's kitchen. She counted very carefully and then stoppered the bottle into which she had spooned the mixture. The street outside was unnaturally still. Half the shops were still closed, their keepers gone to view the grand procession.

She certainly had no desire to join the cheering, ribbon-waving crowd. In fact it was difficult for her to force herself to go beyond the front door, or that swing-gate in the garden behind. Though it had been a goodly number of days since she, trembling in spite of all her efforts at hiding her fears, had stood before the Reeve's court and thankfully heard herself assigned from Jacoba—who stood in a grimy, dingy show of secondhand finery, scowling blackly at her—to Halwice, as neatly gowned and imperturbable as ever. She had watched the coins turned out on the Reeve's clerk table—enough to cover by law her remaining worth to the cook. But Jacoba's whole attitude cried aloud, at least to Willadene, her complete dissatisfaction with the transaction.

Sometimes Willadene could almost imagine herself, out

on some peaceful errand for the Herbmistress, feeling that heavy hand fall upon her shoulder, to drag her back to the inn, even though good sense assured her that this would never happen.

It remained that here alone she felt safe. Though she had one small wish—that she could see Halwice in her fine gown, plain as it was, before Her Grace, a respected member of the guilds.

Willadene had heard a number of descriptions of the High Lady Mahart—that she was so fair of face even flowers seemed to lose their color in her presence, that she was so kind of heart she had fed the hungry with her own hands. They said, too, that she was learned—a very paragon of her line. And now there was gossip that certainly some great marriage was not too far away. It was easy enough to talk, but often rumor belied the truth. Willadene found herself wondering more and more what the ducal daughter was really like. It was against the law for Mahart to ever take her father's high seat, but that she might be won by a prince of some other land and even live to wear a crown was not now considered impossible.

The only tie between the girl whose birthday had sent Kronengred into holiday was the fact that from time to time a page or serving man would appear at the shop for a packet, carefully wrapped flagon, or bag smelling like the whole herb garden behind the shop, to be delivered to Her Grace.

These transactions had become even more frequent from week to week, and although Willadene was always carefully instructed as she watched potions for others combined, even allowed to finish the lesser ones herself, only Halwice ever melded those for the castle and she did it more or less alone—dispatching Willadene to some chore of grinding or the like while she worked at the table, two lamps, even on the brightest of days, giving her light.

Willadene finished her set task and most carefully cleaned the small spoon and set aside the other tools she had had to use. She could hear, even across the maze of streets between, the shouting of the crowds. But she did not venture closer to the door, rather took from a small cupboard a book which she spread open with greatest care so timeworn were its covers.

She had not been totally ignorant when fate had turned her over to the hell of Jacoba's kitchen. In fact, discovering that her scullery maid could not only read and write but also was able to figure had served the cook, in spite of her air of great disdain for such gentry knowledge when she had Willadene make any use of it.

Halwice, learning that Willadene had such abilities, limited though they might be, had set her regular lessons, and Willadene, as someone long hungry, had absorbed all she could. She could close her eyes and recite whole pages of the simpler herbals, but these older records presented puzzles which would often use lamp hours for solving.

What she sought now was a legend, though she was sure the Herbmistress considered it a historical truth—the story of Heart-Hold, that miraculous flower which gave forth a perfume no lover could withstand. No lover—she shook her head—it certainly was not for herself she sought this ancient recipe. *She* was content to spend the rest of her life even as she had the hours of this day.

But—suppose that such a fragrance could be distilled again—presented to Her Grace. Then Halwice would be in high favor and Willadene would have repaid in part her debt of gratitude.

She found the tale—for it was written in a crabbed writing using words long out of fashion, some of which she had to guess at—as a tale and not one of the carefully set formulas of the herbals she knew and used. The single flower found by chance where no other blossoms had ever bloomed, taken up with care and protected in an urn of oil of a kind which Willadene did recognize as being the most costly product of the shop. It was sold only by the drop and only those deep of purse could afford it.

Only—how was one to find any flower? To her clear memory Willadene had never been beyond the walls of Kronengred. Halwice dealt with foreign merchants, but they came to her. She never ventured forth herself to find what they finally delivered. There were a few flowering herbs, but it was still away from the time of year when their buds would appear. And Willadene knew just what those were and their proper use.

She was certain of one thing—such a marvel as Heart-Hold must root well beyond land held by man's labor. And how might one wander into those wilds, where the outlaws now held almost complete rule, on such a searching?

Willadene was reading the scant account for the third time when noise from the street disturbed her. Those who had gone to watch the procession were beginning to drift back. She watched through the open door the Reeve of this quarter and his escort ride back, people scattering before the horses. Willadene put away the book quickly.

In order to reach her proper seat in the Abbey Halwice had had to leave before First Bell with no more than a twist of bread and a small glass of ale to break her fast. The food Willadene had since prepared must be reheated and quickly.

She was gingerly tasting soup from a long-handled spoon when the Herbmistress arrived. There was a knot of neighbors who ringed her round, mainly merchants' wives of the street. Willadene could hear their continuous excited questioning even from where she stood.

Yes, Her Grace was all which was most gracious. And those who called her fair had not been dealing only in flattery. Indeed, the Duke was Star-blessed with such a daughter— But finally Halwice threw up her hands.

"Goodwives all, my tongue is as dry as a cut of salt beef. I have told you all that I can. She is indeed fit to be a queen, and let us hope that if she is, she will also be a happy one."

Some of the women grumbled a little, but at last they let her go and, though the Herbmistress left the door latch out, she came on through into the inner quarters without stopping.

She did not speak to the waiting girl, nor did she make any attempt to take off her fine gown. Instead, she went to the big cupboard where she slept, saying, as her head and shoulders disappeared within its cavern: "Clear the table!"

Hastily Willadene put aside the bowls and food dishes she had set there. She had no more than taken the last piece from the table than Halwice was back, never looking to the girl but putting in place on the well-scrubbed board the object she had held close to her body as she came, as if she would so hide it from sight.

There was a white bowl, perhaps the size of Willadene's two hands set interlapping together, and with that the bag she had seen in this very room once before—that which held the bits of polished but broken crystal.

Halwice next took up two candles Willadene recognized as the kind which gave off perfumed smoke as they burned. On either side of the bowl she set one of these and used a snap light quickly to set them burning. Into the bowl itself she poured a scant amount of the minted water which they used in their work and which Willadene knew to be thrice boiled for purity.

Having done all this to her satisfaction Halwice crooked a finger to the girl.

"Take up those which lie within." She pushed the bag of crystals forward. "Hold them all tightly together for the space of three breaths—long-held ones."

Willadene let the sharp-edged pieces fill one hand and then lapped it with the other, lest some spill from between her fingers. She drew three breaths, holding each, as if she feared that by releasing it she might cause some ill.

"Throw—"

Willadene tossed what she held onto the tabletop. None

of them rolled to the floor as she had feared. Halwice leaned forward, her tight-fitting cap of ceremony having no rolled edge to hide her features, and, for what seemed to Willadene a number of long breaths more, she simply stared at the bits of color where they lay. Then, with a straight forefinger, she worked among them, shoving first this and then that until there lay a single stone of sleek green not unlike a length of water-worn reed.

"Take and hold," she bade Willadene for the second time, and this time the girl silently counted to seven breaths before the next order came.

"Drop it into the bowl—then look therein, girl, with all which lies within you, look within!"

There was no room. She might have been standing on the shore of a very silent lake, watching without even a rippling of the water as shadows passed swiftly or with languid rolling, so vague in outline she could not have said what any of them might be.

But something within her made her try to hold those shadows as they slipped by. The effort she brought to that was like taking a full load of wood across her shoulders, but she held to it, tried and tried to see more clearly.

There was something which dipped and rose—she was no longer aware that this was even water in which it was fighting away. For fighting it was and against odds she could only guess at. It deepened, sharpened. Even as she had watched such on a summer evening winging out for their hunting, so did she see a bat. But that it was injured in some way—though she could not sight its wound—she was also sure.

She had to swallow twice before she could speak, for speaking somehow broke the effort of seeing, and even as she said the words aloud the creature melted into nothingness.

"A bat—hurt."

She was not fully aware of the gasp of breath which came from outside this place, yet something she felt—a twinge of what was both pain and fear intermingled—and she was sure it had not come from the animal she had seen.

"Look on—look!"

The order was so demanding that Willadene forced herself to plunge faster and deeper.

This time the picture came clearer, snapping out of nowhere as if a door had burst open. There were certainly rocks, patterned with lichen, wreathed in part with small fern fringes—yet not rocks of any building in Kronengred that she had ever seen. And in a pocket between the two largest of these, their sides forming an arch over it as if to protect the fragile-stemmed star-shaped bloom, stood what she had imagined Heart-Hold to be when she had read or heard the tale of its gifting to man.

She must have spoken the name aloud, for suddenly her feeling of being otherwise was broken. Hands were on her shoulders steadying her, but not until from that flower had spread to her such a fragrance as she knew that in all her lifetime she would never forget.

"So—that is the way of it!" Halwice's voice sounded from far off and then close. "Let it be— But the path may be long and the way dark."

There was only the table and on it the bowl of water at the bottom of which lay the stone the girl had tossed within. But she had to steady herself with both hands on the edge of the table, for it seemed that she could still catch that scent, as overpowering as the strongest of the autumn ale.

Well above that house and room the Duke sat huddled in his chair, his robes which always looked, when worn by him, as if they had been tailored for another man, creased about him. He had doffed his ducal coronet and held his aching head in both his hands.

Uttobric had never been a social creature, and the older he grew the more he hated these parades of pomp which

were expected. But the power itself—if one has been insig-
nificant and overlooked for most of one's life, the butt of
a scoffing court—power was a heady wine and he was not
about to surrender it. For years he had been a nobody, the
least of his clan. Now he need only affix his seal to a
scrap of paper and one of those who had sneered so openly
would be naught.

Still that was not so—not yet. And he knew it, tasted
it like a sour bile rising in his throat.

"Well," he said now, "was Kronengred suitably impressed?" He had no desire to see the expression on Vazul's face.

"The move was the strongest you could have made,"
the Chancellor returned promptly. "Fortune favored you,
Your Highness, with a daughter who can be a mighty
weapon—if she is properly honed."

Uttobric threw himself back in his chair now, his long
robe crushing against his spine.

"And you will see to that," he commented, watching
the other with half-hooded eyes. "Only keep this in mind,
my Chancellor, it is with me you rise—or fall—"

What he might have added to that was lost as the black
creature on Vazul's shoulder suddenly leaped with a speed
and agility which carried her near across the room. The
Chancellor wheeled to watch her, and his hand was already
on the hilt of the dagger in his belt sheath.

Ssssaaa made straight for the darkly paneled wall and
reared against that, digging claws into the age-old wood,
the usual hissing cry she uttered rising to a high note.

It took but three strides for Vazul to reach that panel,
for the Duke to get to his feet, tearing at the fastening of
his state cloak to free himself from its hampering folds.

The Chancellor's hands sought hidden releases. For a
moment they faced only a dark hole, but into that darted
Ssssaaa and Vazul, blade bared now in his hand, followed.
Then, as the Duke approached the same opening, he heard
an exclamation of pain only a little louder than a moan.

Vazul's back was now once more in the doorway as he retreated into the room, his hands no longer holding steel but rather drawing after him a body which struggled a little as if it would throw off that clutch. Stretching his catch on the floor the Chancellor hastened to reclose the door, while Uttobric stooped over the man who was struggling to sit up but subsided with a gritting of teeth.

"You were followed?" the Duke demanded, glancing at that strip of paneling and then back again.

"I lay there—" The other's voice was a thread of sound. "There was no one following."

"Nor would there be." Vazul near elbowed the Duke out of the way as he knelt in turn, one hand sending the wounded man flat on his back before he busied himself with loosening a greasy, latched jerkin and was able to pull it back and away from the other's left shoulder.

Ssssaaa had crouched by the man's head and with forepaws was patting sweat-stiffened hair. He they worked on closed his eyes and suddenly his head fell to one side. The Duke started back.

"Dead?" he demanded.

"Not yet." The Chancellor raised the rolling head a little and bent closer. "There is the stench—"

"Poison!" Now the Duke backed away even farther.

"It is often a trick of the night prowlers. But caught in time— We must not only save the Bat if we can but learn quickly what he struggled against death to bring us."

"He can be saved?" Uttobric continued to stare down at the body as if he expected to see it crumble into nothingness before his eyes. "You have the knowledge?"

Vazul shook his head. "Not I, Your Highness. But there is certainly one within Kronengred who can return him to life if any mortal can."

The Duke was nodding. "The Herbmistress, yes."

"However," the Chancellor said hastily a moment later, "we cannot leave him here—and tonight is the ball— before that the feasting—at which we must both appear or there will be those who are overinterested as to why we are not.

"The ball will draw the majority of the servants into the west wing." Vazul had now gotten the blood-stiffened shirt free and was loosening a swathing wad which had been stuffed in over the source of the blood flow. "There remains—Black Tower."

The Duke plucked at his lower lip. "Yes, there has not been one held there for half a century or more—not since Duke Rotonbric went raving mad. But how do we get him there?"

"Only by the inner ways, Your Highness. And I must have help to take him, since he is more weight than I can bear that far. Danerx—"

The Duke stared at the man on the floor as if he wished him well away. "Danerx," he said slowly. "At least the man is loyal to me—or I would be dead long since." One side of his thin lip quirked upward. His robe tumbling after him, he went to the bell pull hanging on the far wall and gave two vigorous tugs.

He need have no fear that Danerx, his valet, would not be just where he was supposed to be—two doors away, laying out the garments for both the feasting and the ball. What a deal of time one wasted in this dressing up for such occasions. Uttobric thought fleetingly that unfortunately there were going to be more of them until their plans bore fruit.

The summons for Halwice came after dusk and secretly. Willadene heard only swift whispers at the back door as if the visitor must be gone as quickly as possible. Then the Herbmistress turned to the assembling of certain small boxes, flasks, and jars which she stowed away in a shoulder bag without a word of explanation. It was not until she was done and had reached for her cloak that she spoke at last.

"There is dire need and no one must guess the reason.

I am expecting a shipment from overseas tomorrow. You will open the shop as usual and accept the packet—it is already paid for. If I am asked for, you may say that there is a difficult birthing and I was summoned in the night, you do not know where, nor when I shall return."

She added nothing more, but Willadene was able to guess that it was *not* a birthing her mistress went to attend—she had noted only too well the choice of remedies, and most of them her recent learning equated with wounds.

"Go under the Star—" The girl did not think the woman even heard her, she slipped out of the back door so quickly.

Willadene turned back to eat her bread and cheese. The city was not quiet tonight. Even shut within these walls she could hear the sounds of the crowds. There would be many in the wide square below the castle where there would be free ale and cakes—giving the citizens of Kronengred at least a taste of the feast and the grand ball in the fortress above. Also there would be much to see in the splendor of the arriving coaches bringing noble families to the gathering. Willadene looked around the room in which she sat. Let Her Grace Mahart have all the delicacies, the prancing to stately music, and the rest of the celebrations for her special day; she, Willadene, was entirely content with what she did have here and now.

Halwice had not said when her precious packet was to arrive but when there had been no visit to the shop by First Night Bell, Willadene ceased to expect it. Any emergency which would take the Herbmistress away from her home must indeed be serious. Guesses were useless—if she were meant to know she would learn in time.

She went to bed at the usual hour, leaving only the night lamp burning in case of Halwice's return, burrowing deep into the worn but lavender-scented coverlets of the trundle bed.

It was not until her eyes grew heavy that her memory turned to Halwice's earlier play with the bowl and the candles. And, once she thought of that cleft in the rock and what had raised its proud head there, she tried to hold on to every detail memory supplied. Only, sleep came quickly.

Halwice had not returned when Willadene awoke in the morning and now uneasiness awoke also. Yet she made herself carry out her duties in the same order she would have done had the Herbmistress been there.

She had just taken down the shop shutters and made ready to open for business when a familiar voice hailed her.

"Ha, Willa, how goes it?"

Figis no longer wore the drab rags which had been his at the inn—but rather better clothing such as an apprentice in a small shop might have. He walked with something of a swagger. Though, Willadene noted, neither his bony hands nor his gaunt face was really clean.

"Well enough," the girl answered shortly. She had never considered any beneath Jacoba's roof ones to be trusted, and her earlier uneasiness was growing. "And the inn—"

"*Paugh!*" He actually spat on the paving stones. "There have been changes there—the old sow does not oink very loudly anymore."

Taking that coarse expression to refer to Jacoba, Willadene was interested enough to ask: "Jacoba no longer keeps the inn?" She had heard no such rumor, but sometimes facts outran even gossip.

"It keeps her," he returned somewhat cryptically. "But where's the mistress? Here—I have a packet for her."

He reached within the loosened lacing of his jerkin and pulled out one of those familiar squares so well fastened up in oiled silk.

"She was called to a birthing," Willadene answered promptly, "but she told me that a shipment was expected and to take it in."

He eyed her narrowly, turning what he held around in

his hand as if he were in two minds about relinquishing it. "Don't know 'bout that. Wyche—" He stopped short as if that name had been a warning. "He who sent me said nothin' about givin' this to anyone save the mistress. But then he also said he'd have me ears offen my head did I not do as he told me. Wyche— Jacoba is afeared of him and there are others that come—maybe for orders." Figis grinned. "Seems like he's taken a shine to me. Don't have to go luggin' in greasy pans no more I don't!"

He moved closer to Willadene. "I've learned a lot jus' listenin' around. The Duke, he ain't as safe as he thinks he is—parading 'round like a cock an' showin' off his daughter. There's them as may bring him to heel jus' like that!" He shifted the packet to one hand and snapped his fingers.

"You know what they're sayin' now—that young Lord Barbric has caught Her Grace's eye. She led off with him at the ball last night and then never danced no more. She marries him and we'd see a might lot of changes hereabouts. And me, I'm gonna be ready for the pickin's— that I promise you. Oh, well, take this— I got me other important business—"

He thrust the packet at her and strode off, his thin legs trying to hold the important thud of a district guard but falling far short of that.

Willadene missed that exit, for she was staring down at the packet. This was—evil—veiled but there. She certainly had not forgotten the trap in which she had found the Herbmistress and the Chancellor's man many days ago. Was this another such—something wrong to be planted among Halwice's supplies and then discovered to the hurt of her mistress?

The oiled covering felt slimy to her fingers, and she wanted to rid herself of it speedily. But she had no intention of storing it anywhere within the shop. Who knows— it might even be a source of contamination.

She swiftly sought the herb garden, stopping only to

snatch up some garlic. Weaving broken bits of that about the packet she placed it on the ground on the barren spot where they spread the ashes each morning and snapped over it a flowerpot, pressing that down well into the ground.

This proved to be a busier day than was usual and she had a steady stream of customers—some housewives seeking cooking herbs, the up-nosed maids and waiting women from the castle in search of cosmetic supplies as if the rigors of the forenight's ball had depleted such to an alarming degree.

There were a number of inquiries for Halwice, but Willadene could detect that no one seemed dissatisfied with the reason she gave for the Herbmistress's absence. At the back of her mind was always that potted menace behind the shop, but no guard came marching for a search and gradually she relaxed. Halwice would know how to deal with it—she only wished that her mistress would return.

It was not until dusk gathered in that she did come. Her bag was no longer slung over her shoulder and her face was white and strained. Nor was she alone. By his stride and stance he was a guardsman, perhaps even an underofficer, but he was soberly dressed like any merchant.

Willadene hurried to reheat the kettle, prepared the herb tea she knew that Halwice found sustaining. While she worked she could feel her mistress watching her. The guard remained by the door as unmoving as if he were on duty in the castle.

"That which was to come—" Halwice spoke slowly as if she found even the formation of words an effort.

Willadene paused, teapot in hand. Certainly she must not speak in front of this stranger. She made her choice quickly.

"It has come and is planted," she said deliberately, looking straight into Halwice's tired eyes, "as you wished in the special ashed ground."

It seemed to the girl that there was a spark deep in the

Herbmistress's eyes. But Halwice nodded as if she perfectly understood. She took up her filled cup with both hands as if too weak to risk a single hold.

"Now—there is little time. Take fresh underclothing and your other dress. Also the book third from the right on the shelf. I cannot any longer be away from here, but there will be a heavy trust placed on you. Remember well your gift and use it at all times. The one you must nurse is sore hurt—but he is still with us. He must remain so if we can at all will it, by the aid of the Star. You will go with this guard—" She nodded toward the man who had not spoken. "Obey him, for it is his duty to get you safely to your goal. I have left instructions for you with the one now there. Perhaps—by tomorrow—enough will be resolved that I can see you again. This is true duty, child, and perhaps you are over young to assume it—but there is no other choice."

Completely bewildered Willadene hurried to bundle up her scanty possessions, and the last she saw of Halwice, the Herbmistress was standing by the door watching them cross the garden.

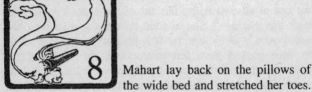

Mahart lay back on the pillows of the wide bed and stretched her toes. She was well aware that sunlight was laying stripes across her from an opening in the heavy curtains, but she felt no desire to pull herself out of this slothful ease right now, though she had been well aware for some time of purposefully soft comings and goings beyond the privacy of the curtained bed itself.

Looking back it seemed to her now that several twenty days of living had been thickly packed between first ball and the promised events, and whenever she tried to sort out a clear memory it slid inexorably into another.

If yesterday was an example of what was going to be demanded of her as to continued patience in the future, she was dubious she could measure up. Then two faces loomed out of her muddled recall— Vazul—what did he really want of her?

She was well aware that his private meetings with her in the immediate past had been in the nature of schooling. Though he had not skimmed far below the surface in any of his accounts of this or that to do with the ducal court, he gave one the impression—perhaps deliberately, Mahart thought now, pursing her lips—that there were darkish depths and traps to be avoided.

He need give her no warnings concerning the High Lady Saylana (and had not, except a dry comment or so). Since Mahart had been a small child she had been well aware of the chasm between that one and her father. She made a face now. Yes, she had led the first dance at the ball with Barbric. He did not quite have two left feet but sometimes, in one of the stately figures they had walked through so pompously, he had given the impression that that misfortune was his. And his hand—she now wiped hers swiftly back and forth across a fold of the sheet—its disgusting warmth and softness was not what one would accept joyfully. She did recall seeing Vazul once watching her as she turned and minced the small trotting steps of the figure. She wished at first that the Chancellor would be more open with her—and then decided it was better that he kept his own counsel. At least now.

But the second figure which she remembered so clearly—the woman among the town council, as stately as any noble lady of the court—the Herbmistress. Mahart had not quite summoned up the courage to invite her to the castle to learn more of her and her wares—though she believed that it might indeed be practical to do so. Yet—

Mahart sat up, pushed away the covering, and set her hand to that crack between the bed curtains through which the sun was coming. She had no idea as yet just how much power she might hold—whom she could send on an errand or demand service from. But that she would meet Halwice sooner or later she was sure.

The sight of her fingers on the edge of the curtain must have been a signal, as it was pulled quickly back and she looked out upon what seemed to her an unwonted crowd of people, all facing her, as if it was now her will to set them in motion for the day.

Julta still stood holding the curtain she had drawn back but at the same time managing a curtsey of sorts. And there was Zuta, a bright note in this time-dark room in her favorite yellow. Beyond her were those two noble misfits who had attended her on that first court appearance. She was completely bored by their company and only Vazul's suggestion that their presence among her retinue might have some purpose led her to continue to greet them each morning with the smiling mask she assumed at the drawing of the bed curtains.

"A fair day, and may the Star favor you." She repeated the formal greeting, thus giving permission to all of them to be about their assigned duties, such as they were.

The Ladies Famina and Geuverir made a bustling business of escorting her to the screens about the bath, accepting the night robe she tossed to them. Julta, however, gave no play of any new awesome service as she stood ready with the big towel and waited for Mahart to draw on drawers and underchemise.

There was a war of scents in the room now: that remaining incense which had burned out during the night, the herbs steeped in the bath, and those less strident odors from the clean linen in which she clothed herself.

She could hear the whispering of Famina and Geuverir, but noted that, as always, Zuta kept apart from those two. What they were whispering about she could guess. Though they had not been friends when first assigned to her service they had bonded quickly, mainly because of a common interest—men. And she knew that both, having been betrothed properly from childhood, were eager to become mistresses of their own establishments, peevishly eager at times. Mahart had asked Zuta why these bridal festivities had not rid her of the two. Zuta had shrugged and declared that in the case of the Lady Famina, it was a matter of dowry—that the father of her lord-to-be was avid for a certain strip of territory to add to his own holdings with the bride's arrival. And there were still negotiations for the Lady Geuverir in progress.

However, this morning it was not men that the ladies were discussing. It was ghosts!

Catching a word or two, Mahart was intrigued enough to summon them closer as Julta brushed and braided her hair.

Of course there were parts of the castle, as Mahart herself well knew, within which the air seemed to enfold one in an ominous, smothering way. And there were innumerable tales of this or that past dignitary (usually one who had lost his or her head through crossing ducal authority) who had been seen pacing some corridor during the hours of darkness.

However, the new manifestations apparently had to do with lights, and, though she was hearing the tale about thirdhand, there were two separate tales, yet similarities in both. The ball had lasted until dawn, and she herself had been so sleepy by its ending that she wanted no more than to find her bed and tumble into it. However, others had more nighthawk blood than she—or else were engaged in such dalliance as they must seek less open ways. And so the reports—

" 'Tis the Black Tower, Your Grace." There was a quiver in Lady Geuverir's voice. "They have always said that it has been cursed ever since the mad Duke Rotonbric hung himself there with a curtain rope."

"Yes," chimed in Lady Famina. "The Lady Horsetha—with her own eyes she saw this *thing* all in white moving along. Guardsman Kylow, he challenged, and the thing disappeared straight into the wall."

Mahart raised a small smile. "The Lady Horsetha, she is, I believe, married—but *not* to a guardsman."

Lady Famina flushed, and she was not one on whom any form of a blush was an attraction.

"They were heated, Your Grace—and went into the open passage for a breath of air. But it is true— Lady Horestha came back shaking so Guardsman Kylow had to support her on her feet. And she swooned again later when Lord Margrave told what *he* had seen."

"Which was?" Mahart accepted the mirror Julta held ready so that she could inspect her back hair before the maid pinned on the shoulder-length veil which was now another hampering bit of her life.

"Well—" Lady Famina tittered, and it was Lady Geuverir's turn to redden as her more talkative companion continued. "There was much drinking, you understand, Your Grace—"

"And he sought a garderobe," returned Mahart impatiently. "But why in that direction—?" And it was her turn to blush. Gentlemen—men—were not always so particular in such matters. "Well, and what did *he* see?"

"Two huge black figures, Your Grace. They came out of the night as if they were pulled from some other world, and then went up the passage. There was a greenish light—a death light—" Lady Famina was now enjoying her own fears. "And they went into the wall also!"

"I suppose His Highness's guard finally arrived?" Mahart commented. "And what did they find?"

"Nothing." Lady Famina paused as if summoning breath to enhance the force of her report. "Nothing—only that door as was barred and sealed after they brought out the mad Duke's body."

Mahart fingered a frosted bottle. She did not believe in specters, she told herself sternly. However, she was sure that she would find good reason *not* to visit the Black Tower was she ever invited to do so—and had any choice in the matter. No—Breath of Lilies was too exquisite to be wasted on any but a state occasion. She opened a cream-filled jar instead, sniffed at the invigorating scent she had so released, and delicately swept fingertips behind her ears and down the line of her throat. Ghosts in the castle? she wondered. What would Vazul have to say to that now?

Willadene had always been so close quartered in the inn and Halwice had kept her so busy in the shop that she did not know this part of Kronengred. Halwice did not deliver her products—her customers came to her. And although those visitors formed a goodly cross section of the old city the girl had heard names of streets, noble houses, and the like with no idea where such might be.

She kept close to her silent guard, even more so when they ran into merrymakers on their way home, steady or unsteady, the last of the revelers of the day before. Willadene found herself elbowed close to the wall, the guard taking his position between her and any body of townsmen who passed. She had pulled the hood of her cloak down so far she could barely catch glimpses of the outside world from under its edging.

The streets and alleys through which they went their way seemed to go on forever. As the night closed in only the decreed lamps lit above each doorway spread small pools of light between dwelling and dwelling. At least the guard matched his swinging stride to her own best pace, and twice his arm with a quick grasp saved her from a stumble—almost as if he had the talent for seeing through the dark.

Above them loomed the castle, and they were drawing ever closer to that. The number of lighted windows in the upper walls marked out most of the outline of the building, and at the foot of the rise on which it stood there was much more light and comings and goings.

However, her guide turned away abruptly from that and brought her into an alley so narrow she wondered if his wide shoulders did not brush the walls on either side. This was worse going, for here and there were refuse bins, primly kept out of sight from the passersby on the main streets. And it was before a large one of these, near the far end of the way, that he came to a stop so sudden she nearly ran into him.

A snap light, shielded by hand, gave her a glimpse of a great tun, so large a one she wondered that any one man might move it. Yet it rolled easily aside when her companion laid a single hand on it.

Willadene could see nothing but stone wall, but he did not look to that at all, rather stamped on the pavement where the tun had rested. Three times his heavy boot rose and fell. Then he crowded back, pushing her with him. There came no warning sound, but a square of the set stones dipped and was gone, leaving a black hole. For the first time he spoke.

"There is a ladder, girl. Get you down quickly."

However, it would seem that she was not about to chance descent into total darkness, for there *was* now a faint glow and she saw the ladder. Hampered by the full folds of her cloak and the bag she had slung over her shoulder by its carry cord, she did as he had bidden her.

There was more light below, illuminating a very small section of a passage which assaulted her nose with a musty, earthy odor. Once they were both down the inner stair, the guard picked up the waiting lantern and started briskly on. She heard a soft thud behind her and guessed that that doorway had fallen shut to seal off this way.

There came stairs, long steep series of them. She kept tight hold on a groove in the wall to her right, which must have been intended as a safety measure, though she did not think it really so.

There were three such flights—each ending in a broad landing before the next began. At two such lanterns had been set, but the third staircase was something of a puzzle. In the first place, it was much narrower, ragged of edges, with chips of stone lying on the floor as if it had been only recently cut.

The stair leading upward was far narrower and her shoes stirred dust which arose to make her cough, even as her companion did. They came to a fourth landing, this very small, so that their bodies touched as they both reached it. The guard raised a fist, and the wan lantern light brought a gleam of answering metal shine—he was using the hilt of a belt knife to rap on the wall.

Willadene smelled fresh oil and guessed that some long-shut way must have been so coaxed to open. Then there was a fair burst of light. The guard's hand on her shoulder propelled her forward into the space beyond while he remained where he was. Before she could glance around she heard a snap of latch.

But her head was up now, for her nose was busy reporting. Above the mustiness and dust of a long-unused room she could smell balms and remedies she was only too familiar with and other odors also, not so pleasant but found in any close-kept chamber where there was illness.

The man who arose from a chair to face her caught her attention first. He gave her no greeting, merely surveyed her from head to foot and back again. And all this time he played and petted with one hand a black-furred creature which curled about his lean throat above the splendid embroidery of his robe as might an extra fur collar.

By the sight of that alone Willadene knew him and somehow forced her legs, trembling a little from that long climb, into a curtsey.

"M'lord Chancellor—"

"Halwice stands hostage for our trust in you." He spoke abruptly. "She also says that you have talent to obey her orders and to keep a shut mouth."

Willadene could not think of any answer to that, but she knew a spark of pleasure that the Herbmistress rated her so.

"You have one to tend, and the tending must be of the best." He turned away, crooking a finger as he did so.

Now she could see the bed, like a huge cavern, draped with curtains resembling the thickest clouds of night. But it was not about that that a row of lamps had been stationed. Rather, resting much closer to the floor and easier to reach, was a trundle bed such as she herself now used. On it was stretched a body. Now and then a hand arose

to push impatiently at the covering. But in the face turned
toward hers the eyes were closed as if he slept.

Nicolas! What trap had caught him this time? she wondered. He seemed a singularly ill-fated young man.

"There." The Chancellor again summoned her full attention, pointing to a small side table on which lay several
sheets of much finer paper than Halwice usually used.
However, they were covered by the even lines of her mistress's script. "Those are your orders. There remains only
this—" He paused and was eye-measuring her again.
"Should he regain consciousness and is able to speak"—
now he went beyond her to the wall and twitched a bell
pull into full sight—"you will use this at once. Do you
understand?"

Willadene nodded. For the past few moments there had
been an interruption to her full attention. She had become
aware of a new scent, thin, hardly to be picked up among
the many others here, yet somehow, she knew, of importance. Her eyes dropped from the Chancellor's to that animated fur collar and another set of eyes met hers—

Here was no evil—the tales in the city about Vazul's
companion creature were belied. But the creature was far
more than any pet. And having once picked up that scent
she knew it was one that she would never forget.

"Do you understand?!" There was impatience in the
man's voice, she realized, that she had not replied
quickly enough.

"Yes, m'lord. If he—" she nodded toward the uneasy
sleeper "—wakes, and if he speaks—then I pull that
loop." She sounded as dim-witted as a real scullery maid,
but that did not matter. Let him think she was like any
servant, and he would consider her no threat to him.

"Here—" Now he moved on to a door. Raising his
foot he cracked his boot toe against its lowest panel, and
it swung outward under that force. "Water, food, aught
else needed, can be delivered so. Leave a note on the tray
if there is such need. There is oil for the lamps in the far

corner—enough for a goodly time. Now—turn your back—draw your hood down!''

So forceful was that order Willadene followed it at once. Nor was she surprised when she turned around to find herself alone in the chamber with the wounded man, though there was no means of exit she could account for, as she was standing between where he had been and that flap-furnished door.

She shed her cloak and draped it with her bundle on a chair carved like a throne but with the velvet of its seat cushion faded to a dull gray. Her first task was Nicolas, of course, though she was sure that Halwice would have never left him if he were still in danger.

Under her hand his flesh felt overwarm, but with a wound some fever was to be expected. There were three bottles, their dosage spoons fastened to them by wires, standing on the floor. She examined each in turn, recognizing it at once for what it was and how it must be used.

Carefully she turned back the top bed cover to inspect the rolls of bandage which pillowed over his shoulder and well down his chest on the right side. There was no need as yet to interfere with those carefully wound bands. Willadene could smell the soporific Halwice had administered. Which left her two things to do. First, she would read the instructions her mistress had left. They were indeed familiar, having only one or two points of which Willadene had not already aided Halwice in using. There was an hour lamp burning, and when the marking reached the proper point she was to rouse her charge far enough to get another spoonful from one of the bottles into him.

Having made sure she understood what she was to do, the girl now was determined to explore this prison. For that she *was* a prisoner kept here for the duties her mistress had set upon her she well knew.

Taking up one of the smaller lamps Willadene began a circuit of the room, first keeping the four walls as her guide. Two of those walls were curved, and she judged that this chamber was part of a tower. There were long narrow windows, but they had been bricked up and generations of spiders had built webs across them.

The furniture must once have been very fine, equal, she believed, to that which might be found in the Duke's own chamber. But it was dulled with dust and showed signs of woodworm visitation.

She had made her circuit and returned, certain that any entrance to this room must be fully secret, even as the way she had been brought here.

Still unsatisfied, for the second time she made this circuit, this time feverishly calling upon what Halwice declared to be her special gift, trying to find some scent of evil as had filled the shop at her first meeting with Nicolas or had always hung about Wyche and his close companions. But nothing save the scent of healing herbs answered her.

She was certain that the Herbmistress would never have lent her knowledge to the use of evil, and she also knew from watching Nicolas and Halwice together on the few occasions the young man had appeared at the shop, that there was friendship, or at least a bond of some sort between them.

A tapping brought her to that closed door in time to see the flap at the bottom being pulled back and a tray pushed through. However, before she could stoop to take it up and perhaps catch some glimpse of who had delivered it, the flap fell again, striking the edge of the tray and jarring it farther into the room.

There were several covered dishes—silver dishes such as might have been lifted from any noble's table—and a pile of folded linen, yellowed by age but clean. Willadene removed this to a footstool not too far from her charge and seated herself cross-legged beside it. Perhaps it was the rich aroma wafted into the varied smells of the room which aroused Nicolas. For his head turned and she saw his eyes, hard as usual, fixed upon her.

There were no signs of the confusion of fever about that stare, and she believed that he was fully aware of who she was.

"Soup—" She balanced the bowl she had uncovered on one hand and with the other reached for an ornately handled spoon.

He frowned and again turned his head slowly, apparently taking in all he could see of what was about him.

"Where?" His one-word question came faint and hoarse.

Willadene shook her head. "Somewhere in the castle. But I was brought here by hidden ways and cannot tell you more. It was by my mistress's bidding!" she finished defiantly as his frown seemed to grow the blacker.

She was remembering the Chancellor's instructions— were Nicolas to regain his senses she must summon aid. Well enough, but it was also plain that the man stretched before her was fighting to keep those same senses and he needed strength to do so. She could give him one of the potions Halwice had left, but the effect of that would be only temporary and the food she now held might do him more good at present. She hitched herself closer and dipped the spoon into the fragrant broth.

"Eat!" She tried to make her voice as commanding as Halwice's could be. Even so, she was secretly surprised when he opened his mouth and allowed her to spoon the stuff into it. Five spoonfuls later he shut his lips firmly in refusal.

"Vazul—" He opened them again only to utter that name.

Willadene crossed to the length of bell cord and gave a vigorous jerk before she returned, this time to indeed take up one of the waiting bottles and measure out a half spoonful.

"It gives strength." She pushed it at that obstinately closed mouth. His eyes offered her neither welcome nor thanks, but he allowed her to carefully spoon the potion into him.

"Ssssaaa—" Luckily he had taken the last drop of that mixture before that hiss startled the girl.

Padding across the floor into the fuller light which rimmed the trundle bed came Vazul's creature, the first time she had seen it apart from the Chancellor. It haunched itself into a part ball, so that its fore body was well above the time-webbed carpets on the floor, its head high as if it sniffed in search of some warning scent. So plain was that action to Willadene that she found herself doing likewise. There were odors in plenty but most of them innocuous and familiar ones.

Her attention had been so fastened on the creature that she was again startled when Vazul loomed out of nowhere into the light. The heavily ornamented and bedizened robe he generally wore was gone and he had instead a plain, much less impressive garment of a dark gray—not unlike that of a working merchant.

"Nicolas?" He paid no attention to Willadene, and she had to scramble out of his way as he came forward to kneel beside the trundle bed.

There was a weak smile on that drawn face, and the eyes looking up no longer pierced like sword points.

"The same, lord Chancellor," Nicolas's answer was clear but hardly more than a whisper. "They did not get me this time either—"

Vazul's hands moved and, with a gentle skill Willadene would not have thought possible in the stiff, reserved man, the Chancellor lifted the other a little and held him supported on one arm while he patted bed linen into a support.

"Ssssaaa—" His creature leaped upward on the bed, darting forward to insert its narrow head under Nicolas's limp hand.

"No," Vazul said with some of his customary dryness of speech, "you will still live to play games, boy. But no luck holds forever. You were found in the passage—"

"At least not in an alley." Perhaps it was a laugh the younger man attempted, but it came forth as a croak. "It was city slinkers who brought me down—and waiting ones."

"Soooo—" The sound the Chancellor made was not far from his creature's hiss. "But what news do you bring?" It was as if for the moment he pushed aside one subject to concentrate on another.

"The best—for our purposes. Prince Lorien chaffs for a fight—he was never one interested in the hunting . . . of animals. He was provided with a guide and certain information. By your look, m'lord, no news has come yet, but I would swear it is on its way. I do not think that the Prince, having his tail tweaked after a fashion, will be bound by any boundaries. That is wild country and easy to cross from the kingdom where no highway posts stand."

Vazul smiled now, stiffly as if such a change of feature did not come easily.

"His Highness will be well pleased," he commented. "And this Prince, what can you tell of him?"

"Young, hot of blood, needing occupation." But Nicolas's voice was dwindling, and Willadene gave a quick glance to the time lamp on the table and dared to interrupt.

"My lord, it is time for a potion. See, he exhausts himself—"

There were beads of sweat now soaking the fringe of dark curls across the wounded man's forehead.

"Well done"—as if he had not heard Willadene, though she was very certain that he had. Vazul's hand smoothed the cover lightly over that bandaged body. His creature seemed to take that as a signal and darted to that arm, curling up to the Chancellor's shoulder.

"I think"—now Vazul did face the girl—"that I leave you in good hands. Halwice has gone hostage for this one."

"I would—" Nicolas tried to move, to raise himself a little. It was Vazul who pushed him back.

"Heal, Bat. Your flights are certainly not yet ended. Give him the potion, girl, and see that he sleeps."

She was already at the table for that and was aware only of a slight passage of air through the room but turned to find the Chancellor gone.

Nicolas eyed what she brought balefully. "How long do I lie here—" His voice quivered as if he was having some difficulty in speaking at all.

Willadene held the very small cup to his lips. "As long as my mistress thinks it well and proper." She was having the last word after all, for his eyes were already closing.

Long before the first morning bell, while the night still held grasp on the four portals to Kronengred, there were travelers heading toward the northern gate—and certainly no ordinary march of a merchant caravan or the pounding of some messenger.

There was one horse between the two of them, and yet neither rode. The horse itself moved with hanging head and there was a rime of dried sweat on its thin flanks. To the right of the clearly near-spent animal trudged a man in border mail and helm, a blood-darkened badge on the sleeve covering the arm he used to hold reins looped once about the saddle horn by which he urged the mount forward.

His companion was in much worse case, head hanging so that his chin near touched his breast, his lower face a mask of dried blood as he snorted for breath through a smashed nose. Instead of mail he wore a jacket of brine-hardened leather, and he certainly lacked both the sword slapping now and then against the other's thigh or any other sign of weapon. His matted hair was gray-white with dust, and twice only the support of the horse to which

119

his hands had been lashed kept him on his feet when he stumbled.

"Holla—the gate!" The voice was husky but the border guard managed to gain the attention he wanted. A lantern swung down from a beam overhead to more fully reveal the wayfarers.

"Who goes?"

"Vacher of the Hawk Liners—with a prisoner."

There was some mumbling from aloft and a wait during which the prisoner would have gone to his knees save for the support of the horse. Then words reached them.

" 'Tis Vacher right enough, served with him on the Burges route, I did. Let the man in, dolt—can't you see he is fair done?"

They did not throw open the great gate but from the postern to the side there emerged light of a kind. A knife sawed through the cords which held the prisoner and he fell, lumpish face downward, while a flask was pushed into his captor's hand.

Two more lantern bearers pushed their way to the scene, one of them wearing the slant bar of an underofficer on his helm.

"Wot you got here!" He came to the point at once, giving the body on the ground a prod with boot toe.

The border guard finished his drink. "That there's maybe something as the Cap'n will be glad to set eye on. Raider—"

Two of the men in that small group snarled, and one went as far as to half draw his sword.

"A raider," Vacher continued, "as may know something as should be shared with honest men—such as why me an' Samnnel an' Jas' was ambushed like they knew we was comin'. The Hawker, he couldn't spare no more men and me, he knew I was woodsranger for Lord Gerorigius a'fore he took and died, so I had the best chance maybe to get through. What I did—an' wi' him along, too."

But suddenly he tottered and would have fallen in turn had he not been caught by the man now beside him.

"Get 'im in," commanded the underofficer, "and have the set bones to 'im. See this other is all properly tight also." Once more he indicated the subject of this order with a kick to the inert body. "I'm for the Cap'n—trust he's back from patrol. Big doin's in the city last night and we was called out special."

They obeyed orders with the snap of well-drilled men. But so intent were they on those very orders that they did not note a shadow lying belly flat on the ground, arm over face to better conceal its pale curve. When one of the guards caught hand in the prisoner's mop of hair and pulled up his head and one of his fellows swung a lantern closer to the blood-soaked face, the shadow tensed. But it continued to lie where it had stationed itself at the first sound of the newcomers until the whole of the party passed back through the postern gate—and for a number of counted breaths afterward.

When the skulker moved at last, it was to squirm on belly back along the wall for what was equal to several strides and then, on hands and knees, scuttle to the protection of a cart. He could hear the snoring of the farmer sleeping above, willing to forgo any better bed in order to be first to the market in the morning.

The shadow did not need traditional gates to pass into the city. Beyond the cart he got to his feet and flitted away from the wall. The past Dukes had prudently had that land cleared of any form of hiding place long since. Yet the watcher found his way unerringly to the vast round of a rotting stump near the size of a small tower. Then came a scratching sound and he was gone.

The First Bell boomed out its daily message when a man, his lean body covered with a patchwork of rags, again came into view—this time not in the outer world but within a room, as if he were thin enough to melt through the cracks between the ancient boards.

"Hobbert." The oiled voice gave his name as the only greeting. "An' wot 'as brought you out of your hole now?"

The man half cringed, almost as if he were greeting Duke Uttobric himself most formally. "News I do have, Wyche."

"That being?"

"One of the Hill Hawks jus' comed in. An' he had Ranny—brought him in tied to his saddle."

"If he came so," the huge man commented, "then the lack wit was still alive—an' . . ."

Hobbert moved a little closer. Once he even dared to glance at the tall tankard which stood within easy reach of the other's hand.

"He—he knows somethin' then—"

Wyche's broken-veined face became a mask of malice.

"What a man knows can bring 'im trouble, Hobbert. Like this—" He pointed to a large roach, foolhardy enough to attempt the top of the table in daytime, and brought his tankard forcefully down on the insect.

"I don't know nothin'," Hobbert gabbled in a hurry. "Only what I jus' come here to tell you, Master Wyche."

The other snorted. "You were a liar since you drew your first breath, Hobbert. But sooner or later"—his hot stare swept the smaller man from head to foot and then back again—"you'll settle accounts. As it is, this time you've used what little wits as rattle around in that lousy skull of yours." His grin was hardly better than his malice of a few minutes earlier.

"Get you to the kitchen an' tell that slob of a Jacoba as how I'll stand you a full belly for once."

Hobbert disappeared—this time through the conventional doorway. The chair, large as it was, squeaked as Wyche shifted his weight. He was neither grinning nor scowling now. 'Twas never really lucky to be caught up in the plots of the nobles. On the other hand—let a city get in such a muffle as the hand of a man was ready for his neighbor's throat—now that meant rich pickings for him as let the others do the blooding while he did the harvesting.

That Ranny was taken suggested perhaps a major danger to those who had his own—temporary—allegiance. But any pile as old as Kronengred had secrets within its walls, and a man could well have his throat slit before he could flap his tongue.

Yes. He took another long pull at the tankard. To pass on Hobbert's message might be to his advantage for the present. He tapped the stained board of the table with his fat and puffy fingers. How—and who—that took some thinking on.

During Willadene's exploration of the room where Nicolas lay and she appeared to be imprisoned for the present she had come across a chest. Perhaps the contents had once been precious—robes of state. The clean odor of cedar had greeted her when she had managed to raise the heavy lid, but the garments, too long folded, slit and tore at her handling. However, she got out enough of them to form a pallet not too far from that of her patient.

By Halwice's reckoning that last dose should give him several hours of sleep. She had hungrily finished the solid food on the tray—rolls stuffed with mince of meat—cold, to be sure, but nonetheless welcome. And she had drunk very sparingly from the pitcher of water. The flagon of wine which had accompanied it she pushed to one side.

For a while she sat on the bed she had contrived and watched Nicolas. It seemed to her that his sleep was peaceful, and under her light touch his skin was no longer heated as much. Halwice's potions worked well, always supposing she could reach the patient in time.

However, it was not Nicolas the wounded charge who interested her now but rather Nicolas the man. She did not know how clever she was at estimating age, but she felt that he could not be too many years ahead of her.

Both Halwice's and the Chancellor's treatment of him had suggested that he was of some major importance to those secrets she knew existed but refused to try to explore. If the Herbmistress wanted her to know something she would tell her—and that Willadene held to.

He was, of that much she was certain, a spy—ears and eyes for the Chancellor and beyond him the Duke. Only someone with strong nerves and quick wits could play that role for any length of time.

She wondered if he still nursed suspicion of her as he had from the first. She—

On her pallet of metallic-threaded rags the girl stiffened, and her head jerked around toward the door—that door which was so securely fastened save for the space at the bottom through which the tray had been pushed.

That space—she regarded it narrowly and as carefully as she could in this dim light. Surely it was not large enough to admit—a man?

However, one hand flew to her nose. So utterly vile was the whiff she had caught that it nearly choked her. There was something outside that portal now—something which was utter danger.

She had her belt knife, yes, but she would be no match physically for a determined killer, and somehow she was sure that who—or what—lingered now without had come to slay.

There was no time to extinguish the lamps. Anyone stooping or kneeling could look through the flap and make sure that the prey was safe inside. Or—

She did not have Halwice's everpresent healer's bag, but before her eyes now, on that tray waiting to be collected, was a pepper mill—perhaps put with all food served as a matter of course.

Willadene half threw herself across the space between, and her hands closed on that most pitiful of weapons. Whatever was waiting without had not moved, of that her nose assured her. She tried to breathe shallowly, fighting the pressure on her that that filthy odor continued to exert.

The pepper mill worked quickly as she turned—savagely but silently as she was sure it might give her away. Then—

The flap was being lifted! Willadene planted herself in what she hoped would be the best position and waited—

Luckily, in spite of the lamps, the trundle bed was out of direct line of anyone so attempting to spy on them. He or she would have to assume the most awkward position in order to view who lay there.

There was a hand on the swing flap and Willadene was astounded. She had expected a man's fist; this was the well-kept hand of a woman, a single red-jeweled ring catching fire from the lamplight.

Hand—then an arm clad in ruby silk, a shoulder, a mass of hair which must have been hastily released from some elaborate headdress, the waving strands hiding the face.

But those strands were no barrier to what Willadene held. She chose what she believed was her best moment and blew. Holding her own nose tight with her other hand against what might drift upward, she puffed the thick coating of pepper in her palm straight at her target.

Her answer was a veritable explosion of a sneeze, enough to strip raw the unfortunate nose which allowed it. What she could see of the interloper jerked back and away. The flap of the door dropped into place. Yet she could hear a series of more violent sneezes, plus a smothered cry of pain. Perhaps some of her improvised weapon had reached eyes as well.

Still, as she crouched there she continued to be aware of that evil smell. For all her torment the unknown on the other side of the door was making no move toward withdrawal.

''What's to do—?'' The words were clear enough for her to understand but slurred. She slewed about to face the pallet.

Her charge was open-eyed now, and frowning again. On hands and knees Willadene crawled to him and firmly placed her hand over his mouth, at the same time nodding toward the door.

There were still muffled sounds to be heard from outside. However, Nicolas seemed to understand her warning and she took away her temporary gag, her fingers brushing over the stubble of his unshaven jaw.

The girl flattened herself down beside him, her lips very close to his ear. "Outside—strove to crawl through the door flap—"

His eyes widened a little and she saw that his lips were shaping visibly a second, single-word question.

"Who?"

She shook her head. This was certainly no time to explain her singular talent. She only knew that the one outside carried that same stench which had sickened her when Wyche had tormented her with his attentions—yet certainly the visitor was not that tavern lounger.

Had she the wealth of products which rested on the shelves of the herb shop—and a little time—she could have perhaps worked out a defense. What she waited for now was to have that one who had come so secretly summon help and force the door.

On impulse Willadene took from her own neck that thong which held her privately concocted amulet. At least she could move, but Nicolas was helpless against any such attack. Or was he? For into that tiny bag, sewn with thickly protective stitching only a fortnight past, there was a very ancient recipe against ill.

Even Halwice had averred that the Old Ones of the past had known more of the power of growing things than any modern herbalist. Much had been kept secret, those secrets dying with their holders. Finding Willadene drawn to what were her own oldest records Halwice had encouraged the girl in her researches.

Heart-Hold had not been the only growing gift for a

world which would recognize its properties—though so much had been lost. Raising Nicolas's head while he stared at her in amazement, she slipped about his throat the cord of the amulet.

But as that left her grasp she bent over, wracked by pain in her middle, bile rising. That stench closed her in, wrapped about her like a blanket. She saw Nicolas watching her, his first amazement fading to something else—a mixture of alarm and concern. Then his hand arose feebly and he pointed past her in the direction of the door.

There the lamplight was very faint, and yet there was a greenish glow drawing a line along the floor, outlining the bottom of the swinging panel. And it was more than light.

Clasping her hand tightly across her nose Willadene scrambled for the remedies the Herbmistress had left. One of those was all she could depend upon now. Perhaps the very fact of her gift made this assault so terrible for her.

She paid no attention to the dangling dosage spoon as her free hand closed about the bottle. Yet she dared not draw too heavily on its contents, for that in itself might bring her down.

Willadene drew a full mouthful from the flask. She held herself taut. This was like taking in coals to lie on the curl of her tongue, and she fought the muscles which would force her to spew it forth again.

She was no longer aware of any except her own pain and sickness, yet Nicolas seemed unaffected by what had come with that curl of green. It was past the door flap now, drawing itself in a snake's form, as if it had more substance than mere light.

Once more Willadene forced herself to move, holding one hand pressed hard to her mouth, feeling as she went as if she were also writhing reptile fashion across the floor.

She would have only one chance and that she would make the most of—

The green line raised its foretip and swung back and

forth as if it possessed eyes and were searching for prey. Willadene could hold no longer. Forcing herself to lean as closely as she could to that thing of the dark she spat forth all which was in her mouth—and the liquid struck true!

It was as if she had hurled a blazing hearth brand on the thing. Twisting, turning, appearing caught in the mess, it struggled wildly and then—was gone.

The girl huddled together. Her mouth was numb but— the smells her tormented nose now gathered in were only the honest ones of what had happened here. The overpowering stench of evil was gone. She silently thanked the Star for the thought which had protected them—that the remedy Halwice had concocted to fight wound rot had indeed been an enemy to this other thing.

She listened. There were no more wheezings from without. But the withdrawal of the Dark's foulness had already assured her of that.

Still sick and shuddering, she longed for the comfort of one of Halwice's soothing potions. Her face was down on her knees as she huddled, her arms tightly about her. There was that to be done—a sickroom must be kept as clean as possible. But at that moment she was too weak to move. She hardly heard the voice from behind her.

"Mistress, what was that which came?" There was no sharp note from Nicolas now.

Somehow Willadene turned her head so she could see him. He had braced himself up on one elbow and was staring at her as if she were one of the night goblins meant to frighten children into better manners.

In spite of the dryness of her throat she was able to give an order.

"Lie—down—would—you—tear that—open again?" Her words came so slowly. But from somewhere she found dregs of strength—enough to push, having to put all the protection her failed energy could summon—a footstool across the door flap. That exertion left her half lying across that would-be barrier, panting.

She must get to that remaining spot on the floor—but before she touched it—lest some of the evil still rest within—she must have her defense.

Wearily she crawled toward Nicolas. "The amulet—" She spoke between gasps as she was forced to rest every few lengths she won. "Give—"

His hand was already at his throat and on the cord. Without being able to lift his head too high from its support he worried it off, and finally it was hers once again.

"What did you do—?" He was certainly more alert than she had seen him since she came here. It was as if watching action itself was playing some part in his healing.

"That which was sent upon us was—evil." She had puddled some of the water in a scarf to hand and rubbed it across her face. The numbness of the potion had faded and her mouth now only felt raw from the ordeal. "Halwice left the kill for wound rot." And kill it certainly was, she thought with a faint flutter of amusement. Now that she was free of the stench she felt curiously light-headed, almost as if all about her was a mummer's play to be laughed away.

"And that was what you spat upon the thing?"

Spat upon the thing, thought Willadene, a most courtly way of describing her action.

"I know not what it was." Now she dared allow herself a drink from the flagon. "But, yes, I think that the dose of my mistress's potion put an end to it. Only—who has such perverted knowledge as to summon such a thing?"

"Vazul—summon him, mistress. What moved through here he must know."

Now Willadene allowed a weak laugh born of shock to break bonds. "Best we bring him a mop and a bucket—"

But she discovered that now she could pull up to her feet with the aid of a chair and, pushing the weight of that before her to keep her steady, she headed once more for the signal rope.

"That is the end of it," Vazul said. "The fellow was mind blocked."

The Duke shifted in his chair. "Who has such powers—save the Star? And no one of the order would betray their beliefs so. You are certain?"

"As certain as seeing a dead man who gasps out his life when the question is put to him can be," the Chancellor returned.

"Then—" the Duke's hand rubbed across his chin and he peered piercingly at his servant "—there is something beyond our understanding. What said the Abbess?"

"She casts the crystals this night, Highness. But remember, those of the Star follow no lord's leadership. They stand apart from any of our worldly disputes—though I believe that she was shaken when she heard of this woods-runner who had a power not authorized by her own orders."

"I trust," the Duke said dryly, "that she is shaken enough to seek some sensible explanation—and that having found such she will share it with us. The Bat—"

"We found him in time, Highness. But that he will be able to carry out any ploy soon is another matter. Halwice affirms that he is past the danger point."

"This girl of hers—"

"As you ordered, Highness. She may guess that she is in the castle, but that is all she knows beside the task she has been sent to do. However, Highness, this other news the borderer brought us. It would seem that the Bat was successful even though he had to suffer for it."

"Losing us only one thing," the Duke returned, "that one who went up from the city and whom the Wolf may acknowledge as master."

"He will acknowledge him so no more. It was a neat bit of night attack. No wonder they hail the Prince as a

SCENT OF MAGIC ~ 131

master of war craft. And so, Highness, we can now move on to the next part of our game."

"It will be no game"—the Duke sounded sour—"if our herald and his escort may be ambushed on the way."

"Our borderer tells us the north road will be watched. The Hawker is calling in all but a thin screen of his forces to ensure that. And he, as is the Prince, is a man who understands this business. I have here—" from somewhere about the folds of his robe he produced a seal swinging from a chain "—the official seal of Kronen. That together with your letter of congratulations and welcome, the message delivered by the herald, will certainly hold the Prince's attention.

"It was masterly, Highness, for you to so subtly suggest that Prince Lorien's advice would be acceptable."

The Duke quirked an eyebrow. "Well, every once in a while I do have a thought or two, you know, Vazul. And if Lorien accepts our invitation to celebrate his victory—"

"*When* he accepts," Vazul corrected him smoothly. "There will be a feasting, a jousting—the Prince has a liking for such entertainment—and, of course, a state ball—the High Lady Mahart to receive him and on your behalf present him with the victor's circlet of the Star."

The Duke's lips pushed forward peevishly. "Another of these balls—!"

"Ah, but as your Highness well knows, the High Lady is in the first bloom of her youth and remarkably well looking. There may be others deemed more beautiful, but she seems to be born with a natural grace of person which makes her noticeable in any company, even if her rank were not known. And balls are the proper meeting places for ladies and their would-be suitors."

He was smiling, but those lips thinned as hurling through the air as if she had leaped from some height and quite a distance came Ssssaaa.

The creature looped herself above on the Chancellor's

shoulder and was plainly hissing into his ear as if giving some urgent report.

Vazul was on his feet, and the Duke looked up at him startled.

"There is trouble in the tower! No." He put out a hand to keep the Duke from grasping the small bell which would bring a quick answer. "Do you want the whole of the castle alert? I shall take the inner way as usual."

He was gone behind the screen that half divided the room, leaving Uttobric to gnaw at his nails, his thoughts summing up every calamity which might be upon him.

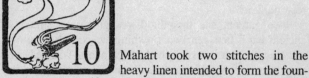

Mahart took two stitches in the heavy linen intended to form the foundation for a new altar panel she had promised to the Abbey in honor of her being advanced there to the role of lady patroness, and then tossed the scratchy cloth onto the table. Her fingers would simply not obey orders today, and in fact her thoughts were very far from conscientious labor at the moment.

Lady Famina bobbed up from her stool. "Your Highness wishes?" she was quick to ask.

For a moment Mahart gazed at her. Yes, there was very much something she wished, but she completely doubted Famina could supply it—and that was information. Zuta had gone to order some more of the restful sleep incense and had not yet returned, and certainly neither of these ninnies was of any use. Perhaps— She frowned, not realizing that Famina might take that expression personally.

In her lifetime so far she had had precious few secrets— and most of them had been so tame as to not hold even her own interest. Zuta was the only one who had shared, beside Julta, those days in the past when she had been her father's forgotten prisoner.

Since life had switched a full way around from quiet to

taking part in the court, they had indeed traded at the rare times they were alone together opinions—most of them derogatory—about the new company into which they had been plunged. But—no, this was something she wanted to think about before she shared it even with Zuta.

"Your Grace—" faltered the Lady Famina, and Mahart realized that the lumpy child must be fearing that she had in some way offended her new mistress.

"It is nothing, Famina." Mahart sketched a yawn. "I find it close and airless here. Shall we take a turn in the rose garden?"

Rose garden, she thought disparagingly—a stretch of ancient earth between two frowning walls with a number of straggly plants over which a gardener watched with deep concern for their continued lives. The fields—the free fields—with their wealth of flowers. And—in the last dream there had almost been another—she was certain she had seen a shadow.

"Of course, Your Grace." Both ladies were on their feet waiting to follow her those decorous two steps behind which etiquette demanded. Thus her own idle words had sentenced her to a period in the open—if there could be any real "open" within these walls.

As she went down the stairs and through the doorway below she eyed those walls about her with a new interest. Yes, she dreamed when she slept—and now looked forward to those dreams. But when she had stirred awake last night, nudged into consciousness somehow by something she did not understand, that had *not* been a dream!

Though all her unordered, unsupervised reading had taught her much about the past, and she thought she knew the castle from its infancy as a traders' command post, to her it had been a place of shelter, certainly not always comfortable.

She had always known that the walls now standing were very thick—thick enough to conceal—what? A small shiver made her pull her shawl the closer. What of the many legendary tales she had read? Not of this castle to be sure—but of others—where were secret ways through such walls.

It was because her own tower had been such a tight part of her life that she had never perhaps thought of such a thing as there being more to the walls about her than she could see and touch at her will. However—she could remember as if she had just heard them moments ago—those sounds behind a wall in her bedchamber. Not the scampering of rats or other vermin—no. Remedies supplied by the Herbmistress as well as an alert corps of cats kept them free of such pests.

But she would take Star Oath that she had heard sounds which had swept within the walls about almost one quarter of her room. They had been strong enough to bring her out of bed—night lamp in hand—to walk along the suspect barriers. Only, they had died out so quickly she could not really center in on them.

Now, standing in the rose garden, she turned slowly around, not to look at the few wizened blossoms showing but at the castle itself. The Black Tower! It was the space of the garden away from her own quarters and for years it had been so shunned that people seemed to have forgotten it.

Ghosts—? She shook her head at her own thoughts. There had been no more stories of specters these past few days. Yet she wanted nothing more than a chance to inspect that section of wall in the fullest light she could summon—have all the heavy window drapes pulled back and several lamps placed to best advantage. Only, to do so would certainly raise questions and ones for which she had no answers.

She was still staring musingly at the Black Tower when Zuta came hurrying down the path, brushing past the two ladies who scowled and pulled aside their skirts. There was certainly no bonding friendship in Mahart's household.

"Your Grace"—Zuta had to pause for a moment to

catch breath—"His Highness's herald has ridden forth
with the invitation. 'Tis said that if Prince Lorien comes
it will be within days!"

Mahart bit her lip. It was a long time since Kronengred
had welcomed a conquering hero, one with all the attri-
butes of this one—a notable feat of arms behind him, of
high birth, likely looking according to rumor, and all the
rest that was ever accorded a legendary prince. She also
remembered word for word—scowl by scowl—exactly her
father's opinion of this event.

She, Mahart, was to make herself so desirable to this
stranger that he could find himself wedded to her—ready
to serve her father's purposes. And she had not the least
idea of how such a deed could be accomplished. Though
she could well guess her life, if she failed, might be far
from even as palely pleasant as it was now.

"Your Grace"—Zuta had drawn much closer—"there
are ways—"

"Charms?" demanded Mahart dryly. "We are not
caught up in some ancient tale."

"Halwice's compounds, Your Grace. There will be the
victory ball and you are to present the circlet of the Star—
Is that not the truth?"

Rumors did spread with lightning speed through this
pile, Mahart knew. "Yes."

"Then, Your Grace, send for the Herbmistress. There are
arts in plenty wrought from the very hearts of flowers and
that which is earth-rooted, which can aid a woman. You are
not aged enough to know much of such matters, but I have
seen ladies well past their bloom turned into maids new
come to court—at least for an evening. You need no such
creams and false enchantments—but there are other ways to
make any man notice one and be led to follow."

That, also, Mahart knew. She loved fragrance for itself
and what it wrought within her—such as her beautiful
dreams. However, she had never tried to use any such as

a lure. But perhaps this was the time she would be driven to it.

"Can you summon this herb wife?" she asked. "I have heard that she does not go from her shop except for some great illness or disaster. Certainly she would not consider the concocting of a new fragrance to be such. I have seen her at the Abbey, and she has the air of one noble born, not to be used as a servant."

"Your Grace." It was the Lady Geuverir who had shuffled forward. Big ears, thought Mahart swiftly, and ready to use them; she must be watched. "Your Grace, she has been within the castle but this morning. It is reported that the Chancellor is ailing and the Duke will have none but her to diagnose his illness."

True enough. Vazul for the first time had not been present when she had had that interview with her father last night. And his absence had been a distinct change from custom.

"Is she still to be found here?" She asked that of Zuta in an attempt to make Lady Geuverir better aware of her lower place—at least in this company.

"I shall discover, Your Grace. And if she is not in attendance on the Chancellor still, I shall bring her," Zuta promised swiftly.

"What was that?" The more he spoke the stronger Nicolas's voice became.

Willadene, inwardly shaken by both her facing of rank evil and her use of the potion, lifted her head with an effort.

"I—I do not know—save it was evil come into sight and body of a sort. Such I have never heard of—save in a hint or two in Halwice's oldest books."

"Ssssaaa—" Something soft rubbed against her arm, and she looked up to see the Chancellor staring about him in open amazement. He quickly averted his eyes from the site of the strange battle.

His creature curled up about Willadene, bumping her

head against the girl's chin, her hiss certainly not a threat but rather meant to soothe.

"What came?" Vazul almost showed his teeth as would a hound.

"Black evil—" Willadene still shuddered. Word by halting word she got it out—what had happened when the flap door had been lifted—her own attack with the only weapon she could lay hand upon—and then that which followed.

Vazul had caught up the flask she indicated, held it closer to the nearest lamp. "And this?" he demanded of her.

"It cleans wounds—there can be no flesh rot—" mechanically Willadene answered.

"Also it very effectively disposed of that thing sent upon us," Nicolas reported.

The Chancellor again regarded the mess on the floor. Repugnance was easy to read on his thin features. Willadene, in spite of herself, held a blush of shame. Then he turned on her.

"Your mistress—"

"Lord Chancellor." The girl no longer felt so lightheaded; it was as if the warmth of the animal now against her cheek was oddly restorative—like a cordial she had freely drunk. "I am new come to Mistress Halwice's service and am one who is but a beginning student of her craft. What happened here I cannot explain—you must ask it of her. Though—"

"Though—" he prodded her when she did not continue.

"There is truly evil here—within these walls. And it lives—and—hunts!" Why she was so sure of that she could not tell.

Her legs had not been strong enough when he had appeared to bring her to her feet; rather she crouched, having to raise her head at an angle to look at him.

"Halwice—" Even as he said that name Willadene's head turned. She had caught that familiar scent in spite of the thick miasma in this chamber. And she was right. Beyond the full reach of the lamps there was a sudden gap of shadow, and she who had stooped to come through that hidden door was indeed the Herbmistress. But she halted even as she came to the lamps, her head up and her nostrils expanded.

There was that about her which kept them all silent as if they shared a feeling that she must not be disturbed. But Willadene could see her nostrils expand as if she would draw in every odor lurking there, recognize it, name it, be ready to deal with it.

Paying no attention to Vazul, who shifted from one foot to another as if he were irritated at her ignoring him, she spoke directly to Willadene.

"Well done." Only two words, but the girl felt as if some chain of distinction had been dropped over her head. Now the Herbmistress did have time for the Chancellor.

"A secret known well enough to bring an attack is strong warning, my lord. Chancellor, Nicolas must be moved—now!"

Vazul had a stubborn set to his mouth. "Where?"

"Think, my lord. 'Tis said you know the inner ways as well as the Bat—" For the first time she looked down at Nicolas with a smile, which he returned. Willadene wondered a little at the change that expression made in his face—it seemed to erase years as well as some of the lighter signs of the pain he had suffered.

"There is the dove loft," Nicolas remarked. Now there was almost a trace of mischief in his tone as he addressed Vazul directly.

It would seem at first that the Chancellor was going to refuse outright, but then he shrugged. "Perhaps you are right—if we can get you there. It can be reached across the roof with supplies. And you will see him there in care," he said to Halwice.

It was not quite an order, as if even he dared not lay any command upon the Herbmistress. But she nodded. And then she turned to Willadene.

"You must hold the shop again. Also, I was seen this

time in the courtyard here. Thus let it be said that I have a patient of high rank—perhaps—'' she half smiled at Vazul ''—even yourself. Or else that there is some other need for me. You are clever with thinking of ploys, my lord, I leave this one for you.

''Now, child.'' Having somehow dismissed the Lord Chancellor as if, being no longer particularly needed, he had vanished indeed, she spoke again to Willadene. ''When you return to the shop, drink deep of the mixture on the top shelf of the second case, that in the amber bottle. Do not eat until evening. But be as usual about the business. I have been summoned to attend someone of high rank, you know not who. The district tax lies in the money drawer, already bagged. Give it to the Reeve's guard, but see also he returns you a receipt even as you have seen him do for me. And—'' Suddenly she leaned forward, stooping a little, and touched Willadene lightly on the tip of the girl's nose. ''Trust your gift always.''

Ssssaaa had unwound and pattered across to claw a way up to Vazul's shoulder. Willadene put her hand up to her throat, still a little warm from that furred body. But she was ready enough to get to her feet and obey Halwice. The sooner she could gain freedom from this befouled room the better.

Yet she hesitated as she passed Nicolas and hunted awkwardly for words. He had always made her uneasy in a strange way she did not even try to understand.

''The Star be with you, master,'' she blurted out.

Again she saw that smile—this time for her. ''And with you also, mistress of many talents.''

Vazul bore down upon them. ''We waste time. I shall get aid and the dove chamber it will be. Also we shall search for the source of that!'' He jerked his head toward the spot on the floor. ''And in that search, Mistress—'' he looked to Halwice ''—certainly you have interest.''

Days seemed to run into each other now as far as Willadene was concerned. Back in the shop, her guard guide dismissed, she obeyed Halwice's instructions for the relief of her body and settled down to rest. The Herbmistress had left the plaque on her door saying that she had been called away and the window shutters were still up. Willadene was not even aware how tired she was until sleep overcame her. And it was the boom of the closing bell that night which awoke her with a start from a sleep too deep even to hold dreams.

Ashamed that she had so forgotten the trust Halwice had given her she dashed her face with the scant water remaining in the basin and tried to order her thoughts. Certainly the Herbmistress had had orders to go out—she always did and those had been made up the day before. If any seeking them had come, they had found the shop closed and would return in the morning. She had better check that such were ready to be handed over—and there was the matter of the district tax also.

She got out of the crumpled and stained clothes she had slept in, washed, and redressed. For a moment or two she stood before the fireplace after she had relaid the fire. There was a pan of mush which could be fried for a quick and filling meal, but an uncomfortable twinge in her stomach dissuaded her from any such effort.

However, it was when she arose from setting the fire that she became aware of something else. She had always been aware and accepted the fact that each human as well as animal carried a personal scent which had nothing to do with cleanliness of body and clothing but was far more subtle and yet such identification could not be wrong.

Halwice she knew well and had from their first meeting. She was certain now that she could trace either Nicolas or Vazul, should the need arise—though she was no hound of the hunt. And in the outer shop there was always a medley of scents.

It was as if all the odors of the herb shop—those native, those introduced—she thought now, lay in levels—some thick and close, others thinning to the faintest of traces.

In Jacoba's kitchen it had been much more difficult, for there foul overweighed fair. Willadene sat back on her heels, her head up, her nostrils high. One by one she sifted through the smells about her—remnants of cookings, stronger yet of herb mixing, close to the closet bed that scent which identified Halwice. She told over on her fingers those she could identify without question.

But—there was something else. Willadene got to her feet. Since she must start somewhere—and where not too many of those layers of smells mingled—she went to the back door. It was shut and barred, and the light of the single lamp which she had brought with her gave but little light. To her eyes there was no sign that that door had been tampered with.

Still—her instinct was *not* wrong. By the Star, she would swear that in this room there had been another presence, one she had never met before. At Halwice's invitation? Of that she could not be sure. However, unease drove her now to pick up the lamp again and march into the shop itself.

Laid out on the counter in a row of various kinds of containers were the orders Halwice had made up. Most of them were usual—flavorings for the baker (who also dealt in special demands for sweetmeats); spices; three separate packets for old Dame Lorka, the Reeve's mother-in-law, who suffered greatly in any chill weather from aged, aching bones; a cough syrup; two pomanders gayly housed in gilt net balls (those Willadene had made earlier in the week), and they would go for courting gifts.

Last of all there was a basket woven of sweet fern, its handle twined around with silver ribbons. That was kept apart from the others—being for the castle and not for the town dwellers. And particularly this time it was intended for the High Lady Mahart herself, bespoke by her in writing of her own hand.

Each of the waiting wares Willadene inspected closely and could find nothing that was not what it was supposed

to be. At last she turned to the basket. There was a violet
wash for the hair, also violet-scented cream for the hands.
And last of all a box of wood, the kind made to hold
nubbins of night incense. The symbol carved deeply into
the cover of that container was a very ancient one, and
the wood was as dark as if it had been put to such use
many times over.

Delicately Willadene pried the cover of the box up. The
scent within was not obtrusive, for what it had to offer
would only come to life when dropped into a charcoal-
heated brazier. But she held the box close to her nose and
her hold on it tightened.

Three times in the days past she had carefully watched
Halwice put together this familiar concoction for the High
Lady. Willadene could repeat easily every ingredient
which went to make up the mixture. Only—today there
had been a change. Through Halwice's choice? Through
the High Lady's orders? Either explanation might hold
the truth.

Yet—taken with the fact that there *had* been a stranger
within the inner room—she could remember only too well
her own experience with that which she had faced in the
Black Tower and could not explain. Or at least had not
had time for Halwice to make clear, though she was somehow sure that the Herbmistress had had no dealings with
such as that serpent of green light.

Slowly the girl closed the lid on the box. Behind her,
on the fourth shelf, there was the very twin to the box.
And in her head was the formula Halwice always used for
its filling. Meddling this might be and the Herbmistress
be angry for it. Yet—

Willadene measured powders, added drops from two tall
bottles and bone-dry peel cut in strips from another bottle
set by itself at the far end of the shelf space. She kneaded
together what she had so carefully chosen, and it resembled nearly dried clay when she had done. Still, it crumbled in large flakes into the empty box as she filled it

pinch by pinch. Breathing a little faster Willadene set it beside the one she had taken from the basket. There was certainly no difference in appearance. And she must believe that what she had done in Halwice's absence was right. Before she could change her mind she repacked the basket.

Oddly enough as she put the rejected box on a lower shelf, pushing it behind a larger one, she felt relieved as if Halwice herself had stood there watching and signaling it was right.

If she was to open properly by Second Bell she must rest now. There had been no promise of when the Herb-mistress would return. In fact, Willadene had been left with the impression that she was to keep shop for perhaps more than just one day. And she was tired. As she folded her clothing over the stool and slipped into the trundle bed she raised her amulet to her nose, striving so to deaden any odor which might keep sleep away.

It, too, had now the faint trace of another. She remembered Nicolas. Vazul seemed very sure of his future protection, and Halwice remained to see him moved to new quarters. But what sword or knife had brought him down? And why? That he was liege man to the Chancellor in a most private way she understood. But— Her eyes closed of their own accord and she slept.

The First Bell in the morning brought her awake. She looked first to the cupboard bed, hoping to see Halwice there beneath the covers, but it was smoothly flat from its last making. The main thing that she herself felt now was hunger, which grew ever sharper as she washed and dressed. All the remaining queasiness of yesterday was gone.

The mush browned in the skillet, and Willadene found herself repeating one of the old rhymes from the ancient herbals:

"Good for the belly,
Good for the day,
In all that cometh,
Star shine the way."

She repeated that last line as she forked the fried mush onto her plate and reached for berry syrup to give it flavor. Four squares of mush later she decided that the good of the belly was well satisfied. And, as she busied herself with the housekeeping duties before the Second Bell, she wondered what this day was going to bring.

When the shutters were down and the door unlatched for business she was restless. Halwice had left none of the simple orders Willadene was allowed to fill written on the slate. She could not weed in the garden for fear that some customer would find her missing from her post.

However, within a few moments she was well occupied. The first of the orders the Herbmistress had left had been called for. She exchanged greetings with the baker's maid—a powdering of flour on the girl's round cheek to mark her service.

However, Realie was full of news, eager to spill it. "He took the *Wolf*—killed him as one stamps upon a bug," she gurgled. "Now the Duke has asked him to Kronengred for a thank offering. Star help us, Master is all which way trying to think of new sweeties, 'cause there will be crowds and parties—"

She was still prattling on when the solemn-faced assistant of Dr. Kemp came in to collect his order. It was he who offered a ghoulish detail or two, supposedly brought in the night to the gate guard about the hunting and harrying of what was left of the mountain outlaws.

So it went through the morning. Much of what she heard, Willadene was sure was far from fact. But two points seemed to remain certain. Prince Lorien had led his men over the border and effectively put an end to the strongest of the outlaw outposts and he was now invited as a conquering hero to visit Kronengred by a missive sent via the Duke's own herald.

At length all the orders were collected, though at times the shop was crowded with those exchanging the latest news. Mistress Lowfard was especially centered upon since her brother was of the gate guard. And if she did not speak much, her few words rooted suggestions.

Only the basket for the High Lady remained. And Willadene's sliver of chalk squeaked on the slate as she was at length left alone. But not for long, as a page wearing castle badge came swaggering in.

"There is a basket for the High Lady Mahart." He leaned against the edge of the counter and regarded his nails as if their condition was more important than the task. "She grows impatient—" He glanced up at Willadene with a sly grin. "You are supposed to be able to make a beauty out of skin and bones—with certain potions—or so they say."

"Your Lady's basket stands there." She found his impudence a little too much after the business of the day.

He tossed a small purse knitted of silken threads on the counter and reached for the basket, giving an exaggerated sniff of its contents as he pulled it to him.

"Your mistress'll have business in plenty," he commented, for some reason of his own still lingering—though Willadene noted that now he eyed speculatively the contents of the basket. "What with the Prince coming in for a grand ball and all. Big times in Kronengred for us all."

"So most this day have said," she returned. "You have another errand?"

She was eager to get rid of this young cockerel, brilliant in his house tabard and clearly very sure of himself. It had been a long day and she was tired. Only the fact that he did come from the castle kept her listening. Perhaps he had even spoken with Halwice and had some message to pass along, was merely tantalizing her out of pure mischief.

"Yes, I was asked by the Lady Zuta to pick up a box of cream. High and mighty as *she* would like to be, she does not run her own errands—yet!"

Zuta—first lady of the High Lady's household. Willadene had picked up enough gossip to know at least her name. But there had been nothing on the counter readied by Halwice bearing such a name.

"My mistress left no such order," she returned.

He shrugged. "Perhaps it was forgotten. I understand your mistress now has weighty concerns—she tends Vazul himself—the Chancellor having gone to his bed with ague."

Willadene was aware he was watching her closely, yet seeming under half-closed lids to have his gaze fastened on the basket.

"My mistress was summoned for her skills yesterday," she answered quietly. "As to whose bed she was summoned I do not know. If the Chancellor ails may the Star grant him swift recovery."

He gave a snickering laugh. "Oh, sooner or later he will doubtless be stalking among us again, that devilish creature of his wrapped around his neck. Perhaps he should take care lest it someday tighten muscles and cut his breath. So—" he picked up the basket "—I am to tell the Lady Zuta I know nothing of her order—or do you?"

"It is not here," the girl replied. "Doubtless it will be made up for her as soon as my mistress returns."

Again he snickered. "Yes, half the ladies of the towers will be sending their own orders. Though by all reckoning it would take Heart-Hold itself to gain them what they want the most—a king's son lawfully in their beds. Your mistress will find her trade growing the closer our hero approaches."

He was openingly sneering as he took the basket and went out. Certainly Willadene could see there was a measure of truth in his scoffing. When Prince Lorien came there would be again a steady increase in the luxury trade.

New robes would be ordered, older ones sent to be refurbished with fresh embroidery and laces, the bounty of the herb shop would be called upon.

Heart-Hold, that one name was strong now in her mind. She hunted out the ancient herbal in which she had read the remnants of the tale concerning it. Certainly, had such a plant still existed, it would have again come into sight during the centuries since that first harvesting. Perhaps the whole story was a concealment for a charm—and the secret of its unraveling long since lost.

The book opened almost of its own accord at the page she had puzzled over so many times. Not only was the writing cramped and faded here but there were names and terms so old she had had to search them out in other guides, and there were a number she could not yet translate.

She was slipping her finger along the edge of that most important page when for the first time she made a new discovery—that this parchment leaf was thicker than the one lying before and the one lying after in the book. She had just drawn closer the shelf lamp and was preparing to light the second when once more the door opened.

That smell was one she could not forget. Willadene pushed the book under the counter and turned to face Figis. Again he seemed to have climbed several steps higher in the world, though the old odors of the inn still clung to him. As before he was wearing more decent clothing—his rags gone—though it was far from clean, dribbles of ale slicking his jerkin. His wild mane of tumbled hair had been partly shorn and there was the shadow of some hairs, perhaps more carefully tended than the rest of his person, across his upper lip.

He stood just within the door, hands on hips and one pointing suggestively at a knife which was more short sword than the ordinary tool worn by all free men. So—Figis must have ended his apprenticeship. He would have been well beaten by Jacoba had he dared to flash steel where she ruled.

Now he was drawing deep sniffing breaths, and then his mouth worked as if he would spit but did not quite dare.

"Master Wyche has him a bellyache," he announced baldly. "He wants something as will take it away. Where's your mistress, girl?"

He swaggered forward to the counter, his eyes still making darting searches of the shop.

"She attends one gravely ill," Willadene answered as she had the whole day through. "As for Master Wyche's ill—"

She did not completely turn her back on him as perhaps he wished, but rather quickly slipped open a drawer and brought out one of the waiting packets they always kept made up. "That will be two coppers." She laid it on the counter.

She wanted him out of the shop. Now she had been able to pick up a faint whiff of that stench which had always cloaked Wyche's fat body—evil. Figis had been spiteful, cruel of nature in the past, but now he was turning into something else.

He dropped the proper coppers on the counter and twitched the packet toward him.

"Your mistress, she's got a lot of queer knowledge." He grinned, showing a broken tooth. "Jus' you hope, girl, as how it don't do her in."

What lay behind that ambiguous threat Willadene was not to learn, for the Twilight Bell boomed over their heads, fairly shaking the walls about them. He looked startled and was out of the door into the dusk. Willadene reached under the counter for the book after she had put up the shutters and set the night bar on the door. With it under her arm she went into the living quarters, trying to shrug off the uneasiness Figis's words had left with her.

11 It was not only Mahart who was to dream deeply and to remember what she so dreamed that night. Perhaps it was the whirl of many scents which had surrounded her all day that now led Willadene to her own deep-held private place. She felt this was so real that the moss under her hands, the faint breeze stirred against her, were as alive and in this night world as firmly as she. Her body was stretched even as she might have rested in her bed, but facedown, on the very lip of a rock-walled drop. Though it was night she could see as clearly as if she had cat's eyes set in her skull—clear sight, even clearer smell.

That crevice in the earth over which her head protruded was narrow; she hardly believed that she could squeeze into it to descend. Still below, there was a pale radiance and as her gaze centered on that her sight seemed to grow even keener.

It was far below, something within Willadene told her that, and she believed that, save for this strange heightening of eye power, she could not honestly see what stood stem erect, leaves fanned out about it. It was no single color, though it was pale as moonlight itself, for the faintest traces of many hues appeared to ripple across its petals.

In form it was not too different from the lilies Willadene had seen carefully painted in the Herbmistresses's books, and its heart was hidden by the bell of petals about it.

Heart—from even that deep distance below her perch Willadene was able to draw such an intoxication of pure scent as made her almost believe that she had been Star-favored with some flower from that future world they were assured waited those of goodwill.

However, against her will, for she would have lain there happily forgetting time, she braced her body upward until she was sitting and the crevice was merely a dark line, the blossom's faint light hidden. But her keenness of sight did not disappear. Instead it was as if she were held by some power and then gently turned, marking about her tumbled masses of ancient masonry overgrown with vines, rent apart by trees—no—they were huge ferns! And she understood that this was a sending, such as she had heard of—a setting in her mind of something to come.

In her tower chamber Mahart thought also of another world. There was a new supply of incense to be burned and to her it was very necessary that it be done this night. She said nothing to either Zuta or Julta concerning it, playing the role of one fain to be left to sleep. However, once the door had closed and only the night-light still gleamed she slipped from the great bed.

For a moment she stood gazing at that stretch of wall. During the day she had had the strange feeling that what she heard there—or thought she had heard—was not to be shared. But it was not strange noises in hidden ways which moved her now. She eagerly set the small brazier by her bed and into it spooned some of the lumpy powder from the box which had been delivered from Halwice's shop. A snap light caught at it quickly, and Mahart sat for a moment on the edge of the bed watching the curls of smoke arise before she cuddled down among her covers and firmly closed her eyes.

Time had no part in these dreams. She could never tell how long it was before she stood in the meadow of flowers. Yes, stood, for tonight she was fully aware that she possessed a body; she did not even have to raise her hands and touch herself for reassurance. Also the colors this time were sharper, brighter, though she did not feel the full rays of the sun which must hang somewhere overhead.

There were birds, and their songs reached her ears, while fluttered about her butterflies of such splendor of color as she had never seen—far different from the few pallid, winged creatures which sometimes could be sighted in the dreary rose garden.

But her inner eagerness was not for the flowers, or birds, or butterflies, making this dream more alive than any she had ever had. It was the fact that she was certain she was no longer alone. However, when she swiftly swung around, she saw no one, just a break in the meadow where a copse of trees encroached upon its carpet.

Now she did fling out her hands, sweeping them through the air, hoping to so touch what she could not see, blindly seeking that other.

It was as if she thirsted for something she could not put name to—a warm feeling which had never been given her? Mahart had no name for the core of that longing. Yet that in time she would find what she so hunted, she swore in the deepest part of her—determining that nothing would turn her from that quest. And, at the same moment she fastened upon that thought, the meadow world was gone.

At first she was disoriented as one awakened roughly from sleep and stared about her in the gloom. This was her own bedchamber in the tower. She pounded her fists upon the roll of the cover over her. No! No! To be snatched away so— Though it had been years since she had cried, having discovered that to allow any hurt to move her so meant little, she felt now the tears in her eyes, slipping out on her cheeks.

Only, in that same moment what must have drawn her

out of that sweetest of dreams, sounded again. She turned her head sharply to face the wall. That rustling sound— and now a single sharp note as if metal had struck the stone. Yet there was nothing to be seen save the three straight pieces of tapestry worked with faded flowers which had been there all her life as long as she could remember.

The strips did not cover the wall. Between them carved paneling made dark bars. Mahart, having shrugged on her fur-lined robe and thrust her feet into slippers, paused only to light one of the stronger lamps, before, with that in hand, she approached the wall.

She shouldered aside the middle tapestry, fighting down a sneeze from the dust that action disturbed, and put her head tightly against the strip of paneling. No, she had not been mistaken. There came a second sound, though much fainter, of metal scraping stone.

Oddly she felt anger instead of fear. If there were passengers in these walls about her very bedroom, had she perhaps been spied upon through peepholes for the past years? She scowled. That thought fed her anger into something approaching rage.

Now Mahart held the lamp very close to that aged wood. The carvings were simple, a vine border which ran along the full outer rim of the wooden slab with a stiff stand of flowers to center it. Yet as she now surveyed the panel closely it seemed to her rather to suggest a door of sorts, rather than the sturdy casing of a wall.

Remembering the ancient legends which had kept her so enthralled when she had read them, she began with one hand to push methodically each leaf of that vine she could reach, thumb hard against the heads of the flowers. If there was an entrance here to hidden ways, she knew she must, for her own safety, discover it.

So far, the panel remained stubbornly immobile. Now she put the lamp on the top of a chest and began trying to insert fingernails under the edge of the panel itself. As she broke a second nail she knew that the problem was not to be so solved. A visit to her dressing table supplied her with a pair of shears, the points of which she tried to lever into that possible crack.

Her anger had given birth to stubbornness—she *was going* to find out what might lie behind. After three jabs she paused as another thought struck her. Once more she visited the dressing table, this time to return with a jar of scented cream.

What good that might do she had no real understanding, but memories of hasps and hinges which had been oiled to make them manageable lingered. With the points of the shears she steadily worked to outline the wooden panel, having to reach well overhead to insert her tool in the line appearing there.

Then once more she used the points, with determination and all the strength she could summon, along the right-hand edge of the wooden panel. Almost she could have cried aloud in triumph as she felt something reluctantly give under that prodding. Instead she turned and, shears in hand, went to the door of her room. Though Julta had never ventured, as far as Mahart knew, to intrude upon her mistress's chamber unless summoned, there was always a chance that an unlatched door could betray her, so she slipped the small bar into place.

A second run along that crack, for she could see now it *was* a crack, opened it yet farther. At about the height of her own shoulder the blades struck a barrier and she wriggled, pushed, jabbed with the scissors. However, it was doubtless chance alone which solved that ancient lock. She felt the shears suddenly slip deeper inward and she gave them a vigorous pull toward her.

The noise which answered was enough to near make her cower, but she neither stepped back nor halted in her task. That harsh grating ended in a snapping sound and the panel swung out, knocking her back toward the bed. Panting, Mahart stared at what she had uncovered.

There was an opening right enough, perhaps not as wide as the conventional door to this chamber but undoubtedly a portal. She was shaking a little now, from both excitement and that uneasiness which struck from the unknown.

Lamp in one hand, the shears in her other, she forced herself into that dark hole. What lay beyond was indeed a very narrow passageway. Even by this feeble light she could see it was carpeted with thick dust. But that dust had been disturbed, stirred, and there was a broken cobweb hanging down the rough wall beyond.

With head and shoulders within the opening now, Mahart could see that, though the passage ran straight along the inner wall of her chamber, not far away there were steps leading up. She withdrew to sit on the edge of her bed and think.

Prudence would dictate that she summon the nearest guardsman and demand a thorough search. Only what if this was one of her father's secrets? What if he had never been as indifferent to her as she had believed and had had some watch kept on her by means of this burrow?

He thought of her as a tool to be used to make safe his throne—she was well aware of that. On the other hand, Vazul, in his roundabout communications to complete her education in the secret eddies of court intrigue, had made it very plain that her father felt he only ruled by sufferance and expected at any moment to have some form of revolt break forth.

She could not imagine the Lady Saylana using such a passage for spying purposes. But the Lady Saylana doubtless had her own eyes and ears to report to her, even as Vazul kept such a system.

Mahart made up her mind swiftly. No, if there were going to be secrets hedging her in, she was going to have a few of her own. She might need them even as a guardsman needed sword and shield—and she had no intention of sharing this one—as yet.

It did not take her long to strip off robe and night rail,

to pull on instead the breeches she wore under her divided riding skirt, a heavy shirt—for the air within that opening was chill—and a hunter's quilted jacket.

Though she had no skill with any weapon but a knife, she chose the longest and perhaps the deadliest of those— a hunter's weapon—and made no attempt to sheath it. A second visit to the outer door assured her that the latch was set, and now she dared to wedge it tighter with a bodkin from her worktable.

Taking up the largest of the room lamps which could be easily carried she lit the flame, reassured by the wash of oil within it when she moved it. So with fire and steel in hand she ventured into the unknown.

There were two choices—right or left. She made a quick selection toward the right and that flight of stairs she could see. Dust puffed under her boots, and once there was a wink of light to her right which she quickly put eye to— a peephole just as she had thought might exist.

The light was very dim, just enough to show two trundle beds. One stripped and not in use and, curled on the other, Julta! So Mahart realized that she had reached the third floor of her tower. But the steps continued to lead upward, and those she followed, trying to keep both her footfalls and her breathing as noiseless as possible.

She stopped almost in mid-step. There was a murmuring from above. Surely voices, but so low-pitched she could not make out separate words. Straining ears, she listened. No, there was no variation in those tones, even as there was no sign of light above— Whoever waited there was not on the stairs.

Mahart drew a deep breath. Retreat would be easy. She was reasonably sure she could conceal all the signs of her night's venture. But not to know who these night crawlers in the walls were—no, somehow she could not turn back from that!

Three steps more. Now the murmuring was louder, but it came from her right, surely from beyond the wall against which her shoulder now and then brushed. Once more she caught a lighted eye hole and it drew her past all thoughts of prudence.

There was more light in this room and it was crowded. It must have been wholly a storeroom until boxes and chests had been dragged aside to clear a place on the floor—a floor which was *not* dusty. Two of those chests, piled one on the other, stood across the frame of the normal entrance. It seemed plain that those within came and went by the hidden stair.

And the room was certainly in use. There were a number of lamps, all tended to give the best light, perched at intervals around where the floor had been cleared and swept. The center of the space was occupied by a thick matting, seemingly put together of a number of faded and even torn bedcovers, folded into a pallet on which lay a man.

Near his head, on the top of a convenient box, there were set out a squad of bottles and one or two jars, most of them now open. For the woman who knelt on one side of the man was busy dressing what Mahart could only guess, from the little she could see, to be a wound. However, the woman had aid in her work, for it was Vazul himself who was lifting and turning the man's body in answer to her instructions.

Having made fast the last tag of bandage, the healer sat back on her heels so that Mahart could see her clearly for the first time—Halwice, the Herbmistress! And Vazul, whom she was supposed to be tending, was in fact the tender of this other at her direction.

"Finished pulling me to shreds, mistress? And what is your verdict— When shall the Bat fly free again?"

"You have the sense enough to answer that for yourself, young man," she told her patient. "Getting you hither undid some of the work of healing. You will go about your business when the Star affords you a stout body again."

The dark head on the pallet turned. Mahart was certain

that she had never before seen that face, half masked as it was now by a dark stubble of beard. Yet here he lay in the very heart of the castle, with not only the Herbmistress but Vazul himself concerned enough to tend him. He was young, she thought, and not too ill-looking for all his neglect of person. Of course she had no knowledge of all her father's servitors—only those who had come under her eyes—and he could even have been one of the courtiers she had not noticed before.

Only why was he concealed here—in the top room of the tower which had always been the quarters of the Duke's daughters? She could not believe that even Vazul could have brought him here secretly without her father's permission.

It was Halwice whose head turned now—until she faced the wall of the peephole through which Mahart spied. And there was knowledge in her face which the girl quickly recognized for that of discovery. Before she could move from her own cramped position, the Herbmistress was on her feet and, in two swift strides, reached the other wall.

There came a sharp click and the panel against which Mahart had been steadying herself moved, making her lose her balance and tumble forward as the woman seized upon her.

"Ssssaaa." Vazul's creature raised her head from the covers on the pallet, gem-point eyes surveying her.

"Your Grace—" It was the Chancellor who found words first. "How—" he began and then hesitated. As during her sessions with him when he had so covertly drawn her attention to the pitfalls of the court, he was watching her with that level, measuring stare.

Halwice dropped her hold on Mahart's shoulder, and the girl drew herself up. She might have stumbled on a secret, but certainly she had done no wrong and she did not intend to be treated like some skulker of the night.

"I found the way—" she made a vague gesture behind

her toward the open panel "—because I heard sounds in the walls."

A moment later she was startled by the effect those words had on the two confronting her. She might as well have said she had been directed by a specter.

"Sounds in the wall?" Vazul broke the short silence first. "What kinds of sounds, Your Grace?"

"Like a brush of something against a wall, and tonight there was also a ring, such as steel makes when it meets stone."

"You say tonight," Halwice broke in. "Then you have heard such before? Enough to awaken you—?" Her surprise was quickly hidden but not before Mahart had seen it.

"And metal against stone—" That was the Chancellor. Now that she could see him clearly, Mahart was well aware that in his belt sheath there was only the customary hand knife, and he would have had to contort his body to bring that in contact with the stones.

"When is a secret not a secret?" The man they had been tending had raised himself a little sidewise, keen gray eyes sharp upon her. "Do we now scuttle for another hole?"

"Mistress"—Vazul looked to Halwice—"what can your skill tell us?"

"Not as much as we could wish. I have talent to be sure, but not such as a true *nose* can summon."

"Do what you can." Vazul's voice did not have the ring of a real order but rather as if he spoke to an equal engaged in a shared purpose.

Halwice pushed past Mahart and ducked through the panel door. From the sounds, for all those within the room were very still, it seemed that she descended a step or so and then climbed those two steps farther up, which must somehow give upon the roof.

"*Ssssaaa!*" Vazul's creature scuttled past Mahart also

and stood just within the opening. Her long neck lifted, her narrow head raised at what seemed an impossible angle.

Then Halwice was back and the creature moved to one side.

"Well?" Vazul demanded.

"Yes, there have been others, at least two," she said with obvious reluctance. "But I have not the power to sniff them out. Only—" She paused and then proceeded, her voice now lacking any tone. "Only Willadene might be able to pick up such. As I have told you, Chancellor, one with her gift is born perhaps once in a century. There are many who can identify separate odors at a sniff but, as you know, she can also sense the smell of evil abroad."

"She has a mighty hand with a pepper mill too." The wounded man gave a small shaky laugh. "But what would you have her do? Line up the full court, nobles and servants alike, and sniff them out? I have heard the old tales of witch-hunting which went so, but those are centuries past."

"No—" Halwice said slowly. "But tonight's happenings must be our guide. Your Grace"—now she addressed Mahart directly—"you have sent to me many orders in the past. Now before us lies a time of fêtes and perhaps much gaiety. Suppose you ask of His Highness that my establishment be applied to for those lures which are available. Then Willadene can be sent to you with such a consignment and perhaps be attached to your household as an expert in such adornments—at least for a space.

"Knowing the High Lady Saylana, she will be first to notice such an addition to your retinue, and also she will be avid to learn what new goods there might be to be offered.

"But if you agree, Your Grace, there is also a warning. Already some of my wares have been tampered with and only due to Willadene has mischief been defeated. Herb craft is a very old learning, and it has its dark side as well—it can kill as well as cure. Therefore I would advise you, should this plan be agreed upon, not to have dealings with any such mixtures as Willadene herself has not passed upon as being free of any meddling.''

Vazul nodded. Ssssaaa had climbed back to his collar again, and there was a very purposeful look on the Chancellor's face.

''It would seem that what you suggest, mistress, is our best answer. Your Grace?''

''Yes, I agree. But also—I do not like hallways and steps within walls, ones through which my own rooms may be easily reached.'' If Halwice recommended this girl she could believe in her and the powers the Herbmistress credited her with. However, she felt exposed to something she could not put name to when she thought about that panel she had so impulsively opened and the fact that there were secrets beyond secrets in the very walls which had once seemed so safe.

Vazul was nodding. ''That can be remedied, Your Grace. The secret inner fastenings of these doors are known to us. You need have no fear of any trouble thereby. It is near morning. After your maid comes to awaken you there will be a message that while you are at breakfast with His Highness there will be workmen in your room. Their purpose will be to install a special new cabinet since your wardrobe will of necessity be continually added to. This will completely barricade the panel so that it will need a squad of workmen to ever force it open again. But first they will plaster the wall.

''Now.'' He looked down at the young man lying at his feet. ''We must also see you safe. Since the wallway seems to be known beyond our own circle we shall place you where you will *not* be discovered inadvertently—in my own suite. In fact in my own bed. For I shall continue to ail for a day or so until you are on your feet again. Your Grace, if you will return to your own chamber—''

Mahart prickled inside. This was as if he were giving some child instructions for proper conduct. However, it would seem that she was not to have any further hand in this particular part of any game Vazul was playing, and she remembered with a start that she must do something to hide the traces of her own activities below. Nodding in agreement she squeezed once more through the secret panel and found her way back to her chamber, where she busied herself hastily with what had to be done.

Willadene awoke, but somehow the fragrance of her dream seemed to last past her duties of the morning—even after she opened the store. Halwice had left on the order slate some instructions for simple remedies which might be exhausted and these she put together even before the Second Bell boomed out over the town. But she longed for the return of the Herbmistress. She herself knew so little and customers would begin to question if she were the only one seen in the shop. She was sure that a number would not trust her judgment—certainly the doctors would not.

But it was none of the doctors who was to begin this day with wreckage. She had cleared away most of the orders as well as prepared three simple remedies herself when there was a stir outside the door of the shop, and a moment later a young man in noble's street finery came in, accompanied by two others of his kind, though not so brightly dressed.

They stared about them contemptuously. One of them pulled down a braided cord of dried stalks, sniffed at it, made a face, and tossed it onto the floor, where one of his companions trod upon it. The leader of the trio leaned across the counter and, before Willadene could dodge, thrust two fingers under her chin and jerked her head up, his thick lips sneering as he looked at her.

"Where's the old witch, slut?" His speech was slurred and, early as it was in the day, she could smell the heaviness of wine—as well as a faint trace of that other thing— the darkness which frightened her.

"The Herbmistress Halwice"—she had pulled away from his hold on her chin—"has been summoned to the castle. How can I serve you?"

He grinned, and that was echoed by his companions.

"Were you not a dirty little serving wench you might just give us a jog or two," he drawled.

"That's telling her, Lord Barbric," commented one of the others. "But it's not getting you anything—"

"So," Barbric said (she had never seen him, but she had heard enough of his roustering, his spite, and his mishandling of commoners to understand who she now dealt with to her inner despair), "look me out, wench, that scent as will make every woman's eye turn toward me willingly. They say your mistress knows it well—Heart-Hold."

Willadene summoned all her courage. "Lord, that is but an old tale. No dealer in herbs has ever seen or heard of it these three hundred years or more."

His hand lifted and before she could dodge he slapped her so viciously that she fell back against the cupboard-studded wall behind her, her cheek feeling fiery with pain.

"You tell your witch mistress, what I want I get and she had better remember that. To give her a little proof—" He gave a sudden nod and the two with him swept from the fore shelf display in the shop the fine bottles, each one one of its kind, to smash on the floor. The fragrances they had held were thick enough to make one dizzy. Over the wreckage Barbric and his friends crunched their way into the outer air.

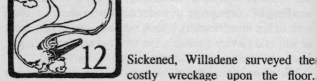

Sickened, Willadene surveyed the costly wreckage upon the floor. There was no use, she knew, as she nursed one hand against her smarting cheek, in calling the Reeve's guard. They would no more lay the hands of justice on that trio than they would sprout wings and fly. The son of the High Lady Saylana was indeed above any complaint a merchant might make. There had been cases before when young drunken lords had preyed upon shopkeepers, but any justice was served quietly thereafter by some responsible member of their House settling outside the Reeve's court with the plaintiff. And somehow she was sure that for this destruction there would be no such recompense.

Slowly she went into the back room for broom and basket and came back to work. The larger pieces she picked up, here running fingers over the back and part of one wing of a headless swan, there sickened by the sight of cracked petals. It took some time to clear the floor. At least no customers intruded. That made her happy at first and then she realized that those in the neighboring houses and shops might well have recognized the vandals and wanted nothing to do with their victim. It was safer to look the other way when one from the Great Houses made trouble for a commoner.

Willadene had swept the floor for the third time, trying to work loose the smallest slivers of broken glass, when someone did at last darken the doorway, and she looked up quickly.

Halwice, her sturdy faring-forth cloak about her, the bulging bag of her supplies in hand, stood there. It was plain she had already noted the half-full basket of broken china and glass, the empty shelves in the street window.

Willadene felt guilty, even though she knew that there had been no way she could have protected those precious possessions.

"Bring a wet cloth." Halwice spoke calmly as if this was a catastrophe she was well used to dealing with. "Lay it across the boards and press lightly. That will bring up some of the splinters, but be careful of your hands. And to whom do we owe this attack—and why?"

She had shrugged off her cloak and set down her bag on the counter while Willadene hurried to the inner room for the cloth she dipped into the water bucket and wrung out. It was not until she returned that the girl answered that question.

"My Lord Barbric, mistress. He was well gone in liquor and there were two with him—nobles also, I think."

"Come here, child." Halwice held out her hand, and now her fingers tightened around Willadene's chin as she turned the girl's face to the full light.

"This mark he left on you also?" she asked. "What was he in search of?"

"Mistress, he spoke of Heart-Hold. And when I said that was naught but a tale he—"

"He seeks that?" Halwice was frowning but, Willadene knew, not at her. "He—or she who sent him, grows bolder—out of strength they have gathered, or because time presses in upon them now?"

Willadene could give no answer to questions she did

not understand. Still keeping hold on her the Herbmistress reached for a pot on a nearby shelf and used her teeth to loose its lid. Then, dipping a finger deeply into the thick jelly inside, she swept that across Willadene's cheek. Though the girl flinched at the pain of the touch, light as it was, Halwice held her head steady until she had finished.

"It is well you will be out of here!" she said forcefully when she had done. "Put down that cloth of splinters and come—"

Willadene quickly obeyed, swift to follow Halwice behind the curtain to the inner chamber.

"Sit—and listen well," the Herbmistress ordered. "There is that which only you can do."

She herself knelt by the long chest, pulling out folds of bedding and garments of a brighter hue than Willadene had ever seen her wear—almost as if some lady's wardrobe had been stored so. As she worked she talked, and Willadene unconsciously moved her stool the closer to listen.

"Your talent is needed, my girl, and it may be of great importance. There is certainly trouble to be sniffed out— trouble such as you have already met by scent among those towers above us. The Duke has his secrets—one you have seen in person—that one who has served him well— nearly to the death."

"Nicolas?" Willadene said the name as the Herbmistress paused.

"Nicolas," confirmed Halwice, "and we should thank the Star that he was found in time. But this is another matter. The Duke seeks a new kind of protection for the High Lady Mahart. She may be in very grave danger indeed, one which only such a talent as yours can sniff out. It is His Highness's will that you for a time join Her Grace's household. To all who question it will be told that you are bringing her some new preparations and there is need in instructing her waiting maids in their use as well as matching certain fragrances and the like to gowns being prepared for the visit of Prince Lorien, the great victory ball and other festivities.

"This you are fully trained to do. If it is possible, gain the High Lady's confidence even in a little. But this is the most important: you must be ever ready with your talent to make sure that no evil draws near her—not only because she is her father's daughter and High Lady but also because she is one who truly follows the Star Path and will, I believe, in the future bring good to this land and its people."

Willadene, remembering that serpent of green light, felt for her amulet, and it was as if Halwice read her mind.

"You will be given what protections are possible, not only for yourself but for her. Above all—learn her personal scent—not just the fragrances she favors—so that you know her in our own fashion as granted by the talent. Now—"

She had pulled a last flat bag from the depths of the chest. Lifting it onto the cupboard bed she unfastened the end and began to pull out a folded length of cloth, all in shades of green varying from that of plants to the leaves of trees. And her stirring of this released the scent of lavender and, what Willadene had come to know as a foreign import of high value, sandlewood.

Unfolded to its farthest extent the cloth was revealed as clothing. The palest green, soft in folds, made up two chemises. There were then two petticoats of a slightly darker shade, and, last of all, two gowns, plain of any embellishment until Halwice lifted the nearest and there was a gleam of deep purple and silver somewhat tarnished by time— High on the left side of the laced bodice this revealed itself fully as a circlet of violets picked out with silver leaves.

Such were no garments for one of Halwice's height nor would those skirts meet around her. She shook out each piece and surveyed it critically as if in search of some flaw and then said: "In earlier days those of our guild

(there were more of us then) had our own robes for meetings and feast days. Now''—she shrugged—''I am known.
Why should I wear livery for myself alone? But these
were my journeymaid dresses and you shall do us proud
at the castle so that none can sneer at your outward
seeming.''

''For me?'' Willadene put out a hand but did not quite
touch finger to the dress Halwice was still holding.

''For you to wear in honest pride. This—'' she plucked
the bodice closer so the girl could see the violets ''—will
serve you as a house badge and none can say you are an
intruder. Now, let us see how well all fits.''

Not only did the Herbmistress see Willadene into the
wealth of clothing, but she took thread and needle and
made some tucks here and there so at last the girl could
almost believe that these had come to her straight from
the seamstress. Their labors were interrupted by calls from
the shop, and she heard from behind the curtain Halwice
deftly explaining to several visitors that the disaster of the
morning had been the result of drunken folly. There was
much agreement that something should be done to curb
such actions, but there was also the undercurrent, the suggestion, that the Duke had truly not the strength to enforce
the law even within Kronengred.

Leaving Willadene to turn up the last hem (luckily her
hands had softened enough under the nightly creaming that
rough skin did not fret the fine cloth) Halwice brought out
from a far cupboard a bag not unlike that she herself
carried when she was summoned to a healing except
larger.

She opened it to display the many pockets inside, and
in each she placed a small jar, packet of oiled skin, or a
thick-sided bottle. As she worked she talked, and Willadene listened with care, for this would be for use of the
Lady Mahart and must, if it were at all possible, please
her.

There was a second row of pockets, near hidden behind

the first, and into these Halwice tucked away certain remedies for minor ills—headaches, sleeplessness, agues and
the like. The extra clothing had a section of its own.

Such medications Willadene had already dispensed in
the shop and knew well. Halwice was reaching for a
packet of well-dried leaves when she near knocked a book
from the tabletop. Picking it up she looked at it closely
and then shot a sharp glance in the girl's direction.

"You have been searching—?" That was not an accusa-
tion but rather a question.

"Yes, mistress. It is the story of the Heart-Hold—there
has been such talk of it I would know more."

Halwice smiled. "How we dream when we are young,
child. I think in the heart of every Herbmistress, since this
tale was first told, there has abode a faint hope that she,
too, might be the Star-favored one to chance upon such a
treasure again. Take it with you— Perhaps you may find
something within to catch the High Lady's interest. It is
said she is one who likes books and has spent many
hours reading."

She placed the ancient book in the bottom of the bag
to Willadene's relief, for she had feared a scold for prying.

This time Willadene's entrance into the castle was not
made a secret to be hidden by night shadows. Instead, one
of the senior pages in full uniform came to escort her,
though she refused to surrender her bag to his hold, knowing that Halwice would not have done so. However, to
walk forward in her new livery, for such she was sure she
could consider the clothes the Herbmistress had supplied,
was an experience to bring her chin up, her eyes light
with pride. Halwice's trust in her was less tangible than a
green dress, but the latter gave Wiladene confidence in
herself and armed her for what she must do.

However, when the climb up the castle mount was behind her and she entered the small posten gate her escort
held open, memory stirred and she looked carefully around

for that tower of dark tales. It seemed that they were bound in that very direction, and she took firmer grip upon her bag.

She was so intent on what lay before her that she was hardly aware of those passing, nor did she note the stares which fastened upon her or heed the murmur which trailed behind her as they went.

The Black Tower was not their goal; instead, she was ushered to another, united to that place of ill omen by a wall, to be sure, but fashioned of lighter stone. The narrow windows were all open to the sun and air, while doves fluttered on its roof. It had every appearance of vibrant life, whereas its neighbor was a finger of gloom pointing skyward.

Willadene was ushered into the lower room, where there was a bustle of servants, and then steered up the stairs to a second and much richer and quieter chamber—though the thin notes of a hand harp not too well plucked could be heard and she caught the scent of some of the pure-the-air preparations such as she herself had fashioned.

Not only were the windows well opened here, giving one side of the room a dazzle of sunlight, but the walls between those windows were bannered with strips of brightly colored ribbons twisted here and there into the form of flowers.

The girl with the harp struck a false note as Willadene came in, and the three others in the room centered their attention on the newcomer.

Willadene sank down in the curtsey Halwice had rehearsed her in, fearful of losing balance as her heavy bag pulled her a little to one side. One waited for the High Lady to speak first, that had also been the Herbmistress's instructions.

"You are apprenticed to the Herbmistress?" It was the girl seated near enough to the pool of sunlight that seemed to put flecks of gold in her hair even though it had been braided in such tight coils, one over each ear, and there were flashes from the jeweled heads of the pins which held it so.

"Yes, Your Grace." Luckily her voice sounded as usual. "I am Willadene, if Your Grace pleases."

The High Lady was certainly not as striking looking as another who sat on a stool nearby, but she far outshone the other two—one being a beanpole with a sourish face, and the other bulging out of her clothes, cream powder ill applied to cover a rising spot on her chin.

"You may be seated—here." Her Grace beckoned Willadene toward her own chair and pointed to a thick floor cushion not too far away.

Somehow Willadene was able to curtsey again and subside as decorously as possible on the place indicated.

"I have long enjoyed your mistress's products," the High Lady continued. "Lady Famina and Lady Geuverir"—now she was speaking to the two other ladies, the plump one having set aside her harp—"we have promised the Abbey the new altar cloth before Prince Lorien arrives. He will undoubtedly go there to give full thanks for his victory. Since your needle skills are indeed to be praised, you may work on that now."

She gestured to the other side of the room where there was set up, stretched and fastened smoothly on a frame, a length of fine, silvery cloth. The two ladies curtsied with elaborate flourishes which led Willadene to believe that there was little liking between them and the High Lady. However, Mahart had already beckoned her other companion to pull her stool closer.

"Now." She was truly excited, Willadene saw, as might be a child before an array of toys from which she must make a choice. "What new things has Halwice concocted with that fabulous skill of hers?"

Willadene undid the cover of her bag. She felt more at ease, for she was sure of the products she had brought and she did know well their uses.

From the first pocket she withdrew a round bell of

opaque opalescent glass which fitted well into the cup of her hand. A quick twist separated it into two. On one side was a paste of palest pink, while facing it was a supply of lily-white cream.

"It is not yet the season of flowers hereabouts, Your Grace. But my mistress has those who bring her scents from other lands. This—" She advanced the pink half a fraction "—comes from the far south—that is dried petals which scents it so—but it is a cream to be used when the sun is high enough to burn the skin exposed to it. Its companion cream can be used nightly to leave the face and hands smooth and clear—"

Thus she spread out those results of Halwice's blending and brewing, giving a clear explanation for each, its use and the care which must be followed in that using. She had drawn out the last of those Halwice had apportioned to her—a small flask fashioned in the form of a tiny, fully opened fan (one of the few treasures which had fortunately escaped that brutal attack at the shop).

"This—" she held it up "—works so." She pressed the small pearl-centered lid and from beneath that spot there came a mist of spray.

Unlike the heavier scents of the other jars and bottles which now were displayed, this was a much lighter fragrance. Willadene herself had been unable to identify its ingredients, though she had been able to tell one from the other.

The High Lady drew a deep breath. "That—! What might it be? Flowers"—her eyes were half closed—"and the fields—the free wind—" It was as if she saw beyond them, this room, out into a place which was hers alone.

"This is Velvet Vine, Your Grace. It is from overseas and Halwice says that this is the last of that she had sent her five seasons past. The vine flowers but once in three years, and the flowers must be harvested within the dawn hour before the night dew has left their petals. It takes,

Your Grace, a full cartload alone of flowers to press for a few droplets of oil.''

Mahart caught it from her eagerly. As delighted as she had seemed with all else Willadene had displayed she appeared most excited with this. Yet the lady who had shared all her interest in the former wares, examining each as Mahart had passed it to her, looked at what her mistress now held with a faint surprise.

"It is very faint—other scents within a room would quickly overpower it, Your Grace," she commented with the freedom of one to whom the Duke's daughter must have at least offered a measure of friendship.

"Think you so?" Mahart appeared openly surprised. "But—" She cradled the small bottle in her hand as if the warmth of her flesh might release even more of the scent she craved. "But to me—" She now shook her head determinedly. "I cannot agree, Zuta. Herb girl—no, it is Willadene they call you, is it not? Can you tell me more of this?"

"Nothing except what my mistress said—that with certain other bindings and fragrances, the velvet vine flowers blend well. There is none other of it now left in her shop—"

Mahart looked down almost dreamily at the bottle. But Zuta hitched her stool forward a fraction.

"There is another fragrance even rarer." Her voice held an impatient note, Willadene thought. "What had you heard of Heart-Hold?"

There was an odd moment of silence in the whole chamber, as if Zuta's voice had been raised enough to also catch the attention of those at the embroidery frame.

"Heart-Hold?" It was Mahart who laughed. "A legend—" Then she suddenly glanced sharply at Willadene. "A legend surely," she repeated, and her tone of voice suggested that she expected agreement with that.

The girl hesitated. "Your Grace, what I would learn of the trade my mistress has mastered so well, comes from constant study. And one thing is always clear—that at the heart of any much-repeated tale there is a core of truth. However—'' Her foot touched the bag from which she had been pulling forth Halwice's work and she remembered that book. But there was no reason to share with the High Lady an account which merely repeated all the old details threadbare by time. "However, in whoever practices an art there lies a deep wish—to find a new treasure, to bring it to fruit and display it. The story of Heart-Hold might well have been born from such a desire.''

The Lady Zuta stirred. "They say it was on the high altar of Ibarkuan Abbey when the northern barbarians broke the fort line in the long ago. To such it would have no meaning and they might only have crushed it into nothingness.''

"That is as many versions of the tale report,'' agreed Willadene. "So to us now Heart-Hold is the unobtainable which those who aspire to deeper depths of knowledge will always seek.''

The High Lady had raised her hands, which cupped the fan bottle, to the height of her chin. She looked, Willadene thought, now as one who dreamed, but when she spoke softly it would seem that she knew very well of what they spoke.

"Who would hold a heart,'' she mused as if to herself, "by something as fleeting as a scent? A heart must be held by what is within one. But''—now she looked to Willadene as if for a moment or so she had been unaware of her presence—"what the Herbmistress has sent us is treasure indeed, this most of all.'' And she continued to hold the fan bottle. "Zuta, if you will summon Julta, I would have all these riches taken to my dressing chamber, and you''—she smiled at Willadene—"can show us when the time comes how best they can be put to use.''

Hurriedly Willadene returned the boxes, bottles, and jars to their pockets in the bag. So this much of her task was accomplished. She was now, indeed, at least a temporary member of the High Lady's household, even as Halwice wished.

When she held out her hand for the fan bottle, Mahart shook her head. "Not this—as yet. I have a fancy to keep this with me." She carefully set her forefinger to the pearl button on the bottle and breathed deeply as the answering mist must have dampened the bodice of her dress close to her throat.

"Tell me," she continued, "how do you harvest your herbs, Willadene? Is the countryside outside the walls of Kronengred well supplied with the flowers and plants you need?"

"Your Grace, that I cannot tell you. This is not yet the season of flowering and I have only been with my mistress for a short time. How or what she harvests when it comes to its peak I do not know. There is a garden behind the shop, but the herbs grown there are for cooking and healing, and when I have seen the Herbmistress concoct such as these"—she indicated the last of those she was packing away—"it was always from her own supplies. Some are dried and not taken from their stems for grinding until they are needed, others are preserved in oils, some come as packets of powder. But how they look in the fields as they grow—of that I have only seen the pictures in my mistress's books. I have never been beyond the walls of Kronengred."

"So it is with me also," Mahart returned. "Tell me— were you always with Mistress Halwice? I know that often herb lore runs in families. Was it so in your case also?"

She seemed to be genuinely interested in Willadene's past. And perhaps it would be better for all concerned that the girl supply at once details which could be easily checked should any find a reason to wish it.

"No, I am no kin to Mistress Halwice. Though she knew my mother who was midwife for the fourth sector.

Even when I was little I had heard of her potions and healing powers. But that was before the plague—''

"Yes—the plague." Mahart nodded. "That changed many lives—for the worse. Did it for you?"

Willadene smoothed the skirt of the finest dress she could now remember ever wearing and thought of how just a short time back she had gone meagerly covered with ragged castoffs.

"I was one of the homeless children. My father was Hakroine, Second of the Rangers' First Squad. He was away—mother nursed those plague-stricken until she also was taken. Then they said my father had been killed by outlaws and I had no family remaining. So I was brought to the Reeve for assigning." She wanted to squirm away from the result of that and she paused.

"And he assigned you to the Herbmistress?"

Willadene shook her head. "There were so many of us and there was so much for the Reeve to be doing. He placed us at the first asking of any who wanted our services. I went as scullery maid to a distant cousin Jacoba of the Wanderers Inn."

She fell silent. How could the Duke's daughter understand such a person as Jacoba or a den as foul as her inn?

Willadene looked down at her hand and the bag she had just finished refilling. What was one who had been a scullery maid to Jacoba doing here, talking with the High Lady as if they might be neighbors? But the sight of the bag stiffened her. So things might have been in the past but they were no longer so. She was Halwice's chosen apprentice and trusted enough to be here for more than one purpose.

"But you have the Herbmistress's favor and are her right hand now," Mahart continued. "Thus things are better for you—even as they are—for me," she ended in a lower voice.

"Your Grace—" The Lady Zuta now stood behind Mahart's chair. "Julta waits to show this one her place of duty and her lodging.'' There was a coldness in that, and Willadene could see the distinct frown on the lady's face. Undoubtedly her free speech with the High Lady was not to the favor of her attendant, but Willadene had only answered the questions Mahart had asked.

She arose from the cushion and curtseyed again. Zuta might be frowning and forbidding, but the High Lady herself was smiling and when she did that she was far more attractive than the dark beauty behind her.

''You must continue to tell me herb lore,'' Mahart announced. ''I do not have the right to demand the attendance of your mistress—especially when the Chancellor needs her superior skills. But you can explain to me little things, and that in itself will be a new form of learning.''

She was to share Julta's quarters, Willadene discovered—leaving her clothing bag beside a second narrow bed in a rather stark room, though there were curtains at the window and a strip of hand-hooked carpet as a runner between the two beds. Over one of which there was a shelf which had been made into an impromptu shrine with a small tinsel Star symbol, such as were sold to raise money for alms.

Julta indicated the basin and jug on a small side table and the way to the necessary from the landing without. Then, with Willadene still lugging her bag of cosmetics, they descended to the chamber directly below which was Mahart's own bedroom.

At present that was in disarray. Though covers had been drawn over the bed to protect its rich hangings, and most of the rest of the furnishings treated so also, there was a musty smell and dust sifting through the air, as well as such sounds as Willadene would not have expected in the High Lady's own private place.

Two men were busy at the far wall, which had been stripped of its hangings, and they were apparently applying a thick coating of plaster, the dust of which made Willadene sneeze, over the ancient paneling.

"Yur lady, she won't get no more cold wind through this." The older of the two men slapped another dollop over the wood. "Takes a lotta doin', it does, to keep up this here old pile of stones. Watch what yur a-doin', lump, the young wench don't want none o' that stuff spottin' her skirts, now do you, missy?"

Willadene had carefully avoided the somewhat wide swing of the laborer's assistant. He had been distracted, she saw, by their own entrance and flushed a dull red when Willadene looked in his direction, leaning quickly over the pot for another load on his trowel.

Julta sniffed. "What a muck you be makin' here, Jonas. Will take us half a seven night to be clearin' it. Mistress"—she spoke directly to Willadene—"now you just set that there bag of yourn in this wardrobe. Ain't no clumsy-footed man a goin' to kick it over when in there."

Willadene obeyed instructions. Certainly in this hubbub there could be no unpacking of her wares at present. Then—she took time to straighten from putting her bag into the dark cupboard Julta had indicated.

Evil! At first she thought that trace came from the interior of the wardrobe. But no, the source was somewhere behind her. She turned to shut the door on her possessions and used that action to give a quick glance about the room.

The room—no, it came from— She made herself look inquiringly at Julta as if waiting further instructions. But she was sure. Just as the evil had touched and clung to Figis from the inn so did it lie here under the sweat and body odor of the red-faced boy. Yet there was nothing about him to suggest the same sly waywardness Figis had always shown.

13 This was not so strong and sickening as had been the assault upon her senses when she had been in that other tower room. And Willadene found it very hard to believe that this Jonas could have anything to do with that hand which had loosed blackness upon them. His hand was not that of a woman nor could she conceive of his being akin to what small sight she had caught of their menace then. Yet she could not be mistaken.

"Lay it on smooth, boy—" The master workman had drawn aside a little when he saw that they still lingered to watch the ongoing labor.

Knowing that a too-quick or unthinking move might reveal her, Willadene somehow produced a look of slight interest.

"Are all the walls to be served so?" she asked. "It is well away now from the Great Cold, which ought to give you time—"

The man laughed, showing stubs of blackened teeth. "All these walls, young miss? 'Twould take a full army of us to do that. No, we put a patch here an' a patch there as we-uns have done, an' our dads a-fore us, an' it serves for a while."

179

She had managed to take a step or two closer to the bucket of plaster. The odors which arose from that—she would take oath that, unpleasant as they might be, none were what she sought. No, her faint warning came from the young man. But what could she do—denounce him here and now? With what proof? It would avail her nothing except to uncover the very secrets she had been sworn to keep.

Before she could make any decision the matter was taken out of her control when the master sent his assistant off for more supplies. As he passed her Jonas did not glance in her direction but slouched out, seemingly intent only on the near empty bucket in his large hands.

"Faugh." Julta spat out what might have been a mouthful of the all-pervading dust. "Stay here, girl, and this stuff will give you a powdering far from any your mistress would contrive."

So Willadene followed on the maid's heels again from the disarrayed room. Halwice had provided her with one way of communication. By the resounding boom of the city bell she could make use of that now and she would, even if she had only a wisp of evidence to offer.

Julta did not seem surprised when she asked the way to the Lord Chancellor's suite where her mistress was supposed to be in attendance. Since the High Lady had dismissed her, Willadene was entitled to at least the freedom of the tower and the chamber she would seek beyond that.

Listening carefully to complicated directions concerning this corridor and that door, Willadene hoped she was memorizing Julta's words correctly.

"It is near noon time," the maid ended. "If you would eat, do so now. You can seek out your mistress after, for Her Grace has not definitely summoned you back."

Willadene's empty middle (she had not been able to finish her bowl of porridge that morning with such an ordeal before her) urged her to follow the maid's advice, and Julta's spare figure, down two flights of stairs, along a corridor, and at last into a room where there was a great deal of noise and confusion.

All the servants of the castle did not eat together, Willadene gathered. Those of the upper class, who dealt directly with the Duke or either of the ladies, had their own trestle table set up at one end of the room, and it was to that Julta beckoned her, making her known, in a perfunctory fashion, to the Duke's head footman and a herald who moved down the long bench enough to let them be seated.

The babble of talk was loud enough to make regular conversation impossible without shouting, thought Willadene, used as she was to the quiet of the herb shop. It rivaled that clamor which hurt the ears of all who served wayfarers in the inn when one of the big merchant trains had just arrived in time for a meal.

After the first few words she had been able to sort out, Willadene gathered that the subject engaging those about her was a single one—the arrival of Prince Lorien and his guardsmen. And her present table companions were certainly loud in their agreement concerning the effect of such a visit on Kronengred.

She broke the crust of a meat tart with the edge of her spoon and sniffed with pleasure. Here was not any too-old meat or second-day vegetables. The food was good and the portions hearty, though a single sip of the ale in the tankard at her place warned her it was far too strong and bitter for her liking.

"They say he brought down the Wolf with his own hand!" declared the footman. "I heard as Sergeant Henicus has said he is like his grandfather—old King Wansal—no hanging around the court, playing the pretty for the maids for him!"

The herald grunted and then swallowed so he could speak more clearly. "They say as how there are them at the court that could do with less soldiering. The High Prince Ranald takes only to the field for the spring maneuvers—"

"And those," cut in the footman, "are largely play, as I have heard tell from one just returned with the last caravan. They have no outlaws to hunt."

"Would we could say the same. Now in Duke Wubric's day it was different."

"Yes," cut in another voice from across the board. Willadene, after a quick glance to identify the speaker, dropped her eyes modestly to her plate while she listened as best she could under the fogging of clamor.

"Yes," the speaker repeated. "Our late gracious lord was a mighty one with sword and spear in his time. Are there any wreckers who dare now to ply their traffic along Southcoast?"

He was a younger man than the other two, slender and dark of hair, and he moved with an odd deliberation, Willadene learned in cautious quick glances. Then he looked directly at her and she near choked on the bite of sweet bread into which she had just set her teeth.

Though he was dressed in the sober rust-brown clothing of a scribe and there was even a spot of ink on the hand holding his spoon, this was—but how could it be?—Nicolas!

Halwice's skills were great, to be sure, but to return a badly wounded man to this apparent unhurt outward seeming was more than Willadene could accept. However, she noted the stiffness of his upper body, that he was eating slowly, as if to raise a loaded spoon or a chunk of bread to his lips was something of an effort.

There was no recognition in his glance at her, and she took that as a warning. However, apparently his comment on their past ruler was not altogether accepted by the other two opposite him.

"You speak free of one of Lord Vazul's household," the herald commented, and the girl could see he was watching Nicolas almost warily.

"Now that is a remark which is interesting." Nicolas shifted a little on his bench perch as if hunting some ease which he could not find. "Certainly the wreckers were of no benefit to Kronen—any more than the Red Wolf of whom Prince Lorien has so prudently deprived us.''

"The coast watch has had half its force withdrawn. What do they now? patrol the harbor streets seeking— what—rats out of ships decaying at their moorings? There are reports from the south that lure lights have been seen again,'' the herald said sourly.

Nicolas grinned. "Oh, but our Lord Duke may have the answer already on his way to us. After a spot of outlaw harrying the Prince might indeed welcome a change of scene and opponents.''

The footman was frowning and the herald flushed. "We shed our protection now until we have to depend upon outsiders for aid. And why? What danger stalks within the walls of Kronengred which the Duke fears so much he must draw all our troops homeward? There is talk in the town—Lord Vazul should know—is he not of a merchant clan? We live on our trade and our Lord Duke—''

He hesitated and Nicolas, still smiling but in a way Willadene could not like, asked: "And our Lord Duke does what is best for the city—even as he swore at his crowning. You speak of rats in ships, my friends. There are such to be found elsewhere also. Who knows what lure lights have been set and where?''

He was deliberately baiting the man now, the girl knew, and she could not guess his purpose. Nicolas was certainly Vazul's man and so the Duke's—but his comments now could be taken for covert criticism of them both. Was he trying to get disloyal answers?

He was getting to his feet, in a manner which might have suggested taking leisurely leave of the company. Only she could read signs enough to guess that only his will kept his body under control. Every healer's instinct made her want to go to him—to make sure that the insanity of his being here now had not again opened his wound. But once more her own need for cover kept her where she was, though her hunger disappeared as she watched him walk away.

"Provocateur." The herald watched him with narrowed eyes. "I say that there are too many talking behind their hands and striving to entangle honest men in nets these days. At least we know that the Prince has no stake in games played here."

He arose in turn, but Willadene did not miss the smirk on the footman's fleshy face as he watched his late companion depart. Instinctively she called upon the higher sense. She did not know what really lay among the words she had just overheard, but that they might have second meanings she could guess.

Now the footman turned to Julta as if the maid had just seated herself. He had been peeling an apple neatly, and now he quartered it and extended one portion to her on the the tip of his knife with a courtly flourish.

"Your lady prepares to welcome the hero?" he asked in a playful tone.

Julta did not appear to notice the offering he would make her; instead she arose abruptly and Willadene was only too ready to follow her.

"As does yours also." The maid laughed with no humor and swept away. As Willadene caught up with her, she said grudgingly, as if she did not wish to share the information but believed she must, "He is of the High Lady Saylana's following—recently come to her from the household of Lord Brutain." Now she smiled one-sidedly. "The High Lady has a liking for lusty men in her livery."

If Julta had thought to rid herself of the footman she failed. Apple and knife discarded he caught step beside the maid so closely that Willadene, now flanking her guide, was able to catch every word he said.

"Hoity-toity are we, mistress? There are them as ruled here before your lady gave her first birth squall. Best watch your manners—"

"And you, yours, lackey!" snapped Julta.

He was still grinning. "Cat claws." He laughed.

"You'd be a handsome piece like as not if you'd give over frowning. Try it some time."

Julta took a long step ahead and reached out as she went to draw Willadene with her. "Now that is the way—"

Ignoring the footman she nodded toward another door than the one by which they had entered.

However, when Willadene turned in that direction, glad to be away from the sly teasing of the footman, she discovered she was not able to escape so easily. For he abandoned Julta and bore down on her.

"You're a pretty little piece—Julta should take lessons from you. And where might you be going now? We've heard as how the High Lady Mahart is housing you for the while— This is not the way back to her quarters."

"She is not of the household," Julta said quickly. "Her mistress is here and she must see her."

"Yes. Old long-tooth Vazul has a rheum. Doubtless that snake thing of his gave him a bite," drawled the footman. "Well enough, as it just happens, young miss, your way and mine run together. I'll just go along with you that you do not become mazed by all the twists and turns in this old pile."

Willadene was at a loss as to how to refuse such an offer. Julta was really scowling, and it seemed to the girl that that expression was divided between her and the footman. Before she could say anything, Julta, with a swirl of her skirts, turned away and was gone, and Willadene hesitated to attract any attention by trying to follow, especially since she had been informed that her goal was in the opposite direction.

"The Lord Chancellor"—before she could move the footman had taken her by the upper arm and was actually propelling her forward—"now one would have said he was forged of steel—never ailed before that I have heard. Bad enough to have your mistress in, is he?"

"I do not know how he fares," she returned and somehow freed herself of his grasp.

Again the footman snickered. "There won't be many

long faces hereabouts if he has taken to his bed for a
space. Has the tongue of Jemu, he has, and that snaky
thing of his makes a man's skin crawl. They say as how
you've come to make a beauty of our High Lady." He
changed the subject and the girl had a feeling that now
he spoke with some purpose. " 'Course no man can say
that the Lady Saylana does not outshine her—"

It was as if he was trying in some manner to pry into her
thoughts. Yet she sniffed no touch of that elusive evil in him.

"I have not seen your High Lady Saylana," she returned evenly.

"But she would like to see you."

This time Willadene was on guard, able to evade his
grab for her arm. Was he trying to drag her off for some
interview with his formidable lady?

"I obey the orders of the Herbmistress Halwice." She
hoped her voice sounded prim enough to make him believe
that he dealt with a simple serving girl. "If the High Lady
Saylana wishes to see me—which I do not think she would
since I am but an apprentice and my mistress would be
better equipped to answer any questions—then it must be
Mistress Halwice who sends me."

"You're an ignorant wench," he returned. "You might
be favored by one far more powerful. Better think on it,
girl. No one ever made a fortune by turning a back on
opportunity when it offers itself. The High Lady Saylana
would be a far better customer for your wares, and even
that flat-faced mistress of yours would agree to that."

The spite in his speech seemed overpuffed, as if he had
been defeated where he had expected no trouble at all.
Certainly their meeting at the dining table must have been
by chance. But then had this newcomer to the Lady Saylana's household perhaps heard some exaggerated chatter
about what Willadene had to offer and decided to please
his new mistress by producing her?

"I go where I am sent," she returned. "And now I go
to my mistress."

"You can go to the Hang Door of Grubber for all of me," he snapped and turned away, but not swiftly, and she had a strong idea that he would follow to make sure she was going to the Lord Chancellor's quarters. However, at present she had to concentrate on the directions Julta had supplied.

That she had been right in her surmise she knew, until at last he did disappear down another hallway, though she could not be sure he was still not lurking on her trail.

Here other footmen stood guard, and perhaps he had no wish to be seen by them. Willadene counted doors and then said to the tall livery-coated man who stood by the third, "The Herbmistress Halwice is my mistress. She wishes to see me."

He appeared to continue to stare over her head, but he took one step to the right so that the door was directly behind him and tapped softly upon it three times.

"Name?" he asked, and she gave it promptly, aware there was now a crack of opening showing. A moment later she was ushered in.

Far from being bedbound the Lord Chancellor sat in a chair nearly as stately as a throne, one meant to have judgments uttered from. Facing him on a far less pretentious seat was Nicolas and, to one side, Halwice was delving into her healer's bag.

She could believe that Nicolas was fighting to keep erect and face his mentor straightly and that that action was drawing deeply on what energy he had left. Halwice came swiftly to him with a small cup in one hand. Paying no attention to Vazul she stood over the young man and ordered: "Drink it—to the last drop!"

By its scent what she had poured for him was a powerful restorative, Willadene recognized. But why in his weakened condition he had gone to the eating hall she had no idea. And it seemed that no explanation was to be made to her, for Halwice's attention was now on the girl as she demanded: "What have you discovered? Has the High Lady accepted you without question?"

"She has accepted me, yes, mistress, and she is much pleased with what I have brought. As to what I have discovered—" She gathered that she was to speak openly in this company. "I was taken to her chamber with that I had brought. But there were workmen there, busied on the wall, and one of them—his master called him Jonas—had the smell, not strong, but he has dealt in some way with the Dark."

Nicolas turned his head to stare at her, and Vazul leaned forward in his chair, though Halwice showed no sign of surprise—she could have been expecting some such report. Around the Lord Chancellor's wrist that wide black bracelet stared, and yellow eyes regarded her.

"Soooo—" Vazul hissed that as if his nonhuman companion had given voice. Now he addressed Halwice.

"Is there any way this wall can be tested, that we may learn whether what was meant to be a protection has been tampered with?"

"Perhaps a wardess of the Star might be able to do so, but it would require a lengthy ceremony, one we could not conceal."

The Lord Chancellor looked as if he were chewing upon something bitter. "Soooo—" he hissed again. "And that we cannot do—yet. Jonas . . ." His attention snapped to Nicolas.

There was a moment of silence, and then the younger man answered as if he had some roll of all the castle inhabitants stretched open before him.

"Jonas—tall, butter fair of hair, giving the appearance of one who is as yet not well trained?" Those questions he shot at Willadene.

"He is tall and fair yes, and the master seemed to be keeping an eye on his work as if some check were needed," she replied promptly.

"Jonas, second son to Wilbar in the Lordship of Vantol. That was—"

"Outlaw taken two years ago, yes!" Vazul replied impatiently. "If I remember rightly it is now wasteland, since their lord and his son are both dead and there is no direct heir. The remaining landsmen and servitors were taken under the protection of Lord Nemunt."

"Jonas came to Kronengred with a road draft last year," Nicolas continued as if he had not been interrupted. "He was assigned by Reeve Laprin as apprentice to the mason Valor, who had applied for the next possible aid. His latest work has been in repairing the balcony of the courtyard opening of the Lady Saylana's quarters."

"By the Star, boy, can you shake out the history of everyone under this roof?" commented Vazul. It would seem that Nicolas's flow of information had indeed pleased him.

The other shrugged. " 'Tis no great feat, Chancellor, to keep watch on newcomers. There is another also." Now he once more turned his head in Willadene's direction. "You came with Julta to the common table. Did it seem to you that she chose her seat there with any care or was it the first open to her?"

"The latter I would say."

"There was a footman there wearing a new badge—"

The girl nodded. "He serves the High Lady Saylana."

Again there was a short silence, and now it was Vazul who took over the questioning.

"Was he cordial to Julta?"

"After Master Nicolas left." She was not quite sure how to address the pale young man now settling even further back into the chair. "He strove to be pleasant to Julta. She would have nothing of his efforts. Then—then—" Swiftly she repeated the conversation she had had with the footman until she had managed to at last lose him from sight.

"He is Ringglen, also out of Vantol," Nicolas said. "But you did not sense this same evil in him, mistress?"

"No. Mistress"—she spoke to Halwice now—"could the evil be carried by an object or must it be part of one's own personal scent?"

"Now that is good thinking, young mistress." Vazul leaned forward. "You have in mind that this Jonas may have brought to place in Her Grace's private chambers some foul danger?"

She was remembering the box she had changed in the shop as she answered: "My Lord Chancellor, once before there was substituted for my mistress's wares something which was not of the proper recipe—though I did not then smell evil. But to change any potion can cause evil, though it is not evil in itself." Swiftly she related the finding of the box of incense.

Halwice drew a deep breath, and an unaccustomed flush arose on her usually pale cheeks. "Never has that recipe been changed since first Her Grace signified that she found it beneficial for sleeping. To meddle so, someone must have entered the shop— Yet the Star blessing was set upon it—walls, windows, and doors—by the decree of the Abbess herself when first I came to be a guild mistress. We—Lord Chancellor—we may be dealing with some dire threat greater than we have thought!"

He was chewing his lip, and Nicolas had straightened again in his seat, until Halwice caught him by the shoulder and held him as firmly as if he had been a wriggling small boy.

The black fur band had uncurled from Vazul's wrist and was now as long as a bowstring. Ssssaaa moved with the speed which near dazzled the eyes. Off the Lord Chancellor's knee she dropped to the floor and then was across the thick carpet in an instant until her formidable claws caught in Willadene's wide skirt and she streaked upward to her shoulder. Oddly enough the Chancellor began to nod.

"Yes, we do have a weapon of sorts to use against the invisible. Girl, can you take Ssssaaa unseen back to Her

Grace's chamber? Once there, let her roam at her will. If anything has been hidden there to do Her Grace ill Ssssaaa can find it. This she has done for me many times over. Which is the way''—he smiled grimly—''I have managed to keep both my office and my life as long as I have.''

Halwice had caught up a discarded shawl and threw it over the girl's shoulder, effectively concealing what rode there now.

''Star Point luck go with you, mistress.'' She was surprised at that encouragement from Nicolas.

But the Chancellor offered a warning instead of good wishes.

''Should one of the High Lady Saylana approach you again—'' He seemed undecided.

Willadene, daring, made answer to what she thought he would say. ''I take orders from Mistress Halwice,'' she returned. ''So my answer would and will be that I am sent to the High Lady Mahart and her I am to serve.''

Halwice smiled. ''Just so. Perhaps such an approach to you might tell us more. There is this—'' And now her voice was that she used when she gave instructions. ''Something moves within these walls which is partly of our kind for learning, partly of menace, and partly of an evil I cannot detect—save it is of that nature. We must delve for the right foot before we pull it forth.

''Now we must all be about what we should do. You, Nicolas, back to your bed and be very sure I leave no restorative within your reach again. Such action is folly I had not expected of you. And, Willadene, I must return to the city. What you can learn—'' She looked inquiringly to Vazul.

''What she learns she will learn with Ssssaaa's aid, and Ssssaaa shall report it to me,'' the Lord Chancellor replied composedly, and Willadene felt that warm fur stir against her neck and cheek as if the creature was assuring her this was so.

14 The many halls and antechambers of the castle were as confusing as the city alleys, and Willadene tried hard to remember her way back to the High Lady's tower. But her concern with the footman who had seemed to be following her had interfered with her concentration, and twice she was sure she had taken somehow a wrong turn.

In these lower passages there were no statuelike footmen beside the doors, and she decided that was a sign she had left the quarters of the nobles and the high officials. But she gave up in despair when she blundered into a room of looms on which several maidservants were busily at work, managing to dodge back into the shadows before anyone glanced away from the task beneath her hands.

Leaning against the wall in the duskiest corner she could find, she pushed away panic and tried to force memory to her command. There was a strange niggling of fear that she should certainly *not* be found wandering about without direction.

That warm band about her throat moved and flowed, still under the covering of her shawl, so that the pointed head now rested on her wrist. She flipped up the edge of the covering Halwice had given her and looked into those small, seemingly pupilless eyes.

Though she did not speak aloud, her lips shaped words—"You know!" And she was as sure of that as if she had heard an answering voice. Daringly she smoothed the silky fur with the forefinger of her other hand.

"The High Lady's tower," she shaped a thought with care.

Ssssaaa's head moved under her light touch. It was plain that that head was swinging to a left-hand hall, dim as twilight, for it had only one or two wall-set lamps and those were flickering, though she could feel no breeze. But Willadene was willing to accept her guide, strange as she might be.

There were doors along the hall on either side, but all were firmly shut and that small nose still pointed straight ahead. That is until—

Willadene nearly staggered she had stopped so short, and she heard a low angry hissing from Ssssaaa. Evil—old—Willadene had a sickening thought of a pool nearby in the dark in which something was rising, a slime of ages of hate and pain, and delight in both.

That nauseating smell came from the door to her right. Ssssaaa's head was higher, swinging to look to her and then the door. Surely the creature which she had accepted in perfect faith as being an ally was not urging her in that direction?

Only now she caught a second scent, this of the physical and not the spiritual world. She recognized it—from overseas. Halwice had had a single shipment of it and had really only acted as agent, for it had been ordered beforehand—a half year it had taken to reach Kronengred—by the High Lady Saylana.

There was sound now, very faint, for the door must be a thick one, and it followed a pattern as if someone recited in a hoarse and croaking voice some verse of ritual.

Willadene could stand it no longer. She felt the evil

rising about her to entrap her, as if she had floundered into some sewer near filled with glutinous refuse which would cling to pull her down.

With one hand she fumbled out her amulet pomander and held it quickly to her nose, though its scent did little to stop that sucking. By the Star—the Star—

Holding up her head, she tried to visualize the Star, brilliant and clear, clean and cleansing, as it appeared in the Abbey. And with that held in mind she took one hindered step and then another.

Warmth seemed to be spreading from Ssssaaa's small body, feeding her Star blaze. Then, somehow, they had won to the end of the corridor. However, Willadene felt as if she had tramped most of the streets of the city below without rest.

She was only faintly aware of the directions from Ssssaaa, but at length she did come into an anteroom she recognized and from it made her way back to the High Lady's tower. What foulness she had stumbled upon she could not guess, save it was from no world she knew.

Again she passed footmen as she climbed to the floor where she had first met Mahart and her small court. But it was the bedchamber above which she must seek now. The door was a little open, and she could hear no sounds from within nor could she pick up the scent of either of the men who had been at work there earlier. A limited attempt had been made to return the room to its regular order—though the freshly finished wall was still uncovered. She approached that, letting the shawl slip from her shoulders and holding out the hand on which Ssssaaa's head now rested.

As far as she could see all marks there were uniform, left by the plasterer's tools. Ssssaaa's head came forward, as if Willadene were aiming a spear at that surface, and swung a little back and forth. Starting as high as she could reach—Ssssaaa could rear, with her support, nearly to the ceiling—she began to sweep back and forth.

In spite of her earnest efforts the girl could herself not pick up any more than the usual odors one might find in a room undergoing repairs. There was no hint of evil.

Yet Willadene could sense that the creature she held was dissatisfied. Her faint hissing now held a frustrated note as if she were baffled. Back and forth they examined the wall clear down to floor level. Willadene could pick up no suggestion of strange evil, nor did Vazul's creature show any signs of discovery.

At last Willadene was sitting on the floor, staring at that expanse of plaster, baffled. She could only believe now that her guess was wrong and that taint had been carried by Jonas himself and not by any material used here.

Ssssaaa uncurled from her wrist and dropped to the floor, scuttling along the baseboard with sharp nose held close to where that met the floor. Suddenly the creature paused and her head swung up and around. No longer was her attention fastened on the wall. Instead she leaped in a series of whirling springs straight for the wardrobe where Willadene had left her bag.

The girl was after her guide at once. Though she had brought nothing noxious into this chamber she had left the bag here, and who knew what might have been added or subtracted from its contents since?

She had the bag out as swiftly as she could and opened it. Ssssaaa reared up on the other side of the carrier so her forepaws also pulled at the edge. Willadene grabbed for the first bottle of cream, her hands shaking a little as she unscrewed its lid. To all appearances it was both untouched and the same container she had earlier shown Mahart—the ball which split in halves to reveal the creamy contents.

Her nose gave her quick reassurance. This was nothing more or less than it should be. But Ssssaaa's actions caught her full attention now. The creature was making no attempt to draw forth or touch any of the other offerings in their strap loops. Instead, she had poured about a third of her slim body over the edge of the bag and was picking with claws at the bottom of the carrier.

Quickly Willadene followed that action by plunging her own hand into the bag, groping along the bottom among her clothes, Ssssaaa's warm fur near entwined with her hand again. Then her fingers caught in something and she jerked free that book which Halwice had put into the bag as an afterthought.

The minute Willadene had it to hand Ssssaaa settled back in a hunched ball on the floor, though those gem eyes were still fast on the girl. Willadene sneezed, for the ancient leather of the binding was flaking into dust at every movement of her eager fingers.

Handling it with all the care she could Willadene searched for that special find she had made—the too-thick page. Were two so fastened together? Or perhaps it could be three? At any rate they were so tightly set that neither her fingernails nor the point of her belt knife could find any opening by which they might be pried apart.

So many of the edges of the pages had flaked away through the years she was afraid of destroying the very thing she sought by too careless handling. Ssssaaa had drawn closer, nose to that thick page. Suddenly, before Willadene could withdraw her find to safety, a long red tongue was busy, running along the edge.

One flick down, a second up before Willadene could pull the book firmly out of her companion's reach. There was now a slight discoloration along the path that tongue had taken, though no stains of moisture spread very far.

Once more Willadene tried the point of her knife. She always kept it sharp, for it could be put to many duties—chopping, paring, skinning stems, sawing roots, and the like.

She was perhaps halfway down the page when the point actually sank in, and when she moved it back and forth with the greatest of care, the stiff old parchment reluctantly yielded to that prying steel. The gap showed her that it *was* truly more than one page made up this place of hiding. But the page in between the two she worked on had been neatly sliced out to give room to conceal finely scraped bits of parchment.

Its concealment so must have preserved it, for the markings on it were far darker than the writing on the two enclosing pages. Only it was no recipe such as Willadene had expected—rather a series of irregular lines which followed no pattern at all with a dot or cross here and there to vary the general disorder. Perhaps it was some code which Halwice would be able to decipher—though it meant nothing to her apprentice.

She searched quickly in one of the pockets of her bag and brought out a small square of soft, fine gauze. The find allowed itself to be folded and refolded. Wrapped in this, she bestowed it for safekeeping within her bodice, where it lay soft between her breasts. So they had made one find—and that not expected—but still they had not searched the whole of the room. Ssssaaa appeared to be of the same mind, as her black-furred length now looped up the dais of the huge bed and was running across the covers, tunneling under the cloths laid to protect the fine fabric from the workmen.

Willadene climbed up also, aware of where her companion in the search was by the movement of the cloth. Ssssaaa had headed toward the tall head of the bed, and now the mound which marked her body was in the center of one of the pillows stacked there.

The girl threw aside the cover and faced those sharp eyes. They swung from her to the pillow and back again. Pillows were often repositories for herbal remedies, as she well knew—stuffed with plants which might give uninterrupted sleep, or surcease from headache or tooth pain. She bent and sniffed the pillow Ssssaaa had indicated.

Yes, more than soft feathers stuffed this. And the herb she could locate was surely an odd one to find here and now.

It was not, as she knew it, a noxious or dangerous substance. In fact, a very carefully distilled liquid drawn from it could be given to fretful and feverish children to good purpose. Only, she was certain the High Lady had never asked for such from Halwice, or she herself would have been so advised.

Willadene brought the pillow into the open and inspected it closely. Beneath its finely embroidered cover it was plainly stuffed with feathers near as soft as down. It took her only a moment to find that one edge had been recently whipped together. With her belt knife she cut enough of those lately added stitches to be able to work her hand into the soft lump, but Ssssaaa was before her and the black head emerged, several small feathers rakishly adorning the slender muzzle, with a small packet in her mouth.

Willadene reached swiftly for a belt pouch and brought out her sewing box, stitching closed again that opening before she examined the packet. It would never do to be caught in the middle of Mahart's bed taking her pillows to pieces.

She took up that small, soft roll so uncovered. It was about the size and shape of her forefinger. The material of its making was common white linen but that had been patterned with faint tracing as if from a pen denied a full carriage of ink. Yet, as she weighed it in her hand and drew several breaths to identify its contents, she could find nothing of the faint nastiness which she had been sure she would scent. Pure herbs only. Still this was for Halwice's judgment, not hers. One thing she did know, though her talent and Ssssaaa had picked up no evil here, she did not intend to leave her own bag of remedies in the wardrobe—to perhaps be tainted. How easy it would be to introduce some one of half a dozen ingredients—and Halwice undoubtedly knew more than a dozen or so more—into a cream already seen and accepted by the High Lady. There were things which would sear the skin, or worse—cause even death!

Ssssaaa had left the bed in one of those arching leaps, one long enough to deposit her coil of body on the still-covered bench of the dressing table. She burrowed under the second wide cloth which had been draped there to completely cover the mirror and the counter below that. Willadene swung from the bed to follow and dared to pull away the covering.

There was an array of splendid bottles and jars, all fashioned as if to further display the treasured scents within. She recognized having seen the equivalent of several in the shop. In fact, it was most of those which had come to a crushed end under the boots of the intruders. The special rose bottle was not there. In a place of prominence, where such might have stood, was a flagon fashioned in the form of tight-bundled ferns.

Fern fragrance arose from it. That was aspen from the north forests, worth far more than its weight in gold pieces were its principal ingredient to be measured in some delicate set of scales. As far as Willadene was aware, Halwice had not had any of that for almost a season—since the territory from which it came was today insolently patrolled by outlaws. Perhaps now that Prince Lorien had put down the Wolf they might be given a chance to secure such a rarity again.

She carefully lifted the small bottle. It was stopper full and by the power of her nose, fresh. Turning it slowly around, the girl hunted for some identifying mark. There it was, staring at her boldly—the cipher of the High Lady Saylana. A birthday gift? Doubtless, but a very costly one indeed and one Mahart had not seen fit to open yet. Willadene set the bottle back in the same place from which she had taken it.

Ssssaaa reared, lifting nose toward the bottle. When she hissed Willadene stared at it again. It had only the appearance of a precious and beautiful treasure; she could scent nothing about it save the fern odor. Now she was truly disturbed. She had come to believe so strongly in her talent that perhaps she had become overconfident. This might be a puzzle only such as Halwice could unravel.

Yet she dared not take it with her. It was too noticeable among the other jars and bottles and might be instantly missed. To make any explanation was to negate the plan of which she was now a part.

Reluctantly she shook her head at the flagon. It would seem that Vazul's creature had also lost interest in it now, for the lithe black form made one of those sudden flying leaps to the floor. Though she headed toward the nearest wall she did not seem interested in that barrier itself, but rather, with another soaring leap, caught at the end of a curtain and wriggled up to the open window there.

Before Willadene could move she slipped through that window and by the time the girl managed to reach the spot and collect a footstool to stand on for a good view, Ssssaaa had completely disappeared.

Only a rustling drew Willadene's attention to the point that she leaned far enough across the sill to see what might be below. Though she had not seen such covering on any of the other walls, outside she found here an upgrowth of vine which she recognized for a particularly hardy and thick-stemmed ivy, one which, despite winter winds, kept tassels of green here and there all year round. There were mats of dead and dried leaves also, and it was through these Ssssaaa had plowed to a point on the left, from which the creature made another spectacular leap to a jut of roof below.

Willadene had not the least chance of summoning her back. In fact, the sooner she removed her bag of simples from the wardrobes and got out of the High Lady's bed-chamber the better. That Julta or the workmen had not yet returned was as much good fortune as she could expect in one day.

With the strap of her bag over her shoulder Willadene

made a quiet exit, peering through a small crack of the door before she ventured out. Since she had not been summoned by the High Lady, only told to follow Julta to her assigned quarters, she might have a breathing space there.

There had been folded coverings left on the edge of the second narrow bed of the room above, so she made it up for sleeping and then shook out and laid aside the second livery dress and underclothing Halwice had provided.

Ssssaaa undoubtedly knew the castle far better than perhaps most now living there. Willadene had a suspicion that she might go roving on missions for the Chancellor, though how could the creature communicate with Vazul?

It must have been that her abrupt departure had signified that she had learned what she had been sent to discover and was on her way with the news. Now what had they supposedly discovered? Willadene sat down on the cot and somehow the small shrine to the Star caught her eye. But instead of feeling that renewal of spirit which such sighting had always brought before, she instead was whirled back for an instant of sickening vertigo to that underpassage and the door from which the scent of evil had issued so strongly.

She had heard enough to realize that the Duke was not secure in his rule—but what force threatened him? There had been gossip in the town about the rights of the High Lady Saylana, and there was the fact that she had produced a son—though certainly Barbric in power would mean no good to Kronen.

The thick edge of the old book she had brought with her dug into her side as she leaned against her bag. Reminded of the find Ssssaaa had made, Willadene brought out of hiding the very thin old leaves. They *were* old, of that she was sure, but their edges were not a-crumble as had been other pages of the book; rather they seemed of some very tough skin even time could not attack.

Skin—she ran her finger across their surfaces with the utmost care. This was a far different texture from any parchment she had ever handled. She slipped along the side of the cot until she was in the full light of the window and held up into the strongest bar of that light one of the two narrow strips.

No, she had not been mistaken—not parchment! What she saw marked there was a faint veining such as might appear on a leaf. But no leaf could so withstand time!

Under this strong light she could see that the markings on it for the most part followed that veining. It was certainly no recipe, for even the most ancient of lore users followed patterns which formed symbols or words. The lines on both these pieces seemed to wriggle and scrawl, as if someone had been idly amusing him or herself with brush or pen, to no true purpose. Halwice must see these, of course, but Willadene could not seek out the Herbmistress again in so short a time without raising questions.

She made again a most careful packet of her find and was stowing it away in her bodice when Julta came in without the formality of any knock, though she must be sure Willadene was there for she said at once: "Her Grace would have you bring your wares. The High Lady Saylana is asking concerning them. Oh—there is your bag? But it was in the wardrobe—" Julta was frowning.

"Many of the bottles are easily broken. On second thought I decided it was better to my hand while workmen were busy there," Willadene answered.

The maid nodded. "Not that those have any care for hand cream—but sometimes such are curious, to be sure. And your mistress's wares are all known to be worth a goodly number of silver pieces. Bring them now—but—" She stood with her fists on her hips, confronting the girl as if daring her to deny what she was about to say.

"What you have is for Her Grace, that was the understanding. The High Lady Saylana can be most pressing when she desires something."

"Of course what is here"—Willadene shouldered her

bag—"is for Her Grace, the High Lady Mahart. It was selected with her in mind by my mistress herself."

She need only hold to that. An apprentice obeyed first the orders of the guild member she was sworn to serve. And she hardly thought that the High Lady Saylana would go against all custom as to try to take for herself some of that Willadene carried.

Julta brought her back once more to that chamber where she had first met Mahart. But now the room seemed crowded to the extent of an audience hall. A second chair of presence flanked the one in which Mahart sat, somewhat stiff of back. Though her face was calm, her eyelids drooped a little as if she would rather not see most of the company around her. The floor was so covered with stools and the cushions for those of lower rank (crowded even back against the wall) that Willadene thought that threading a way through this company without nudging inadvertently some lady or treading on a widespread skirt might be something of an exercise in agility.

However, it was the woman in the second chair who seemed to dominate the whole assembly, just as her brightly dressed and exquisitely turned-out ladies put Mahart's retinue so far in the shade they almost seemed to cease to exist.

She was tall even when sitting and might, Willadene thought at her first sighting, be impressive even without the robes and jewels, the brilliance of which was shared by her ladies. Her hair was dark and braided in a coronet about her proudly held head as if it were a separate crown as, for the many jeweled pins set in it, it might well have been.

In contrast to that dark hair her face was like a well-carved mask of ivory, showing color only at the curve of her full lips. And above her eyes her brows slanted slightly upward toward the temples, a device Willadene believed not to be nature's own work. Her eyes themselves were

almond shaped and she had made excellent use of every
art to give them a suggestion of mystery.

The scent she had chosen was not obtrusive—but Willadene recognized it immediately for what it was, an insidi-
ous charm to arouse the senses. Just as her dress, which
was not in itself too revealing, still made plain that no
feminine curve would be missed by the beholder.

The dress was an odd shade of gray, yet on the seams
and curves it seemed shot now and then with glints of
dark red. A wide collar of rubies, surely more intended
for the ballroom than everyday wear, was clasped about
her slender throat. Age had certainly treated her well—
aided, Willadene was sure, by many of the secrets her
own mistress knew—so that it hardly seemed possible she
had mothered that lout who had invaded the shop.

Saylana was playing with a fan, snapping it open and
shut as Willadene advanced in answer to Mahart's wave,
as if she really had no interest in the apprentice, only what
she brought with her. But Willadene had already caught
it—not as sickeningly heavy as it had been earlier today—
but rather coming faintly, like the taint she had sniffed
about Jonas. It was as if each of them—High Lady and
workman—had brushed against something dark and carried its stain with them.

Once more Willadene went through her pack, bringing out each offering to display it clearly, even as she had for Mahart. The High Lady Saylana showed the slightest hint of an amused smile, as if viewing the posturing of children in some simple play of their own devising—though Willadene heard the rustling skirts of her ladies as each product was brought forth and its virtues extolled. Saylana made no attempt to reach for any of the various potions, and her own personal musky scent was so strong that it blanked out many of the lighter, springlike fragrances Halwice had chosen for Mahart.

"Truly a fine display." Her fan waved back and forth languidly as if she would drive the rival scents from her own vicinity. "You should quite outshine the fairest of the fair, dear child, if it all works as is promised."

Willadene did not miss the flush on Mahart's face. There lurked a bite beneath those words, a suggestion that no means could be used to turn the Duke's daughter into a fabulous beauty.

"I am well pleased," she returned quietly. "All the Herbmistress has sent me for years has been of the best; surely these also will serve their turn. As for being fairest of the fair, dear cousin, you undervalue yourself—look in any mirror and assure yourself of that.''

Saylana smiled more widely. ''Child, you are so new to social wiles and strategies. One does not share the secrets of the dressing table. However, you may be well assured that His Highness will make sure that one of his blood shines. It is a pity''—she closed her fan with a snap—''that the ancient tales we heard as children hold no truth. Then one might bargain with greater powers for what we need the most when we need it.

''Girl.'' Her attention passed from Mahart to Willadene. ''Since you appear to be added temporarily to the service of the High Lady, be sure you give her of your best.''

Willadene hoped that no change or start had given her away to those all-seeing eyes. For with those last words, as if Saylana had somehow released it by will or unknowingly, Willadene had caught a flick of odor laid in her direction like the lash of a whip—the taint—faint, yet not to be mistaken.

''Our thanks to you, cousin.'' Saylana had swung back to Mahart. ''Perhaps when this present round of rejoicing is past Halwice will share some of these with others.''

She was on her feet, a signal all her ladies seemed to have been alert to catch, for they too were standing and then sinking into curtseys.

''It has been a favor on your part, my dear,'' Saylana continued, ''to satisfy my curiosity so, since this apprentice takes her oaths so seriously and would not afford me some moments of her time. But then she is new to this estate and does not properly understand castle manners. Anyway, may she do her best for you—''

''She will!'' There was a sharp sweep as if by a blade in those words. ''And I am pleased that you are pleased, Saylana, since you are well-known to be a mistress of all formal ceremony and courtly ritual.''

But Mahart stood her ground and did not usher the older woman to the door. In the castle now her standing was supreme and it was clear, Willadene was sure, that she intended to make that universally known.

When Saylana and her billowing of ladies had gone Mahart was frowning. With a wave of her hand she dismissed in turn the two of her retinue who seemed to have won little of her favor, but out of the shadows behind her chair came Zuta.

Dressed in one of her favorite shades of yellow the girl could have perhaps even matched Saylana in vibrant and obvious sensual beauty—very different from the cool and more subtle attraction of Mahart.

"Your Grace, she is angry—"

Mahart suddenly grinned like one less than half her years. "When has she not been every time she is in my company? The very sight of me is like wine turned bitter in her mouth. So"—now she looked to Willadene—"she tried to reach you since your coming here?"

Quickly Willadene spoke of the footman. But she did not add that she believed he had spied upon her until she had indeed reached the Lord Chancellor's suite.

Mahart nodded. "So straightway she came hither. Apprentice, what has she to fear among your potions and fragrances?"

"Your Grace, I cannot tell you—if she does fear. For all I have brought with me was of Halwice's own compounding and she does not deal in things of the Dark."

"Saylana is a great beauty," the Lady Zuta cut in. "She scorns you as far less so than herself, Your Grace."

Mahart grinned again. "When one fights one does not always use the tactics and weapons already known to one's enemy. I know full well that the High Lady has every intention of enticing the interest of the Prince. And she has the outward appearance to do so—"

Zuta looked puzzled. "But—"

"Listen here." Mahart seemed to have forgotten Willadene's presence as she began to talk swiftly, as if in fear she might be interrupted before she reached the major points of what she would say.

"The Lord Chancellor has an expert corps of eyes and ears, and at least one of them has spent useful hours at King Hawkner's court. This Prince Lorien is not a womanizer. Oh, he has been in a strange bed or two upon occasion after the way of his sex—but he holds apart from the revels of the court.

"His interest is the training field, or with the hunts, or even trying feats of daring such as climbing Mount Grog, as he did two years past, standing where no man in history had set foot before. He has tamed tree cats and holds one with him at times, even as Vazul holds that Ssssaaa of his. Also he has sent a farhawk aloft in hunting. Most wolf packs he has run down in the north forests so that borderers no longer fear their slinking.

"What makes his heart beat the quicker is a newly forged blade, a fine mount from his private stud. To such a man a woman is a convenience—or sometimes a nuisance. However, there is one way his interests can be caught even by a woman who cannot compete with horse, hound, and sword. It is said that he is one who listens to the bards—especially tales of lost treasure, of strange monsters, and the like. Those carrying such tales are welcome within his hall and questioned most straightly concerning the source of their ballads."

Zuta now appeared completely bewildered. "But why?"

Mahart laughed openly. "Because, I think, in his way he is a dreamer, not one who plucks ripe fruit ready to drop into his outstretched hand, but rather one willing to climb to the frail top branches of the tree for that which remains out of reach. Therefore—to give him what he wishes much—a dream—something so founded in fable that it is well-known but still a dream past present redemption."

"Heart-Hold!" Willadene said without thinking. Mahart

looked at her in surprise. Then the High Lady nodded emphatically. "Heart-Hold."

"But I do not see how that old tale will serve your purpose, Your Grace," protested Zuta.

"Nor am I quite sure how it will—just yet. But we shall see what we shall see, when the time comes."

Time did move, whether to their purpose or its own Willadene could not guess. She had no message from either Halwice or the Lord Chancellor, but she was sure that Ssssaaa had made a safe return and reported after her own fashion. In the meantime she was busied for several hours each day, along with the head seamstress of the castle and the master goldsmith, Mahart serving as final judge of their labors—though Willadene became very aware that the High Lady disliked overelaborate robes and most of the masses of jewels which were urged on her. The high point of all their efforts was to be, of course, her dress for the victory ball where she was to graciously crown Lorien with the victor's circlet of the Star and, if fate were willing, at the same time to center his attention, even if fleeting, for the moment on herself.

On the fifth day they arrayed her, dressed her hair, and lightly creamed her face, so that she might stand with her father at the wide gate of the castle to welcome the young victor.

The whole of Kronengred was in a frenzy, with hourly and then half hourly messengers arriving with news of the advance. By now the High Lady's birthday fête faded into a shadow compared with this.

It was very early on that morning that Mahart had sat up in bed. She had rubbed her eyes and then shivered. No dream of flower-strewn pastures last night—though she had insisted on going to bed early for a rest against the ordeal to come.

Even though she had learned much during these past

months since her father had dragged her out into the world, she still was uncertain. Oh, she had talked confidently before Zuta. However, save for the fact that she had had a private interview with the First Bard, she had really not been able to build up more than the most nebulous of plans. All she might be sure of was that she would play no coy feminine tricks with Lorien. Beyond that she could only follow his lead.

Vazul had visited her once after his "recovery" from the mysterious ague, bringing with him that same wounded young man she had seen in the upper Tower room. In the light of day and in improved health he looked much younger, but there was no lack of self-assurance in him. It was he who had taken over the near whole of that conversation at Vazul's orders, and what he had discussed had been Prince Lorien.

The Lord Chancellor had earlier given her the few details she had rattled off to Zuta and the herb apprentice. Now she heard in depth a character analysis which she would not have believed could be delivered by one man concerning another unless they had been cradlemates or sworn brothers.

This Nicolas weighed each trait Lorien could possibly have revealed and did it so well Mahart sometimes felt she was there at the scene he described. It was plain that the Prince found martial exercise and hunting the major actions to fill his present life. Lorien had not followed the common court custom of having an official mistress; in fact, he had been heard over and over again to dismiss females as clucking hens better avoided.

However, even as Mahart herself had done, he had taken a liking to the ancient legends and tales—first those of battles and titanic heroes, and then more obscure accounts which took on the seeming of quests. Two years earlier he had indeed fought his way up Mount Grog, losing two companions to exhaustion along the way, for no reason he had ever made clear—except there was indeed in his li-

brary an account of an early lord who had dared such
slopes and returned with vast knowledge which aided him
to control the kingdom before his death.

However, Lorien was not reaching for any throne. He
held his three brothers mainly in contempt for their court
life, yet did nothing to belittle the heir. Rather he sought
fellowship with far travelers, mercenaries from overseas,
and now and then, to the surprise of all, an elderly scholar.
Yet he would put down a book and reach for sword hilt
on the instant.

"He is two men," Vazul said as Nicolas paused for
breath. "If he unites them he shall indeed be formidable.
In the meantime, Your Grace, remember what interests
him the most but do not discuss matters you yourself are
not well versed in. Rather lead him to talk and then listen—for a good listener ranks high in any company."

Listen, she reminded herself now in the gray of early
morning. Any speech they would exchange during the occasion to come would doubtless follow the full formula of
court ceremony. And she had no idea when this very
important listening could be arranged.

Then Julta was at her door, behind her the herb apprentice. The maid superintended the setting up of the big
screen and the establishment of the bath behind it. Afterward, as Willadene moved toward the array of cosmetic
soaps and the like Mahart spoke on impulse.

"I have never tried the fern lotion. It is so rare that
perhaps it is best for this occasion."

Willadene picked up the fern-leaf–shaped bottle and instinctively held it to her nose. The scent was certainly
right and she knew that no one else—unless it be Saylana—would be wearing it today. She nodded and held it
out to Julta.

That enticing odor clung to both Mahart's skin and the
hair Julta dried, first with a series of towels, and then
combed until dampness was only a faint trace.

"Nothing else, I think," Mahart said when they were

done and she sat in lacy chemise and petticoat to eat the breakfast which had been delivered to her chamber. This was one morning she would not have to face her father in the dining hall.

"Yes, Your Grace," Willadene agreed. The scent clung to her own hands. "Save some cream beneath the eyes— let them seem the more lustrous—"

Mahart laughed and licked a drop of honey from her lower lip. "Oh, yes, trump me up as fine as Saylana— except I am not her. Keep that in mind." She looked more sober now.

It was many turns of the timing glass later that Willadene was free from that room where the rustle of fine fabrics and the many scents of extravagant fragrances made it seem that they were in the midst of a crowd of posturing ladies. Though Saylana did not appear, two of her ladies came to stare and, as Zuta said later, to snoop, their ostensible mission to present Mahart with a lace-bordered kerchief to be fastened to the chatelaine at her belt. And, of course, to present their mistress's best wishes on this joyful occasion.

Mahart's gown was of a dull blue, close to that of the sky of evening. And it did have the advantage of showing not only its wearer's slender form, but, in addition, the clearness of her skin. She had allowed only a touch of the rouge brush, Willadene agreeing heartily with her abstinence, while she chose to allow her hair to be braided as if she were truly younger than her years. However, among her brown plaits had also been woven with care silver chains studded with moonstones, a small tiara and a collar of the same stones providing her jewel display.

Willadene could well believe that the High Lady had deliberately chosen gown color and stones to be in contrast to the usual rich display Saylana seemed to favor. And, looking critically at Mahart, as two of the undermaids under Julta's hawk eyes adjusted the robe of state, she knew that indeed the Duke's daughter had chosen wisely to make her appearance in what might be termed sober garments.

The ladies Famina and Geuverir picked up the far edge of the heavy train, making an odd pair, as they assumed haughty masks and went to play their own parts in the day's pageantry.

Willadene saw to the ordering of the dressing table. The fern scent was certainly a staying one and somehow, during these past hours when it had been ever in her nose, she had found it less to her liking. But at least it was not of the heavy muskiness the other ladies favored.

She had already made her own plans for the morning. There was no hope, of course, of gaining any good vantage place below from which to watch the arrival of the young conqueror. But the day before she had marked a tower window from which, standing on a stool and leaning well forward, she could at least get a bird's-eye view of the ceremonious meeting before the castle gateway.

Now she slipped quickly along, hoping that no one else might have had the same thought, to find her favored lookout. It was necessary, she discovered, that she lean well out to view the swirling mob of colorfully dressed commoners, and she gave a start as the trumpeters used their instruments with full force—only to feel a hand behind her seize her girdle.

"Easy does it, mistress—" She did not need that voice to identify who stood behind her. As usual her nose supplied the proper name, though she glanced around at him.

On impulse she said, "The footing is wide enough for two, Master Nicolas." Though why she suddenly felt so at ease with him she could not explain, even to herself.

"Wise woman." He chuckled and then was up beside her. To her eyes he moved lithely, and she wondered at his speed in recovering from the wound which she had seen in all its depth and width as she had helped to dress it. There was, she decided, a certain pallor under his tanned skin but otherwise she could see no trace of ill about him.

He was up beside her now, but he had not removed his hold on her girdle and somehow she did not resent his touch, knowing it for no gesture of familiarity but meant to steady her in place.

" 'The Prince cometh—' " he quoted from the beginning of an old ballad. Indeed, the crowd had parted, or were swept back by the Duke's guards, to allow an open way for a man on horseback, followed with a parade-ground stride by a number of men who could never be mistaken for anything else but expertly trained armsmen.

The Prince himself was mail clad but with a brilliantly patterned tabard over that mail. He carried his helm before him on the saddle horn so that his head, with its dark curl of locks, was bare. Willadene could not see much of his face from above, but it was as if her present companion could read her thoughts for he said, "He is comely enough, mistress, truly a prince to win any lady's eye—if not her heart."

There was something in his tone which caught Willadene's attention. "You do not find him as they see him, then?" She gestured toward the wildly cheering crowd below.

"I do not find him," he returned. "No, I shall not tease you with riddle, mistress. It is only that he is not open to any man's reading. In many things he excels—he is such a fighter as perhaps Kronen has not seen for generations; he can induce in those who follow him such a loyalty as has no price."

"Still"—she pushed, reaching behind his words to his tone—"you find him flawed."

Nicolas frowned. His lips shaped an answer she could not hear, so he moved the closer. Now his breath was warm on her cheek and she could catch, through those cheers, "Not flawed, perhaps more unknown. I have seen him, in battle against outlaws; as a representative of the

Duke and from a House of name I have shared field rations at the same fire; we have spoken of old lore. He has a liking for such, which is one of the stranger sides of his character. But I think that the real man is guarded far inside him and no one has yet seen that Lorien.''

''They say the Duke would have him wed with the High Lady.'' But she felt a moment of cold. The court was no place for openness (in fact, now a very fleeting thought of the strangeness of Nicolas's sudden frankness with her also struck), but the Mahart she had come to know deserved much better than a man who guarded his inner self past all knowing.

''Those of high blood do not do their own choosing,'' Nicolas commented. Then, as if he would change the subject quickly, he pointed with his other hand to a splash of rainbow colors to the rear and the right of the Duke, now advancing (giving his usual impression of being encased in someone else's finery) with Mahart a dutiful two steps behind him.

''There,'' Nicolas continued with no note of any deep respect for his rightful ruler's retinue, ''stands the so-called 'glory' of our court—Lord Barbric and his companions. Note their mail, their swords!'' He was openly scornful. ''We would have rid ourselves of the Wolf and his kind long since and not had to wait for an over-border fighter to do it, had those slink hounds been of the old Duke's like. They have their own ways of fighting and it is never clean.''

Willadene remembered that morning in the shop—the smashed glass on the floor—the threats openly made.

''The Duke is the Duke,'' she said slowly. ''And also Chancellor Vazul is no weak-willed man.''

''One cannot build a fortress on sand with shifts underfoot, ready to swallow its stones,'' he said wearily. ''You know—did not Ssssaaa report—that there is a growing rot within here?'' He struck the stone ledge with his palm. ''Your mistress thinks it something such as has not struck before. Perhaps the plague itself left some foul seed to sprout in later times. Have you heard talk of an old nurse of the High Lady Saylana who is given lodging and care by her solicitous mistress?''

Willadene shook her head. ''Julta does not gossip, but the Lady Zuta continually brings news to the High Lady. She has never mentioned such.''

''The Lady Zuta.'' He repeated the name. ''Now look you—see that young sprig in violet blue, third to the right of Barbric?''

With some effort Willadene was able to place him. She was far more intent on what Nicolas had to say now than she was in the protracted ceremony in progress below.

''He is Lord Hulfric—note the name—it possesses the ducal ending. But he is very, very far removed from any hope of possession. Lately he has shown some interest in your Lady Zuta during her toing and froing in search of gossip. He is certainly a drinking comrade to Barbric upon occasions and yet not to the fore of that lord's companions. Watch Zuta if you can, mistress. Ah—Lorien is officially welcomed. I trust all the guardians of protocol are relieved that all went so well.''

He was pushing back from the ledge when Willadene put out her hand and caught at his sleeve. ''You hint much but say nothing clearly,'' she said soberly. ''Just why did you seek me out?''

''Mistress, you are among our High Lady's close companions for now. And I remember a night when I saw you defeat something which should have had no existence in any sane world. There are very few under this roof who can be truly trusted, and I think that you can be counted among that number. Watch your mistress—the Duke's plans are known, and opposition to them simmers. We must be prepared if it comes to a boil.''

His eyes were like steel points again as his gaze met hers. These skulking night games were his—yet Halwice trusted him and Willadene would trust the Herbmistress to the death.

She nodded, and then he slipped away and was gone, almost as if he were able to vanish into the wall. For a second or two she felt very much alone.

There would be the state banquet now before Mahart would return to her quarters to start the lengthy preparations for the ball this night. That the High Lady must accomplish two such ceremonial occasions in one day and then look forward to a night on display made Willadene very glad that fate had not called her to such a destiny.

Mahart stretched out on her bed and resolutely closed her eyes. Her feet ached, her back ached, and she felt that she had aged a lifetime since this morning. Also, she *never* wanted that fern scent around her again! At least they had to agree that she be allowed an interval between that never-ending smiling, listening (though she certainly had heard nothing but formal platitudes from the Prince during that interminable meal) to refresh herself—if such a thing were possible—before she need once more appear in full glory at the ball.

However, she longed for the right to just go to sleep— with Halwice's wonder incense beside her—to wake in that place of fields and flowers. She turned her head back and forth on the pillows now, trying to find a comfortable resting place. At least her hair had been freed of its banding with all the eyelike milky stones which they had strung upon her.

Only—there was the Prince. Did anyone ever call him just Lorien? she wondered. He smiled, yes, but never with his eyes. He spoke, but only the set, correct comments with a compliment which she was sure he did not mean thrown in now and then.

He was handsome, yes, and his warrior trappings distinguished him in an interesting way from the fops of the court. Though she had been seated next to him at the high table—Saylana at least three spaces away—he had been far more attentive to her father's halting bursts of speech, delivered as if the Duke were finding it difficult to remember he *must* carry on a conversation.

There had been a number of questions from her father about the attack on the Wolf's stronghold, of course. But it seemed to her that the Prince answered those in the most general fashion, not enlarging on any aspect of the engagement. He had admitted that they had taken some prisoners who had been duly turned over to his host's guard several days earlier, and that statement had appeared to render her father more than usually thoughtful.

Vazul had been duly presented to the Prince but then had kept his distance, not appearing at her father's shoulder like a bulwark as well as a dispenser of advice. However, Mahart did not doubt that the Lord Chancellor and the Duke had rehearsed many of the questions her father asked now.

Since she could add nothing to such a conversation on swords and deeds, she had indeed been reduced to listening. But after a while she detected a kind of pattern in her father's questions. While he outwardly was rejoicing over the downfall and erasure of the Wolf, he appeared also to be unduly interested in any men taken in close company with that outlaw—though he made no direct demand concerning them.

At length, it had all been over. She had found the rich food little to her taste and the company frustrating. Only one fact had struck deeply: the High Lady Saylana had kept a close eye on Lorien—or perhaps on the two of them. But, youthful as arts might make her appear, Saylana was far too old for the Prince—or was she?

Stranger matches had been made in the past. If a lord, to further some scheme, married a green girl near young enough to be his granddaughter—could not a lady with all the practiced allure of Saylana be able to attract this prince—notably not attached elsewhere? And what a blow that would be for the Duke—to have his tortuous plan go so awry—that his sworn enemy attract the very ally he had hoped to net!

Mahart dug her fingers into the softer coverlet. She had sent them all from her—Zuta, Julta, the Herbmistress's girl. But her period of freedom would be short. The ball—did her father actually believe that she could in any manner be a rival for Saylana should that High Lady set her snares?

Who was *she*? The Duke's daughter, yes, past seventeen years of age, until recently kept as if in slumber as far as the world was concerned. She knew nothing of the games within games which the courtiers played. And to her they seemed a stupid waste of time for the most part. In the old books things proceeded in a much more exciting fashion. High Ladies often even took up swords and fought battles for their rights. She thought of herself confronting Prince Loren with a sword and suddenly giggled.

No, she was Mahart and as Mahart she was determined to do the best she could for—herself! Let Prince Lorien caper his way about the ballroom (though she could not imagine his stiff figure performing any kind of a caper); she would watch and, as they had bade her, listen.

Pulling the coverlet tighter about her shoulders she finally drifted away as the aches of her body eased and no plans stirred to keep her from slumber.

Green—not the fields of her longing but giant ferns, curling tips well above her head. Around her was a green gloom, and a humid wind pressed against her, though she was sure that in this place her real body did not exist.

What did exist was a force which drew her past any will or ability to stem, and it seemed the farther she was into this murky gloom the thicker was this growth, as if the giant plants around her were attempting to pull her into fragments, absorb her into their own lush growth.

Mahart had known nightmares in her life. When she was younger shadows had come to grisly life and pursued her down dark corridors. However—this had a difference, a kind of reality which left her stiff with fear.

For a moment the ferns before her either parted or faded into nothingness and she could see a face. Old—old with such a map of wrinkles that even mouth and eyes seemed overborne by their depths. But the sparks of eyes—the malignity in them was like a physical blow.

Behind this monster wrought by the changes of great age there was another—but only a column of mist—though she noted that it had a darker core. But it was those evil eyes which held her nettled. Two claw hands, wrapped by twisted and gnarled bone, arose—pointed—

"Your Grace!" It came like a shout and the fern forest was snapped into nothingness by its force—with it that which had confronted Mahart there.

She opened her eyes to find that she was sitting up in bed, panting as if she had raced through corridors the prey of some fear.

Zuta's hand was on her shoulder and Julta stood at the foot of the bed, the herb girl with her. They were watching her wide-eyed, and the herb girl was holding out an amulet in her hand.

"You—you are all right, Your Grace?" Zuta asked.

Mahart's heart was returning to its proper rate of beat and she drew a deep breath. "It was a dream!" She said that defiantly, as one who refused to be caught by any night-born fancy.

16   "You are overtired, Your Grace."
Zuta gently pushed Mahart back on
the pillows. "Herb girl, have you no restorative? Her
Grace has but a short time now before the ball begins."

Willadene made for her herb bag. Yes, no one was
immune to nightmares, but the High Lady seemed to have
met with one deeper than usual terrorizing level. The smell
of fern was very strong. It was lingering unlike any fragrance she had had contact with before, and she wished
strongly for Halwice. For she was plagued by the belief
that whatever talent she might indeed have was being overshadowed now by something else. Yet there was no betraying evil stench she could pick up.

Mahart seemed to agree with her, for when Willadene
returned with a small cup of honey-flavored liquid, the
High Lady was already out of bed and seated before a
small table on which was a tray with a light meal.

There was another dinner to be served this night, but
only for the male members of the court. The ladies were
too intent upon necessary hours of primping to waste
time so.

Mahart was running her fingers through her loosened
hair.

"Willadene"—she addressed the other's name as she might one close admitted to her company. "Is there any way this fern smell can be lost? I find that it now is near stifling at times. If I bathe again—is there another way of overlaying this scent or at least aborting it?"

"It can be tried, Your Grace." Willadene was attempting to call to the fore of memory what Halwice might suggest for such a service. Though usually any smell to be banished was an unpleasant one, and she had no sure belief that *that* procedure could work. It was only because she herself found the scent so oppressive that she could really understand Mahart's desire to rid herself of it.

Bathing, yes, with certain nullifying crystals added to the water. But they did not have much time. At Mahart's orders Willadene took over and set about seeing once again to an even more elaborate program than they had earlier followed this day.

However, the fern smell did fade when Willadene saw to a strong use of orangeflower water for both bath and to rinse the hair. It was a simple scent, but she had added to it with a reckless hand some spices from overseas. The results were certainly not those usually sought by ladies bound for an evening of pleasure, but when they had done Mahart caught Willadene's hand and squeezed it.

"I may smell a little like a midwinter feast pudding"— she laughed, the shade which had been on her face when she had awakened gone—"but is there not an old saying that the way to interest a man is to attract his desire for food? I hope the Prince has a liking for mince tarts!"

"Your Grace—are you sure— Perhaps there is some other remedy. What could be, herb maid?" Zuta was frowning as Julta saw Mahart into the fine underlinen which clung to her body. This had been carefully taken from a wardrobe fortunately not opened earlier, and they had all agreed none of the fern fragrance clung to it.

The dress she was laced into was far more elaborate than she would have chosen, but it was of her father's ordering. Willadene had sprayed it well with orangeflower essence. In color it was not, Willadene thought, really becoming to Mahart.

The High Lady looked her best in cool, delicate shades. And this robe was stiff, golden brocade which tended to conceal the slender, youthful lines of her body and made her look almost clumsy.

Because Mahart's hair was still somewhat damp they towered it under a net headdress so beset with gems as to belittle her delicate features and make her hair more resemble some unfortunate dowager's wig.

At least, since she was to lead the dancing—with the Prince of course—she need not suffer in addition the weight of cape train and her skirts did not sweep the floor.

"Faugh!" Mahart stood before the long mirror Julta tilted to a proper angle. "I look like a fête doll. Saylana will, I think, be properly pleased." However, she did not appear to find that of any great importance.

The great hall, which had been cleared for the occasion, was three stories high, and two of the balconies above were packed with such of the major servants who were not on active service so allowed to watch the pageant below. Behind their carefully preserved lines there was a shoving lot of lesser rank. Willadene had hoped to see Halwice somewhere—knowing that the plain robe her mistress favored would be more conspicuous amid all the finery about than it usually was. But there was no sign of her.

Her own clothing and hair held some of the strong scent Mahart had demanded her ladies to use and she noted that those on either side of her withdrew a little whenever she moved as if they found close company oppressive. However, Julta was with her and the maid had fared no better from their efforts.

Below on the first of the balconies were stationed the musicians. Since the Duke had small liking for music, those who had served his predecessor had to be hunted up again and quickly rehearsed—to what result they would soon see.

On the dais at the north end of the long hall the Duke had already taken his seat, as if by being to the fore he could somehow speed up the procedure.

Mahart was already making her way up to the second highseat a step below her father's, and close behind her came the Lady Saylana, her sea-green robe patterned with a webbing of silver in which were caught pearls, while such jewels lay in costly loops across her white shoulders, quite openly revealed, and aided in lacing her bodice and as well were threaded through her hair, giving stability to a miniature tiara which bore a far too startling resemblance to the Duke's coronet.

Beside the Duke's throne stood a squire of the body resplendent in a ceremonial tabard bearing Uttobric's arms and holding with care a cushion on which lay a circlet of silver so tipped and inset with diamonds that it appeared to outflash nearly all other surrounding jewels.

There was a fresh blast of trumpets, even more ear torturing here within the confines of the hall than they had been in the open. The throng of courtiers standing below the dais quickly parted, rippling as all bowed or curtseyed to the solitary figure on whom centered all eyes.

This time the Prince did not come in gear of war but rather, much in contrast to the other men there gathered, he wore breeches of a gray which was near black. A tunic of the same drab color was, however, near hidden by a tabard worked in such a splendor of metallic threads and gems as to nearly blind the eyes of those who watched him advance at a steady tread.

The Duke twisted in his chair. Vazul had stepped forward to announce the Prince. Willadene was too far away to really distinguish the expression on the faces of any below, but she had the feeling that the Duke's hatred for display was working on him, as, with a jerk of his hand, he summoned the squire into position beside his daughter.

Mahart could see faces, but she wondered more about the thoughts behind them. She had heard her father sneeze twice and could well believe that he had waiting for her later a blast of anger for the spices which certainly clung jealously to her.

Saylana was as blandly smiling as ever. But that smile was certainly now centered on the Prince, and Mahart herself viewed him as Vazul droned on concerning the mighty victory and the debt that Kronen owed this over-the-border stranger.

Without his mail trappings Lorien did not seem as difficult to assess as he had been at the banquet. Only the brilliance of his tabard somehow made the man fade a little—he also could be one wearing, a little awkwardly, borrowed robes.

"Kronen has known many heroes"—that was her father. "It is our greatest privilege at this hour to welcome a new one to those ranks—to the fore of those ranks! That one who is not bred of our land has yet cleared it of a growing evil is certainly an act designed by the mercy of the Star. And it is the Star's own gift which is now offered him."

On the cue she had been waiting for, Mahart got to her feet and with both hands lifted the glittering circlet which the squire held ready. Lorien would not kneel, of course, since he owed no liege service here. But he did stand on the lower step of the dais, making it easier to settle the coronet on the head he bent slightly in her direction.

Now, her flesh was tingling, since *she* was the one to give honor there would be no flourish of sword but another and far more personal part of the ceremony. The stiffness of her sleeves seemed to bind her arms as she lifted her hands so that they closed on Lorien's gem-collared shoulders. Leaning forward (he might help her a little, she

thought with rising irritation) she managed to give the kiss
of honor, her lips barely brushing his cheek.

He smiled, but it was but a form to suit the occasion,
she was sure, as she drew back. Did his nose seem to
twitch? Perhaps the spices wore on him even as they did
on her father.

But the Prince was holding out his arm and her father
had already signaled the musicians above. She set her fingertips with the proper lightness of touch, allowing him
to lead her down to the floor and into the stately march
about the space left clear for dancing, which was the
proper beginning of the ball.

To Willadene above, that march was a rainbow round
of color upon color. But her attention was mainly upon
the High Lady and the Prince. How did it feel to meet so
with one with whom one was to share all the favors and
ills of life?

At least he was young and well looking, and his men
were bonded to him. But did a conquering hero make a
good husband? Perhaps only High Lady Saylana could
answer that in truth, and certainly rumor had stalled over
the many whispers of how she and her late lord conducted
their private moments together.

The stir of lesser servants behind Willadene pressed forward, and Julta spat a warning as she was jostled. Already
the grand march had drawn to an end and the dancing was
to begin. Lorien dutifully led Mahart to form the first
square, bowing as deeply as she curtsied in return.

Perhaps swordplay in excess, Mahart decided, had
something to give a man in the nature of grace in dance.
Lorien did not caper as she had half expected, awkward
since he was so rumored to avoid such occasions at his
father's court.

And he continued to show a pleasant face, keeping his
attention on his partner in a very complimentary fashion.
She found that their patterned steps appeared to fit in a
fashion she had never experienced before with any lordling

in a duty dance, and she was both surprised and a little disappointed when the music ceased and their waving chain of dancers came to a halt.

Once more, her fingertips on his wrist, he led her back to the dais where another chair had appeared without undue stir, placed beside her own. She flushed a little at that blatant hint that Lorien was to be considered her property. Still he showed no surprise. Had they already been arranging her future—Lorien, her father, and Vazul? A spark of anger as strong as her spices flared up at that thought.

Somewhat frantically she tried to frame a sentence which might lead to conversation, but their worlds seemed suddenly so far apart that she could think of nothing, which added to her frustration. The more so when she saw the very confident and compelling stare Saylana had turned on her taciturn companion. Of course, since the Duke did not dance, it was now up to Lorien to lead out the second lady of the kingdom. And, as the musicians struck up again, he arose, bowed to Mahart, and went to Saylana, whose smile had all the heat of a midsummer day.

Saylana had no trouble in finding some subject of conversation, Mahart noted as she watched the two meet and part as dictated by the courtly dance. And plainly Lorien was paying attention to *her*. Twice he smiled broadly and once he even laughed. Yes, this was a game Saylana knew well how to play.

Mahart was suddenly not sure of anything. She had accepted her father's plans for her eventual marriage, as she had accepted all of his other decrees concerning her actions. Somehow in her mind, until this night, any suitor had been but a kind of puppet set up to dance at the bidding of her elders. But Lorien was real in a different way—though her knowledge of men was certainly very narrow, limited mainly to secondhand information received from Zuta. Now she had a fleeting doubt as to whether all she had been told in the way of gossip was indeed united to truth.

Suddenly even this large room seemed overheated, and she wanted to be free of it and all the company around her, allowed quiet to sort out this new jumble of thoughts. Above all she wanted to arm herself so that no action of hers, made in ignorance, would arouse the tittering amusement of those she had long ago guessed had no true liking for her.

Willadene watched the circling, all the bowing and curtseying, the touching of fingertips to fingertips, and decided that certainly a court ball could be a tedious affair—unless one was playing some part of it. She was hungry and she was tired after her exertions to de-scent Mahart. Descent—something new to her experience and one she would greatly like to discuss with Halwice.

Once more she studied the line of upper servants along the front of the balcony. Somehow she had thought that the Herbmistress would certainly be among them. But her dark gown could not be seen among the glitter of house badges and brilliant colors they affected. Even Julta had donned a rust-yellow dress, discarded her apron, and crowned her graying hair with a wisp of beribboned lace in place of her usual tight cap.

A man in the livery coat of a footman had pushed up on the other side of the maid and was talking to her, but the music was an effective cover to conceal his words. Willadene did not recognize his house badge, but that did not mean that he was not indeed an old friend of Julta's. She saw the maid nod and then turn to her—

"There is a feast in the serving hall. My friend Jacham says that table is worth the visiting. Would you go with us?"

Willadene shook her head. She was very sure that such an answer was one Julta wanted, and when the maid swiftly wriggled through the crowd with her escort she was certain—though the thought of food did have some appeal. She need not force her company on the two already preceding her, but she could follow and lose herself in the company of those others who must be headed there.

She had reached the door of that eating place when a whiff of more than roasting meat and pungent sauces caught her attention. There was a burst of giggling not far away and she saw one of the lower maids, her cap hanging by its string on her plump shoulders and her foolish face flushed with what Willadene guessed was already more than a prudent portion of the strong ale.

She was clinging to the arm of one in the dress of an upper groom, grinning up into his face and now and then digging him in the ribs with her free fist. But—

Figis! What was that disreputable townsman doing here? The last time she had seen him Willadene had noted that he certainly no longer presented the appearance of the ragged kitchen lad she had known. Now he was even more dressed like one who had a rightful place in some noble household.

He tickled his companion under her ample chin and then gave her a smacking kiss which the maid appeared to accept as her just due. Now that Willadene could see her closer she recognized her— Hettel was one of the maids assigned to the High Lady's apartments to collect the used linen and see that it was laundered. Usually she was a silent shadow, trained with the rigor of all palace servants. Her freedom of conduct tonight came as a small shock to Willadene, especially the person of her companion. But before she could answer her first impulse and shove through the crowd, to come close enough to perhaps hear what they were saying, a wedge of laughing, singing others had come between and they were gone.

Yet Willadene now found it hard to follow her first plan and reach the table. She did not take time to try to find an open place on the benches—those were all occupied. But she did reach around one footman, who had half collapsed and was humming to himself, to catch up a meat tart and an apple.

There was no sight of Julta, and the girl had little liking for the increasing freedom of manners in progress about her. So, with supplies in hand, she went back to her own tower chamber, substituting water from the pitcher there for any of the mind-clogging ale.

She ate slowly as she tried to solve the problem of Hettel and Figis. How had the latter managed somehow to insert himself into the ranks of the palace servants (which in itself was usually impossible—the servants were the sons and daughters or other kin of those who had gone before them, and seldom if ever was a stranger admitted to their closed circle)?

Even more strange that someone such as Figis had achieved such a rise in status. Willadene needed a chance to relay this information, as trivial as it might turn out to be, to either her mistress or the Lord Chancellor.

Halwice, she was sure, must spend some time in the shop once again and perhaps Willadene could go there on the pretext of restoring supplies. It was the best resolve that she could come to at the moment.

Wearily she undressed and drew on her thin night rail. Luckily her bed was well blanketed, as she had discovered earlier the single panel of glass in their own narrow window could not be entirely closed. The vines which were fast covering the wall about the High Lady's chamber just below had found good holds now on the upper stones as well. She discovered as she looked out into the night that there was indeed a cloudy mass of growth between her and the small balcony of Mahart's chamber.

Her hand sought her amulet, and the familiar feel of that was soothing enough so her eyes closed and she was asleep.

Willadene awoke to utter darkness. The night lamp which was always set to burn through the night had somehow been snuffed out. There was something else, a warm band across her throat, a soft hissing in her ear. While about her—yes—the stench of evil was strong.

"Julta?" she called and was answered from the other bed by a thick snoring. Steadying Ssssaaa against her with a tight hold, Willadene slipped her feet from under the covers and felt with her toes for her slippers.

Now that her eyes had adjusted, she could see that there was the faint oblong of dim glimmer which marked the window. With that as a guide she moved out into the room.

It was easy enough to feel her way along the wall now to the door, though she had one pain-filled encounter with a stool. But the latch did not lift to all her tugging. At last she had to accept the fact that she was locked in by some means she did not understand.

Now she crossed to Julta's bed. The woman had not even undressed but lay as Willadene had never seen her, a sodden lump still clothed and with no coverlet over her.

Drunk—or drugged? In any case the maid would be no help. And she had located the source of that aura of evil now—from under her feet as if it arose from below—from the High Lady's chamber!

Ssssaaa hissed in her ear again, and she realized that the creature was urging her to the window. She shivered in her night rail as she balanced on the stool and looked out.

This was a moonless night, but from the castle below there arose a faint haze as if not all the festive lamps and torches had yet been extinguished. She reached out and caught at what seemed to be the thickest loop of the ivy, pulling at it. It gave for only a small tug and then held. She was so sure now that her only way to reach Mahart's threatened chamber was down that crude ladder and onto the balcony a floor below.

Perhaps it was just as well she had to depend more on her sense of touch than her sight, for Willadene had never had any easiness with heights. Ssssaaa slipped from her, down her arm and into the mass of ivy. Skirts were not

meant for such action. She swept her hands back into the
gloom of the room until she found her bed and rooted out
from beneath her pillow there her girdle. Having clasped
it and its tools for daily use about her waist she used her
table knife to rip up the lower part of the night rail until
she had two strips she could wind about her legs from the
thighs down.

So prepared, she jammed the window open to its fur-
thest extent and somehow forced herself out, clinging desperately to the ivy, fighting for finger- and toeholds. Bits
of long-dead leaves and the sharp ends of stems made it
far from easy.

What was worse was her knowledge that some dark
danger waited below that was even more terrifying. There
was light shining out on the balcony as her bare feet
thumped on the icy stone. Nor was the room beyond
empty.

She could not catch any words, but she could see at
least four dark shadows looming up beside the platform
bed. One swung suddenly around so a faint touch of lamplight showed her Halwice's face. With a cry of relief Willadene staggered into the room.

Suddenly she saw Halwice do something which startled
her and halted her mad rush toward the Herbmistress. For
Halwice had simply pointed a finger at a candelabra on
the dressing table and the wicks of four waiting candles
had burst into instant flame, giving much fuller light to
the scene.

She saw Ssssaaa's body humped on Vazul's shoulder
which was barely covered, as his dressing robe had slid
under the animal's squirming ascent to her usual perch.
There was no mistaking that most of this company had
been hurriedly summoned from rest, though the light
glinted from the bared blade of a short sword arming one
of the figures clothed, even masked, in tight black garb.

It was the sudden quick movement from Nicolas, for
her talent had put name to that black night skulker, which

drew her attention to the bed—or rather the wreck of the bed!

Where mattress and covers had lain smooth she now saw a tangle, with a hole in the center into which the furnishings of the bed dangled downward as if they had been sucked from below, while from that hole came the stench of evil.

Halwice moved away from the other three by the bed. Her hands now dropped on Willadene's shoulders. "You have been much with her these past days—you know her!"

Shivering, trying hard to fight against the sickening stench, Willadene understood very well. Mahart's personal scent was well set in her mind. Even evil could not erase the traces of it now from the bed.

"So—here is your hound and one which can be well trusted."

Willadene could see Nicolas's mouth set tight above his stubborn jaw, and she wondered how much he agreed with her mistress's serene recommendation. Vazul was smoothing his creature the while, watching the girl with narrowed eyes. She, however, could read no doubt in them. Then the third person who had been standing at the foot of the destroyed bed came into better light.

Though he had also thrown off his finery of the ballroom, Prince Lorien's measuring stare was centered on her.

"I know nothing of such things." His voice was harsh and he was frowning.

It was Halwice who replied. "To each his own talent, my Lord Prince. Yours is rooted in steel and the use of it. But there are others of equal power. Tell me, why are you here?"

His frown had faded and he stared about him as if he suddenly realized where he stood. "I— There was a need—a dream—"

Halwice nodded. "Just so. To every act there is an

answer. Something was wrong here tonight—a troubling such as even we who are steeped in the Old Laws do not understand. I think, my Lord Prince, that you were also meant to be prey—but that those who play this game are still only students. They loose powers they do not fully understand—which no sane mind can deal with.''

"Me—prey! For whom and why?'' His face flushed and his fists grasped at the bedpost by which he stood as if he would use it as a weapon.

This time Vazul made answer, but in a roundabout fashion. "Your Highness, if in the morning your officers found you gone—and perhaps also clues that you were in danger—what then would they do?''

"They would take Kronengred apart stone by stone,'' he returned simply.

"Just so. But there would be a period of desperate searching, of hatred sown. You have delivered us of that monster the Wolf. But there are others behind him and they want no part of you and your well-trained men. They would sow discord and Kronen would bleed because of it. We do not know just how their plan failed to be fully realized, but that they have the High Lady there is no dispute.''

Ssssaaa hissed and the Chancellor turned quickly to Halwice. "Time is again our enemy, Guild Mistress. We had best be on the trail.''

Halwice's hand lay warm and comforting on Willadene's shoulder. "There are preparations—one cannot go off a-searching without what may be needed the most.''

With that Nicolas placed one hand as if he were making ready to vault into that hole in the bed, but Vazul spoke first.

"You do not hunt without your hound,'' he said.

Nicolas shot a glance at Willadene, and, though she could not read his masked face, she was well aware of how little he liked that order.

But Halwice had already pulled her to one of the great

wardrobes and jerked the door open just far enough so it could afford a screen. She pulled and pushed at the array of gowns and finally came forth with a divided skirt such as ladies might use for riding in the country, which, by its looks, had never been worn. There were other garments made to fit with it and when Willadene had pulled them on, the Herbmistress helping with laces and ties, she found this new clothing far less confining than ordinary dress. It was richer than anything she had ever worn and Halwice used her scissors to snip off a shoulder and breast badge so that the pearls and small gem beds forming them fell heedlessly to the floor. Nor did she stop there but gathered an untidy bundle of other clothing which she stored in a pack.

Willadene did not dare object even when Halwice caught up her coil of hair and sawed away until in length it merely brushed her shoulders. The Herbmistress had been silent throughout, but now she pushed forward the pack with her foot.

"Yours," she commented. "There are aids that you know in there—use them well when you have to. But remember this, only your nose can bring aid to Mahart and perhaps safety to all Kronen in the end."

Mahart was dreaming, of course, yet it was a dream which seemed very real, and frightening. For she could not see, and when she tried to raise a hand to her blinded eyes, it would not obey her command.

She was not alone either, for she could hear now and then a muttering of voices and she was certainly *not* in her own bed into which she had remembered crawling already dazed with the need for sleep.

There was a smell also, or at least a warring of smells. Some remnants from her choice of spices still seemed to cling to her, but there was also a sourish, musty odor and something else she could not have put name to but which made her shiver.

The dream drifted into the deep dark again. It was pain which aroused her the next time, the grating of her shoulder against harsh stone. But even as her eyes and hand, her voice would not obey and she was captive of this complete dark. When she tried to sort out one sensation from another the dull pain over her eyes became sharper.

Now—a spell of what she sensed was swinging in the air? And her helpless state of body made her icily afraid. Once more she struck against something—this time with her already spinning head and it was darkness and forgetting.

Sound awakened her, sound and a new smell, one she had once been able to identify.

"Fool!" The voice snapped and it was followed by a similar sound but no word, and she heard a sharp cry in answer.

"Highness—not there—only her—" The words slipped and slid away from her before she could force meaning from them.

"Hold him, Jonas." Somehow that voice was able to penetrate and make full sense. "What you are sent to do, you do!" Again that slapping noise and then a shrill scream of pain. "Do you understand? If we can save anything from this bungled night's work we must move fast. How long have we, Wise One?"

Fingers touching her, girdling her limp wrist. They believed her helpless, Mahart began to understand. Therefore, until she learned more, that was just what she must be.

"Another sniff—" That was not the sharp voice. Mahart nearly cried out as a grip tangled in her hair, jerking up her head at an angle which increased the band of pain. Then there was some wad of cloth pressed across her mouth and nose so willy-nilly she inhaled and straightway was again in the mindless dark.

Only, the dark was not empty. She began to sense that through it other things moved, if she did not. Mahart strained to hear any sounds which might give her the knowledge of where she was and—why.

Perhaps it was something in that mixture of scents which had clung to her body and hair after the herb girl's efforts which kept that dark hold from being so intense. Once more she was aware of her own body, of the strangely slow beat of her heart, of breath which her lungs fought to capture. The sensation of other things in motion about her was gone. Did that mean that she had been abandoned, helpless to await some fate for which the darkness was normal and had no hindrance?

Though the dull pain in her head persisted, Mahart began to try to piece together the few bits of information her hampered senses could bring her. It seemed easier to breathe as the moments passed and her heart resumed its steady beat.

She concentrated on a finger—the smallest portion of her body she might reasonably hope to control. And—it moved! Only a fraction, yet still it moved. So she was encouraged to continue her battle for returning self-control.

In the end her slight body was slick with sweat and the pounding in her head was so much she could no longer endure it. Fearing one more slide into nothingness she added up swiftly what she had learned.

Though she could move her fingers, lifting her hands was beyond her power. She believed that she had not been struck blind but rather that a blindfold half masked her. Yet how had she come from her safe bed to this place? Who had brought her—?

Sound—those were surely footsteps, heavy, suggesting a large body. There was a puffing of breath also, and she caught the fumes of strong ale. Never had she wished more for anything in her life than at this moment that she possessed the talent Willadene had willingly demonstrated to her, to assess by scent alone much which lay about her. The heavy-breathing foot stamper brought with him smells enough to keep a squad busy snuffing—old grease, unwashed body— But he was not coming straight to her as she had first feared. Rather, she heard a sort of squeaking sigh as if he had settled some bulk in a protesting chair.

Seated himself only to rise again as two other pairs of footsteps sounded for Mahart.

"Give you fair day, Wise One," rumbled a thick voice.

There was no answer save for the light patter Mahart realized was now approaching her. Scent again but this—this was something she had known before. Into her mind swung a hazy picture of a graceful glass bottle in the form of a cluster of fern leaves, some drops of oily green liquid moving sluggishly as the bottle tilted a little. Aspen! Once the odor had enticed her; now she found it sickening.

There was another odor also, but far from fragrant—musty, earthy, as if it arose from delving in sour sod such as the blighted castle garden possessed.

Pain struck suddenly as a blow sent her head rolling aside.

"Well, leader of rats"—the voice was a cackle like that of a raven relishing some jest—"now you have her. What do you think to do?"

"Master"—there was a third voice now from some distance away and she had heard no footsteps—"the hunt is up! That thrice-damned dabbler in potions—"

"Ah, boy, you'd better not ill-speak your betters. Them as does sometimes finds themselves in a worse state"—that was the cackling voice. "This must I tell you, rat master, she has had all the potion I can give her—the next will mean her death. For all of that—she may be mind dead now—the girl has no training nor has she been given any antidote. I would say if you would find her biddale by these street scrapings such as serve you you had best move her soon."

"Out of the city—the fourth way!" It seemed to be an order. "Get you Jonas and Orthon and move! Or your back'll be raw liver for a week. Think you, the High Lady's lash was no love tap—your eye does not look so good to me—it is nothing compared to what you will feel if you don't get on the move—and *now*!"

There was a period of confusion. Mahart was so afraid of revealing that she was conscious of much about her that she spent her will on trying to remain utterly limp and unmoving. Hands pawed at her after a short space. Her body was lifted and she felt the harsh edges of metal—perhaps a mail coat—against her cheek.

They had reached a lower level. One of her hands

bumped painfully against a railing and once caught, to nearly bring a cry out of her as that was snatched with an oath and slammed across her body. Once more she had the feeling of being in a confined place, perhaps underground, and then was heartened by the sight of a dim light nodding up and down before her. So in spite of her blindfold she could see that much, or perhaps that potion they had used on her was wearing off.

Twice she was dumped painfully on an uneven surface, and she could hear the heavy breathing of him who had carried her. At the second of these occasions they were joined by another man.

"An' jus' where is we to take 'er?" he demanded when the orders of her disposal were repeated. "We ain't takin' no one to th' Raven's tower—not less I hear that from th' master hisself. Didn't get that gormal of Prince, did he now, wi' all the stir up. Now he we'd takum gladly—knife in his gullet an' 'im throwed out where those bullyboys of hissen could find him in a day or so. No, you brings us this here slut—"

"The master may think as how he can bargain with her in his hand—" suggested the younger voice.

"Well, he ain't gonna plant her where we've gone to earth. You want your head on a spear—or does 'e? We 'ad a good plan go' until the master got hooked up with th' idea of playin' lords' games. I say we lay low an' wait an' see what them high-ups is gonna do."

"Where so we take her then?" The third voice must be of the man who had carried her here as it was much closer, as if he was crouched not too far away.

"To Ishbi—for all I care!"

Someone drew a deep breath. Then, "You'll do the tel' of where you planted her to the master, then?" the high voice asked.

"Well, sure as the sun is in the sky, no one is gonna come snoopin' there," the other declared. "It'll only take a couple o' men to hold the pass, and no one in his right

mind has gone into that maze since the clock of Kro-
engred was set—a goodly sum of seasons ago.''

Once more Mahart was picked up. Ishbi—she tried to
pull on memory and found it heightened her headache, so
set herself to endure.

Having passed Halwice's inspection Willadene was
about to take up the bag the Herbmistress had indicated
when she remembered her amulet and that other which
she had bound with it—the leaves from the far past. Those
were still with her, as they always were, but she had no
time to ask Halwice concerning the find in the book, for
the woman shut the door of the wardrobe to reveal the
room.

On the floor by the dais of the bed lay the mound of
covers which had been roughly pitched away to uncover
the hole in its surface. Nicolas was lying belly down on
what was left of that surface, holding out over that ominous black break a lantern. Though dawn was beginning
to creep into the room they still needed such light as they
could gather.

Both Vazul and the Prince had also joined him after a
fashion, the Chancellor still anchored with a tight hold on
one bedpost but leaning forward at a perilous angle and
the Prince on the other side of the bed, kneeling on the
edge of the dais and striving to see into this secret way.

" 'Tis fresh cut,'' Nicolas announced. ''Perhaps they
broke through just before they seized her. And there is no
such way on the plans, Chancellor.''

"That is needless to say,'' commented the Chancellor
with a snap. ''Well, mistress, will this maid of yours serve
our purpose? Let her close, Nicolas.''

He obediently squirmed to one side, and Willadene very
gingerly joined him. Evil—she must pierce through that
overpowering evil to reach the far-more-difficult-to-pick-
up scent.

"What does she?'' Lorien demanded as Willadene

stretched her head and shoulders over the hole. The lantern showed broken beams of wood and glimpses of what might be stone walls.

"She seeks," Halwice returned calmly. "For she has been favored by the Star with the strongest talent I have ever touched. Each of us carries from birth our own particular scent which has naught to do with our physical body or its condition, or what covers it. Those who have the Great Talent can trace any they know, even as the great hounds can follow tirelessly a forest track."

Willadene fought to shut their voices out of her ears, their words out of her head, to catch only scent. That first layer, evil—below it traces of the heavy spiciness which Mahart had chosen to cover the fern fragrance, then—as one might sight a single thread in a piece of woven stuff— she caught and held that which was Mahart alone. Yes, she had passed this way.

That was only the beginning. Nicolas, swinging the lantern about his neck with a cord, leaned farther over to test the first of the battered beams. And Willadene followed his descent, not happily but because she must, being who and what she was.

The lantern displayed another hole beneath the beams which had been half broken away, and Nicolas was already swinging his light into that. The air was choking with dust when they moved, but Willadene dared not cover her nose lest she lose that precious thread they must follow.

"Ah—" The light was stationary now, but hands reached up and caught her about her waist, swinging her down. "So that was the trick of it." Nicolas sounded almost as if he were admiring the labors of those who had burrowed here. "But they must have had a guide—" And now his voice turned somber.

Once more he picked up the lantern and swung it around to give them better sight of where they were. They stood, as far as Willadene could see, in another of those stone-walled passages, but around them was a mound of broken rubble and above they could still see the light from the room. It was plain that this was no normal opening to the inner ways but one which had been roughly broken through.

"But no one heard—" She spoke her amazement aloud.

Nicolas had picked up a piece of rubble, but as quickly as he had touched it he threw it from him with an exclamation of pain. She could see no mark of blood on his fingers. She could—

Fern fragrance—but with it something else—something she had never known before. She caught at Nicolas's hand to hold it closer to the lantern light. Across the tips of two fingers there were patches of red.

From those she looked with fear at the jumbled and broken bits of ancient wood about their feet. He moved quickly away from that rubble, jerking her along with him.

"What—" She was beginning, and tried to pull away from his hold, but he kept it tight.

With her other hand she worried at the herb bag and somehow got out the small jar she sought. "This thing is—it eats, I think," she explained, and he was willing to stand still while she smeared across those blotches the cream from the jar. "There was a ship's captain a year ago who came to Halwice. He had but three fingers on one hand. It came of a seaweed washed aboard in a storm which ate—ate at the ship itself. When they would have thrown it over those who touched it barehanded also were maimed. I do not think your slinkers dug here—the sounds would surely have been heard. But had they some mixture which would eat at wood and stone—"

She had never heard of such, but there were always new things to be encountered. He gave a swift nod. In this dim light and in his black clothing he could hardly be seen, yet she was very much aware of him.

"That is why the bedclothes hung over! But why would something which feeds so not have taken that also?"

"You may guess as well as I can as to that," she returned, slinging her bag over her shoulder. "Now—" She had taken several more steps away from the rubble into the darkness and raised her head, calling upon her talent.

"This way." The evil clung in that path also as did the spicy undercurrent. But she was careful not to be diverted by either—she sought and found Mahart's own trace.

Nicolas matched her stride. He had the lantern, but some trick of adjusting its panels brought the light to a very thin beam. This he kept swinging slightly back and forth so that it would reveal the largest area that could be. But all they could see were the stone walls much like those of the other passages Willadene had traveled, not in secret.

She half expected Nicolas to question her, certainly about their way, but apparently he was willing to accept, at least for now, her decision. It was not until they reached a sharp turn in the way and scaling off there a second passage, that Nicolas went into action. He stooped to study the thick dust. It was well muddled here as if there had been a scuffle of some sort.

"There—?" He pointed to the side way.

Willadene stood, closed her eyes, tried to center all her energy on her sense of smell. The evil stench had thickened and it was near desperately hard for her to pierce that for her beckoning thread.

"No."

His black clothing was now so well coated with dust that she could see him better. He had taken two side steps into the way he indicated and was flashing the lantern downward. Even from where she still stood she could see the disturbance of dust. There had certainly been recent passage along that way. But—

"No." Resolutely she started forward on her own along the main passage. This slanted downward, and there was a damp which collected in the air. Willadene judged that he did not agree with her, but after a moment or so he followed.

There were no stairs here but a distinct downward slope.

Then the light from the lantern caught on a light patch on the wall. Nicolas swung the thin beam around and what she saw brought a gasp out of Willadene.

The stone of the wall had been hollowed here into a niche, one barely large enough to house what stood in it behind a netting of rusting metal bars. Those bones were so thin and delicate, the whole skeleton so short, that Willadene could only believe this ancient horror had had a child for its prey.

"Athgard!" Nicolas's hand, protruding from the dusty black of his sleeve, looked as pale as the bones before them. "So this was his ending—"

Athgard? And who was or had been Athgard? Willadene swallowed and swallowed again, trying hard to see only bones against an ancient wall and not the fleeting vision in her mind of what had once housed those bones.

"Five hundred seasons—maybe more—" Nicolas's finger was pointing now to the skull which, loosed from the spine, had fallen forward to rest against the metal of its imprisonment.

There was another look to that bone—a circlet of time-darkened metal. What had once been set to the fore of it had been pried away, leaving only twisted prongs they could barely see in this frail light.

"Athgard, son of Wisgard." Nicolas's palm straightened up in a kind of salute to the long dead. "So this is where the House of Gard came to in the end. But"—it would seem now that he was addressing the bones themselves—"rest in peace, knowing that those of Ishbi were brought down in their time—and bloodily—to the last remaining member of their house. Get we safely through this venture, and freedom will come also to the last of Gard and a place beneath the Star will be opened."

"Ishbi—" All Willadene knew of the past was what she had picked up from hints found among Halwice's meager library and that had been mainly only herbal lore.

"Ishbi!" There was a vicious twist to Nicolas's mouth.

" 'Twas all because of the King's daughter—Nona. She drew men to be taken by her enchantments, one after another, all the lordlings and their households. There were others that she summoned and the Star was forgot, another power arose—one drinking blood.

"The last Duke of Gard was poisoned at his own table, his heir was gone—Nona's Hag mistress ruled. But never are the scales weighing good and evil so badly balanced that they do not even out once again. It was from the same north that Vulsaden rode and with him those who had hatred for Nona's beliefs bred into their bones.

"And in time she fell, for those of the Star called also upon greater powers. There came out of the skies an answer which rocked all the land. Vulsaden pulled together the survivors, and all who had been liege to Nona were hunted down to the death—though their Hag mistress was never found. So the House of Den ruled for two generations, and then the last Duke was sonless and his sister married into the House of Bric from which came a new line to the throne."

Swiftly Willadene made the sign of the Star before the pitiful thing they had found. "Yet still we struggle—" she said.

"Just so. And in that we have a part. Do you swear, mistress, that this way is ours?"

She forced herself to turn away from the imprisoned bones, to forget what imagination made only too vivid for her.

"Yes—this is the way."

It seemed to her, however, that the stench of evil which had struck at her so earlier had somehow slackened. Either that or she was getting used to the pollution. But she was certain that she still held to the thread which had led her this far, concentrating on it with all her power.

There were no more evil surprises along their way, though the narrow corridor they walked continued to slope downward. Now the dust was not so overpowering, for there was moisture in the air, yet it was still thick enough underfoot to muffle their going.

Stench of another sort wafted to them once or twice as they passed slits set where the walls met the roofing over them.

"We are under the city," Nicolas half whispered. "This way leads along the great sewer. Hold this—" He pushed the lantern toward her and she grasped it firmly. His hands were busy at his belt and then she saw that he had taken out of some hiding place among his clothing what looked not unlike a riding whip. With that in one hand and his bared knife in the other he started forward again.

"Slime eaters," he said briefly, "though they mainly keep to the waterways."

Moments later he pointed out disturbances in the damp dust which were undoubtedly tracks of some creature. But those were also overlaid with the marks of boots, proving her assertion that they did follow a recent trail.

There were runnels of water down the walls, seeping out of those high-placed openings, and the smell was near overpowering. There came a shrill squealing and Nicolas, with his shoulder, pushed her back against the opposite wall.

"Mistress," he said and his voice was the steady one of an armsman going into a familiar battle, "have you anything in that charmed bag of yours which can be a defense—a quick one—there is"—and he spoke now with a grim note of humor—"no pepper mill here."

She counted over hurriedly in her mind all Halwice had furnished. There was one thing which at the time she had hardly believed necessary but now it might just work. Setting the lantern on the floor between her feet, she searched until she found the proper pocket. Also the thin, greasy glove which was wrapped with it.

"It—they must be near. And do not let it touch you."

The squealing had grown louder; now she caught movement in one of those wall slits. Holding her improvised

weapon carefully in her gloved right hand she swung up
the lantern with the left, and now she could truly see the
head of the thing working its way through the slit.

For one second she thought of Ssssaaa, for this creature
seemed to have the same long and limber body and short
legs. But it lacked the luxurious fur of the Chancellor's
pet, and the scent she picked up from it was that of filth
and decay—its fur ragged in patches with sores showing
greenish on the bared skin.

It fell with a plop to the pavement some distance away
from them. Nicolas waited for an attack. His lash rose,
whistled through the stale air, and wrapped its fore length
around the beast, jerking its writhing body toward him
where he stood with ready steel. Only Willadene moved
first. She had taken a pinch of the powder she handled
with such care and raising her hand to the level of her
lips she gave a puff of all the breath she could summon.

Motes which seemed to spark as if they were born in a
fire filled the air. She had aimed as well as she could and
luckily Nicolas was still some distance from his intended
prey.

The motes sifted down upon that scabby hide. A hideous
scream seemed to fill the passage at a near ear-torturing
level. Nicolas gave his lash a shake and the twisting,
writhing thing, now looking like a coil of dull fire, struck
the wall and rebounded a step or two but lay unmoving.

Only there was already another head showing aloft. It
did not move swiftly as had its fellow, rather crouched,
viewing—its long neck well stretched—that crisping body
just below.

Its squeal became a screech but it ventured no farther.
Nicolas spoke to the girl. "Can I draw this cord through
what you hold?"

"Yes, but take care." She had already opened the shutter of the lantern to give them more light to counter any
attack, and now into the wider beam she held her gloved
hand.

Nicolas peered closely at the powder resting on her flattened palm, and then swiftly and with the ease of one knowing well his tool, he pulled the lash through that small lump.

Just as when the motes had taken spark life in the air when Willadene had blown them free so now did the length of his lash glisten with pinpoints of fire.

With one lithe bound he crossed the passage and aimed that lash upward. It did not catch quite as true as had his first use of it, but it did flick deeply into the waving head above, and again that piercing scream sounded in their ears.

The creature did not fall on their side of the wall; it had been far enough back in the slit to retreat the other way. There were two more of those terrible screams while Nicolas stood on guard below. But no other head appeared.

After a long moment he looked to Willadene, holding the lash some distance from his body. Though most of the motes had disappeared there was still a tiny flash here and there.

"I do not think they will move on us again," he said. "The one which fell back may well have carried the contagion to its fellows. How do I free my lash?"

Carefully the girl restored to her bag the pouch and what remained in it. Then she held out her gloved hand.

"Draw through this, slowly."

When he had obeyed her order the lash was clear of any sign of spark—though there was a scatter of such on her glove. She hated to lose that protection but this was not time or place to go through the long procedure of cleaning it into safe use again. So she drew it off gingerly and dropped it on the muddy way, grinding it deeply into that thick surface with her boot.

"It is still our way?" Nicolas questioned a few moments later when they came to two dark arches on the opposite side from that wall which gave upon the sewer.

Willadene had stopped short. There had come out of

the further of those two doors that exultation of odor which had struck her back in Mahart's chamber. There was certainly the unmistakably clean and enticing smell of fern—but with it the warning stench. She drew a deep breath, then fumbled for her amulet and sniffed it deeply in hopes of clearing her head. The thread which was Mahart—no, it did not lead this way. But there was something which did make some use of that passage—something which was wholly evil!

Once more she raised her head high as if she could so outreach that stench. Mahart—she must be right! Evil held here but that which signaled the High Lady was still straight ahead.

How long they had been in this warren of passages and darkness she had no way of telling. She saw Nicolas take a small disk from his belt pouch and hold it close to the lantern whose beam they had again reduced to a slit.

"We are very near to the walls—the walls of the city itself," he reported quietly.

There was no slope downward this time; rather they came to a flight of stairs leading up and they climbed cautiously, listening for any sound.

Their ascent ended on a small landing and they faced a door. It was latched on this side, but could it also be on the opposite?

Nicolas lifted the small bar and silently set it to one side. He placed his palm against the wood and, knife in hand, exerted just enough pressure to open the door a crack and thus assure them that they were not locked in.

Willadene caught suddenly at his arm, drawing his body closer to hers so that she could whisper in his ear.

"This is the Wanderers Inn—or rather its cellar. Never in my life can I forget that!"

18 Cold, she was so cold—and her mouth felt as if she had had ashes forced down her gullet. Mahart tried to summon up energy enough to raise even a finger. Dark—her face was nearly covered with a nasty-smelling slimed rag.

She was so thirsty she could have croaked aloud for water, but even that was denied her. The cold flowed about her like fingers of wind tearing at her.

Outside—surely she was outside, beyond the maze of ways they had dragged her like a horse pack.

Ishbi—he said it—

Somehow those words had penetrated through the torments of her inert body to reach her mind.

"Sling her over the pack mare an' let's get a-goin', then."

She had been lifted with no gentleness and then had landed hard, facedown across some kind of a frame. However, that maneuver had in a fraction served her a little. The cover on her head had caught on some projection and been jerked free. Those who had left her ignominiously slung over a pack animal had not seemed to notice.

The daylight had hurt her eyes. And all she could see was one horse leg lifting up and plopping down again as

251

she was carried joltingly forward. But there had been no
cobbles under that hoof, and the wind which still ruffled
across her body, lashed as it now was like a deer carcass,
had carried no city taint. They were certainly out of
Kronengred.

She had heard voices, but now the words did not hold
in her mind but faded in and out—and she had slipped
again into the waiting darkness.

Mahart flinched from a dash of water in her face. She
could blurrily see figures moving about her. One knelt and
now caught fingers in her matted hair, pulling up her head
and bruising her lips by the force with which he pressed
a cup against them.

"Grissand damn you fools! *She* wants her alive—not
dead— One cannot bargain with nothing! Get a cloak about
her and have some of that stew ready— If she does not
make it to Ishbi you'll soon find out who will answer for it!"

He let her drink and then held the cup away, though
she protested weakly. Someone she could not see dropped
folds of a traveling cloak about her, and she realized that
her night robe was near a tattered net now.

They had propped her up, maybe with the pack saddle
at her back, and, as the water revived her, she could see
more of this company. He with the water bag filled the
cup again and held it for her.

"Sip only, or it will come up as fast as it went down!"
he warned her.

Though he wore a mail shirt under a quilted leather
jerkin and a bowl-smooth helm he was certainly not of
the guards she knew. A bush of yellowish beard sprouted
wirily from his chin, and above his thick-lipped mouth his
nose was dented as if it had been broken in some long
ago encounter. There was certainly no sign of compassion
in his eyes, the lid of one drawn crooked by a scar. She
might have been some animal he tended under orders.

There were at least three others who passed back and
forth about what appeared to be a temporary campsite.

Over a fire a pot was heating and she could hear the stamping of horses not too far away.

"Got a fancy for her, Rufus? She ain't much of an armload. But it ain't every Tenth as can say he's had him a High Lady for bedding—"

Suddenly her mouth was dry again, her eyes intent on that face not so far from hers. The man who had come up behind him was much younger, with a sharp set of features as might suit a rat. He wore no armor but rather a travel-stained and smudged set of livery— Blue—silver—

Without a word the man by her side set down the cup and arose with agile ease to backhand the boy, who uttered a loud cry of pain and rage.

"Stow it, trash," remarked the soldier. "Got that stew ready, Jonas?"

Another young man with a small bowl dipped and brought it half full. Steam filled that air and just as thirst had earlier held her captive now so did hunger arise in her hollow middle.

Mahart discovered that her hands, her arms would now obey her. If she had been roped those bonds had been removed, if something else had held her it had faded.

She held out her shaking hands to cup the bowl.

"It's hot," Yellow Beard said. "Take it easy." Now he turned on the others who had gathered around the fire and were waiting for their own shares. "You listen and you listen good. We has our orders. Want to argue them out with *her*?"

There was a murmur from the young man he had buffeted. "I be for Wyche—"

Yellow Beard laughed harshly. "Now, I'll just make believe, 'cause you're young an' green, as how I did not hear that. Your Wyche may be a strutful man in town— but only 'cause *she* wills it so for now. An' to get on *her* wrong side—" He paused. "Now that is something as I wouldn't wish on my worst enemy! We has these orders: to take this wench to Ishbi and turn her over to the guard—no more no less. An' she had better be alive when we do that turnin'.''

Having so made plain their orders, he came back to Mahart.

"Now, you. *She* wants you—that's enough for me. Can you stick on a horse? Riding like a pack won't do you much good.''

"I can ride." She could not be sure of that, but if there was any way she could escape the trials just past she would will herself to the greatest effort she could summon. She made her first move by levering her shoulders away from the support, bracing her arms on either side of her body.

The world slung around. Mahart bit her lip until all settled down. Certainly she was far from all she had ever known. There were trees towering around this small glade and a sense that her kind did not belong here. She watched those by the fire. There were five of them, including Yellow Beard who was clearly in command. She had recognized now the livery worn by the youngest man—Saylana's. This "She" Yellow Beard kept mentioning—the High Lady Saylana?—somehow it was near impossible to think of her as being associated in any way (in spite of all the strangest rumors) with these outcasts.

Ishbi—the name continued to haunt her— From her reading in the past— Ishbi—

Only there was something more important now—the journey which apparently still lay ahead of her. That there would be any reason or hope for appealing to her captors she quickly put aside. She must school herself to patience and watch for any act or chance that might work in her favor.

Luckily they lingered for some time over their meal. Unfortunately, they did not appear to be too talkative a lot and she could not hope for answers to the questions which she tried to push to one side.

However, when they were ready to move on Yellow Beard ordered a pack frame to be left and a blanket placed instead on the back of a head-hanging horse, the lead rope of which he took into his own charge, drawing her up beside his own mount, the others behind them.

Mahart held her cloak as closely as she could about her, not only for protection against the wandering breezes but also because she realized that it was now nearly the only garment she possessed.

They went at a steady pace but not a swift one, and twice they halted while one or other of the party detoured to one side to inspect the trunk of a tree, as if they so followed some mark, for it was very apparent they were not on any used trail.

At last the countryside about them began to change. There were fewer of the tall trees and more brush, the thicker patches of which they had to avoid. But there were also outcroppings of rocks. These bore no resemblance to the stones of Kronengred, for those were dull gray while these had a greenish cast and were also veined with wider stripes of the same color but of a darker shade.

Some arose like miniature cliffs walling them in at times, and there was life here—lizardlike creatures who clung head downward to the stones and seemed to watch them intently with beady eyes, as if they were fully aware their territory was under invasion. There were birds that wheeled and soared overhead also, sometimes swooping so close to the earth as if to alight on a rock outcrop— though they never did.

Mahart's body ached from head to foot. They had stiff leather bottles of water hung from their saddles, and from time to time Yellow Beard offered her a drink from his.

She judged by the light that sunset was close, and yet they made no move toward setting up camp. How long had it been since she had lain herself down on her own bed in Kronengred? She had no way of knowing.

At last the passage ahead began to narrow, those standing crags drawing in closer together until they seemed to form two walls between which their party rode. However, here there was a change in those rocks. The deeper-colored veins did not run smoothly but bore deep incisions here and there, almost as if they were meant for inscriptions.

Then came one space where the dark-green vein was near as wide as the rock which bore it and that had surely been worked upon by some intelligence, for Mahart found herself staring at a face.

It was of natural size and that of a woman, though there was no indication of any hair framing it. The features were clear-cut. It was beautiful in its perfection—but the perfection itself— Mahart shivered. She had heard them say that the Herbmistress's apprentice could actually smell evil—well, now she was sure she saw it!

There was movement from beyond that face. A mail-clad form, wearing a very strange helm which completely hid all features, stood in the way before them.

Yellow Beard twitched the lead rein of Mahart's horse, drawing aside so the animal could pass his own mount.

"This is the one," he said.

That helm-masked figure reached forward and took the lead rein. There was no answer, merely that jerk on the rein which brought the horse on. But neither Yellow Beard nor any of the others accompanied her. Ishbi—had they at last reached their goal? She had passed that face; had she been any taller she might have brushed against it. And her flesh tingled at that thought. No, it was not Saylana who brooded over the way which led ahead—but someone greater and far more powerful.

Willadene kept her grip on Nicolas, straining to hear any sound emerge from the opposite reach of this cavern where the stairs to the upper floor lay. The fact that there was a lantern set on top of a barrel by the foot of those was warning that someone either was here or intended to shortly return.

Nicolas edged a little to the right where he could get a better sight of those stairs. Save for a distant drip-drip of water there was no sound to be heard.

Suddenly Willadene caught that—the thread of scent which had drawn her along. With all the care at separating one odor from another she could summon, she drew in two deep breaths.

Yes, it was certainly stronger here, as if Mahart had been some time in this place. Either that or—Willadene swung a little away from the stairs. Her fingers were claw sharp in Nicolas's flesh now. He did not try to shake her off but followed as she went—not toward the steps and the light, but back into the gloom of the huge cellars she had never explored in those days when it had often been her task to hunt some dust-ridged bottle from one of the tottering shelves.

Around two of those shelf towers she pushed a way. Then the beam of their own lantern caught on something and she grabbed up a tatter of cloth, still white enough to be easily spied in this gloom.

The stuff was silk, soft between her fingers, and she did not really need to raise it to her nostrils to know that it was a piece of Mahart's body linen—her night shift doubtless—which had entrapped her scent so deeply.

The rag had protruded from what looked like solid wall. She could hardly even see the crack from which she had freed it. Nicolas deliberately shifted the shades of the lantern, using the light as he might a sword blade to draw some pattern.

"Ssssaaa—" He uttered a hissing noise not unlike that which Vazul's creature might sound. "Hold—so—" He thrust the lantern into Willadene's hands, and she watched his gray-dusted hands run fingertips back and forth across the wall—first up and then down from the place where she had found the rag.

"Here!" She concentrated in answer to his urgency, holding the lantern beam on the end of one block of stone which seemed to her eyes to be no different from its fellow. Nicolas had knife in hand now and he seemed able to insert the slender point into a pattern of invisible slits.

Noiselessly a narrow door opened, showing another dark way into which the lantern's beam seemed swallowed up. Nicolas turned to her.

"This way?" She did not need that rag, though she stuffed it in her jerkin to preserve the faint person-scent. Now she nodded in answer to his question.

He was muttering to himself, and from one or two words she caught she knew he was cursing—but who or what was the object of that anger she had no idea. At least the way was straight, and oddly enough the thick dust they had found in the other passages did not seem to lie here. Their lantern beam flitted across a pile of tree-knot torches, as if this was a much-used path.

It continued straight, though twice there were other openings, but the clue she followed lay in neither direction. However, they were in sight of a third when they saw dim light ahead and a rumble of voices distorted by the passage.

Nicolas whirled her into that side passage. He pushed shut the slide on the lantern, and they huddled shoulder to shoulder waiting.

"Got the city hummin'," commented one voice. "Tell you it weren't no good that that head-chopping Prince of theirs weren't taken. That demon-birthed Vazul will somehow git him into it and not like was planned, neither."

There was a rough laugh in answer and now the light was plain enough that Willadene could see the two of them. *That* fat lump of spoiled lard. She might not know Nicolas's more colorful estimate of their situation, but she had her own words for what she found nauseous.

That was Wyche bellowing along. "Let 'em turn the city top to bottom." He spat loudly at the near wall. "They ain't goin' to find th' wench—an' without a-knowin' who has hands on her they ain't goin' to push too hard. The High Lady now, she has an eye for the Prince—like as not she'll make a full meal o' him afore he knows which side is up."

Willadene could feel Nicolas's breath on her cheek and

the heat of his anger. "Wyche I know too well," he gritted out.

"This Ishbi place now—" Wyche's companion was beginning when the other lost all signs of joviality. "Shut your mouth, slime toad." And because he spoke without any tone of anger somehow that made it more threatening. "You ain't never heard o' that—understand?"

They were well past the entrance to the side way now, leaving the two in thickening darkness. Willadene had felt Nicolas's body tense at the mention of that queer name.

"Ishbi?" She made a query of that as they came again to the main corridor.

"If they think to take her there—!" He had quickened his pace until he was almost running, and Willadene had to scurry on as best she could at his heels though the weight of her bag seemed to be heavier with every step she took. Would they ever be out of this place of dark and able to rest for a moment?

There were no more breaks in the wall, but they kept listening for a sound which might mean other wayfarers. Nicolas seemed possessed by the need for speed, and the girl began to lag in spite of all her efforts to keep up.

Suddenly he dropped back a stride and put his arm about her waist, lending his strength to hers. It was not soon after that that the passage did turn to the right, and ahead there were patches of light which were the honest ones of day and not from torch or lantern.

They came out through a mass of brush which Nicolas held aside for their passage. Willadene breathed air fresh enough to renew her energy a little. She looked around and saw that they were in the vine and shrub overgrown ruins of a small building.

Nicolas had released his hold on her. In spite of all her will to continue, she crumpled to the ground, only her bag keeping her from total collapse. Her companion stood, hands on hips, looking around. Suddenly he gave a sharp nod.

"So—this is their long-sought passageway! Now listen, mistress"—he stared down at her with those compelling sword-bright eyes of his—"answer me truly—did the High Lady indeed come this way?"

For the first time Willadene was at a loss. The scents crowding in around her were so many, a number entirely new, and she must sort through them. Rather forlornly she pulled that rag from her jerkin, sniffed at it, and then sat head up and eyes closed for a long moment.

Slowly her head turned, though she did not open her eyes. "I think they laid her there. But there were horses—"

"As might have been seen!" he snarled. "Now listen, I must carry what we have learned to the Lord Chancellor. Also we must have supplies, mounts. You must keep yourself out of sight here until I return. Can you do so?"

She nodded. As far as she was concerned at that moment she could not have crawled a step farther. Her throat felt parched but she had a small supply of cordial which would allay her thirst for a while.

He urged and partly dragged her back into where two ruined walls met and then shook the brush into place before her. That done he was gone with a hawk's speed and she was left alone.

The Duke was huddled in his great seat, an untouched goblet of wine to his hand along with a platter of crumbled but untasted biscuits. A map of Kronengred was spread before him, but he stared not at the recently chalked marks there but rather at the wall where messenger squires stood to attention, ready to dart off upon command.

"Prince." He did not turn his head toward the man he addressed but continued to stare ahead. "There was a plot—in half it failed, for you were not taken. Mahart is in their hands, but there is hope that they will—"

He hesitated. The younger man spoke.

"They will attempt to use her as a bargaining piece?"

"There are a hundred—a thousand places in this city," the Duke continued tonelessly, "where they can keep her so no searchers of ours can find her—"

"She is no longer in the city." Both men turned heads.

Vazul, his creature hissing loudly in his ear, came to the other side of the table and looked down at the map. His always gaunt face had now the look of skin stretched tightly over bone. "The Bat's network is to be depended upon."

"And the Bat?" demanded the Duke.

"Nothing as yet. But there is something else— Your Highness, the High Lady Saylana has also disappeared—and with her not only some of her ladies but also the Lady Zuta. If they left the city it was by no normal means. And the Herbmistress would speak with you—"

"I grasp at any straw—meanwhile deal as you can with the affairs of the flight of these women. Let the Herbmistress come."

Just as age had seemed to ensnare the Lord Chancellor overnight so did Halwice's features appear the sharper.

"Your Highness"—she did not wait to be addressed but swept into speech at once—"and you, Prince Lorien. We have come to fight more than one woman's desire for power. There were hints of this long ago when the House of Gard was brought down here in Kronen and your own people fought a battle with mountain raiders— Remember you Ishbi, Prince?"

He was leaning forward, one clenched fist on the table before him.

"Demon spawned that was, mistress. But in the end we prevailed."

"Did we?" she said slowly. "Or perhaps the enemy only withdrew for a space to rearm and strengthen. Prince Lorien, my craft puts those who follow it on a very narrow path between Light and Dark. Within these past few days I have learned that we face powers far stronger than any steel forged, any learned knowledge. I speak of Nona—"

"A legend—" But the Duke's hand flailed out and upset his wine across the map.

"Ishbi!" Now Prince Lorien's fist slipped across the map making the wine river there run the faster. "I am of the blood who was there and others may forget—we shall not as long as we breed sons. It is the cursed—"

"Or are we?" Halwice's voice cut through his rising one. "By what once was ruler of spirit there?"

The Prince was on his feet. "If somehow that evil beyond evil is a part of this, then, Lord Duke, your quarrel is also mine." He hesitated and then added in a lower voice from which the hot wrath had died a little, "May the Star Rays be about your daughter, Duke, if she is captive to such."

The Duke put his head in his hands and those hands were trembling. Mahart—she had been just a name to him not long ago, a small irritation to be endured, but of no great value. What was she now? He could not have truthfully said, save all his sly connivings and schemes were like tattered webs torn apart and of no value.

There was a stir as through the door came one of the squire messengers, but what he had to add he took to the Lord Chancellor not the distraught Duke.

Vazul unrolled a small strip of paper but he did not hold it up to his own eyes—rather to those of Ssssaaa, and within a second or two the creature's hissing became so loud it drew all their attention, even the Duke's.

"They have taken her out of the city." Vazul had all the appearance of one translating his creature's hisses.

"The Bat says, mistress"—he inclined his head a fraction toward Halwice—"that your maid insists the trail leads on. He gathers supplies and mounts to follow. There has been talk of Ishbi."

And that final word echoed through the chamber as if it was as strong as the clamor of one of the city bells.

19 The heavy fragrance about Mahart enclosed her like a score of blankets wadded one on top of another. Even the air here seemed to hold a green shimmer as the horse plodded after that metal-encased figure who led it. The rock-walled trail they followed suddenly widened out onto what she first thought was a ledge and then saw dreamily was the first of a series of very wide steps, easy enough for the mount who carried her to descend, leading down into thick greenery.

Each step was deeply incised with a symbol and her guard-guide led the horse so that the animal walked directly over the heart of each as they went. Mahart could see now that all that greenery below was no normal trees and scrubs, rather a rank growth of ferns taller than her head even as she rode toward them.

There was no wind here, nor any sound of bird or insect. As they reached the last of those wide steps he who had brought her stepped aside. When her mount drew level with him he looped back the lead rope over the saddle horn. Nor did he even raise that helmed masked face to look at her. Instead he halted. The horse continued to plod at the same pace straight ahead.

So like a dream was all of this that Mahart felt she

could demand no explanation, offer no protest. Still, she knew inwardly that she was headed now toward some peril she could not begin to imagine.

At first the wall of ferns seemed to be just that, a barrier to warn any intruder away, but as the horse approached at its slow amble those fronds, without the urging of any breeze, split apart and opened a way for them. There were, she began to notice, strange breaks among them here and there—a scrap of wall, a sharp corner. While there was no sound, the thud of her mount's shod hooves sounded on stone, even though underfoot seemed only a green carpet of moss.

Mahart cried out. A frond to her right had appeared to bow away, and she looked for only an instant of pure horror into a face. Not one of beauty such as had been engraved on the wall, but rather one which might have been rudely hacked from the bark-scaled side of a dead tree. Then it was gone, as suddenly as she had seen it.

However, the further they advanced the more and more obvious became those signs of handiwork, the remains of very ancient structures, while the growth of ferns began to thin out.

At last they were through the final fringe of green plumes and into the open. What was spread before her was a calm-surfaced lake crowded round with ruins of the green-veined stone. The ferns had dwindled to a moss which resembled in part a vine as its tendrils crept outward over the stone yet sparingly as if that plant found little liking for the support it was forced to accept.

Centered in the lake was a massive heap of rubble—perhaps even a castle overthrown to nearly the shape of its native stone. There for the first time she saw movement. Things came out of the water, stirring it with small ripples, darting up among the stones. They moved so fast she could not, in this strangely drowsy state into which she had fallen, really distinguish them well, though she had an impression that they had four limbs and a wide blob of head, which appeared to sit on their shoulders with no rise of neck between.

In color they were nearly the shade of the stones, so that once ashore when they halted, they faded into the mound of rubble enough so that she could no longer spy them.

Her mount brought her to what once might have been a pier stretching into the lake and then halted and stood with drooping head. It gave a doleful wheezing sound and began to shiver under her, as if her weight somehow exhausted it.

Sore and stiff the girl slipped from the mount's back and found that she must hold to the edge of its blanket in order to keep her feet, so dizzy she had become.

With a second deep sigh the horse went to its knees and she was swung off until she was brought up painfully against a fragment of wall and clung to that for support.

Now the animal lay on its side, its wheezing breath coming in great gasps. She backed away, not sure what fate was claiming it and whether she would be so taken also.

The horse's head was down. As far as Mahart could see it no longer was breathing. She dug her nails into the scrap of rock wall, pulling herself unsteadily back from the animal she was now sure had died. Her mouth was dry with thirst. Yet she had no desire to drink where those island things swam.

Using one hand for a grip to drag her forward a step, and then another, Mahart started to work her way back from the edge of the lake, though she knew she could not bring herself to fight a way into the ferns.

"Light of Star,

"Path of bright." Her tongue was so dry she could hardly shape the words. "Star of Mercy, Star Above—" Slowly she recited the Five Points. Few nowadays believed in miracles, in outward aid in time of peril. She was not Abbey bred and did not even know well any of the Great

Petitions. However, in this place somehow Mahart caught and held to one memory—that of the shining light with which the Abbess had welcomed her on her pilgrimage. "Star—" she croaked hoarsely.

She tripped and fell over a portion of wall near as high as her knees, landing painfully so she could only lie where she was for a space. Flowers— Flowers—and a field—and someone to come.

The heaviness of the fern scent seemed to fall away, as, from not far from her head, there was a much sharper and cleaner scent. She looked at her hand, it was sticky red—not with blood, for the smell drew that hand to her mouth.

Lamman fruit—and ripe, though this was not the season. But she did not question that as she combed through the vine leaves and crammed the berries into her mouth, almost swallowing them whole. Her first hunger so satisfied, she looked about. Her tumble had somehow deposited her in what had once been a garden. But—Mahart shook her head dizzily—it was all wrong! Even she who had never trod farm soil or been at a harvest could see the medley of vigorous plants around her were all ripe when, by nature's law, they should be months apart in development.

Her broken nails filled with rich soil as she grubbed for the long podlike roots of salassa, crunching their meatiness between her teeth until the juice ran down her chin. Now she could see a row of low-growing bushes not too far away, their branches bending under a wealth of plumferts all in golden ripeness. Even the Duke had never had such a feasting as this!

Mahart's wonder grew stronger. Most of the fruit crowded in such a wealth around her at this place usually attracted both insects and birds. She saw neither. But beyond the plumferts there was a still higher jut of wall and from there came sound—

She got to her feet and went toward that. Now she could see, as she rounded the largest of the trees, that there was a hollow in a tall spire of stone. It was like a pocket and no daylight appeared to reach into it and yet it was not dark. Set into the wall well above the center of the cleft was a gleaming crystal.

Mahart went to her knees and for the first time all her terrors and fears struck her and she answered them with tears such as she would, if she could, never show her enemies.

From the bottom point of the crystal water flowed in a stream no wider than her smallest finger to fill a basin. Over the edges of that poured in turn the overflow, to soak the ground and vanish, but not in any visible stream.

Somehow she crept to that basin, bowed her head before the shining of what hung above it. Mahart had come to believe that this was a place of evil, yet within it, as a stone was within a fruit, there was good! That such could dwell together she could not believe—she could only accept.

She would not sully the flood in the basin with her muddy hands, rather strive to wash them with that which flowed over the edge until they seemed clean and she could cup them to bring water to her mouth. She drank. There were no longer any words—words were not for this place—there was only abiding peace as if soft arms gathered her in and held her close in a comfort she had never before known.

Willadene hunched against her bag and tried not to think of bowls of honied porridge, slabs of fresh bread spread thick with butter—all of them more meaningful now than the remnants of the feast in the castle. She had sparingly used the cordial, merely wetting her fingertip and touching it to her tongue. Its restorative powers she had witnessed many times over, but it did not now entirely satisfy her aching middle.

Judging by the light—and a single patch of bright sun which touched the top of a mound of debris a little farther from her improvised den, it must be midafternoon. They were now hours behind Mahart and her captors. Once more she held that rag of night rail to her nose and fastened all her will on seeking the right thread of scent.

Only she was tired and had to fight to keep her eyes open, her mind centered on what she would do. However, she was completely shocked awake when she felt rather than heard the beat of hooves, vibrating through the ground. Her only answer was to squeeze farther back into the scant covering and wait.

What she heard then was no longer just the jolt of hoof on earth and mossy stone, but a hissing. The bush before her shook as a slim body found a path between branches and leaves, and then she was looking down at what could only be Vazul's furred companion, now raising her forelimbs from the ground and rearing up as far as she was able to reach.

"*Ssssaaa—*" There was no more movement; certainly the Lord Chancellor had not made an appearance. But the creature now leaped for her, and then was almost instantly circled about her shoulder, even as she favored that choice of position with her master.

Willadene was smoothing the head which rubbed now and then against her chin when she saw the blot of black, standing out clearly in the sun, which could only be Nicolas.

He was leading three horses, two of them saddled for riders and the third weighted with a brace of pack bags. Willadene crawled out of hiding and stood up, her muscles aching from that long crouch in hiding.

Two of the horses Nicolas made fast by their reins to piles of rubble, but the third he busied himself with, loosing one of the bags, bringing out a coarse napkin which bulged with a promise that made the girl lick her lips.

So far he had not spoken, but he handed the package to her with a snapped "Eat up!" She noted that his eyes were never still and she thought he was reading all which was about them as a scribe might read a book.

She sat down on a jut of stone wall and eat she did, striving to do so in less than frantic gulps. There was also a small flagon which a sniff told her was one of Halwice's herb teas and she took a measured sip from that.

Nicolas was on the prowl about their rough camp. Twice he went down on one knee to study what seemed to be a bare patch of ground. When he came back to her he wore that usual frown she had associated with him since their first meeting. She licked her lips and retied the package over about a third of its remains. Now was the time when she must sink herself even farther in his sight.

"I do not ride—" she said boldly and looked at the nearest of the tethered horses warily.

His frown grew the sharper and he muttered a word or so she did not really hear. Then he answered her as if he was one who had full power over her untutored body.

"You will ride! At least there is a trail which can be followed for a woodsrunner—even if you can no longer play the hound. Hold on to the saddle horn; give me the reins. We shall be greatly hindered but we shall go."

Boost her up into the saddle he did. She felt a disquiet which almost made her dizzy—the ground looked far down and hard. Her bag he had stripped from her shoulder to fasten behind her saddle. The horse shifted weight under her and she fought to keep her balance. But she followed orders and took a firm hold of the saddle horn, her nails near biting into its surface.

Now it was Nicolas who led the way on foot. He held the reins of her horse, which luckily seemed of even temperament and willing to accept her as a burden, and, having looped his own reins on the saddle of the second mount, it fell in behind as if well trained to this form of travel, the pack pony bringing up the rear.

At first all Willadene could think of was her precarious position, but as nothing appeared to shake her loose she began to watch Nicolas. From time to time he would leave her for a moment or two.

His eyes turned ever from ground to bush, to the trunks of trees around which they wound a way which seemed to him to be as clear as a beckoning scent might be for her. At length she spoke softly.

"You are travel trained." She had heard back at the inn of the guides upon which merchants had come to depend whenever they had need to turn off the main highway. "What do you read as might a scribe from what is about us?"

To her surprise and inward relief he looked up over his shoulder at her and there was a quirk of a wry sort of smile about his lips. He had discarded that half mask and so seemed in an odd way closer to those she knew.

"I read—so—" He pointed to a scuffed patch in the carpet of last year's leaves. "This is an easy trail, for some of those we follow are city men and have no idea how one hides one's passing. See that branch ahead—it was stupidly broken off perhaps because it raked some-one's cap awry or the like. But there is one with them who knows the open country and he leads."

Willadene could not have told whether they were headed north or south, east or west, at this moment. Except that westward lay Kronengred and she was sure they were not headed back toward the city.

"Where do they head?"

A trace of that frown returned. "North. But if they think to take refuge in some hole of the Wolf's they are lack witted. Not only did our doughty Prince clean out the main headquarters but he left one body of men, together with such trained rangers as the Duke had not recalled, to hunt out all other lairs. And the Prince is moving again—north. His scouts are indeed well trained and track tested. Look now what I do."

He went down on one knee where a tuft of tough grass sprouted from between the aboveground root ridges of a very tall and old tree. Delicately, he used his knife and, separating the grass, he cut about a half dozen stalks.

Keeping them carefully in one hand, with the other he
stroked the lump of green upstanding again. Though it was
difficult for Willadene to see at this distance from her seat
aloft she could guess that a trained eye might well catch
the disturbance.

The fresh stems of grass he twisted and then reached
well up so he near had to stand on tiptoe to touch a mass
of dried bird's nest from the previous season. Into that he
tightly wove the grass—but only to one side so there was
a small spot of green facing the direction ahead of them.
Then he turned to her with a laugh.

"I play the montebank now, mistress. Such skills are
not needed—as yet. But take note of what I do, for the
time may come when it is necessary for you to use hands
and eyes to follow some road and leave a message
behind."

He allowed her rest from riding as the dusk began to
close in and she needed that, thinking of a certain cream
among her store which would ease chafed and burning
skin. The campsite he had selected was not far from a
brook, the sound of which was soothing, too.

Here one of the great master trees of this dwindling
forest had fallen in some storm, taking with it several
lesser brothers and sisters. What fronted them was not
unlike the untidy nest along the trail but blown up to
accommodate a giant bird. It was into this that Nicolas
cut and broke a cunning way. The horses he picketed
nearby, explaining that their mounts could well give first
alarm if anything came in their direction.

Willadene paced stiff-legged back and forth, trying to
release cramped muscles. She went down to the stream
where she joyfully found a generous stretch of cress just
coming into ripeness. But remembering Nicolas's caution
she put into use one of his lessons. She did not pull the
plants raggedly from their bed, leaving full sign that they
had been so harvested, rather picked and chose in the
twilight, hoping to make sure that the opening left by what

she took would be, as far as she was able to arrange it, covered by what remained.

When she had done she was startled to find Nicolas beside her. Those eyes which had always seemed so easily turned into weapons looked different somehow.

"Mistress," he said slowly, "I welcome you to the trails."

20

"Picked him up jus' like we was told in Brown Bessie's." The metal-enforced booted toe of the squad leader indicated the object at their feet with a hearty prod which made that bedraggled heap moan and strive to pull himself even tighter into a ball. Prince Lorien regarded their catch with a scornful lift of lip, but the Chancellor leaned forward in his chair to regard their captive with a measuring look.

"Look at me!" he suddenly commanded, and reluctantly that tousled head did lift, so that shifty, watery greenish eyes met the probing ones of the Chancellor.

"You serve—whom?" If those words had been a whiplash they would have bitten that forlorn youth on the floor. "Or is that coat you wear a castoff?"

"Find your tongue, scum!" commanded the squad leader. He grabbed the fellow's hair in his thickly gloved hand and jerked the captive's head even higher, near bringing him off the floor.

"I—be—messenger—" But it was plain that he was trying hard not to yield to the concentrated forces of their wish.

The squad leader shook him and he uttered a small,

broken cry. Tears slipped from his eyes and runneled the grime on his cheeks.

"We have no time to waste"—the Prince's voice was as chill as a pail of ice water to douse their prisoner— "and there are many ways to sharpen a man's memory and loosen his tongue. You have heard the Chancellor— Whose messenger are you?"

The youth on the floor was sniffing, a flow from his nose adding to that from his eyes.

"Hers—"

"And *she* being?" continued the Lord Chancellor.

"The High Lady. She sent to Wyche—I was his man then—and said she must have someone sly and cunning—"

He was interrupted then by a short bark of laughter from the Prince as he paused to gulp.

"And thus you helped to set traps—" Vazul continued.

"I carried messages to Wyche—he sent me into the burrows," the prisoner half sobbed. "An' it was me as was to get the bed wench outta th' way. But, I swears, by the Horns of Gratch, I only took orders—"

The Prince had been watching him with narrowed eyes and now he pounced with the speed of a hunting cat.

"Took orders—and the High Lady Mahart—is that not so?—is out of the city—in whose hands now?"

The captive cowered as well as he could with that torment of tight hair hold on him. "They said—Ishbi." His answer was hardly more than a whisper.

"For what reason?" Vazul took up the interrogation. "Give us facts which are the truth and you can hope for a quick death. Keep secrets and learn there are other and long, painful ways of leaving this world."

"I don't know!" Now the prisoner's voice arose to a sheer wail of pure terror. "I got me orders—I weren't told nothin' else."

"Ishbi," the Prince said slowly. "This High Lady you ran errands for—where did she go?"

"Lord Prince, how do I know? Me an' Jonas an' Gorger, we got the other High Lady out as we had been told—an' we held her—along the north trail till the news came as she was to be sent to Ishbi. But me, I did not go with 'em as took her—I came back here, 'cause I don't know the land ways. And I was a-waitin', as I was told, until your squad picked me up."

"I think," the Prince remarked, "that we have here a very small fish where we had hoped to enmesh an oartooth. He may supply you with a little more knowledge, my Lord Chancellor, but nothing more really pertinent to our search. Meanwhile—" He had been playing with a slender pick of a dagger, such as might enter a full mask helm to find a vulnerable eye. Now he slipped the weapon into its own sheath which was a pocket on the belt of his sword. "We ride north. I have already ordered out the scouts and if there is a trail to be found, be sure they will chance on it. Also, your Bat is playing a part in this and"—he smiled—"Lord Chancellor, I have the greatest respect for the talents of that one."

"His Highness has asked for an audience at the Abbey; that is where he has just gone. Having come into his holding sidewise as it were, there may be things he should know of the past, so he goes there to discover them."

Prince Lorien nodded. "Wise enough. Meanwhile, Mattew, remove this offal and release it to my Lord Chancellor's men. They may have some further use for it."

In spite of a rise of wailing two of the squad obeyed the wave of their leader's hand and their captive was dragged away.

Mahart regarded the scanty rags which were all that was left of her night shift. There was the blanket still girded about the silent horse outside this area of safety—but the cloak which was her only possible covering she could not find, and night would soon bring cool breezes to roughen her scratched and begrimed skin.

It would have to be the blanket, she decided, nerving herself into what she was sure was peril in leaving this garden. The gentle peace held her still but also it was as if a part of her mind had awakened from some drugged state and she was able to think as well as feel once more.

She paid a second visit to the basin and once more washed both hands and face from its overflow and then, before she might be cowed into reconsidering, she struck out for that lower place in the wall over which she had fallen.

The sun was gone now and there was a dusky twilight. She had crossed the wall when she heard a splashing from the lake. Those things of the island—and she had not even so much as a belt knife! Yet she needed that blanket before night finally closed in.

Stooping Mahart picked up a short length of stone. It was smooth and rounded, with broken, jagged bits at either end. Plainly it had once been part of a much larger carving. With it in hand she crossed the long tangled moss toward the pier.

Out in the lake it was as if moonshine—though that orb was not overhead—had been caught and held in the broken rubble. Only it was greenish in hue rather than the clear gem beauty she knew. And there was a great deal of movement there now. The creatures were even more difficult to see by that strange radiation, but they were taking to the water which along the shore she could see was splashing, well churned by their entrances.

Setting her jaw and grasping her heavy, improvised club with both hands, she hurried to the horse. For the first time a new emotion awoke in her—pity. It had been as much a captive of those who had sent them here as she, and, though she did not know what killed it, she was angry as well as sad.

She knelt by the inert body and, laying her club within reach, she tugged at the buckles which held the blanket fast. Then—Mahart had no idea why she did this, but she found herself edging forward, taking its head on her knees and pressing her palms against the rough hide just above the half-closed eyes.

There was no healer she had ever heard of who could reverse the hold of death, no herb grown which could draw back a thing already departed.

Still there was something rising in her now, a strength she had never felt before. And she found herself crooning, an old, old swinging of words that came out of her own past when once she had had a nurse from the north country who had treated her as the lonesome child she was and not an untouchable High Lady.

There was a huge sigh, ruffling some of the tatters of her nearly vanished shift. Out of her—even as the water curled from the basin—was running energy and the animal was responding. Perhaps not death had claimed it after all but rather overwhelming fatigue.

As its head rose from her knee there came a shrill ear-paining scream which was echoed and reechoed from the water end of the pier. Things were scrambling out of the water, yet in the air they hesitated, bunching together instead of advancing as she expected them to.

Mahart, club in hand, was on her feet, barely aware that the horse was scrambling and kicking its way upright also. Her attention now was for the things from the lake. Though the greenish glow of the island seemed also to cling about them, here she could see them much better.

They were certainly unlike any animal she had ever heard of or seen fancifully pictured in the old books. Each had four long thin limbs. Those at the upper part of their bodies—for once out of the water they were now actually standing—appeared to have not paws but digits webbed together into hands. Their heads were large and round, balanced in size by the lower portion of their bellies, and their features resembled those of a toad she had once seen bewilderedly lost in the sorry waste of the castle garden. The eyes were very large, as was the mouth, the nose only a slit in between. They had no covering over slick greasy-looking skin, and she could not guess their sex, though she had an idea that both male and female made up that ever-growing crowd.

Still, to her complete amazement, they made no attempt to approach her closely, though the arrival of more and more from the lake pushed the first comers forward. Yet she was certain that they intended her no good and must be planning an attack.

A place of refuge? The garden? The horse blew and now gave a high whinny. It, too, was facing the water things, the whites of its eyes showing, and it stamped on the mossy stone.

Mahart reached out with one hand and caught at the dangling reins. The mount did not try to elude her, instead shouldered against her as if she supplied some idea of safety.

Slowly Mahart made the trip back to the garden wall. But was the expanse within large enough to hold them both without the horse destroying the wealth of food? It seemed to know what she would do. Pulling the reins from her loosened grasp, it withdrew a little and then leaped the low wall with ease.

Behind them from the lake arose a wailing which appeared to contain the beat of words. Mahart caught at the wall. She was being pulled upon, urged back to where they waited, and it was all she could do to resist. Her grasp on the wall top was anchorage, and she dragged herself toward that one step and then another until she could throw herself over, to lie once again facedown in the thick growth of ground fruit. Instantly that compulsion ceased.

The wailing continued for the space of several breaths and then died away, and she could hear once more a splashing of lake water. The creatures, she hoped, were withdrawing.

Turning she saw that the horse was moving around the

inner edge of the wall, seeming to purposefully avoid the plants. Finally it came to a patch where it lowered its head and began to graze with greedy haste lest this somehow be withdrawn beyond reach. She was able to get the bridle off awkwardly, snatching also the blanket having loosed the last of its buckles.

The coarse cloth smelled of horse and dust but it was warm. Drawing it about her she went back to the fountain. She spoke aloud now as if the sound of her voice would bring the answer she needed.

"What am I?" she asked and somehow aimed that question at the crystal from which the water so steadily dripped. "There is that to be done—that I can understand here." She touched her breast and then her forehead between her eyes. "But what am I—surely not what I always believed myself to be."

There was no answer out of the niche— No, she must learn the answers in another place—inside herself. That strong sense of waiting which had haunted her so long in dreams of the flowered meadows was upon her. But the time was not yet. She found a place farther along the wall where the damp, diffused flow of the basin did not reach and she pulled the blanket closely about her. The sleep her body demanded came quickly and easily.

There was a face—or rather a pair of compelling eyes fastened on Willadene. Inner power lurked in those eyes even as she had always felt it lay with Halwice. Only, this threatened—it was not just holding her in judgment. Old, old eyes like pits of whirling, ever-burning fires into which one might fall and be consumed—

She fought not with fists but with her will, her thoughts—

Then she was sitting up in the dark and into her ear sounded the soft hissing of Ssssaaa. Warmth, more warmth than such a small body could really hold, seemed to spread from where the creature had fitted itself to the girl's curve of shoulder. There were no eyes—only the dark, and by her someone stirred so that her hand went to her knife hilt.

There was a hand heavy on her shoulder now and a whisper even lower than Ssssaaa's hiss to be heard.

"Be quiet!"

But the girl did not need that warning. She had caught those other sounds through the night—from beyond the brushy cave they had fashioned for themselves. Horses—the grasp on her was released and he was gone. Her sight had adjusted a little to the darkness and she reached up a hand too late to stop Ssssaaa, who was also leaving her.

Whoever rode the night took no precautions to muffle their passage and they were farther away than she had first believed. She heard the splashing of water as if their mounts had taken to the stream, but there was no way of telling how many of them there might be.

It was there, also, the stench of evil. She fumbled for her amulet bag and held it to her nose. Fastened to it now was the small packet of the two leaves she had found in the herbal, and twisted around it all the scrap of Mahart's night rail. She had a strong feeling that each of these drew strength from the other and that they must be kept as one.

The sounds made by the horses faded. They had not approached this brush heap which had been their shelter. But—within her Willadene knew and her grip tightened on the amulet—one at least among that company had sensed the fugitives. Why they had not been rooted out she could not tell—

Nicolas crawled back in beside her. She could see the light blur of his face, but the rest of him melted into the night.

"We have fellow travelers—"

Over the branch arched Ssssaaa and she was once more with her.

"Some one of them knew of us," she told him and was sure of what she said.

"They are either pressed for time or"—and now that

chill which she had so often seen in his eyes seemed transferred to his whisper—"think us so easy prey that we may be gathered up in leisure. Ssssaaa managed to keep our horses quiet—surely Vazul has an excellent ally there. But it was plain that they ride a known path—five men and two women—"

Without understanding why that particular name came into her mind Willadene said, "One the High Lady Saylana."

Again she felt the pressure of his fingers closing about her upper arm.

"How did you know that?"

She had buried her nose in that untidy bundle which her amulet had become.

"There was the scent of aspicen fern—that and black evil!"

"They did not try to cover their trail." His grasp on her eased somewhat. "West—west and north. The Prince broke the Wolf but he did not gather up all his followers. They would scatter until summoned again. West and north—toward Ishbi."

"What is Ishbi?" she demanded at last. The word appeared to hold some dire power for anyone she had heard say it.

There was a long moment of silence as if Nicolas was considering what he would say, and when he did reply it seemed to her that he was evasive.

"You have looked upon the Star—in the Abbey?"

She remembered well her one trip there with Halwice when she had been left in the place of worship while her mistress had withdrawn to confer with the Abbess. But then she had been filled with such wonder of the place that she could not call to mind any detail of it. Except—except that fragrance—that richness of scent to calm heart and mind and which had rolled upon her, encased her, so that Halwice had actually had to shake her when she'd returned to bring her once more to the here and now.

However, it was that wonderful scent which held fast her memory—and she had only a dim mind picture of something shining at the far end of the long room.

"Our world," Nicolas was continuing slowly, as if he still searched for the proper words, "lies open, even as do we from our birth time. There are ever choices for us and also for the world. Sometimes those choices seem to be governed by a will beyond ours. What would your life have been had the plague not struck?"

Willadene felt the soft fur of Ssssaaa. "I—my mother was a midwife, known to Halwice, my father a border guard. In those days of the old Duke people were pushing north. There was good grazing land for sheep and even talk of building a town to center the guard and their families and provide a trading post for the new settlers. My father had signed for duty, my mother thought it a chance for new service." Strange, she had not thought about that for years—the slavery in Jacoba's inn had beaten such hopeful memories out of her.

"So your life would have followed another path and thus formed by the path you would have been another person."

His hold on her was no longer tight and compelling, it had instead some of the warmth Ssssaaa always provided. Now she dared to ask the balancing question.

"Who would you have been?"

"My House was old, once reckoned among the noble names of the duchy. But—we served at the fall of Ishbi. It was said a curse lay upon us thereafter, even though we fought under the Star. Thus we dwindled in numbers. Also the raids from the far west cut into our holdings and we had no funds to hire fighting men as our own band dwindled over the years. Sons and daughters died young and without offspring save for a few—until it came to my own time. My father had been crippled in a fight with an orsbear that had been raiding our last horse herd and he could no longer lead or attract men to his following.

"The outlaws were growing stronger, and just before the coming of the plague they struck. Our hold fell and in the flames of the great hall my father and mother died together. But the plague had already been rumored and they had fostered me with a ranger up in the hills, for my father could see no future lordship for me. For his common sense I shall be always thankful. However, we had a distant blood tie with Vazul and when the plague was over and I was left, I dared to put that to the test. Vazul is a man of many talents, far more than even his worst critics can suspect, and I have no regrets for becoming his ears and eyes in strange places. That is my story, mistress. If the outlaws had not taken Farholm, or if I had not been sent to the rangers for training, or if I had not hunted out the Lord Chancellor—then I would not be what I am today."

"Ishbi," she said slowly. "What is this? They do not speak of it in Kronengred, or if they do I have never heard of it."

"We are back once more," he answered, "to the balance of Dark and Light. Generations ago there arose a power in the west which dealt with forces ordinary men could not understand. There was a woman—Nona—of the Royal House of Harkmar, who they tell—though that is perhaps only story—was not of completely human breeding—though how such a monstrous thing might happen who can tell. This force from the west was drawn to her and she to it, and she took with her those of a like nature and they founded a strange hold—Ishbi—

"For a measure of time they were nearly forgot—and then they tried their powers. But those of the duchy and the kingdom under the Star put as they thought an end to such dealings with the Dark. And there was a final battle when that which was in body was slain. But whether it was all defeated no man knew. And now one hears rumors that the plague was of such devising that we might be weakened for a second such trial of arms."

"What do they want with the High Lady Mahart? A hostage?"

The dawn was coming now and she could see him far more clearly.

"Perhaps. But it is plain that by those who have passed us this night—the High Lady Saylana is minded to ride for Ishbi and there lies the rotten core of all our troubles."

Once more she pressed her amulet to her nose. For a moment it was as if she stood with the High Lady Mahart, so strong was that whiff of scent.

"Then so do we go also," she said and knew that she could do no less.

They ate of the traveler's provisions he had brought. She went by herself to the streamside and pulled off the divided skirt and the loose drawers under it and worked as well as she could, using as little of the cream as possible, to soothe her chafed skin.

It was a bright morning and the sun dappled the water of the stream through the tree branches. Willadene was aware of life all around her—the sounds of birds, the rustling of what could only be small animals in the grasses. Ssssaaa crouched by the stream and drank and then made a lightning fast slap with a forepaw and brought out a flapping fish which vanished quickly save for a bone or two.

"They have left us a full trail," Nicolas told Willadene when she returned to the campsite, "and they ride northwest making no attempt to cover their passage. Therefore we go on alert. For since they have no fear we may well find peril of one kind or another. The outlaws are scattered but they are outworld men and they know this country well."

She hated to be in the saddle again but there was no other way, and she was as sure as Nicolas that there was a good reason to hurry. Ishbi waited—or something waited there.

21 The slim scout, his dappled clothing difficult to see even when he moved into a path of full sunlight, looked up at his commander, ready with his report.

"It is true, Highness, but there are three trails which muddle one another. The last is ranger set."

Prince Lorien took a carefully measured pull from his saddle bottle. "Ranger set?" he questioned.

"By one who knows many trail tricks, Highness. There were those among the outlaws who have such knowledge but for them to deliberately leave signs of travel, as well hidden as those are, that I do not believe."

The Prince grimaced. "No, for any following from the town now would not have the wit to read such. Therefore we may believe that you spot the directions of Trufors, the Lord Chancellor's man. And before him two parties who made no attempt to hide their going?"

"The second rode hard and in the night, but they must have known the way well, Highness, as if this were indeed an open trail."

"Send out the summons, Trufors, but also alert the scouts."

"We are going, Highness?"

"Undoubtedly to Ishbi," the Prince replied. He was well aware of the shadow on the other man's face. Trufors could not be judged by any man to lack courage, but he, also, was of the Old Blood. Men of his name clan had marched this way full two hundred years ago to a bitter and near devastating battle.

The scout saluted and was gone, swallowed up by the foliage as if he had never been there, while Lorien was left to stare down at the hoof-cut dead leaf tracks among the trees. That a man could not leave untreated an unhealed sore on his body—that was the truth. Nor could those who were of the ancient houses leave a festering wound within the land itself. His father—well, he had sent his squire to carry the message to him. But it took time to assemble a force to sweep this rugged country, full of cuts and draws, thick trees, and hills rising to the mountains.

There were the forces from Kronengred, and he was certain that Vazul had enough influence over his master to see that they would also be on the move. But already there had been rioting in two sections of the city. A whole street of merchant warehouses burnt— Odd that that should have appeared to start in the Herbmistress's shop. She was a strange one, but in her way she was like Vazul, strong of spirit and knowledgeable in other ways. And now she had gone to the Abbey. They said prayers strengthened a man's sword arm—if so they would need those in plenty.

That they took the girl appeared to weigh the hardest on Halwice as the hours passed. Hostage, he was sure, bargaining piece— He looked down again at that churned road they had left. She was very young and from all accounts she knew very little save what had been her home. He tried to remember her face—but another seemed ever to form between—that of the ripe beauty who had openly tried to pull him into her net. One memory did float through his mind—of that dance which should have been

so stiffly formal to follow custom but had suddenly become lightsome as any frolic while her hand had been in
his. It had never happened so before— And she had been
taken from the safety of her bed, where she should have
been in peace. Lorien's jaw squared. Ishbi—no, such inno-
cence belonged not in Ishbi, nor could the Dark be allowed
to take it so.

Dawn had come and the first tinges of pink shone in
the sky when Willadene, hoping to hide her shrinking from
another day in the saddle, allowed Nicolas to help her to
mount and they rode away. But he did not follow the open
trail of those who had passed earlier. Instead he threaded
a parallel way among such cover as there was. Now and
then he halted and she sat shivering nervously as he left
her to cast over to that other trace. He was not just making
sure of it, she was certain, but rather setting some of those
subtle signs such as he had called to her attention yesterday, and of this she accused him when he returned.

"Just so. The Prince's scouts will be out. Those we
follow now ride freely, for they believe that any picking
up their traces will be of their own kind and perhaps will
gather to accompany and support them. But the Prince will
be not too far behind—if we are lucky his scouts may
reach us." However, it would seem that such luck as that
was to be denied them. They did halt at intervals and
Nicolas allowed their horses to graze or drink at streams
and springs he seemed to know of old. He was very quiet
this morning and was short in answer to any talk she tried.
It occurred to Willadene that he was perhaps regretting
his openness of the night before and would welcome no
more confidences concerning the past, or more than surface acquaintanceship for the present.

She kept the amulet packet in one hand, though the
other was tight on her saddle horn, and sniffed at it from
time to time. Always she feared that that scent which was
Mahart's own had been dissipated by the time or distance

and she could not be sure they still followed on the track of her captors.

Yet, even when Willadene attempted with all the will she could summon to keep her senses fixed upon the matter which had brought her here, she still was aware that the country around her was slowly also becoming a part of her. The scent of all the rich growth about her, the sounds of insects and of birds—it was almost as if she had been in a box all her life and now was free.

Those faint memories she had recalled for Nicolas—those lost almost for good behind the horror of Jacoba's kitchen—had held such things, and she had known them before. Had she really gone with her mother out for the harvesting? It could well have been, for her mother was well-known, and she had been called to attend cases of illness beyond Kronengred's walls. She did not fight to pursue those faint suggestions of memory. What counted now was their quest. The High Lady must be finding this open world as strange as she herself did. Willadene hoped with all her heart that Mahart's captors had thought her too valuable to be ill-used.

Ssssaaa was hissing almost sleepily in her ear, and on impulse she reached up with the amulet so that small, pointed nose could sniff at what she cherished. Before she could withdraw her hand needle teeth closed on flat leaves she had found between leaves of the ancient book.

"No!" she said with such vigor that Nicolas turned his head to look at her. Gently she pushed Ssssaaa's head away from the folded silk and forgot her hold on the saddle horn as she spread out its length. She could see the teeth marks in the silk, but the two strange leaves remained intact.

"What is it?" Nicolas had now moved in beside her.

"I do not know—" Swiftly she told him of how Ssssaaa had freed it from the glued pages of the moldering herbal. He did not try to take it from her but leaned the closer.

"Leaves—" Willadene was saying. "See here the

veins. I have seen many dried plants but none as old as this which did not crumble at the touch. Yet I have carried it since I found it and there shows no break.''

His brown finger touched her hands lightly as she held them palm up, the leaves resting on them. And she yielded to that touch, letting him draw nearer to her.

"You say," he said after a moment, "these are leaves—"

She felt her talent questioned. "But it is true, anyone can see that!"

"I say it may be a map. You speak of Heart-Hold— could this be a clue to its rooting?"

Quickly she drew her hands back and folded the silk about the leaves. "We do not seek flowers!" she said firmly. "Heart-Hold was given to the Star until—"

"Until," he interrupted her, "those wolf heads came down from the western hills and there was no more an Abbey. If evil is again astir, so must be good. How many years was that pent up in that book of Halwice's unfound? Why was Ssssaaa able to free it intact?"

She made a careful business of rewrapping the amulet and its two appendages. "You would have it that we do not move by our will, but another's!" Her voice sounded a little shrill.

Halwice, yes, Willadene would answer eagerly any request that the Herbmistress would make of her. Was she not now enduring the agony of riding because it was asked of her talent? But somehow she shrank from the thought that some will beyond her comprehension now used her as she might use a salve to cure an ill.

Nicolas shrugged. "Mistress, this much I have found out in my life. Nothing comes purely to us by chance alone. That which you hold is perhaps greater treasure than any in the Duke's locked coffers. Take good care of it."

His hand came up and brought her mount to an abrupt stop.

It was the silence which warned. An instant earlier two birds had been singing lustily from a tree not far away. She instinctively used the talent. Yes, there was man smell—and one she knew. Her hands pressed the amulet tightly against her breast and she swallowed.

Man smell, and evil, and the evil had grown the thicker since the last time she had picked up that scent. She saw Nicolas glance at her, and with her lips she shaped a name: "Wyche."

He gave only a shadow of a nod. They could hear the thud of hooves now, sounding as clearly as those of the party who had passed them earlier. And then that thick voice reached her.

"We was doin' good in th' city. She should have let us be. That spindle-shanked Duke is overready to be booted to Head Hill an' shorted by the one on his shoulders."

"You overrate yourself, city scum." That voice was cold, so cold it might have been a lash of sleet in their faces. "She has need—that is all you need to know. Had your followers not blundered so we could have had the Prince also." Willadene could feel the rage in that.

"Now he's out hunting and we have no time left for the sport of tracking him down in turn."

The voice sounded farther away as did the sound of hooves. Nicolas grinned. "The tunnel snakes seek refuge—"

"He said that the town was fighting—" Willadene now had full hold of her saddle horn again.

"Yes, we have known that this would come—only not when. There are those who serve the Duke with swords they do not wear in public. Wyche is a boaster and he has been allowed much rope that we might learn through him how far this web might spread. We move to stand face-to-face with that which would swallow us all and it would not be nice in its feeding—for it will like to turn upon those serving it who are no longer of value. Thank you, little one—''

The girl saw he spoke to Ssssaaa. Then he added, ''This one is a protection greater than any armor forged. We are privileged that she was loaned to us. And let us now be about paying for that privilege.''

She still nursed the packet against her as an armswoman might raise a shield. Nicolas urged the horses into a slow walk again, but now they angled a little more northward, slanting away from the route those other two were taking.

It was a whiffling sort of noise which brought Mahart fully awake. She looked up into a sky which was sun bright and yet hazy as if some veil had been drawn between its rays and where she lay. She sat up, her blanket covering falling away. The horse was not too far away, grazing eagerly at the moisture-soaked growth about the edge of the basin, showing no desire to drink directly from it.

Her steed was certainly not any finely cherished mount from the ducal stables. She could see the outlines of ribs on the side nearest her as if it had not been adequately fed for a long time, though it seemed to be making up for that now.

Food—she roused and moved toward the nearest of the miniature trees and selected two well-rounded plumferts for herself. But as she returned to the blanket Mahart was forced to think of the here and now, and also what might lie ahead.

''I was favored. Star,'' she said and made the proper hand sign of thankfulness, yet this time not courtesy but in truth. ''I have been brought out of the hands of my enemies and into this sanctuary, but for this there must be some reason.''

The murmur of her voice died away. Without turning her body she tried to see as much of the enclosure in which she had taken refuge as was possible. The strangeness of all these growing things ripening together—that was beyond any guess she could make. She licked plumfert juice from her fingers and tried hard to add together what she did know.

Had she been taken as a hostage, a weapon to be used against her father? She could remember little of that journey under the depths of Kronengred now. Then there had been that camp where they had forced her on horseback, still prisoner and the word *Ishbi—*

Thought seized upon that word. She closed her eyes for a moment and was back in the musty, shadowed depth of that library where she had roamed undirected, taking here a chronicle, there a journal, reading with a careless lack of any directed interest. Legend slid into ancient fact, fact faded into legend—monsters warred with heroes and treasures spilled out in dark caverns for anyone fortunate or strong enough to take them.

Ishbi—yes. Mahart suddenly grasped the second plumfert so tightly in her hand that its skin broke and the pulp squeezed between her fingers.

Something from the west—yet none that had written of it had given it a name—only hinted that it was not of human kind—in fact that there lay a vast gulf between it and humans and it strove to cross that gulf—to take—

There had been a woman— Mahart shook her head as if to settle her memories into a proper pattern. Now—*she* had been human. Or *had* she? There had been talk of some taint in her bloodline. But she had not been of Kronengred—rather of the kingdom. Nona—

It was as if a chill finger had touched her forehead. She shivered. Yes, it had been the flawed one, King's daughter though she was, who had made that pact. And it was the keep Ishbi that she and her followers had raised as a focal point to draw on powers perhaps only the Abbess of the Star could begin to understand.

Mahart's sticky fist thumped down on her knee in exasperation. All this she had dismissed in her disorganized reading as legend. If she only knew more!

She went to the basin and washed her hands and then on impulse gathered up some tufts of coarse grass which grew along the wall and gingerly began to try to groom the horse. To be doing anything here and now was a relief of beating memory. She was an inept hostler but the animal blew, then shook its head from side to side, as if, Mahart hoped, it was expressing some liking for her ministrations.

There was still no appearance of sun, nor, as far as she could see, any other sign of life except the patient horse and herself. No insects buzzed from flower to flower, no birds sang. Though she knew so little of the outer world she was sure that this was somehow wrong.

Having done her best for the horse, she went to that lower section of the wall over which they had entered this place. She could see the pier and beyond it the island. Though it was not dark yet there appeared to be a sheen of a faint green aura about it. But the water was motionless and she caught no sign of the creatures who had scuttled among the rocks.

The fern forest surrounded these ruins on three sides. The tumble of stones had been reduced to such piles as one could not tell if these were the remains of a border keep, a castle, or a town. Though if this *were* Ishbi it could well be all three. However, she had no intention of leaving the safety she had found to go exploring.

Mahart regarded herself. Though the night rail she had had on had been of triple thickness, as was necessary in the chill of the castle, the material selected had been purposefully soft for the ease of the noble who would wear it. Tags of lace still held by a thread or so, but there were also rents and tears which left only a mass of rags.

Her hair had been braided for the night, but those braids had snagged on briars and twigs. She began to work with it, loosening what she could, picking out the leaves and

twigs caught in it, feeling the soreness of her scalp where
those had pulled. Once loose about her shoulders she could
do no more than use her fingers as ineffectual combs and
try to pull out all the debris she could reach.

When it hung in as good order as she could achieve
Mahart shed her rags, gathered them in a bundle under
her arm and went back to the basin. After all there was
only the horse to witness her bare body.

Around the foot of the basin had been growing a
spongelike plant which caught and held a measure of water
and felt soft in her fingers. Mahart gathered two handfuls
of this and began to bathe as well as she could, wincing
at the smart of scratch and chafe but proceeding grimly
in spite of such discomforts.

When she was through the pleasant warmth seemed to
dry her skin as well as any towel toasted before the fireplace and, finding a fairly open space, she spread out the
remnants of her only garment to survey them critically.

For a moment or two she was elsewhere again—back
in the castle facing the long mirror of her chamber to
survey the glory of her ball gown—a ball gown—her eyes
were closed. Once more she felt a firm hand closing fingers about hers, leading her into such lightness of step she
had never believed possible. She drew now a face out of
memory. How could she who had known so few men in
her life say whether he was handsome? She only knew
that to meet his eyes, answer a smile of his with hers,
gave her warmth and pleasure.

From beneath the closed lids of her eyes now moisture
gathered; she was brought back to the grimness of the here
and now by a tear slipping down her smarting cheek.

Fool that she was! What was past was past and there
were no real memories in it. This was no legend of ancient
chivalry—what would bring any riding after her except
those who were her father's liege men—and, she wondered, bleakly, how many of those could be trusted now?

There remained the matter of clothing. The long sleeves,

one of which was split near half its length, could be torn out. She stood up and held the full length about her.

Some judicious tearing would give her at least a kind of loincloth for underwear and a sleeveless slip reaching near knee length with strips to belt it in snugly. Mahart set to work. Solving those alterations without scissors or even knife as an aid, was a formidable task.

At length she tried on again the awkward garment she had managed to produce and was very glad that this time there was no long mirror to make visible her shortcomings as seamstress.

She had been so intent upon this labor that she was startled when she realized that the hazy light which had signaled day was fading. Surely, and she was fearfully sure of this, it was not yet night—she had not lost that much measurement of time.

The horse's head came up. It had seemed to be dozing against the wall. Now it snorted, looking out over their wall of safety. Mahart hastily scrabbled in the hollow where she had spent the night until her hand once more closed about that length of smooth stone she hoped could be a weapon.

With that in hand she made a careful circle of the entire wall, looking out at all she could see of lake and that loom of fern forest. Her feet found grass and plants easy enough to tread, but she stumbled in some places painfully over stone and knew that she must find some form of foot covering also.

The curious stiffness of this place appeared to take on menace now. She heard the horse whinny and saw it back into a corner of the wall and stand shivering. It must have struck the animal first—now it reached for her.

There was a need—she must go—the need was great—there was nothing else in the world other than that need!

Before her eyes the ranks of ferns split apart, to form an open portal. At the far end of that there was something of their same green, but it was no plant. Some trick of light, or of that *thing* which moved against her, made her sight more acute, far-reaching.

No ruin. There were intact walls, crowning them a bulbous round of roof. That same haze which haloed the island was also here, but it did not hide that the building had an open door and in it stood a figure, a figure who beckoned, who called without audible voice, but rather so on the far limit of hearing, that Mahart's improvised club near slipped from her hands. She was ready to vault the wall to answer.

"Come—!" It was a plea—or was it an order?

Mahart had brought her foot down on one of those handfuls of spongy plants which had provided her with a bath. She turned and half threw herself at the basin. Dropping the stone she plunged both hands into the water gathering there, threw it into her own face so that runnels ran down her hands, dampened her hair, spattered on her shoulders.

Now she clung with both hands to the edge of the basin, trying to force herself to turn to look again at that one who waited, who called—

Who demanded! Of that Mahart was now sure. Trap—a trap and only by the grace of something greater than she could understand, had she not fallen into it.

22 This was a hunt of sorts and every man—moving as noiselessly as possible through the thin woodland, avoiding any open space—might be moving in on game. For some time now the land had been gradually rising, first in such gentle slopes one would hardly notice it, and now with hills which led yet higher.

Lorien crouched behind a rock and listened intently. He had not been mistaken, for that low trill came again—the food-find cry of a black jay to assemble its kind to some unexpected feast. Only that particular sound had not sprung from any bird's throat. Mattew was more to the south—it was Jasper and Timous who flanked him on the right.

There had been many protests but he had hammered home his point—if they spread their advance squad sparsely and kept in touch with well-known signals, they would be better able to locate any trails fresh made. And that he fully intended to be one of the trackers, he had used all his authority to enforce.

The tracks he followed had been older at first, but suddenly there had been a swing of riders from the south, pounding with no care for hiding their trail. Five of them—

A glint of color caught his eye suddenly. There was a wall of thorn brush offering an impenetrable barrier there. The riders he followed had had to turn their path because of it and flank the wall of brush. One of them had paid a forfeit for coming too close.

Lorien loosed the scrap of fine linen. No woodsrunner, not even a gallant of the court would wear such. Without knowing just why he held it to his nose and smelled the remnants of a scent he had met before. This was not the spicy, almost nose-prickling odor that he had been slightly surprised High Lady Mahart had chosen for the ball. It was somehow like clear water, the frosty air of an early winter morning— The other High Lady! She of the beckoning eyes and the ripeness of body so subtly defined by her dress of wine and gold—just such a gold as the lace he held.

He had had no desire to be pulled into the intrigues of the ducal court. But the Chancellor had appeared to believe that the High Lady Saylana was at the core of this trouble. He could not imagine her riding the woodlands, but it was plain she had. Tucking that scrap of lace in his belt he angled around the end of the thorny thicket to answer that call which had sounded for the third time and which he dare no longer ignore.

As he slipped from tree to tree their growth thinned. Here were rocks and boulders but of a color he had never seen before—dull green. And they were veined with lines of an even deeper shade. Now he could see ahead the sharp rise of an escarpment and farther beyond that mountains—two of which marked land over which he had hunted, though he had never come this far into a neighboring land.

There was a faint movement to the right, a signal of his own devising. He kept to cover since he had not been openly hailed and that should mean trouble. It was good that he had advanced so cautiously, for he came out on the edge of a break in the land as if someone with a giant ladle had scooped up the earth.

Jasper lay belly down on the edge of that drop, his eyes shifting quickly from Lorien as the Prince arrived to something below. It was a hump, but it took Lorien a full minute before he recognized that as a crumpled body wearing the forest dress of his own guard.

"Timous—" He breathed the name. "Who—" Anger was hot in him.

"I found him so, Highness. He is dead—" There was a flatness in that answer.

"A fall—?" But even as he said that Lorien was sure that such was not the truth. Timous—unless—unless he had been pursued would never have ventured so near the sharp edge of this drop.

"Traces?" His next question made more sense.

"There is a trail—only his," Jasper returned.

"Get you to Mattew, bring up a full squad."

"You stay alone, Highness?" There was a quick denial in that.

"I keep watch. You will find me here. But be quick— then tell Mattew ropes—there are such on the pack ponies."

The scout looked as if he would still deny Lorien's right to remain, but he had served too long under the Prince not to know when his commander had determined on something.

Jasper had spoken of a trail. Lorien averted his eyes from that broken figure below. Timous had been a quiet man with skills which had served them all well. But he had always seemed to be ill at ease when praised and somehow he had never appeared to have any close friend in the squad. The plague had ended a life he never spoke of, and it had seemed to the Prince that he had always been locked out of comradeship in a manner the others did not understand. But Timous was *his* man—he had served with loyalty and skill. And there was now a death to be paid for, as Lorien did not believe this came by accident.

He himself began to move warily along the rim. The trail could not be too far away or Timous would not have fallen here.

There was a trail, yes, and Lorien hunched over it, unable to read meaning in what those tracks told him. Someone—a single someone—had run this way unheeding of what lay ahead. There were broken branches, evidences that the runner had fallen and risen, to throw himself on at frantic haste. Yet as Lorien began to trace the way back he could find no evidence that there had been any pursuit. No other tracks covered those left by Timous.

He was well away from the edge of the cliff. To his right the outcrops of stone were rising, seeming to seek to stand shoulder to shoulder. Ahead they appeared to form a wall. But Timous's tracks led on along that wall.

Lorien drew his sword. He was a fool to go farther, yet the need to know what had happened at the beginning of this trail drew him in a way he could not explain. Then Timous's frantic prints overlaid those of horses, and those pointed straight away to where there was an opening between the walls of green stone which was like a gateway.

Lorien stopped. His good sense had battled that pull of compulsion. But without thought he stepped out onto the open trail, trying to see what might lie beyond that cut.

Movement— He slipped quickly right, his shame at his own folly feeding the anger which had come when he had sighted Timous's body. He was scout trained, considered a canny fighter. Prudence said slip back, away—

Only, though his will commanded, his feet would not obey. For a moment he realized the horror of that—but if that strangeness held him, it did not control the rest of his body. His sword was out—

That which subtly threatened came out into the open. For a moment relief touched Lorien. An armored figure, even if it did wear a helm which completely masked its features, was nothing new. What puzzled him was that it did not seem to bear any weapons—there was no sword, no axe raised to contest the way.

But the guard—if guard it was—raised its arm so that its hand now lay on its own left shoulder. A second later, and that arm moved in a throw and through the air came a vivid, flashing line of green. With it—

In spite of himself Lorien near cringed. There was just a line of light rippling through the air, but before it came darkness, death, and worse than death. He could move his feet now—the thing wanted him to run. Instead he stood his ground. That was no spear, no arrow, and the armored one had not released another like it.

Lorien swung his sword. He was now fighting pure fear, fear which shook him as he never believed it might. His sword flashed through the air. It should have struck the green shaft, broken it—

Instead that line caught upon the sword, wrapped itself about the blade as if no sharpness of steel edge could cut it. And Lorien, moved by fear and an inner wave of horror, hurled the sword from him before the thing which claimed it could touch his hand. He tried to retreat.

The guard made no attempt at a second attack. He merely stood waiting as if he had no doubts of what was to follow. As the blade clattered on the rock and hit the ground the green length shook itself clear. It was no longer airborne, but it was still on the move, swiftly across the ground like an adder set for the kill.

Lorien hunched against one of the tall pillars of rock, then tried to slip around it. There was a blank moment of complete shock, and he realized that here also was another drop—not as wide as that which had swallowed Timous but one which battered him in spite of his mail as he fell. He had a fleeting thought that the green length would follow him, and then his helmed head hit hard against an outcrop of stone and there was nothing but darkness.

*   *   *

The long fingers of the woman seated at the table were very busy. She had at either hand a row of small bowls dark with age and long use, each with its powder filling. But she was not mixing them in any careful measurement, as had always been her way. Instead, she had before her a square of stone in which were embedded here and there tiny sparks of light, as if one looked up into a night sky to sight stars.

"You understand," Halwice said quietly, "that what I do is a thing forbidden and it can only be done once. I have been absolved and have fasted, and spent my night in penance before the Star. Now—it is no longer in my hands, I am only the instrument."

The Duke chewed at his lower lip and said nothing. But the Lord Chancellor moved a little in his chair, opened his lips as if to speak but remained silent.

Pinches of powder, some ash gray, some the red of dried blood, some the green of leaves still alive, some the blue of the sea, some the white of the sand or of ground seashells.

She worked with care and built her picture lines across the Star sheet the Abbey had with such reluctance loaned her. Halwice had always known that her line—mother, daughter, mother, daughter—had talents. Some of them had not chosen to pay the high price of bringing those to life. She had been so—taking pride as a healer, trying for nothing else until this hour.

The pinches of powder shifted of themselves, appearing to link or avoid those sparks of light. Those of red and gray gathered together and kept apart from any touch of spark. They still moved grain by grain and they were building a picture. Both Duke and Chancellor leaned forward now, hardly daring to draw breath lest in some way they disturb what was happening.

Just as the gray and the red were attracted together, so did the other colors find what seemed to be their bond mates. And then the three were looking down at what was truly a picture.

"By the Star!" Halwice's voice was a command. There was no more shifting dust.

She was looking at a head so well portrayed in the red and gray that it might have been fresh from the painter's brush.

"Saylana," breathed the Duke. But only for a moment was he right. Beauty was fading, flesh was wrinkling, falling away, a mouth puckered where there were no more teeth to hold it firm. And yet there was a life still in the eyes which had become pits.

And that life stubbornly remained. While from the lower section of the slab, stringing in glistened threads from one spark of light to another, were the other colors—and those remained vibrant and alive long enough for all of them to see them well.

"It is no longer in our hands." Halwice had fallen back in her chair. On the slab the colored powder arose forming rainbow dust motes and then was gone. "They carry the sword and the fate lies upon them, not us. Clean your dukedom, Uttobric—that task remains to you. What chances elsewhere you shall only know in time."

Nicolas slackened pace and Willadene was devoutly glad for that pause. In spite of the treatment she had applied again that morning to her chafed legs she felt ever-present burning pain. She did her best to smother that discomfort with full concentration on the sights and smells around her. And once Nicolas had brought them to a full stop on the edge of a small clearing in which a tawny-coated ober-bear reared erect against the bole of the largest tree which formed the wall about that opening, drawing its great claws in a sweep into the tough bark. Luckily what breeze was blowing was toward them and she smelled the rank taint of bear, but they did not attract the beast's attention. Then he dropped four-footed again and waddled south.

"He marks his hunting territory," Nicolas explained. "There may be a younger one of his species hereabouts. If such chances on the tree and cannot easily reach those claw signs he will prudently withdraw."

Ssssaaa stirred where she curled about Willadene's throat. She thought at first that the creature had been disturbed by the smell of the bear, but instead that needle nose flipped up the edge of the amulet package which now rode on the outside of her jerkin.

Aware that Ssssaaa had her own way of communication the girl lifted the bag to her nose. Through the rank animal odor which still lingered she suddenly caught the stab of another scent. It lasted only for a second or two but it was enough to bring her head around at a sharper angle. Then it was gone, but that had been like a cry for help— she reported her belief. For a moment she thought that Nicolas was not going to put any credence in that—his eyes were sword bright again. Then, briefly, he nodded and changed course, even hurried their pace a little.

The forest around them thinned and now rocks arose. Beside one which towered above him even though he was mounted, her companion reined in. She was startled from her examination of that spur, for its color was unlike anything she had seen elsewhere—dull green, not, however, from overgrowing moss but in itself—and across its surface, drawn as straightly as if one had pulled a line taut was a band of darker green.

"Ishbi lies ahead—the accursed."

She still held tightly to the amulet, but now she closed her eyes and used her talent. Layer by layer, she sifted scents, putting aside those which were born of the world about her—the animals, Nicolas, what she held in the amulet. It was a hard stretch, a struggle, as if she sought out through the dark in all directions, grasping, grasping at filaments so fine they slipped through her frantic hold. Out and out, down and down—

Suddenly she stiffened. There was an answer born of darkness and fear. The scent of spilled blood! Mahart? Had that sudden thrust of her scent meant that she had been bodily threatened? No—somehow she was sure it was not the High Lady. But it was blood and pain rooted together and not too far away.

Willadene's eyes snapped open.

"There is someone hurt!" Inept as she was at any skill on horseback she caught the lead rope Nicolas held only loosely now and somehow headed her mount at an angle which led behind that upthrust spur of rock.

Luckily the horse picked its own cautious way. She felt the warmth of fur against her hand and saw that Ssssaaa had sped down her arm and was now flattened against the neck of her mount. Perhaps—no, she was sure—the creature was in control of the beast. But almost as soon as she had made that discovery they came to an abrupt stop.

The ground broke away only a few paces ahead, the way she had taken ending in a ragged cleft in which the rocks seemed as tumbled together as if they had been hurled by some great force. And she heard a moan.

Swift as she was to quit her saddle she was still awkward enough that Nicolas was before her, working his way to the very edge of that cleft. A moment later Willadene had loosed the bag of her healing simples and joined him.

Though the spur of rock threw much of what lay below into shadow, the girl caught a glance of what seemed to be an arm, the hand scrabbling on one of the tumbled stones as if in effort to draw its owner up.

Nicolas was gone swiftly, even as she knelt as close as she could to the edge to see how the injured one could possibly be reached. The walls, for the most part, were indeed cracked and riven; an agile man might very possibly descend at one place only a little farther along. Whether she could attempt it, hampered by skirts—even those divided for riding—she was far from sure. Then Nicolas was back, a black blot against the spur, around his arm a coil of rope.

With the girl following his instructions they worked as swiftly as they might. She was vaguely aware during their tugging and knotting that Ssssaaa had deserted her, and she caught a single glimpse of a sleekly furred form on her way down the drop as easily as if she trod a straight, smooth road.

Nicolas knotted a sling in the end of the rope, testing it with all his strength many times over. The other end he fastened to the saddle horn of her horse, as he allowed the sling to dangle down the fall, ending by putting in her hand the lead rope.

"When I say 'pull,' lead away," he commanded. Then with almost as much ease at finding helping holds as Ssssaaa had shown he was over the lip of the rock and was gone.

She saw him land some paces away from the now inert and almost hidden body and disappear into the rubble which half concealed it from above. Quickly he appeared again, half bent over, boosting up into full sight a body weighted with mail and a short surcoat devoid of any badge. The head moved feebly, its mail coif still in place but the helm gone, and smears of blood across a white face masked it.

Nicolas steadied the body against the propping rock, then the murmur of his voice reached her. Their find must be conscious enough to understand some order, for she saw two hands in mailed mitts come out on the rock, enough to hold the man while Nicolas busied himself collecting the rope. He dropped the loop around the injured man, lifting one of his hands and then the other to pass them through the loop so that now the rope belted him just above the waist.

Nicolas's head went back as he looked up to her.

"Pull—" he ordered, and the word echoed in that narrow place, "slowly."

She had already drawn the horse around, facing away from the cliff, and now she led it forward. There was a moment before the rope snapped taut. Then she slowed but still urged the beast outward and away from the spur which guarded that trap. She could see the movements of the line—at times it appeared even to slacken and then grow tight again, as if he who was being so raised could at intervals aid himself by some hand- or foothold. Yet the time before Nicolas and then that bloodied head emerged into her sight seemed very long.

The rescued man was plainly of the Prince's forces, yet he did not wear the clothing of a scout intended to fade into the foliage but rather half armor, and there was an empty sword sheath at his belt.

However, he seemed to be able to keep his feet, although Nicolas put an arm about his broad shoulders as he stumbled out.

"Here!" It was Willadene's turn to give orders, and she pointed to an open space where he might stretch out so that she could see the extent of his injuries. That he had not broken a limb from such a fall was a miracle.

Her healer's bag to hand, she poured a portion of water from the bottle Nicolas held and proceeded to wash the drying blood from the face turned up to hers. Nicolas had loosened the coif and she found a bump just above the hairline and a cut almost as if the edge of the helm had slashed there.

"Who—" His eyes opened as she dribbled into the cut some of Halwice's remedy against infection. Then his gaze narrowed. "The herb girl—"

"True, Highness," she answered with an outward show of composure. "No." She planted a hand firmly on his chest to keep him flat when he would have pulled himself up. "Let me finish."

Stripped of all his court trappings he seemed a younger

man, yet still one very sure of his own abilities. But how had the Prince come alone into this wilderness? She certainly had not expected to find him here without any escort.

Nicolas had withdrawn a little, was rolling up the rope to be once more stowed away. Then he seemed surprised at something he saw and went out of her sight for a moment while Prince Lorien frowned up at her.

"They said you could trace her—the High Lady—as might a hound—" he said slowly. "Is that why you are here—she is somewhere near?" And there was a shadow not quite of fear, at least for himself, on his face but rather a rising flush of anger.

"Near, but how—and where—that must be learned."

There was a hiss and out of nowhere Ssssaaa jumped on her shoulder, nuzzling her cheek until she turned her head while the Prince watched narrow-eyed. "Beyond—" Was it her talent or something else which supplied that? She could not have taken oath on either.

Nicolas came back into sight holding—well away from his body, she noted—a sword. The brightly honed steel was darkened, smoky in color in an odd fashion, as if something not unlike a rope had been wound around it. At the sight of it the Prince sat up abruptly.

"Get rid of it, man. It is poisoned by the accursed!"

Nicolas tossed the sword from him and, when it rang against one of the rocks, it broke into shards along those smoky lines and lay like a battlefield weapon abandoned years ago.

The Prince pushed Willadene aside when she tried to prevent his getting to his feet. He was looking beyond both of them, his attention up slope where she could distinguish a wall-like formation of the stone and in it a break.

"Back." The Prince swung on the other two. "You do not know what guards here—"

"But you have met it—or him," Nicolas said calmly. "Share then what you know."

Though the Prince never took his eyes from that break in the wall, he began to talk in short sentences which had the harsh notes of battle orders. He told of finding Timous and of the broken trail the scout had left as if he had been hunted by something monstrous, of the armored figure who was faceless and carried no weapons until he had plucked out of the very air that green ribbon—

When he spoke of that Willadene gasped, and somehow she found that her hand had gone out to clutch at Nicolas as she remembered only too well that meeting with evil in the Black Tower when the Bat had lain helpless and she had done only what she could. Even now the nausea of that battle arose in her throat as she fought down the desire to vomit.

The Prince had paused at the sight of their two faces and now he asked, "This weapon is known to you?"

Willadene felt that she could not even lose enough control to nod in answer, but Nicolas was ready with his version of that meeting.

"But that was in Kronengred—in the castle. And you say it was destroyed," he said. "How then came it here?"

"A month ago, Highness, when I brought you the news which led to your settlement with the Wolf, I found one of our border guards, a man so placed that he would have easily seen who came and went from that hole. He was dead and around his throat there was a ring of burnt flesh which had near cut his head from his body. Then I knew of no weapon which could cause such a wound—but I think that which crept upon us in the Black Tower, which hunted your scout to his death and tried to slay you, was alive. Do not poisonous snakes give birth to more than one of their kind?"

"And if we dare that gate again—" the Prince said slowly. "You have seen what it did to a sword forged by our greatest of smiths—and flesh is much less than steel."

Nicolas had a strange little smile. "If this *was* Ishbi in its time, then there was more than one entrance. I have been thinking—the rangers and scouts of the border pass down much which has long been forgotten elsewhere. Mistress"—he spoke now to Willadene—"there is the map."

Her hands were at an instant over the amulet in protection. "It is a fancy—" Yet even as she touched that packet she knew that it was true. She had always secretly believed it might lead to Heart-Hold. But Heart-Hold was of another time long past—

"A map?" The Prince was looking now to her. "A map showing what, Bat?"

"Perhaps another entrance to where we would go. For Ssssaaa had a hand in its finding and her will lies always with that of her master who wishes nothing more than that Kronen have peace."

Slowly Willadene displayed the leaves, standing back a little while Nicolas and the Prince spread them with care on a flat ledge of rock.

Suddenly the Prince cried out, "But that line—it is surely the Vars near its source. Last season I traveled with the border scouts of the kingdom to check our old maps, finding many of them inaccurate. But that is the Vars—to it I will swear by the Star."

"You have men on the way," Nicolas said. "We can lead a detachment thus—"

And what, Willadene thought, if they found other guardians with outré weapons to forestall them? In her heart she knew that for her there was only one entrance to Ishbi as it lay up slope from her now. But she said nothing, withdrawing within her mind to form her own plans. Mahart was ahead, and not too far. She had dealt once with the green serpents, she could do so again. A flask of the same liquid rode even now in her bag. Yes, she had her own plans as far as she could shape them.

23 They had retreated from the near vicinity to those rocky spires and established a temporary camp. Willadene made a show of checking the contents of her healer's bag, though she did not need to touch any, for all were already well set in her mind. She had done her best for the Prince, whose mail hood, loosely laced, lay back on his shoulders while a neat bandage covered the forepart of his head.

She brought out trail provisions and insisted that they eat, even though she had to fight continually against that tug within her to be done with all this and about what had drawn her here. Ssssaaa had curled herself in a dark pool on the top of a stone nearby, but the girl noted that those eyes were ever on the alert in the direction of the break in the wall. Somehow she felt entirely secure for the moment with such a guard.

The Prince and Nicolas almost seemed to forget she was there, so interested they were in the leaf maps. While Lorien had been able to locate one point of reference, so Nicolas found two more, discovered during his own scouting for outlaws.

If many of those had escaped the clean-out of their den, then they must have fled southward, for the three by the rocks seemed now to be in a deserted world. Nor had there been any sign of that armored figure the Prince had faced.

As they finished the limited store of their rations which Willadene had portioned out she saw the Prince go to stand, looking down at the shatters of his sword blade. He looked up at her as she returned the package of food to the saddlebags.

"Mistress, I know that you who deal in herb lore know many things which are strange to the rest of us. Have you any thought as to what that serpent thing might be?"

"Highness, I am but apprentice to herb lore, not born into the knowledge by blood as many are. This I know—that it is utterly evil and it answers to another's mind."

"The High Lady Saylana?"

She would have assented to that but something made her hesitate. Somehow in her mind Saylana stood for the Dark, yes, but there was—what—another?

"Highness, I cannot say. But surely she meddles in this, and I would swear it was her plotting that was the seed from which this grows."

"I have watched you—you look there!" He looked up at the distant doorway in the wall.

Suddenly Willadene was impatient. "Highness, I was set upon a trail—and willingly, for what I had seen and learned of the High Lady Mahart makes me desire to help her. I believe she is in great danger."

"As a hostage?"

Willadene shook her head. "It is of another kind and one I do not understand. I only know—she is encompassed by evil."

"We shall have her forth—" She thought he sounded far too confident, when suddenly there was the chirping call from the Bat and a party of the Prince's men was upon them. Willadene pulled back, on impulse taking her bag with her, while Lorien went to meet the newcomers.

"Ssssaaa." The black-furred one landed on her shoulder. And that was like a cry for help. From the amulet arose once more that single scent which was Mahart's alone—like an appeal.

There was the guardian of the gate. One of the evil weapons might well have been vanquished—he could have another. So—she would be prepared. Her own answer rode within the top loop of her jerkin lacing. She had worked on it quietly and apart while leaving them to their play with the map. A strip torn from her undergarments had been woven as tightly as she had been able to handle it about the end of a broken branch. This she had soaked until at least half of that potent liquid she carried had been absorbed into the cloth.

There was a great deal of talk below. Two scouts had been dispatched to round up more of the Prince's men, while he and Nicolas studied the leaves. From time to time one of the waiting men was summoned to view their find in turn.

Willadene lifted her pack to her shoulder and settled it with the familiar shrug. Ssssaaa did not try for a ride but was winding sinuously among the stones ahead, and Willadene depended upon her for warning.

At least she was not riding, she thought with a small sigh of relief. Rather, she picked her way among the stones, at the best pace she dared take, up and up. The wall arose to her right—she could see clearly the dark mouth of the opening ahead and she watched it carefully for any movement.

There came a sudden shout from down below, and she did not even glance back but plunged forward, drawn by that ever-increasing need which lay ahead. Nothing moved, there was no armored guard, it was as if the gateway had been left deliberately open.

Perhaps it had, but there was no gainsaying now that compulsion which forced her ahead through its shadow, Ssssaaa weaving a way before her. And, once she was within that opening, there was only utter silence. The shouting was cut off as if some barrier behind her had been slammed shut.

Willadene grasped her stick with its well-soaked rag. There was pavement of sorts under her, and stones rising on each side with only one way left—straight ahead.

Nicolas flung himself forward. He was fleet of foot— that was part of his training. Then his straining body struck against a solid surface with force enough to hurl him back at the men at his heels and bring them all down.

"Willadene!" Somehow he got enough air back into his lungs to shout. He struggled to his feet, but the impact of that force with which his body had met the obstruction made him unsteady.

Obstruction? He could see nothing but that dark entrance. Nor did any guardian stand there, ready to hurl him back again. But the Prince was still on his feet. His hands outstretched, he was running them back and forth through the air as if he fingered some surface. A moment later Nicolas had joined him. It *was* there! A wall not to be seen, not to be breached by any means they knew, as they proved during the next frantic moment, throwing rocks heavy enough that two men had to lift them, bringing up a tree from below to use as a ram like to burst the strong gate of a keep.

They could see nothing, only feel—locked out and helpless to follow.

"It seems," Nicolas said bleakly at last, "that we are now left only with your hope, Highness: that we come into this cursed place from another point."

"Cursed, double cursed." Lorien wiped sweat from his smarting cheeks with the back of his hand. "Ishbi has secrets—we have only the minds and wills of men. But"—he looked to Nicolas—"once before men cleansed this place and there are no walls before our will. We shall see what the map can do for us."

Why had she been possessed by such folly? Nicolas's

hands curled into fists. In that moment if Willadene stood before him he would have had a hard time restraining himself from striking out at her. They said there was witchery in herb lore—certainly what she called her talent had brought them here. And it was witchery of an evil kind she might be facing now beyond that barrier, while there was nothing for them to do but strive to find a forgotten path which might bring them too late to what she had gone to confront.

But they rode out. Nicolas took the lead, for he knew best these forest ways, always gnawing at him within the memory of that green crawling thing in the Black Tower and the growing fear that even worse might be ahead.

Mahart cupped her hands and drank deeply of the water in the basin. It seemed not only to fill her mouth and throat but somehow seep into an inner part of her so that it washed the fear away.

She turned away from the small fountain to face the garden. It seemed as it had always been since she first had had the good fortune to stumble into it. The horse had ventured out of the corner and was grazing quietly again.

The girl forced herself back to the wall and once more began a slow circle of it, intent not on what lay within but what stood without. She stopped several times and rubbed her eyes, for there appeared strange shafts of haze between her and those stands of ferns. It was almost as if, for an instant or so, she could see the outlines of buildings, that she could be caught in some fancy of Kronengred or Bresta. But always the ferns gleamed a brilliant green again, and those flashes of other sights grew less until they disappeared.

At last she settled herself in a nest she had made on the horse blanket and handfuls of grass from near the wall, but she had been careful not to pluck too much of the plants flourishing in that untended garden. A need to relax, to sink into the warmth of sleep, settled on her and at last she could no longer withstand it.

Crying, crying which hurt the ear, even as might that of a brokenhearted, forsaken child. It filled the darkness, filled her with the need to answer. Mahart opened her eyes and found she was already sitting up, straining forward. That crying was no part of some dream—it was real—heart tearing.

She was on her feet, stumbling a little, as they were so bruised by going unshod and she had not yet taken time to devise footwear. But that was no matter now—only the crying.

"Where are you?" she called. "Where are you?" But not even a rustle from the ferns answered her. She had reached the lower part of the wall and scrambled over.

The lake? Could it be that others—not only those toad things—lived here and that some child had fallen into their hands? There was pain now in the desolate voice.

However, the sound drew her past the end of the pier. She looked to the lake. Its surface was untroubled and she saw no movement among the rocks there. No, it was in the other direction. Limping a little, she rounded an end of the garden wall and suddenly realized that she was now facing that place where the ferns had parted to show her a road into darkness. Mahart half expected to find them parted again. But their wall was not broken; only the crying continued.

"Where are you?" she called helplessly. She could not just plunge blindly into that jungle without any guide.

There was no weapon left to her save that length of stone she had chanced upon—and her hopes of using that effectively against any real attack were very thin.

"Your—Your Grace—" Mahart was startled by movement at the very edge of the ferns. A black blot appeared to be crawling, breaking a way through that barrier into the open. The voice was harsh, cracked, that which might come from an aged throat.

Mahart edged back until her shoulders rasped against the surface of the wall which was too high here for her to attempt to climb.

The crawler moved slowly with obvious difficulty, and though that piteous crying had ceased there was almost a similar note of heartbroken appeal in the voice which came again.

"High Lady—pity— From your heart give me pity—"

The hunched form had stopped its advance, was huddled together so that she could not make much of it. Then a stick-thin arm showed, sweeping back what appeared to be the edge of a muffling cloak, to uncover head and shoulders.

About that half-revealed body was an eerie greenish glow, as if some of the substance of the ferns was formed of light particles and had rubbed off against it as it fought its way through their clutch.

Mahart gasped and her hands flew out to form the ancient ward-off sign of evil.

"Star Shine!" Her own voice was thin and ragged, and she began to edge along the wall, still facing that—that thing—as if constant watch could keep it away from her.

"Lady—" The word ended in a piteous wail. That skin-and-bone arm fell beside the bundle of body.

What she saw crouched there must certainly be part of a dark dream. Because, in spite of the skin pouched and wrinkled beyond belief, the white streaks in the matted hair—Mahart did know! And knowing— She swallowed. This was in its way like confronting one of the toadlike creatures out of the lake—only worse—far, far worse.

She had to try twice before she could shape the name she knew so well.

"Zuta—" Only this could not be her companion from girlhood. This was a wizened, age-sapped threat of what years could bring.

There came an incoherent cry from the thing. Now both arms had freed themselves from their covering and were huddled about a body still covered by a shapeless cloak or robe.

The plague—that one terrible misfortune Mahart had heard of for what seemed most of her life. Had it somehow lingered here to fasten greedily upon a fresh body again? But Zuta—had they taken Zuta also—though who had taken her?

Mahart forced herself away from the support of the wall. Zuta was too much of her past, she must—

"High Lady!" That call was swallowed by a loud hissing such as was challenge. Ssssaaa brushed past her ankles and slipped out into the open to face the thing out of the ferns. Zuta—but how could this be Zuta?

Mahart's own arm was grasped firmly and she was held away from the crawler.

She looked around and there was no mistaking that other—the Herbmistress's girl. Willa—"Willadene—" Triumphantly she produced that name aloud.

Mahart waved helplessly toward the crawler. There sounded weeping again, the hopeless cry of a child—or the very old—the abandoned and lost.

"Zuta—" She looked hopefully toward Willadene. "Is it—the plague?"

"It is utter evil," the other replied. "Stay you here. If it is well that you come I shall call—"

The other girl had released Mahart and now she advanced toward the hunched body. Around it, forming a circle, Ssssaaa was running. However, when the furred one reached Willadene she leaped and climbed, claws catching in the girl's clothing, to once more ride her shoulder.

Willadene had allowed her healer's bag to slip from her shoulder; her hands were busied in holding out the amulet she wore about her neck.

The thing who might be Zuta gave forth a loud scream and sank forward until the head touched the ground not too far from where Willadene stood.

"It is not the plague we have known, Your Grace," the

herb apprentice said steadily, "but keep your distance for now." She still made no attempt to approach Zuta any closer—rather she was opening her bag to bring forth something which seemed to catch from nowhere a clear bright light. This she held out but no closer than the circle Ssssaaa had drawn.

She was so ignorant—Willadene felt like spitting her frustration aloud. This was evil, the stench of it was sickeningly strong, but a new evil—or was it so new? That which had caught in her nostrils when Wyche had been her bane—here it was also but to a far greater extent. What she was trying now was again another old wives' tale which she had never heard of being put into practice. Yet Halwice had packed this bag, and Willadene trusted the instincts of the Herbmistress above all else.

What she held was a mirror of sorts—not burnished metal as was usual, but rather clear crystal. The backing was a slip of night-sky blue. Willadene no longer watched Zuta; rather she concentrated on that scrap of mirror.

What it caught and held first was that shrunken, aged body—a body so old it might have risen lych fashion from a forgotten grave. Then—the greenish tinge about it grew stronger. She actually saw only a shadow, but what seemed like a coverlet or netting had been draped over Zuta. That was feasting—feasting!

Ssssaaa's hissing arose to an almost deafening crescendo. What she faced, Willadene could not have put name to, but she used the only weapon she could think of—that she had prepared against the green serpent of Prince Lorien's venture.

Holding tightly to the mirror with one hand so that its crystal was still turned to Zuta, Willadene cried out with all the force she could summon—enough to drown out the hissing.

"By the Star, for the Star, against the Dark that devours and waits, let there be light, let there be life—let there come an ending!"

Reaching forward, over the edge of the circle she touched Zuta's contorted body. In her other hand the crystal of the mirror appeared to burst into a flame, but there was no heat within it to threaten her hold. Where the stick with its soaked rag had touched there sprang up light.

For a long moment Willadene could smell the fragrance which was part of that which answered her, something not of this world—something that evil could neither taint nor touch.

Zuta had stopped moaning. Suddenly her contorted body stretched out as if she had sought her own bed to rest. They could no longer see through the haze, but below it something liquid spread, smoking, and the flashing of the mirror, although Willadene did not move her hand, caught at that and it was gone.

They heard it go—a blast of air, of smell, of power which bent the ferns before it as it withdrew. Then for a long moment out of the time they knew they saw Zuta, Zuta in all her languorous beauty, lying at her ease. And there was peace about her. Until the haze balled together and when it was gone there was nothing left.

"What—what was it?" Mahart somehow found voice enough to ask.

"By some chance"—Willadene was seeking her own explanation, fitting one scrap of knowledge to another—"your lady lost her youth, her life energy to something—which still waits there." She nodded toward the fern forest. "Your Grace, we seem to have fallen into a world of legend and ensorcellment which it has been said for generations does not exist."

Mahart dropped down beside Willadene. "I am Mahart, and you are Willadene. In this strange world you speak of let there be no birth rank, for perhaps with your knowledge you are the stronger of us both. Zuta—" She found it hard to talk now. "She was my own friend for years. Yet there was a part of her I always felt I never knew, and perhaps she had the same to say of me. That she is in peace, Willadene, I thank you. The Star Shine grants us much, and more than that final peace we cannot ask for.''

"That you were not also such prey—'' Willadene found her hands were shaking now. The rag she had tied about her stick for defense flaked away, burnt so that it was already breeze borne ahead, while the crystal of the mirror was dull and quenched.

"It—it tried. But—come—please come—there is safety here!''

Thus Willadene found herself brought into the garden. Mahart was right—the feeling of safety, of warm and loving enfolding, closed about her. But that did not mean, she was sure, that any battle had been securely won—it was only a skirmish they had survived.

Prince Lorien eyed the rugged escarpment before them now. Unlike the oddly green-veined rock of the other side of this stretch of country, they were facing normal grayish stone as might form a jutting prominence of any normal height. Yet their path had led along the rise of wall ever since they had left the ill-omened and guarded gate.

Their party had grown, as Lorien's own men drew in to be briefed on what they faced, and with them a handful or so of border rangers who turned to Nicolas for enlightenment. The main difficulty now was the need to know the true nature of the enemy. Twice during the day they had wiped out handfuls of men—badly armed and yet ferociously determined to die if they could take with them at least one of the enemy. Some of them used weapons awkwardly, as if they were more used to the stealthy knife in the back rather than strike of sword blade on sword blade. These, Nicolas was sure, were slinkers from the city who had somehow made common cause with the few outlaws who fought frantically. Their own party took no prisoners, for the enemy refused to either surrender or be taken even when badly wounded. And Nicolas, used to

the wolf-barking cries of the outlaws, was disturbed by
the utter silence in which they fought.

Now that wall they had followed all day had taken a
sharp angle to the north and its rough surface promised
for the first time a chance to climb. They had consulted
over and over the leaves, and at last Nicolas and the Prince
had agreed that they had appeared to reach a point which
was marked as the end of the chart they had followed.

However, a climb in coming dark was not indicated—
at least for their troop. But Nicolas considered himself free
of any allegiance to the Prince's orders and he had already
paced along, spotting this handhold and that toe crevice
which could be used.

Somehow he knew well that Willadene had not won to
any safe place. This was the end of the second day since
she had made her own reckless choice and there was nothing he could do about it—yet.

The Prince moved up beside him, his metal-reinforced
glove striking against a knob of rock.

"To go alone—"

"To go alone," Nicolas answered without turning his
head to look at the Prince, "is what I am trained for,
Highness. Because I know a little of these powers which
Halwice and Willadene appear to be able to summon from
what seed, roots, and growth, I believe that the High Lady
is here. And for no good purpose. There are forces we
have not seen before—"

"Against which steel is no weapon. But then, our
schooling has been different, my friend. Nor are you liege
man sworn to me. If it is your choice—" He hesitated.
"Leave a trail—with morn's light we shall not be far
behind you."

Nicolas's choice of weapons were few and certainly not
cumbersome. He carried his favorite long belt knife, together with a slightly smaller blade sharing a double
sheath, and around his waist was a loop of tough cord,

knotted expertly here and there—a silent killer and a deadly one.

For the rest he depended upon his years of skulking, and those had never been wasted. His body, toughened as well as he could exercise muscles most men did not even guess they might possess, served him well. His side was still tender from the healing wound, but that had united well under Halwice's tending—in fact so well he found himself believing that the Herbmistress had brought more than the lore of her trade to his aid.

Impatiently he shared the scant rations of the troop, and the dusk was near night when he began his climb. As he had hoped, the surface of the cliff was rough enough to give him good holds and he soon pulled himself over the top, his side aching a little but still able to move with his old agility.

He found a place between two spurs of rock and tried to see what now lay before him. There were stars and a rising moon tonight, and he had always had the gift of keen night sight, even as his namesake, for much of his prying and scouting had always been kept for the dark hours.

Below him was another drop into this mysteriously guarded land. However, surveying as carefully as he could he began to realize that he had not reached the top of a cliff but actually the top of a wall—designed and firmly set by sentient beings for protection.

The crag beside which he had paused was not an outcropping but the remains of what must have been a watchtower. So—if there had once been guards here then there must have been a way for them to come and go. Guards—ones such as the man of metal who had held the other approach? He hefted a good-sized rock in one hand and hoped that his tender side would not prevent him from making one of those well-aimed throws he had so often practiced. Then he moved out.

It was the extraordinary silence of the space below

which impressed him first—no drone of insect nor even the sound of a breeze rustling. He might be moving through a place of the long dead. But it was an excellent warning for him to make his progress as silent as possible.

Find the way down to the lower land he did. It lay in the core of the second sentry post he chanced upon—a stair which was hardly more than a ladder of sorts, and which he used with the utmost care though the narrow treads were firm enough. Then he came through an opening in that confining wall into the open of the night.

There was a wide space here, occupied by ruins. He might have dropped into a city such as Kronengred after some major destruction had struck. Here again, all was silent, though he would normally expect to hear the scuttling of night hunters, the cry of a dire hawk, the many other sounds of life.

Instead, there arose ahead of him somewhere the sound of a thin cry—such as sent his hand to knife hilt. And then that was drowned out with a rustle which grew thicker and thicker as if a giant broom were sweeping back and forth across the land ahead.

The ruins gave way. He smelled a scent of fern heavier than he had ever encountered before, and he could catch in spite of the dim light that there were indeed ferns before him but such as he had never seen elsewhere. These were as tall as well-grown trees and seemingly packed so tightly together that their territory could not be invaded.

Nor had Nicolas any wish to attempt that—at least by night. A swift glance right and left showed him that there was a space of fallen and broken rubble along the wall, and he chose to track a way through that.

He had been listening steadily for that distant wail, but it had not sounded again. Willadene— Firmly he closed his mind against fears he could do nothing now to aid and kept on his slow advance through the debris, the wall he had followed from the other side now arising again to guide him.

The swishing of the ferns died away and he was aware of his own growing fatigue. He could not keep on without rest, without a small sip at least of the flask of cordial Willadene had provided him with as restorative before they had parted.

It was easy enough to find a place into which he could wedge his body so that no one could come at him from behind or either side, facing out at the ferns. He was used to ranger's sleep, which consisted more of short dozes and quick awakenings. Thus he established himself within what he was well aware was enemy territory—though no outlaws might prowl it this night.

But if Nicolas slept even this lightly, there was that here which had no wish for rest, for further meddling with its plans, which seethed with rage of what was already lost.

24

"Willadene?"

She did not feel as if she had really slept on their shared makeshift bed, but now Mahart's hand on her wrist brought her fully awake—awake enough to feel wary, as if she faced some task she had unfortunately forgotten.

"What is it?" she asked, trying inwardly to trace the cause of that uneasiness.

Mahart sat up. The scanty rags which had given her some body protection had been exchanged for what extra clothing Willadene had brought, though there were still twigs caught in her hair and she was far from appearing the High Lady of the past.

"Do you not feel it?" There was a quaver in that question. They had talked much together since they had won back to the garden—sharing sometimes thoughts they had never believed they could reveal to another. And Willadene knew at once what she meant.

There was a change in their sanctuary. The misty light which one could hardly term day was surely not as bright. As if drawn by a cord Willadene turned toward the water basin. Mahart was already heading toward it. That ever-flowing water lapping over its sides had stilled; there was no longer any drip from the tip of the crystal.

Yet there was no warning stench of evil. Instead, Willadene breathed deeply, to draw in not only the mingled fragrance of all which grew there but also that of another, far more subtle presence.

Mahart was staring down into the now-quiet bowl. What water remained in it was mirror bright. What did they see there? Neither girl could ever afterward describe it clearly; perhaps the evoked pictures did not even match, altered by their separate natures.

"No," Mahart voiced in a half whisper, retreating a step back.

"We must!" Willadene answered and knew the touch of fear. For some reason this sanctuary was closing to them; there would be no turning back now.

Willadene reached out and up, daring against instinct to touch the crystal from which the water had trickled, her hand groping as it might for the clasp of a protector.

There was a ringing—a sharp flash of light—as if she had touched the root of a storm. The crystal splintered, its bits falling like hailstones into the basin. But in her fingers remained what she looked upon in amazement, for it might have come out of one of Halwice's shop drawers—a well-rounded seedpod.

Without conscious thought she held it up between them, and that elusive scent which had tantalized her from her awakening was for a breath or two comfortably strong.

"Star gift—" Mahart said softly. "Surely Star given." She reached out as one greatly daring and laid fingertip to the pod. Again that whiff of strengthening fragrance. Then she looked to Willadene.

"So we must serve." There was that in her voice as strong as any altar-given oath.

They ate, perhaps for the last time, from the bounty of the garden. Willadene shouldered the bag of remedies and they once more climbed over the dip in the wall, rounding along it until they faced the fern forest from which Zuta had crawled.

Their coming seemed a signal—the ferns swayed apart, opened a path, however, one which would wall in any venturing there. The scent of the ferns was very strong but not enough to cover that other—the rising stench of evil. Underfoot were moss-covered blocks of what once might have been a street, and through the fern veil they saw now and then the loom of ruins.

Mahart looked back over her shoulder, closed her eyes for a moment, and then resolutely faced ahead. The fern way had closed behind them as if they moved through a pocket which adjusted itself to their faring.

So they came out of the misty green of the ferns at last into an open space. If all else here had been age bowed to ruin, this structure rising before them had endured untouched.

Three wide steps led up to a portico with roof-supporting pillars, deeply engraved in some language surely long forgotten in the outer world.

There was a single great door on the portico and from that rolled the evil stench so strong as to be almost visible. Yet what lay beyond and within lacked any light.

Willadene's hand met Mahart's, and both their palms closed together about the seed of the fountain.

As armswomen might march on order into battle they climbed the steps. Now the interior before them slowly developed a glow. There was a compulsion urging them forward, and still they must yield to accomplish what they came to do.

The long hall they entered might well be an audience chamber of some Prince. As the light about them brightened gems glowed, metals burned, and there were figures which still appeared blurred as if those must remain hidden from their eyes.

"Well come at last!"

She who sat on the throne near the end of that chamber

leaned a little forward. Her green robe was heavy with gems and silver lining; in fact, it seemed to weigh on her body, just as the youth she wore as a mask was beginning to crack.

"What do you wish of us, Saylana?" Mahart's voice did not falter. They had come to a pause a little way from the chair. Willadene could see now that there was a body lying limply on the floor on either side of that chair of state, and she recognized death—but death of a new kind which was more to be feared than any sword thrust or poison cup. Yet still she held, knowing that her strength added to Mahart's, even as Mahart's helped to root hers.

"What do I wish of you—?" Saylana cackled. No silvery laughter this time. "Life, my sweet, life—yours—and it seems by the grace of the Dark Old Power, you have also brought with you another—this wench who has been given more than any human should rightfully have. Thus, my feasting shall be doubly sweet—" Once more she cackled and then suddenly she half turned her head as if she had heard her name called.

It was at that moment that Willadene, who had been so overwrought by the pressures on her since her awakening, remembered Ssssaaa whom she had not seen since their awakening. However, it was not the Chancellor's creature who had attracted Saylana's attention.

She turned back to them, grinning, showing blackened stubs of teeth.

"By Drimon, all things come to them who wait. We shall indeed have a feasting!"

Her right hand moved with a speed Willadene would not have thought possible. Out from her fingers slapped a length of green light. They did not have time to move, but at least this horror was not intended to really bring them down now. Instead, it formed a hoop which grew larger and larger in diameter as it whirled up into the air and then came down to ring them about, while Saylana nodded and grinned. Both girls could understand that for this moment she considered them safely captive.

Nicolas roused before the first streaks of dawn light cut the sky. And he roused alertly as one battle ready, for he well knew that pinch of awareness which had so often saved him in the past, the premonition that danger waited ahead. He already had knife in hand when that dark line of fur came flowing fluidly among the tumbled debris to leap for him.

"Ssssaaa!" He stroked that head which butted against his chin. He never knew where Vazul had found the creature or how the Chancellor had bonded with her. But her utter faithfulness to those she selected—and such were very few—as well as her service to Vazul Nicolas had understood from their first meeting.

However, now Ssssaaa preceded others by only a few minutes, long enough for Nicolas to leave his improvised shelter. It was no surprise that Lorien led the short file of men along the same general trail he had taken. But the company was a small one, some half dozen of the Prince's own men and three of the rangers. Catching sight of Nicolas, he joined him quickly.

"There is some power," he burst forth, "which I do not understand. We began the climb, only these—" he waved at his followers "—could make it. The others were as bound when they tried. If this is Ishbi then we deal with old evil awakened."

"We deal with those who have the High Lady," Nicolas returned grimly, and then in a slightly different tone of voice, "also Willadene—"

"But she chose—" the Prince began, and Nicolas laughed grimly.

"Your Highness, no man controls such a woman. She has that in her to make her stand free and go the path she has chosen as rightfully hers. Look you"—he stroked Ssssaaa's head—"here is one to tell us so. And what she seeks lies there''—he nodded toward the stands of fern, scowling, as it seemed to him the very air was rotten with their heavy scent.

Making himself head boldly for that green growing wall was one of the hardest things Nicolas believed he had ever done. Yet there was no visible peril ahead. Only those cursed ferns and beyond them—somewhere—the two girls. For he was oath-certain that Willadene had somehow reached Mahart.

''Lord—down with you!''

That shout had come from one of the men slightly behind. The Prince took cover no more quickly than Nicolas, who was berating himself that another had picked up the danger he had not seen.

Over their heads, as they pulled themselves among the scant protection of the crumbling walls, an arrow sang. But that had not been aimed in their direction, rather from behind, flying toward some mark among the ferns.

For a long moment there was utter silence—no foot stumbled among the scattered stones. The ferns stood tall and untouched by any breeze.

Nicolas put out his hand and touched Lorien's forearm, nodding toward the wood. He did not doubt that the Prince had indeed a goodly store of woodlore, but this land was his own running place and he was sure no one could put its every advantage to use.

Lorien stared at him fiercely, and Nicolas was sure that the Prince had no wish to surrender any scouting to him. Yet finally Lorien nodded and Nicolas swung to the left, making a bellywise crawl toward the nearest spur of the forest. He tried to shut down all thought, to concentrate only on what he must do. Let Prince Lorien advance as he pleased, he would find Nicolas before him.

He had half expected to be met by a cloud of those tormenting midges which hung thick about normal forests, but there was nothing here. Only—

He flattened himself to the ground, peering through the

fingers he held up to shield his face. His black night-fitting suit had been so well grimed that it was the color of the stones about and he could play one of those rocks with ease.

What he was watching was a man or else a body which had slipped down, half supported by the ferns around. The arrow? No, there was no sign of any shaft—still he was certain the man was dead.

Had that stranger been alone—a solitary guard such as the mailed figure at the first valley entrance? This one wore no armor, and he was curiously drawn together, his knees up to his thin chest, as if he had been huddling hopelessly, waiting to be brought down.

No sounds—just that bundle lying there. But they must learn who or what had killed him or they themsleves could go the same route. Nicolas crept on, the cursed fern scent almost stifling about him.

But—he knew this victim! Not for nothing had he himself prowled the nightways and hidden places of Kronengred as well as the open lands beyond the city. The contorted face, expressing both fear and horror intermingled, he had last seen in the city. Willadene had spoken of him—Figis—a bit of refuse washed up by the plague, kinless and masterless— No! The fellow had been with Wyche when Nicolas had last caught a glimpse of the youth. And as far as they had been able to discover Wyche had disappeared out of Kronengred on the same night the High Lady had been abducted.

Where there had been one man there well might be two. Ssssaaa flashed past Nicolas to the body, sniffed, hissed, and was back again. A promise of no danger here?

However, caution had been too deeply bred into him for him to reveal himself more than he possibly had to. The longer he stared at the dead man's face the more he was aware of a strangeness. Figis had died in great terror, of that Nicolas was sure, but he still could not see either the sign of a wound or of spilled blood.

And the Figis he had seen before had been young, carrying several years fewer than his own. But in spite of the print of fear on that face there were other marks—deep-set wrinkles on either side of the nose, a shrinking about the mouth. And surely he had had a full head of hair then, much more than the scattered locks now covering part of his head. This was Figis, to that Nicolas would swear, but it was a Figis upon whom age had settled in a matter of a few days.

Ssssaaa was weaving a path back and forth before him as if to urge him on. And one of those swings gave him a glimpse of another figure farther beyond. Nicolas froze. He could not control Ssssaaa as the Chancellor was able to, and she now changed course, heading toward that other shadowy blot. With all the precautions he could summon, Nicolas again followed.

It was Wyche this time, caught among the trunks of the ferns. The huge bag of the man's paunch and body were shrunken—he could have been a famine victim. Even as Figis, he too wore a look of terror. Death had come hard to Wyche, and perhaps not swiftly.

Both men were clearly dead and their killer or killers made this territory theirs. If Prince Lorien were to come marching in unknowingly he would find no familiar outlaw den but a peril they could neither understand nor foresee.

Yet—Willadene and the High Lady—or were those two already reduced to such papery shells as that which confronted him now? He could always remember the bite of anger, but he had learned early to make it serve his purpose and not lead him to open and unthinking action.

Nicolas returned as quickly as he could and squatted down with Prince Lorien and the squad leader. The thought of a death which could suck a man dry was not encouraging, and he could see the shadows of doubt on the faces before him.

Ssssaaa had followed him back and now gained his shoulder. As she so often did with the Chancellor she placed her sharp muzzle close to his ear and began a hissing near as low as a whistle. He was trying to guess what message she brought when Prince Lorien spoke.

"We have already discovered something also, Bat. I alone can advance without danger to the edge of the forest; none of these others can."

"What hinders them?" Nicolas found this new item difficult to fit in with what he had seen—that the fern forest had been clearly penetrated.

The Prince's helm shadowed much of his face but did not hide the square determination of his jaw. "It is like a wall—just such as our larger party met with below. We are being whittled down. And unless you know some forest lore, we are to be deterred by thin air alone—or a wall no man can see."

He had hardly finished speaking when there came a sound from the forest—a scream of torment and fear. Nicolas was on his feet. The girls! If he were the only one who could enter there, so be it. But as he ran, Ssssaaa clinging to him, he saw that Lorien was drawing even with him and they both crashed through the first rank of ferns together. Nicolas fought for control even as a second cry sounded. To run headlong into the unknown was the mark of a fool—he had learned that lesson many seasons ago.

He paused and caught at the Prince. "That way?" His forefinger pointed straight ahead. Lorien nodded, breathing hard. However, even as Nicolas he slowed his pace.

For the third time that sound reached their ears; now it was hardly above a gurgling moan. It might well be bait in some trap, but they could not turn aside now.

Through the ferns loomed up the remains of a building—roofless so that the green wands grew inside—still giving more light than within the forest itself. The ferns within the wall had recently been scythed after a fashion, so their fallen lengths made an irregular carpet for the place. In the middle of this there remained, still sturdy set on its base, a pillar of the green-veined stone. It had been put to use.

The body roped to the pillar was still alive, twisting and turning, trying to find some small hope of a yielding bond. This was no stranger either as far as Nicolas was concerned. There were old slights and snubs he had taken impassively, taunts which had not drawn him to answer by brawling.

Barbric might be out of the straight line to the throne as far as the law declared, but no one who knew Saylana's son could think that he did not have some ideas of his own about who was to wear the ducal coronet.

Only, his expression now was that of one near the edge of sanity, as if he had witnessed something none of his senses could accept.

Directly before him stood that mailed figure who had denied Lorien passage through the gateway. Around one armored arm a green snake length coiled, but he now moved to attack.

"For—for Star's sake—!" Spittle exploded from Barbric's lips as he made that plea. "Let her not feast on me! I am her son—or was her son—for I believe that she who bore me is long gone out of that body which has begun to fray about her like a too-worn dress. This was her place once—when men called her Nona—and she would have it back again."

Speech appeared to be giving him back a measure of control. "Don't you understand? She sucks life from the living—and now she readies herself for a new body—Mahart's—one young enough to give her many more years."

"You supported her," Nicolas returned. He was keeping more than half his attention on the metal figure and that snake of light, not sure when either or both would attack.

"I did not know what she would do. Take the throne

from that bumbling old fool, yes, but that she had made
a pact and then paid for it—that I learned too late.''

"A pity we do not have more foresight," remarked
the Prince.

Barbric showed him a snarling face. "Be not so bold,
hero. Your strength will be an extra feeding for her, and
do not doubt that she is waiting for you with those she
has already gathered in.''

"She has them—the girls—'' That was no question but
a statement from Nicolas.

Barbric nodded. "Landed them as neatly as if she fished
them forth from Gladden Stream. Nor, as you will now
discover, can you return to save yourselves either!''

Suddenly his scowl became sheer terror. A single fern
which had escaped the massacre of its kind around the
pillar bowed as if under a blast of wind. When it arose
upright again there were filmy threads floating through the
air, the green of the ferns and yet nearly invisible.

Barbric screamed and screamed again. Ssssaaa jumped
from Nicolas's shoulder and hurled herself like a fur-
coated arrow straight for the metal-clothed guard. The un-
expectedness of such an attack from so small a creature
appeared to completely master its reflexes for a moment.
It took a ponderous step backward and stumbled over one
of the cut ferns, crashing down on its back while the green
thing it had nursed traveled up its arm and shoulder and
seemed to pour itself into one of the dark eyeholes of the
metal mask. The snake did not reappear, but Barbric was
fast entangled by green ribbons which wound about him
in spite of his frenzied struggles.

Nicolas moved with his knife and the Prince with the
sword he had taken from his squad leader. But those
blades, keen as they were, simply rebounded from the
heaviest blows the two could aim.

Then the lines uncoiled and became a single ribbon
heading on into the forest. The shell of Barbric hung as
ancient bones against the pillar.

Though they still went at a wary pace, Nicolas, at least, felt the necessity for charging ahead. What they had heard from Barbric was out of all reason—except they had seen what they had seen—that Saylana had somehow been possessed, her body worn as clothing by a sorceress out of legend was near past any serious belief.

Still something had withered Figis and Wyche, sucking life from them, and had done so to Barbric. The collapse of the metal guard was as puzzling. Had he been punished in some manner for allowing Nicolas and Lorien to find Barbric and learn as much as they could of this tangled web?

Once more the fern trees were thinning out, and not far ahead they could see open sky and a tall building which had all the austerity of a temple. Nicolas did not doubt that it was here Saylana, or she who seemed Saylana, now held court.

25 Neither girl had attempted to try fortune and strength against that green ring barrier. The light in this long hall appeared to surge and then fail a little. Willadene was intensely aware in a strange way of that seedpod she and Mahart clasped between them. Almost she could believe it was to be an aid, though the time was not yet.

Saylana huddled back into her throne, her bulky shirts appearing now far too much for her slender body to support. Her eyes, sunken into caverns of her skull, were closed, and the withering of her face and now too-much-revealed shoulders continued before their eyes.

Willadene did not believe this power was asleep, or even worn to exhaustion. It was rather as if that failing body had been left for a space while what animated it went elsewhere. Now would be their time to move, but in which direction and how the girl could not have answered.

Mahart's shoulder was against hers now. Instinctively they had drawn together as shield mates ready to meet an enemy charge. Fear, yes, there was the scent of that, and she believed that they shared that equally, but it did not rise to panic in them.

The body on the throne gave a twitch of returning en-

ergy as a skeleton-thin hand arose to the wrinkled forehead. Loosened by its touch a long lock of dusty black
hair separated from the skull and slipped along Saylana's
shoulder. But the age-puckered lips were smiling, and she
opened her eyes to regard the two before her gloatingly.

"A feast—by the very roots of Yaster, the ever-cursed,
a feast!"

She surveyed the two before her as one might face children who had repented of their naughtiness and now
waited to be forgiven. Within their close-clasped hands
the seed was warm. Willadene was aware that for an instant they stood in a place of cool, pleasant odors, a mixture of grass, flowers, sun-warmed earth—

"You are Nona," Mahart said as if some problem had
been solved for her.

That raw cackle of laughter answered her. *"Nona?* My
girl, you reach back far in time for that one. I cannot
remember well everyone who has provided me with proper
clothing. I gather Nona left something of a memory here—
think how much more your services will be marked."

Then that ghastly, tooth-baring smile was gone and she
sank again to the back of the chair. Only this time there
came a change. In their sight her flesh appeared to firm
and the wearing of too many years was erased.

When she addressed them again she was once more
Saylana, but a Saylana who might have aged a score of
years from the time Willadene had seen her dancing in
the great ballroom.

"Well, well," she commented. "So dear Barbric did
have unexpected strengths in him after all. Like a true son
he is now with his mother." She gave a pat to a breast
which once more filled out the low-cut bodice properly.

"Now, my dear, more visitors—whether you shall find
them welcome, I do not know. But they will serve my
purpose very well indeed."

A slim shadow crossed the floor from behind that throne
in great bounds. It came toward the girls until it was within

a handsbreadth of the ring about them, and there whirled and crouched, its head uplifted to the highest point in order to view the throned woman best.

"Mahart!"

"Willadene!"

So close together came those names that they near blended into one. As had Ssssaaa, Nicolas came around the dais with the wariness of a lurker. And keeping close was a man in mail and half armor, a drawn sword in his hand.

"Stop!" Again a single warning from two throats but it halted that race toward them. Nicolas gave a quick glance to the floor, sighting the green ring, and then threw himself before Lorien to halt the other's stride.

Willadene had been working with her free hand at the fastening of the healer's pack she had refused to abandon. She located a bottle by touch, hoping that she was guessing right, raised the flask hastily to her mouth, and worried loose the cork.

She wondered at Saylana's forbearance. That she had been allowed to so arm herself must mean that this—this enthroned thing had full confidence in its own powers. Perhaps her thought of some intervention was merely an added fraction of amusement to the game it intended to play.

The cork was gone. Willadene spun the bottle in her grip and hurled what was left of its contents as well as she could toward the nearest portion of the green ring. Most of the stuff splashed short, and for a stiff moment of fear, she knew failure. Then she noted a curl of steam from that green ribbon—nor did it hold to its circle shape any longer, but rather beat upon the floor and fell into two parts, cut by those drops which had reached it.

Avoiding the writhing lengths with a mighty stride Lorien was with the girls, a hand out to Mahart. Nicolas did not turn his back on the enthroned figure, rather approached the other three in a sidewise fashion.

"So—" The caricature of Saylana spoke. "You have learned something from that weird-wife after all." However, she did not show any great surprise as she spoke to Willadene. "Welladay, you shall be a juicier morsel for the taking if that is so."

Though her hands still rested on the arms of the throne the lower part of her body began to twist and turn. The fullness of her bedraggled skirt swelled and swayed, and from beneath its hem there showed tips of brilliant green.

These lengthened, moved purposefully toward those below. They had the appearance of leafless vines, growing at such a rate that that process was visible. Lorien moved between the girls and those advancing vine serpents.

Again came that cackle of laughter. "Yes, mighty slayer of outlaws, use that blade of yours. You have already lost one to the crawlers—do you think you shall be any luckier this time?"

The Prince's mouth tightened, and Nicolas and Willadene could guess that he was remembering what had happened at the pass. One of those crawling ribbons flailed out to the far side and then began to draw in again. Nicolas was now being herded closer to the others. He gave a glance upward—at least there was no netting visible there ready to descend upon them.

The need for action worked upon Mahart. She managed to keep her voice steady, her courage high.

"We stand in the Light of the Star, you who are of Darkness. Thus we are a greater company than you see."

The gaunt face of the woman flushed a dusky red. "Call upon your puny light, High Lady. I do not think you will be answered—"

"Oh"—that was Nicolas—"but then again she might be, as once before the Star answered here and—"

"Be tongueless! That was long ago. One learns more with every year's passing. The Sisters of your Abbeys sit upon old lore as a hen does upon eggs, afraid to use even what they know. I do not think that any of you have something new.'' She raised one hand and made a gesture.

That green vine which had neared Nicolas's side slapped over. Willadene gasped. She had been so sure that it would have a stranglehold about the Bat, but a swerve of his body left him free, as it brought him up almost shoulder to shoulder with her.

"Quite a little chipper you are," their captor observed. "Try all you can, all of you—the longer you strive to hold off fate the sweeter my feasting shall be. Will you now try that sword, Prince? How do you know—perhaps this new one you carry is somewhat tougher of blade.''

Willadene caught a small flash of movement from the corner of her eye. Saylana had been concentrating on her human captives—perhaps she had forgotten Ssssaaa entirely. What weapons the creature might possess the girl could not guess, but at least she was moving purposefully, and straight for the throne.

"Ah, Prince, you disappoint me—'' Saylana had gotten that far. The vine which had herded him lifted up from the floor and was swinging back and forth like the blind head of a giant worm.

Lorien made no attempt to use steel on that wriggling threat. Instead, his left hand went to his throat and he yanked from under his mail a chain on which swung a piece of glittering crystal. His next move was quick and unexpected, as he whirled the chain about his head and loosed it so that the spark of glitter swooped through the air and struck the ever-thickened body of the vine.

"By the Power of the Star," his voice rang out.

The spark of flying light was lost to sight almost in the same moment they had seen it. Saylana's grimace made her aging face a mask for a monster. Both of her hands swung up and out. The vines writhed, began to whirl, formed a waist-high wall about the four before her, herding them close together. There was no use for Willadene to depend upon her herbs now. Those she had used against the earlier attack were gone.

Saylana was rocking slowly back and forth, a patch of whitish foam at one corner of her mouth, foam which spattered as she cried out in a tongue none of them understood, doubtless some curse from another time and place.

There was strain in every line of her distorted body now as if she fought more than just those helpless captives.

Avoiding the flailing cords of green with supreme agility Ssssaaa was closing in on the foot of the throne. Willadene grew aware of a new element in this struggle. She still gripped hands tightly with Mahart, between their palms that pod. There was rising warmth against her flesh; she caught a hint of that unwordly fragrance.

On her other side she had a glimpse of Nicolas's slender hands, busied with his knife. But no steel would stand against the noxious weapon which was beginning to rise again after a brief halt. What would he do?

On the throne Saylana's body convulsed. She raised her right hand and pointed it at Lorien. "Fool, you have not brought me death—but you shall be the first to pay for your folly!"

To his right the green wall sent forth a long whirling tendril. Before he could avoid it, it fell upon his shoulder and encircled him. He had moved in the only direction left him, separating himself as far as he could from Mahart.

Just as Lorien had swung that splinter of crystal, so did Nicolas now flip his knife in the direction of their enemy. But Willadene saw no bared steel blade—somehow he had twisted about it a sheath of dull clay color.

It landed cleanly, dispatched by long-practiced skill, on the billowing lap of the woman.

Her scream was such as to deafen all of them. Her face was hardly more than a skull with living eyes. Frantically she brushed the weapon away. But it left smoldering patches on her torn and twisted robe.

The heat in that pod Willadene shared guardianship of

was growing ever stronger—much higher and it would sear her flesh. She turned to look at Mahart, whose eyes were all for Lorien. The Prince stood statue still, his body braced as if he were enduring some powerful struggle against unnatural strength.

"Mahart!" Willadene lifted her enclosed fist with a jerk which brought the other's attention back to her. "Now!"

She did not understand whether the same mental command had reached the other girl or not, but somehow she was sure that it had. Together their arms swung and they loosed the pod into the turgid, rancid air of the chamber.

Only to see it fall short as if it had hit against some unseen barrier. Mahart gave a small broken cry, but Willadene was intent on something else. Ssssaaa's sinewy black body was there even as the pod fell short of their target. Seizing it between sharp teeth she made one of those extraordinary leaps and landed on the body of the thing on the throne whose energy and flesh appeared to be giving birth to ever stronger and longer tendrils.

Saylana's skull bowed for an instant as she viewed this new attacker and what she bore. She raised both hands and grasped Ssssaaa about the middle, whirling her up in the air, but that which the creature had brought remained with Saylana.

Now she screamed. Not only was that cry one of pain but it was overlaid with terror, such fear as none of them had ever heard from any human throat. The small black body flew through the air.

Willadene was aware of movement from beside her. Leaning out at a perilous angle over the wall of green, which luckily had stopped its advance for the moment, Nicolas managed to catch the limp black body and bring it to nestle to his breast. But there was no answering sound or movement out of Ssssaaa.

Another and still more tortured scream burst from the thing before them. From where the pod lay on Saylana there was a flicker of light which grew brighter with every breath they took.

The green wall about them trembled, strove to close in and engulf them entirely. But that last surge failed. Instead now the green tendrils were being hurriedly withdrawn, brought back to she who had given them birth. Once more her figure filled out, she became closer to the human woman they had always known, except for her face. For that now bore the features of that carving which guarded the entrance into its sorcery-ridden land.

She was making no move to rid herself of that ever-growing patch of light which was now near breast high, only sat watching its growth with wide eyes.

Lorien stumbled and might have gone down as that vine withdrew its hold on him, but Mahart was close and quick enough to steady him. His face was gaunt and grayish, but slowly he shook his head as if to rid himself of some nightmare vision and gave his attention, with the others, to their enemy.

That which rested on her lap might have found her its proper soil for rooting. Now, through the haze, they could see the rise of a stem, the uncurling of long leaves. And the veins on those leaves blazed gold, sharply defined as had been the ones on the leaf map.

Only her face remained clear, unmoved—her face and the eyes which sought them one after another with a piercing glare that in itself was a curse.

Up grew the flower. Willadene drew in a deep breath of delight. Not in all the world had she expected ever to find such a perfect fragrance. Not in the world—yes, because this was not of this world—it was never meant to be.

"Heart-Hold!" Mahart had kept her grip on Lorien though he no longer needed steadying.

The mask of perfect beauty, which was the last unchanged bit of the throned one, cracked, shattered, fell in powdered dust. There was a great wind about them, first of northern cold—a threat, and yet one that weakened steadily—and then one of summer as their earth knew it.

This was no hall. Mahart threw wide her arms, wanting to embrace the flower-embroidered fields before her. Her dream made real. And that one she had waited for—here he was—his hands reaching out to catch at hers.

Willadene balanced on the edge of a cliff among rocks, looking down at that white star standing tall below. Heart-Hold. But she had no wish to pluck it. Heart-Hold was of the heart and grown within one.

There were arms about her and she smelled that particular scent which she knew for always would mean security and warmth for her. Soft fur brushed her cheek.

Then the worlds they had found apart for an instant whirled about them all and they were back in Ishbi. Only here also was change. There was no body on the high seat; that had been cracked and reduced to dust.

A pillar of light hung there in the air. Though they could not see within it, they were certain there was a flower at its heart. While above all the putrescence of this place had been cleansed away and a scent born in a world apart from theirs, yet welcoming, impregnated them all.

Slowly, not quite sure they were still not caught in another dream, they turned and went out of the mass of ruins which was hardly more than rubble. Where the ferns had stood there was open land, fields dotted with the remains of a city which would never be again. And they were hailed with exuberance by a party of men who stood in those fields, staring wide-eyed and near unbelieving.

"Will—she strive to come again?" Mahart asked, as they went to join those others.

"Evil begets evil," Lorien answered her. "This time we must keep watch."

"But how?"

He looked to Willadene who was murmuring to Ssssaaa cradled in her arms, Nicolas, light-footed as ever, beside her.

"Old knowledge," said the Prince slowly. "The stuff of legends which have been allowed to rust away. Talents exist still among some of us. Those must be found and cultivated—put on guard—"

Nicolas laughed. "A new form of border watch, Highness? Do not be surprised if you find your suggestion may come true. Swords and spears, yes, but beyond those, weapons which will not shatter and cannot tarnish."

The room was stuffy and Mahart felt as if she had been thrust into a cell, her hard-won freedom gone. But that was one of the things to be decided here this day. She was aware of Lorien, just as she knew he was well aware of her, though he did not look in her direction but rather gave his courteous attention to the Duke.

It was an oddly formed party which had gathered in the castle to perhaps decide the whole future of Kronen to come. Vazul, of course. Though he looked oddly bereft these days for Ssssaaa had not rejoined him. The Herbmistress's apprentice was here also, as well as Halwice herself, and in a place of honor the Abbess who so seldom left her own place of rule. Nicolas no longer wore that black which melted in the shadows but rather the rust-brown uniform of a captain of border rangers.

In the center Duke Uttobric squirmed as usual in his chair, eternally uncomfortable.

They had unfolded their stories, woven them together in detail. And as strange as those tales had been no one had doubted that they told what was the truth. Now that they were through the Duke spoke first to the Abbess.

"Your Holiness, it would seem that evil rooted itself heavily in our midst and we felt nothing but uneasiness. Is there no way we may keep watch and ward on that which lies in the hearts and minds of men and women?"

"Such invasion is also of evil," she said quietly. "However, the truth is that we must now set wards. Already our Abbey scholars are seeking out the very earliest accounts, looking for any reference as to how such Darkness can be detected before it grows. What we learn we shall share with all.''

''By the Star, Holiness, we give you thanks for that.''

She looked past the Duke to Prince Lorien, a long, measuring look as if she must make some decision but was not completely sure of her ability to do so.

''This amulet which you used against the evil one,'' she asked, ''what was its nature?''

His hand went up close to his throat as if he would reach for something which was no longer there.

''It was my vow crystal.''

The Abbess nodded. ''And even the touch of that was enough to buy you time. Therefore, it would seem, Highness,''—once more she addressed the Duke—''that the Star has accepted our need. But more greater—'' Now her attention fastened almost equally on the two girls. ''That which used your aid to bring it into life was long lost. It has withdrawn, perhaps, from this world again, but a part of it will remain. Heart-Hold is not for one man or woman but for all of us who live and die and strive to better what lies about us.

''Heart-Hold''—now she regarded all four of those across the table with some of the same searching she had turned upon Lorien earlier. ''Heart-Hold appeared to you—knitting you into such bonds as no shadow can hope to break. Your Highness wishes wards—I do not think that there shall be another stirring—at least in our lifetimes—but there are your wards.''

Her wand staff had been lying across her knees; now she raised it and slowly swept it by the four. The crystal on its tip blazed high, and Willadene sighed with delight, for the fragrance settling around her was that of the other world—the world of fair dreams, safe days, and quiet happiness.

However, the Abbess was not finished. ''Halwice''— the wand dipped in the direction of the Herbmistress now, and once more its tip flared—"you are of the Old Blood, though out of prudence you have denied it, using but a small part of what lies within you to give. Now, I say here, loose the bonds laid upon you by earlier generations before your birth. Be what the Star meant you to be!

"Highness." It was the Duke's turn to meet her eyes. "In this woman you shall find such a guard as whose like has not been known since before the days of the House of Gard. It was their denial of such talents through narrowness of mind which brought an end at last to their rule and house. I think it is already in your mind what else is to be done.

"These tell us Ishbi is cleansed. But it was tainted. Choose you another site for your watchers. There also shall be a Call Cell of the Abbey, for it is time we must also be alert."

She laid her wand once more across her knees and was silent.

The Duke cleared his throat and held out his hand to Vazul, to have a sheet of parchment, laden with seals, passed quickly to him.

"Highness"—it was the Prince he first addressed—"you are not of our Kronen blood, you have no reason to wish to take on any burden of another land. But we can do no more than ask. This"—he gave the parchment a little wave—"creates on the north border—that wildest and harshest portion of the duchy, the place from where danger may watch and wait—a holding. Those who man it must be warders indeed, not only ready to patrol against outlaws but against the rise of Dark. If you will be one with these three who are of our blood and so are surely called to the duty, our gratitude will be great."

With one hand Lorien accepted the charter, but with the other he caught at Mahart's and felt her fingers close tightly about his in return.

"Your Highness," he said firmly, "I think that such

anchorage here has been set on me as I can never deny. Thus I agree."

Thus the four signed the charter, Willadene already planning a session with Halwice to discover how information might be exchanged between them; Mahart, feeling free in spite of the castle walls shelling her in; and Nicolas, shooting glances at Willadene and then at his former master, the Chancellor. There would surely be much to be done and most of them green to the doing of it. It might be another form of employment than he had known for the past few years but not the less absorbing. And—he looked to Willadene once again—it would be new not to be alone—new and, he believed, rewarding.

But there was one more thing he must say to Vazul before they parted, and that he did as they arose to toast the new venture from the golden goblets of state which appeared at the Duke's summoning.

"Ssssaaa—she was gone after the Heart-Hold." Knowing what the small creature had meant to the Chancellor, he hated to say that. However, to his surprise Vazul smiled and clapped him on the shoulder.

"Do not worry. But send me the pick of her litter when her whelping time comes. I find myself quite chilly at times without a champion in fur."

Thus was the Border March of Kronen brought to life and appeared thereafter proudly on every map as Wardland. Perhaps those of Kronen might not understand truly what roots it had, but to those who held it there was always the strong fragrance of Heart-Hold to be met now and then on a wandering wind.

We hope you've enjoyed this Avon Eos book. As part of our mission to give readers the best science fiction and fantasy being written today, the following pages contain a glimpse into the fascinating worlds of a select group of Avon Eos authors.

In the following pages experience the latest in cutting-edge sf from Eric S. Nylund, Maureen F. McHugh, and Susan R. Matthews, and experience the wondrous fantasy realms of Martha Wells, Andre Norton, Dave Duncan, and Raymond E. Feist.

SIGNAL TO NOISE

Eric S. Nylund

Jack watched his office walls sputter malfunctioning mathematical symbols and release a flock of passenger pigeons; his nose was tickled with the odor of eucalyptus. Inside, the air rippled with synthetic pleasure and the taste of vanilla.

"I need to get in there," he told the government agent who blocked the doorway.

"No admittance," the agent said, "until we've completed our investigation on the break-in."

Puzzles, illegalities, and dilemmas stuck to Jack—from which he then, usually, extracted himself. That gave him the dual reputation of a troubleshooter and a troublemaker. But the only thing he was dead sure about today was the "troublemaking and sticking" part of that assessment.

The agent stepped in front of Jack, obscuring what the others were doing in there. National Security Office agents: goons with big guns bulging under their bulletproof suits. And no arguing with them.

Today's trouble was the stuff you saw coming, but couldn't do a thing about. Like standing in front of a tidal wave.

Jack hoped his office *had* been broken into, that this

wasn't an NSO fishing trip. There were secrets in the bubble circuitry of his office that had to stay hidden. Things that could make his troubles multiply.

"I'll wait until you're done then."

The agent glanced at his notepad and a face materialized: Jack's with his sandy hair pulled into a ponytail and his hazel eyes bloodshot. "You have an immediate interview with Mr. DeMitri. Bell Communications Center, sublevel three."

Jack's stomach curdled. "Interview" was a polite word that meant they'd use invasive probes and mnemonic shadows to pry open his mind. Jack had worked with DeMitri and the NSO before. He knew all their nasty tricks.

"Thanks," Jack lied, turned from the illusions in his office, and walked down the hallway.

From the fourth floor of the mathematics building, he took the arched bridge path that linked to the island's outer seawall. Not the most direct route, but he needed time to figure a way out of this jam.

Cold night air and salt spray whipped around him. Electromagnetic pollution filtered through the hardware in his skull: a hundred conversations on the cell networks, and a patchwork of thermal images from the West-AgCo satellite overhead.

Past the surf and across the San Joaquin Sea, the horizon glowed with fluorescent light. Jack regretted that he'd stepped on other people to get where he was. Maybe that's why trouble always came looking for him. Because he had it coming. Or because he was soft enough to let little things get to him. Like guilt.

Not that there was any other way to escape the mainland. Everyone there competed for lousy jobs and stabbed each other in the back, sometimes literally, to get ahead. He had clawed his way out with an education—then cheated his way into Santa Sierra's Académe of Pure and Applied Sciences.

But it wasn't perfect here, either. There were cut-throat maneuvers for grants, and Jack had bent the law working both for corporations *and* the government. All of which had helped his financial position, but hadn't improved his conscience.

He had to get tenure so he could relax and pursue his own projects. There had to be more to life than chasing money and grabbing power.

Now those dreams were on hold.

His office had been ransacked, and the NSO had got too curious, too fast, for his liking. Had they been keeping an eye on him all along?

He took the stairs off the seawall and descended into a red-tiled courtyard.

In the center of the square stood Coit Tower. The structure was sixty meters of fluted concrete that had been hoisted off the ocean floor. It had survived the San Francisco quake in the early twenty-first century, then lay underwater for fifty years—yet was still in one piece.

Jack hoped he was as tough.

The whitewashed turret was lit from beneath with halogen light, harsh and brilliant against the night sky. Undeniably real.

Jack preferred the illusions of his office; sometimes reality was too much for him to stomach.

No way out of this interview sprang to mind, and he had stalled as long as he could. The crystal-and-steel geodesic dome of the Bell Communications Center was across the courtyard. Jack marched into the building, took the elevator to sublevel three, and entered the concert amphitheater.

On the stage between gathered velvet curtains, the NSO had set up their bubble.

Normal bubbles simulated reality. Inside, a web of inductive signals and asynchronous quantum imagers tapped the operator's neuralware. It allowed access to a world of data, it teased hunches from your subconscious, and solidified your guesses into theories. They made you think faster. Maybe think better.

But this wasn't a normal bubble. And it was never meant to help Jack think. It was designed for tricks.

THE DEATH OF
THE NECROMANCER

Martha Wells

She was in the old wing of the house now. The long
hall became a bridge over cold silent rooms thirty feet
down and the heavy stone walls were covered by tapestry or thin veneers of exotic wood instead of lathe and
plaster. There were banners and weapons from long-
ago wars, still stained with rust and blood, and ancient
family portraits dark with the accumulation of years of
smoke and dust. Other halls branched off, some leading
to even older sections of the house, others to odd little
cul-de-sacs lit by windows with an unexpected view of
the street or the surrounding buildings. Music and
voices from the ballroom grew further and further
away, as if she was at the bottom of a great cavern,
hearing echoes from the living surface.

She chose the third staircase she passed, knowing the
servants would still be busy toward the front of the
house. She caught up her skirts—black gauze with dull
gold striped over black satin and ideal for melding into
shadows—and quietly ascended. She gained the third
floor without trouble but going up to the fourth passed
a footman on his way down. He stepped to the wall to

let her have the railing, his head bowed in respect and an effort not to see who she was, ghosting about Mondollot House and obviously on her way to an indiscreet meeting. He would remember her later, but there was no help for it.

The hall at the landing was high and narrower than the others, barely ten feet across. There were more twists and turns to find her way through, stairways that only went up half a floor, and dead ends, but she had committed a map of the house to memory in preparation for this and so far it seemed accurate.

Madeline found the door she wanted and carefully tested the handle. It was unlocked. She frowned. One of Nicholas Valiarde's rules was that if one was handed good fortune one should first stop to ask the price, because there usually was a price. She eased the door open, saw the room beyond lit only by reflected moonlight from undraped windows. With a cautious glance up and down the corridor, she pushed it open enough to see the whole room. Book-filled cases, chimney piece of carved marble with a caryatid-supported mantle, tapestry-back chairs, pier glasses, and old sideboard heavy with family plate. A deal table supporting a metal strongbox. *Now we'll see,* she thought. She took a candle from the holder on the nearest table, lit it from the gas sconce in the hall, then slipped inside and closed the door behind her.

The undraped windows worried her. This side of the house faced Ducal Court Street and anyone below could see the room was occupied. Madeline hoped none of the Duchess's more alert servants stepped outside for a pipe or a breath of air and happened to look up. She went to the table and upended her reticule next to the solid square shape of the strongbox. Selecting the items she needed out of the litter of scent vials, jewelry she had decided not to wear, and a faded string of Aderassi luck-beads, she set aside snippers of chicory and thistle, a toad-stone, and a paper screw containing salt.

Their sorcerer-advisor had said that the ward that protected Mondollot House from intrusion was an old and powerful one. Destroying it would take much effort and be a waste of a good spell. Circumventing it temporarily would be easier and far less likely to attract notice, since wards were invisible to anyone except a sorcerer using gascoign powder in his eyes or the new Aether-Glasses invented by the Parscian wizard Negretti. The toadstone itself held the necessary spell, dormant and harmless, and in its current state invisible to the familiar who guarded the main doors. The salt sprinkled on it would act as a catalyst and the special properties of the herbs would fuel it. Once all were placed in the influence of the ward's key object, the ward would withdraw to the very top of the house. When the potency of the salt wore off, it would simply slip back into place, probably before their night's work had been discovered. Madeline took her lock picks out of their silken case and turned to the strongbox.

There was no lock. She felt the scratches on the hasp and knew there had been a lock here recently, a heavy one, but it was nowhere to be seen. *Damn. I have a not-so-good feeling about this.* She lifted the flat metal lid.

Inside should be the object that tied the incorporeal ward to the corporeal bulk of Mondollot House. Careful spying and a few bribes had led them to expect not a stone as was more common, but a ceramic object, perhaps a ball, of great delicacy and age.

On a velvet cushion in the bottom of the strongbox were the crushed remnants of something once delicate and beautiful as well as powerful, nothing left now but fine white powder and fragments of cerulean blue. Madeline gave vent to an unladylike curse and slammed the lid down. *Some bastard's been here before us.*

SCENT OF MAGIC

Andre Norton

That scent which made Willadene's flesh prickle was
strong. But for a moment she had to blink to adjust
her sight to the very dim light within the shop. The
lamp which always burned all night at the other end
of the room was the only glimmer here now, except
for the sliver of daylight stretching out from the half-
open door.

Willadene's sandaled foot nearly nudged a huddled
shape on the floor—Halwice? Her hands flew to her
lips, but she did not utter that scream which filled her
throat. Why, she could not tell, but that it was necessary to be quiet now was like an order laid upon her.

Her eyes were drawn beyond that huddled body to
a chair which did not belong in the shop at all but
had been pulled from the inner room. In that sat the
Herbmistress, unmoving and silent. Dead—?

Willadene's hands were shaking, but somehow she
pulled herself around that other body on the floor
toward where one of the strong lamps, used when one
was mixing powders, sat. Luckily the strike light was
also there, and after two attempts she managed to set
spark to the wick.

With the lamp still in hands which quivered, the girl swung around to face that silent presence in the chair. Eyes stared back at her, demanding eyes. No, Halwice lived but something held her in thrall and helpless. There were herbs which could do that in forbidden mixture, but Halwice never dealt with such.

Those eyes— Willadene somehow found a voice which was only a whisper.

"What—?" she began.

The eyes were urgent as if sight could write a message on the very air between them. They moved—from the girl to the half-open door and then back with an urgency Willadene knew she must answer. But how— Did Halwice want her to summon help?

"Can you"—she was reaching now for the only solution she could think of—"answer? Close your eyes once—"

Instantly the lids dropped and then rose again. Willadene drew a deep breath, almost of relief. By so much, then, she knew they could still communicate.

"Do I go for Doctor Raymonda?" He was the nearest of the medical practitioners who depended upon Halwice for their drugs.

The eyelids snapped down, arose, and fell again.

"No?" Willadene tried to hold the lamp steady. She had near forgotten the body on the floor.

She stared so intensely as if she could force the answer she needed out of the Herbmistress. Now she noted that the other's gaze had swept beyond her and was on the floor. Once more the silent woman blinked twice with almost the authority of an order. Willadene made a guess.

"Close the door?" That quick, single affirmative blink was her answer. She carefully edged about the body to do just that. Halwice did not want help from outside— but what evil had happened here? And was the silent form on the floor responsible for the Herbmistress's present plight?

With the door shut some instinct made the girl also, one-handedly as she held the lamp high, slide the bolt bar across it, turning again to find Halwice's gaze fierce and intent on her. The Herbmistress blinked. Yes, she had been right—Halwice wanted no one else here.

Then that gaze turned floorward, as far as nature would let the eyes move, to fasten on the body. Willadene carefully set the lamp down beside the inert stranger and then knelt.

It was a man lying facedown. His clothing was traveler's leather and wool as if he were just in from some traders' caravan. Halwice dealt often with traders, spices, and strange roots; even crushed clays of one sort or another arrived regularly here. But what had happened—?

Willadene's years of shifting iron pots and pans and dealing with Jacoba's oversize aids to cooking had made her stronger than her small, thin body looked. She was able to roll the stranger over.

Under his hand his flesh was cool, and she could see no wound or hurt. It was as if he had been struck down instantly by one of those weird powers which were a part of stories told to children.

THE GILDED CHAIN
A Tale of the King's Blades

Dave Duncan

Durendal closed the heavy door silently and went to stand beside Prime, carefully not looking at the other chair.

"You sent for us, Grand Master?" Harvest's voice warbled slightly, although he was rigid as a pike, staring straight at the bookshelves.

"I did, Prime. His Majesty has need of a Blade. Are you ready to serve?"

Harvest spoke at last, almost inaudibly. "I am ready, Grand Master."

Soon Durendal would be saying those words. And who would be sitting in the second chair?

Who was there now? He had not looked. The edge of his eye hinted it was seeing a youngish man, too young to be the King himself.

"My lord," Grand Master said, "I have the honor to present Prime Candidate Harvest, who will serve you as your Blade."

As the two young men turned to him, the anonymous noble drawled, "The other one looks much more impressive. Do I have a choice?"

"You do not!" barked Grand Master, color pouring into his craggy face. "The King himself takes whoever is Prime."

"Oh, so sorry! Didn't mean to twist your dewlaps, Grand Master." He smiled vacuously. He was a weedy, soft-faced man in his early twenties, a courtier to the core, resplendent in crimson and vermilion silks trimmed with fur and gold chain. If the white cloak was truly ermine, it must be worth a fortune. His fairish beard came to a needle point and his mustache was a work of art. A fop. Who?

"Prime, this is the Marquis of Nutting, your future ward."

"Ward?" The Marquis sniggered. "You make me sound like a debutante, Grand Master. *Ward* indeed!"

Harvest bowed, his face ashen as he contemplated a lifetime guarding . . . whom? Not the King himself, not his heir, not a prince of the blood, not an ambassador traveling in exotic lands, not an important landowner out on the marches, not a senior minister, nor even—at worst—the head of one of the great conjuring orders. Here was no ward worth dying for, just a court dandy, a parasite. Trash.

Seniors spent more time studying politics than anything else except fencing. Wasn't the Marquis of Nutting the brother of the Countess Mornicade, the King's latest mistress? If so, then six months ago he had been the Honorable Tab Nillway, a younger son of a penniless baronet, and his only claim to importance was that he had been expelled from the same womb as one of the greatest beauties of the age. No report reaching Ironhall had ever hinted that he might have talent or ability.

"I am deeply honored to be assigned to your lordship," Harvest said hoarsely, but the spirits did not strike him dead for perjury.

Grand Master's displeasure was now explained. One

of his precious charges was being thrown away to no purpose. Nutting was not important enough to have enemies, even at court. No man of honor would lower his standards enough to call out an upstart pimp—certainly not one who had a Blade prepared to die for him. But Grand Master had no choice. The King's will was paramount.

"We shall hold the binding tomorrow midnight, Prime," the old man snapped. "Make the arrangements, Second."

"Yes, Grand Master."

"Tomorrow?" protested the Marquis querulously. "There's a ball at court tomorrow. Can't we just run through the rigmarole quickly now and be done with it?"

Grand Master's face was already dangerously inflamed, and that remark made the veins swell even more. "Not unless you wish to kill a man, my lord. You have to learn your part in the ritual. Both you and Prime must be purified by ritual and fasting."

Nutting curled his lip. "Fasting? How barbaric!"

"Binding is a major conjuration. You will be in some danger yourself."

If the plan was to frighten the court parasite into withdrawing, it failed miserably. He merely muttered, "Oh, I'm sure you exaggerate."

Grand Master gave the two candidates a curt nod of dismissal. They bowed in unison and left.

KRONDOR
The Betrayal

Raymond E. Feist

The fire crackled.

Owyn Belefote sat alone in the night before the flames, wallowing in his personal misery. The youngest son of the Baron of Timons, he was a long way from home and wishing he was even farther away. His youthful features were set in a portrait of dejection.

The night was cold and the food scant, especially after having just left the abundance of his aunt's home in Yabon City. He had been hosted by relatives ignorant of his falling-out with his father, people who had reacquainted him over a week's visit with what he had forgotten about his home life: the companionship of brothers and sisters, the warmth of a night spent before the fire, conversation with his mother, and even the arguments with his father.

"Father," Owyn muttered. It had been less than two years since the young man had defied his father and made his way to Stardock, the island of magicians located in the southern reaches of the Kingdom. His father had forbidden him his choice, to study magic, demanding Owyn should at least become a cleric of one of the more socially acceptable orders of priests. After all, they did magic as well, his father had insisted.

Owyn sighed and gathered his cloak around him. He had been so certain he would someday return home to visit his family, revealing himself as a great magician, perhaps a confidant of the legendary Pug, who had created the Academy at Stardock. Instead he found himself ill suited for the study required. He also had no love for the burgeoning politics of the place, with factions of students rallying around this teacher or that, attempting to turn the study of magic into another religion. He now knew he was, at best, a mediocre magician and would never amount to more, and no matter how much he wished to study magic, he lacked sufficient talent.

After slightly more than one year of study, Owyn had left Stardock, conceding to himself that he had made a mistake. Admitting such to his father would prove a far more daunting task—which was why he had decided to visit family in the distant province of Yabon before mustering the courage to return to the East and confront his sire.

A rustle in the bushes caused Owyn to clutch a heavy wooden staff and jump to his feet. He had little skill with weapons, having neglected that portion of his education as a child, but had developed enough skill with his quarterstaff to defend himself.

"Who's there?" he demanded.

From out of the gloom came a voice, saying, "Hello, the camp. We're coming in."

Owyn relaxed slightly, as bandits would be unlikely to warn him they were coming. Also, he was obviously not worth attacking, as he looked little more than a ragged beggar these days. Still, it never hurt to be wary.

Two figures appeared out of the gloom, one roughly Owyn's height, the other a head taller. Both were covered in heavy cloaks, the smaller of the two limping obviously.

The limping man looked over his shoulder, as if being followed, then asked, "Who are you?"

Owyn said, "Me? Who are you?"

The smaller man pulled back his hood, and said, "Locklear, I'm a squire to Prince Arutha."

Owyn nodded, "Sir, I'm Owyn, son of Baron Belefote."

"From Timons, yes, I know who your father is," said Locklear, squatting before the fire, opening his hands to warm them. He glanced up at Owyn. "You're a long way from home, aren't you?"

"I was visiting my aunt in Yabon," said the blond youth. "I'm now on my way home."

"Long journey," said the muffled figure.

"I'll work my way down to Krondor, then see if I can travel with a caravan or someone else to Salador. From there I'll catch a boat to Timons."

"Well, we could do worse than stick together until we reach LaMut," said Locklear, sitting down heavily on the ground. His cloak fell open, and Owyn saw blood on the young man's clothing.

"You're hurt," he said.

"Just a bit," admitted Locklear.

"What happened?"

"We were jumped a few miles north of here," said Locklear.

Owyn started rummaging through his travel bag. "I have something in here for wounds," he said. "Strip off your tunic."

Locklear removed his cloak and tunic, while Owyn took bandages and powder from his bag. "My aunt insisted I take this just in case. I thought it an old lady's foolishness, but apparently it wasn't."

Locklear endured the boy's ministrations as he washed the wound, obviously a sword cut to the ribs, and winced when the powder was sprinkled upon it. Then as he bandaged the squire's ribs, Owyn said, "Your friend doesn't talk much, does he?"

"I am not his friend," answered Gorath. He held out his manacles for inspection. "I am his prisoner."

MISSION CHILD

Maureen F. McHugh

"Listen," Aslak said, touching my arm.

I didn't hear it at first, then I did. It was a skimmer.

It was far away. Skimmers didn't land at night. They didn't even come at night. It had come to my message, I guessed.

Aslak got up and we ran out to the edge of the field behind the schoolhouse. Dogs started barking.

Finally we saw lights from the skimmer, strange green and red stars. They moved against the sky as if they had been shaken loose.

The lights came toward us for a long time. They got bigger and brighter, more than any star. It seemed as if they stopped, but the lights kept getting brighter. I finally decided that they were coming straight toward us.

Then we could see the skimmer in its own lights.

I shouted, and Aslak shouted, too, but the skimmer didn't seem to hear us. But then it turned and slowly curved around, the sound of it going farther away and then just hanging in the air. It got to where it had been before and came back. This time it came even lower and it dropped red lights. One. Two. Three.

Then a third time it came around and I wondered what it would do now. But this time it landed, the sound of it so loud that I could feel as well as hear it. It was a different skimmer than the one we always saw. It was bigger, with a belly like it was pregnant. It was white and red. It settled easily on the snow. Its engines, pointed down, melted snow underneath them.

And then it sat. Lights blinked. The red lights on the ground flickered. The dogs barked.

The door opened and a man called out to watch something but I didn't understand. My English is pretty good, one of the best in school, but I couldn't understand him.

Finally a man jumped down, and then two more men and two women.

I couldn't understand what anyone was saying in English. They asked me questions, but I just kept shaking my head. I was tired and now, finally, I wanted to cry.

"You called us. Did you call us?" one man said over and over until I understood.

I nodded.

"How?"

"Wanji give me . . . in my head . . ." I had no idea how to explain. I pointed to my ear. "Ayudesh is, is bad."

"Ask if he will die," Aslak said.

"Um, the teacher," I said, "um, it is bad?"

The woman nodded. She said something, but I didn't understand. "Smoke," she said. "Do you understand? Smoke?"

"Smoke," I said. "Yes." To Aslak I said, "He had a lot of smoke in him."

Aslak shook his head.

The men went to the skimmer and came back with a litter. They put it next to Ayudesh and lifted him on, but then they stood up and nearly fell, trying to carry him. They tried to walk, but I couldn't stand watching, so I took the handles from the man by Ayudesh's feet, and Aslak, nodding, took the ones at the head. We carried Ayudesh to the skimmer.

We walked right up to the door of the skimmer, and I could look in. It was big inside. Hollow. It was dark in the back. I had thought it would be all lights inside and I was disappointed. There were things hanging on the walls, but mostly it was empty. One of the offworld men jumped up into the skimmer, and then he was not clumsy at all. He pulled the teacher and the litter into the back of the skimmer.

One of the men brought us something hot and bitter and sweet to drink. The drink was in blue plastic cups, the same color as the jackets that they all wore except for one man whose jacket was red with blue writing. Pretty things. I made myself drink mine. Anything this black and bitter must have been medicine. Aslak just held his.

"Where is everyone else?" the red-jacket man asked slowly.

"Dead," I said.

"Everyone?" he said.

"Yes," I said.

AVALANCHE SOLDIER

Susan R. Matthews

It lacked several minutes yet before actual sunbreak, early as the sun rose in the summer. Salli eased her shoulder into a braced position against the papery bark of the highpalm tree that sheltered her and tapped the focus on the field glasses that she wore, frowning down in concentration at the small Wayfarer's camp below. They would have to come out of the dormitory to reach the washhouse, and they'd have to do it soon. Morning prayers was one of the things that heterodox and orthodox—Wayfarer and Pilgrims—had in common, and no faithful child of Revelation would think of opening his mouth to praise the Awakening with the taint of sleep still upon him.

The door to the long low sleeping house swung open. Salli tensed. *Come on, Meeka,* she whispered to herself, her breath so still it didn't so much as stir the layered mat of fallen palm fronds on which she lay. *I know you're in there. Come out. I have things I want to say to you.*

The camp below was an artifact from olden days, two hundred years old by the thatching of the steeply sloped roofs with their overhanging eaves. Not a Pilgrim camp by any means. No, this was a Shadene camp built by the interlopers that had occupied the holy land in the years after the Pilgrims had fled—centuries ago. A leftover, an anachronism, part of the heritage of Shadene and its long history of welcoming Pilgrims from all over the world to the Revelation Mountains, where the Awakening had begun. Where heterodoxy flourished, and had stolen Meeka away from her. And before the Awakened One she had a thing or two to tell him about that—just as soon as she could find him by himself, and get him away from these people . . .

Older people first. Three men and two women, heading off in different directions. The men's wash house was little more than an open shed, though there wasn't anything for her to see from her vantage point halfway up the slope to the hillcrest. The women's wash house was more fully enclosed. That was where the hotsprings would be, then.

Where was Meeka?

The sun would clear the east ridge within moments, and yet no man of Meeka's size or shape had left the sleeping house. In fact the younger people were hurrying out to wash, now, and there were no adults whatever between old folks and the young, so what was going on here?

Then even as Salli realized that she knew the answer, she heard the little friction of fabric moving against fabric behind her. Felt rather than heard the footfall in the heavy mat of fallen palm fronds that cushioned her prone body like a feather-bed. Well, of course there weren't any of the camp's men there below. They were out here already, on the hillside.

Looking for her.

"Good morning Pilgrim, and it's a beautiful morning. Even if it is only a Dream."

She heard the voice behind her: careful and wary. But a little amused. Yes, they had her, no question about it. She could have kicked the cushioning greenfall into a flurry in frustration. But she was at the disadvantage; she had to be circumspect.

"How much more beautiful the Day we Wake." And what did she have to worry about, really? Nothing. These were Wayfarers, true, or if they weren't she was very much mistaken. But there were rules of civility. She had meant to get Meeka by himself, without betraying her presence; but she had every right to come here on the errand that had brought her. "Say, I imagine you're wondering what this is all about."

A fantasy, a love story, a summer of change...

The China Garden

By LIZ BERRY

AVON
tempest

"Like a jewel box with hidden drawers and
compartments, this finely crafted, multilayered
novel holds many secrets...richly laden with
mystery and suspense, in which the ordinary
often masks unexpected interconnections
and the extraordinary is natural to the story's
wildly imagined terrain."
—PUBLISHERS WEEKLY ☆

Avon Books Presents
SCIENCE FICTION AND FANTASY
WRITERS OF AMERICA
GRAND MASTER

ANDRE NORTON

BROTHER TO SHADOWS
77096-2/$5.99 US/$7.99 Can

THE HANDS OF LYR
77097-0/$5.99 US/$7.99 Can

MIRROR OF DESTINY
77976-2/$6.50 US/$8.99 Can

And in Hardcover

SCENT OF MAGIC
97687-0/$23.00 US/$30.00 Can

AVON EOS PRESENTS
MASTERS OF FANTASY AND ADVENTURE

CHANGER
by Jane Lindskold   78849-7/$5.99 US/$7.99 CAN

THE STONES OF STIGA: A NOVEL OF SHUNLAR
by Carol Heller   79081-5/$5.99 US/$7.99 CAN

SHARDS OF A BROKEN CROWN:
VOLUME IV OF THE Serpentwar Saga
by Raymond E. Feist   78983-3/$6.99 US/$8.99 CAN

WARSTALKER'S TRACK
by Tom Deitz   78650-8/$6.50 US/$8.50 CAN

FIRE ANGELS
by Jane Routely   79427-6/$6.99 US/$8.99 CAN